BOUGAINVILLEA
BLUES

Dublin Galyean

ISBN: 149351119X
ISBN-13: 9781493511198

For my birth family
For Suzanne

ACKNOWLEDGEMENTS

Natalie Goldberg, Ray Bradbury, and Brenda Ueland all fundamentally advised the same thing: just write.

Friends, students, and colleagues encouraged me simply by asking when they would get to read this book.

Finally, Phil S., Writers of the Purple Page, and the men who gather on Thursday nights had a part, some large (P.S.) and some small, in getting me to the end.

CHAPTER ONE

San Diego 1962

BILLY KNOCKED ME DOWN like a lineman blindsiding a quarterback. He outweighed me by at least fifty pounds, so my head slapped the ground hard. But all I could think of was that the thud of my head might wake up his parents, who would want to know why I was outside their daughter's window in the middle of the night.

With his knees on my back, he pushed my face into the ground and rolled it around. Then he was quiet for a few seconds like he couldn't quite decide what else I deserved. As I caught my breath, he grabbed my shirt, turned me over, and pummeled me everywhere but my face. Was that out of respect for our friendship? He was grunting something unintelligible. When he got off me, I rolled to my side and started crying.

I couldn't see what he was wearing but once he got home from school, he usually put on jeans and a cutoff sweatshirt that always had grease stains on the places where his stomach overflowed his belt. I had on pajamas and my sneakers, which I polished to keep white. I even mustered up a little anger that he was getting them dirty. (In the bathroom later, I would discover a nosebleed, some scratches on my neck, and the beginning of a large bruise above my right eyebrow.) I felt like I had been trampled by the town mob in *Frankenstein*. Would he start kicking me next, or was he satisfied with the punishment already administered? With a snort of disgust or to get my attention, he decided to shove me with his foot like you would kick a piece of trash to the curb. "Go home, you emaciated pervert, and don't let me ever catch you even near here again."

I wanted to say that would be hard since I lived next door, and, as self-conscious as I was about being skinny, I was slightly amused at his use of the word "emaciated." I wanted to explain that, while I might be thin, I was far from being that undernourished, but I kept quiet and struggled to climb the fence. I expected him at any moment to push me over, but he probably liked hearing me groan as I scraped places already made tender by his fists. I didn't look back until I got inside the door to the garage. It was too dark, even in the moonlight, to see whether he was still watching me, but I half expected to see his eyes flaming inside the dark outline of his body.

Billy had completely surprised me when he tackled me, since I had been standing in the dark for about an hour. I hadn't seen Sandy do anything that I should have been beaten up over. In fact, she was only there for a few seconds. She had turned on the light, picked up a paper off her desk, and then left the room. Of course, I had hoped that she would return and begin to do something more interesting, which is why I had been standing there so long.

I had gone to bed early because Mom and Dad were having one of their usual arguments (Mom called them "discussions") about how little Dad was involved in our lives. I slept only briefly before waking up in a sweat thinking about Sandy's nose. Really. Sandy had this perfect nose, not long or slightly crooked like mine. Though she was not as gorgeous as Marilyn Monroe or Sophia Loren, she was close, and about as far out of my league. Tall and slim, Sandy had the legs of a dancer but the upper body of a stripper. Even back then I probably couldn't have described her face in much detail, but I do remember, in addition to her nose, she had this perfect jaw line, just like Sandra Dee's. She was so well known at school for her resemblance to the actress that Billy was called Brother Dee.

As much as my body ached over the pounding, it was the shame that bothered me most. Of course this was nothing new. I was ashamed about a lot of things. I was barely mediocre at sports. I was the only boy on the block without a girlfriend, one incontestable proof of maleness for a wimpy kid. *And*, as Billy alluded to so imprecisely earlier, I was skinny. At least I was right about his misuse of the word. Emaciated would be the description of a death camp survivor, not a well-fed, middle-class white boy like me. Still I was thin, and I would have given anything to be heavier, even if it meant looking like Billy. But most of my shame, though I didn't know it then, had more to do with voyeuring, that I thought this was the only way I could get close to someone I was attracted to.

And it's important to point out that the voyeuring wasn't as innocent as I'd like to make it out to be. At that time there was little access to porn like *The Last Tango in Paris* or *Behind the Green Door*. I mean, I had seen only one

Playboy, a special issue that Billy, ironically, had showed me just a few weeks earlier. It was the first: Marilyn Monroe with only a few carefully placed *Playboy* logos to keep her "decent." By present standards it was nothing, but then, for someone like me, who had never seen anyone nude (except for my mother, but we'll get to that soon enough), it was quite, shall we say, stimulating.

I hope I'm not coloring what happened too much by this retrospective look. I know an autobiography can be more fiction than history. Of course, I now understand Billy's indignation. I am a father. I don't trust boys who just show interest in one of my daughters, much less want to be her boyfriend. I know I am capable of doing just what Billy did to me if I caught some kid sneaking a look in their bedroom window.

Just thinking about it now makes my blood buzz, as much as it did when I stood outside Sandy's window that Saturday night. Not that I had an opportunity to do anything more than look, but in the Southern Baptist Church, mere proximity could get you in trouble. I still laugh at the old Baptist joke Dad liked to tell about the pastor who caught two of his flock doing it. "Well, at least they weren't dancing," he said.

Psychologists might say that the desire to see the female form unadorned is just an example of normal sexual curiosity, especially for a boy entering puberty. The church leaders begged to differ. They hold us Christians to a higher standard, though it is a standard regularly breeched by some of the most vocal and visible evangelists. All I knew then was that looking at naked women gave me a rush that obliterated all my insecurities and, at the same time, made me a degenerate sinner. I believed I was condemned just for thinking about it.

4

I have no idea what first gave me the idea of looking in windows, except that I had been overexposed to my mother's body for years. Maybe it *was* just innocent curiosity at first. More likely it was a desire to see the forbidden and in that viewing partake of the intimacy that nudity implies. Even with all my reading on the subject, I still don't know what got me started. But when I think of my own daughters, I only see it as creepy. Even so, a little empathy sneaks in whenever I hear of a Hollywood star caught in some XXX movie theater engaging in what is ambiguously described as "lewd conduct."

As I said earlier, the night of my whupping, I had woken up in a sweat. It was May but had not cooled off much by bedtime, as it usually does. Since everybody in my family—Debbie (my older sister), Maw-Maw (Mom's mother who had lived with us ever since Mom went to work), and my parents—closed their bedroom doors at night, I didn't consider opening it for ventilation. Of course, this was long before we had anything resembling central air. The desire for privacy at night seems almost funny now, but back then, when I was twelve, I missed the irony.

I don't remember having spent any time planning it out. I had seen Sandy, Billy's sister, when she came home from the beach earlier that day and couldn't get her out of my mind. She had had on a short overdress that covered her swimsuit for when she was not working on her tan. It was light yellow with tiny blue flowers and contrasted nicely with the pink two-piece that showed through in places. She was always friendly to me the way older girls can be to boys whom they would never ever consider dating material.

I kept thinking about how her bedroom was just over the fence from our garage. So when night came, it occurred to me to see if she might still be up. I don't even know if I wanted to see her undress at first. I think just watching her do stuff she might even do in public would have been fine. Watching her secretly through her window seemed risqué enough. For cripes' sake, girls at my junior high were sent home if, while kneeling, their skirts didn't touch the floor, and a girl who merely french kissed got a reputation for being an easy lay.

Of course, my sensibilities around sex suffered from this constant war between what Mr. Testosterone was telling me and what I heard in church. So the Baptist dancing joke wasn't always that funny to me. I was a good Christian and believed what Jimmy Carter revealed in his *Playboy* interview: the Bible taught that thinking about doing something, which was prohibited, was tantamount to doing it. Had I been a little better at rationalizing, I might have concluded that, with as much time as I had spent thinking about it, it wouldn't be any worse if I did it.

I suppose it doesn't take much spiritual insight to realize the truth in this, that someone who hadn't committed adultery but obsessed on the possibility was not a lot better than those who actually did it (because his thinking would sooner or later lead to the action anyway). At the time, I not only felt guilty for going against my Christian beliefs, but, even worse, I knew that the temporal punishment for sex outside of marriage was the ultimate shame: ruining the reputations of the pregnant girl, our two families, and me. Then there was the eternity-in-hell part.

One time I had accidentally gone into the girls' locker room and only realized my mistake when I heard voices that, even in junior high, were too high to be boys'. I stayed just long enough to see a tall girl with a creamy tan and a glistening white butt walk toward the showers. Unlike the boys' locker room, which smelled of rank socks and unwashed jockstraps, the girls' room smelled of perfume and shampoo with only the slightest whiff of sweat. For months I fantasized about similar "accidents" that only increased my guilt for the original mistake. To this day I still find the smell of recently shampooed hair to be erotic.

So, with my overactive imagination, I was lying in bed sweating and thinking of Sandy. This time I was pretending we were on the beach and discussing whether it was time to go back out and catch a few waves. What makes this hilarious is that at that point, I had never surfed. In fact, I had seen a documentary on sharks during one of the few rainy schedules at school a few months before and was terrified of going into the ocean. It's not that I couldn't swim. Backyard pools were fine. I could even jump off the high dive at public swimming pools. But the idea of something underneath the water just waiting to take a chunk out of me was too much, especially when that chunk could be the lower half of my body. As an adult, *Jaws* kept my family from vacationing near the ocean for a good ten years. So, even in my imagination, we stayed on the beach, but the more I thought of her in that pink bikini, the more I was building up the nerve to slip out back and look in her window.

Had I gone back to sleep the dream might have sufficed, but, still awake, I decided to go for the real thing. (The "real thing." Geez, I sometimes think I'm just an amalgam of trite commercial slogans.) In the hall, I slowly closed my door and stopped to listen for anyone who might have heard me. Thankfully the thick carpet, a must for all of our homes, muffled the sound of my steps. I was going out the kitchen into the garage before I realized I couldn't remember if I had closed my door. I tiptoed back and heard what I thought was music coming from Debbie's room. She would often go to sleep with her radio on, so I figured I was safe. Then it occurred to me that even if she were awake she would be listening to the music and certainly wouldn't hear me padding down the hall. I even paused for a few moments to admire my reasoning.

In the backyard the pepper tree looked spooky against the half-moon sky. I kept hearing some scratching near the oleanders that I hoped was one of the neighborhood cats, but imagined it was a man trying to do what I was planning. My imagination often got the better of me. I mean I watched *Alfred Hitchcock Presents* only once, and I wasn't even alone in the house. I think it was actually a show about this guy looking in windows. He would torment them at night by slipping in and out of view and then, when they felt safe the next day, he would kill them. I still get a little nervous as I'm writing this. So I was overcoming possible murderers and the almost certain condemnation of God, just to climb over the Bradleys' fence to get a chance to see Sandy.

The conditions were perfect, until Billy arrived. The moonlight was strong enough for me to see my way to her window, but once I was close, a trio of palms with wide stumpy trunks hid me from view. Sandy's windows were hung with sheer curtains that seemed to invite me to look in. To soothe my conscience, which I did unconsciously, I pretended I was watching a movie, that she was an actress, and that I was looking at her like anyone else in the audience.

I finally made it through the night to Sunday morning. When I got up, Dad had already taken a bath and was sitting at the kitchen table in a sleeveless undershirt and dress pants. I didn't appreciate him, especially with Mom's constant carping about him in my ear. I didn't even like the way he looked. His nose was too long and crooked, and he had dents on each side made by his glasses. I didn't like his pale body and trucker's tan. I didn't like that he wasn't tall like our neighbor on the other side of the Bradley's, Captain Carroll. Maw-Maw used to talk about what a handsome couple Dad and Mom were in Texas, especially when he was in uniform, but I wasn't convinced. One thing I did like about him: he wasn't skinny.

"Want some Grape-Nuts?" he said as he gestured with his bowl.

"Okay. But right out of the box." Dad usually softened his for a few minutes in milk. Uggh.

He looked up with a banana in his hand. "Want a few slices of—" He looked at me for a few moments. "What happened to you?"

"I'm not sure. It's weird. I had this dream. I was watering the oleanders." Mom was always complaining that Dad never watered them enough and that's why five years after they were planted, they still didn't hide us from the neighbors behind. "So I think I might have been sleepwalking." This was sounding lame, but I hoped just mentioning the oleanders would throw him off.

He began to put banana on my cereal even though I hadn't agreed to any. "You ever sleep-walked before?"

Mom arranged almost everything that had to do with doctors, church, school, and extracurricular stuff like music lessons and often admonished Dad because he didn't do his part, or at least remember what had happened. As a result, Dad could sometimes be fooled into thinking that he had forgotten something. But he would see sleepwalking as a pretty big deal, so this would be one thing he knew he would have remembered.

"I think I did it once on an overnighter with the Royal Ambassadors." They were like a religious Boy Scout group and something Dad was not likely to check out with Mr. Bodenhamer, our sponsor. Dad looked at me for a few moments, like he recognized me but couldn't remember where he had seen me before. "Soooo. How do you think you got that bruise?"

I had thought up the oleanders to explain the scratches and forgot about the bump that felt like it was swelling as we talked. "I don't remember anything when I was sleepwalk-ing—if I really was." (By sounding doubtful, I could soften Dad's possible opposition. Such a smart cookie.) "But in the dream, I got scared by something in the house and ran right into the fence behind the oleanders." I shrugged as if to say, "Who knows what can happen when you're sleepwalking," and poured some milk on my cereal.

Right then I wondered if I should try to throw up so I could both stay home and avoid any more questions about how I looked. I knew I couldn't lie my way through the whole day, especially once Debbie, the most skeptical per-son in the universe, started interrogating me.

I got Dad off the sleepwalking subject by asking who he thought might come close to Roger Maris's homerun record this year. I hurriedly finished my cereal while he talked about Mickey Mantle and Willie Mays. I put my bowl in the sink and said, "Thanks for breakfast. I'm gonna get ready."

In my room I was scrambling for ideas. If I told Mom I didn't feel well, she would want to take my temperature and I would have to find a way either to raise it artificially or to convince her I was sick even though I didn't have a fever. Throwing up would do it, but I was always lousy at anything but gagging when I put a finger down my throat.

I went over my story a few times in my head, revising it slightly before I had to tell it again to Mom. I wouldn't have to sell it to Debbie because she was deathly afraid of getting sick and would stay away from me once she found out I was nauseous. She hated missing anything to do with her acting and was already in rehearsal for a small part in a musical at the Starlight Bowl. Not that she wouldn't be suspicious, but I was betting she wouldn't take the chance to get close enough to a diseased body to investigate. Since Mom would drive us to the emergency room at a moment's notice, I had to walk the narrow line between something serious enough to miss church over but not serious enough for a doctor.

I rubbed my cheeks real hard to make my face look flush, put on an old Cub Scout handkerchief to hide the scratch marks on my neck, and got into bed. I started to fake shivering but knew it would be hard to make it believable without a fever, so I got up and started spinning in a circle to make myself dizzy, hoping I would either throw up or at least look dazed. I did get dizzy and felt awful enough that I actually had to lie down.

"We're leaving soon," I heard Mom yell through my bedroom door.

I tried to yell back while sounding pitifully weak at the same time. I should tell Debbie that would be a good exercise for her acting class. Instead, Mom just couldn't hear me. She knocked and opened my door before I told her to come in.

She said, "Let's go, buddy boy," before she noticed I was in bed and immediately looked worried. "Are you sick?" She had on everything except her blouse and skirt, which was not surprising since she was usually walking around in a bra and slip while making sure everyone else got ready.

Sometimes she would ask me to zip up her dress. She even had me snap on her bra a few times.

She was strikingly beautiful but gradually becoming overweight. She would add a few pounds every year until it not only hampered her looks but also made her mostly immobile the last years of her life. Her large brown eyes were framed by dark eyebrows and thick eyelashes that needed no makeup. Her body was as close to Marilyn Monroe's as you could get without being blond and slimmer. Mom's hair was dark, almost blue-black like you see in some Japanese women, and she had olive skin that never seemed to get sunburned. She had a large smile that reminded Dad of Mary Tyler Moore. But probably what got her the most notice was the gracefulness of her movements, like she was a ballet dancer or Fred Astaire's partenaire de danse. Maw-Maw used to talk about all the men who were after her in Beaumont, especially after Dad had done something to irritate her, like telling that joke about the pastor finding the couple having sex. Mom still turned heads even as her upper arms began to flab and bulges were starting to form between her ribs.

This was the crucial moment. She would decide in the next few seconds to stay home and take care of me or to see through my ruse and force me to go. If Mom hadn't promised to shepherd a new family through their first church service, I think she might have stayed, but commitments were sacred to her, especially those that involved people in need. In fact, most of the terrible arguments between Mom and Dad started with Dad wanting to change his mind about something Mom had decided to do for someone else.

"I'll get the thermometer."

"No, I'm okay. I mean, I don't have a fever. I just feel a little queasy."

Mom felt my head and agreed. I knew she was very sensitive to stomach upsets and considered it a valid reason to forego almost anything. "I didn't sleep well last night, so I think I'll be fine with a little more rest." This was the other half of Mom's therapeutic approach. The first was to take our temperature and, if we had a fever, speed us to the doctor. The second was to order us to bed.

She didn't ask me what kept me awake, so I didn't have to get into the story. Besides, she used to tell us about her father sleepwalking at night, which is why I came up with the lie to begin with. It was good I could avoid going into details because she would likely think of some weird precautions to protect me in the future, like locking my door from the outside. Dad wouldn't be likely to bring it up because he tried to avoid things that might upset her.

Debbie had been listening in the hallway and walked in when Mom left. She asked me to explain once more what made me think I had been somnambulating. She liked any excuse to show off her vocabulary. After I gave her the revised explanation, she looked at me like she wasn't convinced either but said nothing. You would think she would find ways to stay home, too, since she had come to doubt our church's theology. But she liked the hypocritical attention she got from the deacons since she was as attractive as Mom but younger. She reminded people of Sophia Loren with blue-gray eyes.

Maw-Maw stopped in too. She was already wearing her usual floor-length dress. She had at least a dozen. Most were some shade of blue and had pockets where she kept a tissue and gum. Her sensible black shoes had laces and a one-inch heel. Her hair puffed out like a furry helmet over an equally puffy face that was beginning to obscure her Katherine Hepburn jaw. She told me she would pray for me to feel better, which just made me feel doubly guilty.

As soon as I saw that the car had turned the corner, I settled in the living room to watch Mighty Mouse cartoons, trying to avoid thinking about Billy and his sister.

CHAPTER TWO

Sunday Night

EVEN IF I WAS the only one who heard Mom open and close the bathroom door and then click on the light, it still didn't seem right that no one else got up to help. And was I also the only one who could hear her moaning? Standing in the hall outside the door, I waited for a pause in her breathing to knock.

"I'm okay," she said, before the moaning began again, but softer.

"Mom, it's Joey."

"I know, honey. Go back to bed. I'll be okay."

I did not move.

"Really."

Maw-Maw had said she never knew anyone that could tolerate more pain than Mom. She said Mom had severe morning sickness when she was pregnant with both Debbie and me but wouldn't take anything. She once walked fifteen miles with a high fever during a Louisiana hurricane to beg a doctor to come help Maw-Maw, who couldn't stop vomiting. Just before she graduated from high school, she had a tooth pulled without the anesthetic because they were barely squeaking by after her father died. So I knew she was really hurting if she was making noise.

I opened the door slowly because she was usually on the floor. She was naked, but I was used to it by now. Her knees were pulled close to her chest and, when she saw me, she apologized and asked for a towel. I grabbed one from the rack and hesitated, because the towel couldn't cover her completely. She grabbed it with a grimace and spread it over her legs. Then she began to rock back and forth like she was trying to do sit-ups on her side.

"Thanks, sweetie. Now you go back to bed."

At first, she always refused help. To show that I was sincere, I had to repeat an offer at least three times. Which I did.

"Okay, but don't stay up too long. You need—" She sucked in air to deal with the next stab of pain. Sometimes the pain would subside when she threw up. Sometimes she just needed to lie quietly for a while. There usually wasn't much for me to do. She mostly wanted support. If she needed relief with an enema, then I held the bladder until all the water emptied into her bowels.

Tonight I was standing in the corner near the door. When she was finished, I wet a washcloth and placed it on her forehead, like she did for us when we had a temperature. I tried not to look at her too much while I was doing this.

I know it's disturbing that this boy was allowed in the bathroom with his naked mother, but, like I already said, I wanted to help. Since she didn't think it was strange, neither did I. Back then I was just upset that no one else was concerned. Super rebellious, smarter-than-anyone Debbie could barely stand to be near Mom, even at the dinner table, so there was no way she would play nurse. But not even once? Dad got up very early and was the soundest sleeper in the whole house, but did he really sleep through it *every* time?

"Thank you, Puppy. You're such a good boy." My face felt hot. I was called Puppy because of this dog I tried to save. I would come to hate this kind of attention, but then it sustained me. (Mom's nickname for Debbie was Her Majesty.)

She took a few, deep, slow breaths and smiled, either to convince herself or me that the worst was over. "I'll be all right. Now give Mommy a kiss."

I leaned down to her on the floor and tried to kiss her on the cheek, but she guided me to her lips. I shudder at the memory. No wonder I still have trouble with intimacy. I remember hearing that dentists have lousy relationships because they spend so much time in the faces of people whom they aren't close to emotionally. I understand. These days I have an arrangement with my hygienist that I will take at least two breaks before she finishes cleaning my teeth. She thinks I have bladder problems.

"Turn out the light before you open the door."

I flipped the switch, stepped outside, pulled the door almost shut and reached back through the opening to turn the light back on before I shut it completely.

"Whoa, whoa, whoa, Mr. J." Debbie held out her arms to keep me from walking into her.

"Shhh. You're gonna wake up—"

"Who am I going to wake up? Mom's already up. Maw-Maw's in snore city without her hearing aids, and you'd need a cannon to rouse Dad before his alarm goes off."

17

She was right. But I wanted her quiet anyway, out of respect for Mom, I guess. Debbie was wearing one of Dad's yellowed T-shirts and some flannel Christmas pajama bottoms with tiny candy canes. She had cut off most of the legs to make them provocatively short. Her black hair was tied back tight enough to pull her forehead taut. She had on Minnie Mouse house shoes that had no practical purpose whatsoever.

I said, "I'm sleepy," which was a lie because my heart was pounding even before I ran into Debbie. "And I'm going to bed." That was true. When I started to walk past her, she cut me off like she had learned to play defense with her feet from a basketball coach.

"Were you in there with Mom?"

Since she was standing here when I came out, she was either asking because she didn't believe it or because she felt something was wrong with it.

"Mom's sick," I said, not hiding my annoyance.

Debbie shrugged her shoulders, leaned her head forward, and shook her head with her mouth open, as if to say this was the most obvious statement anyone had ever made. She responded by walking past me to knock on the door, a lot louder than I had done a few minutes earlier.

"Mo-om? Can I come in?"

Mom didn't notice it was a different voice and said that I had done enough already.

The hall nightlight was dim, but I could see that Debbie was looking back at me as she said to Mom, "It's me, Debbie."

"Oh. Ah. Not yet." Even through the door I could hear a hint of eagerness in her voice—her daughter finally showing her some concern. "Just a minute."

Debbie did not stop looking at me while she waited for Mom to let her in. Once she went in, I knew I should go back to bed while I could, but I was too curious to see what Debbie would do. I could hear talking through the door but couldn't understand anything other than hearing my name a few times. When Debbie stepped out, I could see that Mom had put on her robe and was leaning forward on the commode with her head in her hands, like she was gathering the strength to go back to bed, or to go on with her life.

Debbie frowned as she closed the door behind her. Her look was all the more menacing because she wore mascara and eyeliner to bed. Every time she complained about some tiny pimple on her face, Mom would tell her how she was so lucky to have such dark lashes and eyebrows that she didn't need makeup. But Debbie was always given to extremes, especially if Mom counseled against it.

In the hall she shook her head slowly, like it hurt for her ponytail to move with her head. She stared at me. "Mom asked me to wait so she could put on her robe, didn't she?" She waited all of a millisecond for an answer. "What the hell is going on?"

To Maw-Maw using the word "hell" was tantamount to saying the Lord's name in vain, and I had heard Dad say it only once, but we were at a baseball game and the men around us were saying much worse.

"Geez, Debbie. She's sick. What's the big deal?"

I knew this would not be enough to get Debbie off my back, but I wanted to make her feel as guilty as possible before she let me have it over I did not know what. Besides, I was annoyed that she was suggesting I was doing something wrong when it was everybody else, including Debbie, who weren't doing what was right.

Even if Billy hadn't attacked me, I knew that standing in the dark outside Sandy's window was wrong. But what could be wrong with helping your mother? She was always putting herself out at church, at my junior high where she worked, and even for strangers on vacation.

On one trip to Texas, she actually had saved a woman whose family was staying in the room next to us at the El Camino in El Paso. By the pool, in the afternoon, Mom heard the woman coughing. Debbie already had a circle of boys around her, and one of them was the woman's son. When Mom asked him if his mother was okay, he said that she coughed like that all the time. That day she must have smoked at least a pack of cigarettes just while I was noticing. Mom had gotten Dad to stop only a few months before even though he still would light up a pipe after dinner now and then. The woman asked Mom to recommend a Mexican restaurant, and they got to talking. In between coughs she said, "My doctor wants us to move to Arizona if my lungs don't clear up soon, but my husband has too good a job to leave."

Mom said, "I know. And you hate to uproot the kids from school and their friends." They chatted a while longer and Mom didn't think any more about it until later. A little after midnight, the woman's coughing woke us up. Mom knocked on their door, and the panic on the son's face when he answered made Mom ask if she could come in. The woman was red-faced and gasping for breath. Mom couldn't get through to the front desk to ask for an ambulance, so she had Dad drive the woman to the hospital. They knew where it was because Dad had been stationed at nearby Fort Bliss before we moved to California.

The woman survived and thanked Mom by inviting us to stay in her guesthouse in San Antonio whenever we came through that part of Texas. When they sent us a sofa the next Christmas, Mom found out that she and her husband owned a very successful furniture store. Seriously. Apparently during their poolside conversation, Mom had mentioned that ours had been ruined by a small fire on the Fourth of July and we couldn't afford a nice replacement. When the woman's father died, Mom sent flowers.

That's not all. A man at church had been injured on a construction job, and Mom brought his family dinner every night for a week, right after fixing dinner for us. She said it was no trouble because all she had to do was double the recipe. Then, from the money she was saving for our next vacation, she paid for materials for the set of *The King and I* when Debbie, in tears, said someone had stolen the money the drama class had raised the summer before. When I was invited to fly with the all-San Diego elementary school orchestra to Chicago for a national competition, Mom paid for my plane ticket and hotel by using the money she had been saving for her own trip to her twentieth high school reunion in Beaumont. And she had been a star there: homecoming queen and valedictorian. She never did go because Dad got laid off, and she had to work extra as a cashier at Fedco just so we could afford the basics. Every night she fixed dinner even though she was exhausted after getting home from work. Otherwise, Dad would insinuate that Maw-Maw was taking Mom's place.

She did even more for me: always telling me how smart and talented I was and that I could do anything I wanted. This didn't jibe with how I felt, so I both clung to it and denied it. I felt that helping her tonight was what we should all be falling over ourselves to do.

Debbie had her hands on her hips, arms akimbo, in her best offended-adult imitation. "You're a grown boy." That's

21

not how she usually characterized me. "Well, almost grown, and young men don't help their mothers in the bathroom." She blinked slowly so I could watch her eyes disappear and reappear like a reptile's. "Please tell me she had something on under the robe."

"Look, I'm tired. Let's talk about this tomorrow, when we've both had some rest." I almost laughed because I was repeating exactly what Dad said to Mom whenever she wanted to continue arguing near bedtime.

"Joey, did she have ANYTHING on under her robe?"

Since Mom often went around in her underwear, even if it was no more than a negligee, that was a reasonable question. I was stuck. I could lie, but I could only be convincing with a lot of preparation. Without it, my blushing face and shifty eyes always gave me away. That's probably why Dad seemed to doubt the sleepwalking story yesterday. I decided the safest response was to say nothing and hope she would let me go back to bed.

"Joey, why do you think Mom allows you in there like that?"

Now the lecture was coming. Probably based on something she had read in some stupid book. I had to admit, she was probably the most well read person I have ever known, which included most of my professors in college. Her obsession had begun early. She had already read all the books in the small elementary school library by the end of fifth grade. That summer the Books on Wheels had a stop only a few blocks from our house. She was given permission to check out ten books every week. How? The mobile librarian agreed to give her ten the very first time as a trial. Debbie proved she had read them by orally summarizing each book. We found out because the woman called Mom to congratulate her. By high school, she knew more about a lot of things than most adults, including our parents.

She leaned close to me with her hands on my shoulders. I could smell the chocolate she had eaten while in bed. I wanted to tell her she forgot to brush her teeth.

"You don't know about the Oedipus complex and all that Freudian stuff," a condescending understatement to be sure, "but this is beyond weird." She shook her head again—this was a regular habit—raising her eyebrows at the same time for emphasis. It's hard when you're smarter than everyone else and still not even old enough to vote. "A boy in the bathroom with his naked mother?" She used her Texas accent, so she actually said "necked," as if saying something insightful in a dumb-sounding drawl made it sound more profound.

"I don't know what an octopus complexity is"—she started to interrupt, but I went on quickly—"and I don't care." I was angry now because I knew she had me. I was all the more uncomfortable because I was still dealing with what happened last night. I simply turned away from her and walked into my bedroom, locking the door behind me. She said something that included the words "sorry" and "weird," but did not try to come in.

Back in bed I was hoping that Mom would tuck me in as usual, which she sometimes did on these stomach-bout nights. I wanted to know she was okay, but I wanted more for her to tell me that there was nothing wrong with what I did. I couldn't sleep, but not only because of what Debbie had insinuated. I would doze off and dream of Billy telling Sandy what I had done. I would wake up and then sleep long enough to imagine him telling his parents. I would fall asleep and wake again, each time with Billy telling someone else. The last group was the Carroll twins, who lived on the other side of the Bradley's, Billy's family. I should have been worried about what my family might think or the people at church, but I didn't dream about them. I knew Maw-Maw would give me up to the devil because the only people she despised more than drunks were people obsessed with sex. When I found out years later how my grandfather, her husband, died, it is not all that surprising.

So I lay there wondering what I would do. I started thinking of other windows I could sneak a look into, like the Twambley girls', who lived on the opposite side of us from the Bradleys. There were four girls plus the parents, and three of them were quite striking. Well, they all were, but one was too young. Instead I did what I usually did whether I was upset or not. I imagined Sandy undressing for bed until I could get that exquisite release.

I must have slept some because I almost levitated when Dad knocked on my door to get me up for school.

CHAPTER THREE

"Who's our hickey man today?"

Greg Skinner wasn't referring particularly to me. It was just how he, notorious in the ninth grade for all the girls who wanted him and for being bigger than most of the teachers, liked to start his day at Douglass Junior High. He inspected everyone who walked from the main entrance down the hall. Like a modern Neanderthal, he had enough facial hair for a full beard and his neck was so thick it was hard to tell where it ended and his head began, which was probably why he always wore shirts with collars. To him everybody but his friends were pencil-neck geeks. A few of us referred to him, way under our breaths, as the no-neck monster from what the children were called in *Cat on a Hot Tin Roof.* I was on my way to English class when he stopped me.

"Buddy boy, you better have a talk with your girlfriend 'cause it looks like she was looking for blood not love." He laughed like a snorting donkey that was trying to catch his breath.

I think the point was that this hypothetical girl I made out with was so inept she could manage only scratches, not a decent hickey. Or that the only girl who would have me would be a vampire looking for nourishment. He had no idea how flattered I was that he thought a girl was responsible.

"She do that, too?" he said, pointing to my head.

I shook my head, forgetting my usual defense of ignoring him.

"Oh, I know what happened." He turned to his buddies to make sure they were watching. Then he walked toward the janitor's closet, hit the door with his foot to make a loud noise, and, at the same time, jerked his head back. His timing made it look so real that I wanted to ask him if he was okay. His fellow hunks thought he was hilarious. Of course, they all had girlfriends on hand, who were beautiful, stacked, or both. One of them, who was compassionate and courageous enough not to go along with Mr. Neckhead, made it worse by giving me that look people use for kids with polio.

Now, don't get me wrong. School was mostly tolerable. Sure, I had to deal with being called Mrs. Popeye by the guys in PE, usually the ones who already had an abundance of pubic hair. If more guys had known how well I did in the classroom, I might have fared even worse. So I didn't talk about how much I liked my teachers, how much I enjoyed learning, and how proud I was to get good grades. Mom helped there, and she had high standards since she had excelled in school. But, alas, academics didn't get me babes or even the grudging respect of guys, most of whom, I bet you're not surprised, did not do so well in class. That was what made sports so important.

By Saturday, most of what Billy had done to me was not so noticeable. This was the day of the big game. I was pitching and therefore the center of attention for half of each inning. We were playing the Elks, known for their three-year win streak and the exploits of the twins.

"Want to warm up in the backyard first or go early to the field?" Dad had just finished breakfast. He had on his usual weekend outfit, yellowed white dress shirt and faded khaki slacks. Mom and Maw-Maw were still in bed. Debbie left an hour ago to rehearse all day for *The King and I*.

"I don't know. What do you think?" I wasn't being polite. I really didn't know which might be better. But if one was, I would do it.

"I say we go early and work on the mound you'll actually be pitching from." Dad said this in spite of having done everything possible to make the mound in the backyard a replica of the one we used in our games.

I poured some milk on a bowl of Trix, which, at almost fifty percent sugar, was guaranteed to get me charged up. I put on my baseball uniform and tennis shoes, carrying my kiddie cleats (no metal studs allowed), my glove, and the catcher's mitt for Dad.

Aside from the hickey silliness at school, no one in the neighborhood had seemed that interested in my Billy-inflicted injuries, but all the kids knew about the big game and everyone, except the twins and their parents, wanted them to get beat. Even Billy wished me good luck yesterday. I hoped that meant he didn't hate me anymore.

Even if I wasn't ever as good at it as I wanted to be and was far from being as good as the twins, I had always loved baseball. Dad and I watched games together on TV before I could even walk. The year I became eligible for Little League, I was second in line to sign up, and that was only because Dad's alarm malfunctioned. Instead of arriving at 6:00 a.m., we were an hour late, but registration began at 9:00 a.m., which is why I was *almost* first.

Hitting a round ball with a round bat required years to master, even for the talented twins. Since we had no T-ball option that enabled us to hit without a pitcher, it took a lot of courage, too. We had to face kids who could throw that very hard ball about as poorly as we could hit it. Three guys on my first team quit during the first week, one after being hit in the middle of the back because he turned the wrong way when he saw the ball headed for his body, the other two when they had to duck to keep from being beaned. I might have quit, too, if there weren't so much at stake. Afraid as I was every time I went to the plate that first season, even when the coach was pitching in practice, I forced myself because I believed that it might somehow lead to a date.

Except for Billy wishing me luck yesterday, I hardly saw him all week. It was not that difficult at school because he never had advanced classes. When I got home in the afternoon, I would rush into the house and stay in my room until I finished my homework. The imminent game gave me a good excuse to practice in the backyard rather than play in the street with the guys. It also meant Billy didn't need to explain why he might not want to play if he was the only one of the four of us who declined. So each day this week I did an hour to two of homework and then was either by myself throwing through the tire Dad had hung on the pepper tree or pitching to Dad himself once he got home. He knew what was at stake with the Saturday game, so he caught me at least some every day, even with Mom nagging him about the yard. And he never brought up the sleepwalking.

When Mom asked about the bump, I took Greg's cue and told her I had walked into my door on the way to the bathroom. She seemed convinced, maybe because she had done it during one of her night stomach bouts. I think she believed the part about the oleanders causing the neck scratches because they were a kind of nemesis of hers, being so uncooperative to grow tall enough to shield us from the prying eyes of our neighbors. Of course, she blamed that on Dad for not preparing the soil properly before he planted them and for forgetting to water without her constant reminders.

Our Little League played at a field built for the community by Convair, the aeronautics corporation where Billy's father worked. I was on the Miramar Jets and the Carroll twins, Jerry and Terry, were, as I already mentioned, on the mighty Elks. Miramar was a naval air station (yes, the *Top Gun* one) and their father was a captain in the navy. Even though he wasn't a pilot, he had plenty of juice as a ship commander.

Billy hated the twins' success almost as much as I did, so I hoped that a victory over the Elks might smooth things out between us. It wasn't likely, but miracles do occur to those who love the Lord, as Maw-Maw reminded me whenever I complained, especially about how unfair it was that I was so skinny.

I had hated and admired the twins ever since the four of us neighborhood boys were all in third grade. We played our first game in the street then, but it was football, not baseball. Of course, their dominance was not limited to any one sport. Billy was a little slimmer then and, since we knew each other before we met the twins, he suggested that we be on one team and the twins on the other. We were all about the same height so it seemed fair.

"Who's got a coin?" Billy said. We looked at him like he wanted to borrow money. "For receiving and going uphill," Billy explained as Terry handed him a quarter. He flipped it so high in the air I started to get a bad feeling about how this would go. He let it drop on the ground like the beginning of an NFL game. Billy and I won, so we chose to receive. The twins chose to face downhill on our quiet little cul-de-sac.

They "kicked off" by throwing the ball in the air. Again the height gave me pause. I caught it and told Billy to follow me close so I could hand it to him to go around me while I blocked. I didn't even get to turn toward him to hand off because Jerry was already tagging me. He smiled like he was having lots of fun.

On our first play from scrimmage, they blitzed and tagged Billy in the backfield. That's right, we're playing two-man teams, and their whole team rushed the quarterback.

"Could you do a little blocking?" Billy said to me rather perturbed.

"Both of them?" I shot back.

"All right, let's switch. You stand further back, and I'll fake a block and go long."

Billy did get behind them, but I couldn't throw it that far, and Jerry intercepted my pass. Terry ran interference for him, until he made it into the end zone, which meant past the manhole cover of our dead-end street.

"Well, at least we didn't have to worry about blocking," Billy said as we walked back to receive the kickoff again.

I liked Billy for that and, until the recent tussle outside his sister's window, we got along real well. We played for only twenty or thirty minutes because by then the score was already sixty to nothing. From then on, they suggested Billy and I should be split up. I don't know if they were being merciful or just found it boring to win with so little resistance. Or maybe being fair like good Christian boys was actually more important than winning.

Not that they had to miss out on much winning from then on. By the time they began junior high, they already had the broad shoulders and slim waists of grown men. They were not quite as advanced as Greg Skinner, but then he had a few years on them. They had begun pumping iron in sixth grade. A diet of protein shakes they mixed themselves, puberty, and daily workouts in their garage gym made them into Adonises at twelve. They had serious guns (what the hunks liked to call biceps) and a chest-lat-shoulder combination that rivaled experienced surfers. As was the fashion in those pre-hippie days, their hair was military short. Both were blond, which gave them an Aryan look. Terry had a crew cut with a white cowlick that looked like he had bleached it. Jerry wore his hair in a flattop. I had a flattop, too, but it never seemed to cooperate, even with tons of Butch Wax. Besides I had this permanent bump on my head that meant the hair in the middle of my scalp had to be extra short so the top of my hair would be even with the rest of my head. Another reason to hate them. Even more annoying, they were overly polite to adults and honest even when it gave them no advantage, like finding money in the street. They made a point of telling Billy and me that they would give it to their church if they couldn't find the original owners.

Girls cooed over them the way they did over movie stars. Their parents didn't allow official girlfriends until high school, but we knew that they had some on the sly. They were so fast that they had finished one-two in the all-junior high PE class100-yard dash, which meant they beat the eighth and ninth graders, too. The high school coaches (football, basketball, and baseball) were already inviting them to games, tempting them with the promise of starting them as freshman and asking where they wanted to play in college. And this was in seventh grade! God I envied them, so beating them in one Little League baseball game would mean a spot in my glory hall of fame.

"Got everything?" Dad was calling to me as I walked off the front porch.

I nodded as I patted my shoes and equipment. I looked to see if the twins had left yet, but their car was still in the driveway. I smiled until it occurred to me that maybe their father had already dropped them off, and he had brought the car back to get his wife. Billy was standing on a milk crate leaning over the engine of his jeep. Yes, he had his own car at twelve. His father let him drive it when they went off-road in the desert, and it would be his when he turned six-teen. Sandy in a pair of shorts and a puffy blouse sat on the porch eating a Popsicle, a bright red one. I tried not to stare.

I put my stuff in the trunk and got in the car. I didn't know what would happen today, but I always felt confident on the ride over. Though I believed Mom about Dad most of the time, I suspended criticism of him when we were involved in baseball, like watching a Dizzy Dean telecast of the Yankees or pitching off that custom mound in the back-yard. He worked for the city as an engineer, so he knew how to build things to exact specifications. He measured and remeasured not just the height, for which he used a level, a protractor, and a series of metal plates, but also the slope of the mound so it would be the same in every way as the one at Convair Field. He spent almost as much time measuring the one at the field and drawing up plans as he did build-ing the one in our backyard. But the rest of the time, I was influenced by Mom to believe that he was irresponsible like most men, while I was a wonderful exception.

Dad and I arrived early for the game, getting there about fifteen minutes before my manager arrived, in just enough time to warm up and throw about thirty pitches off the mound. Dad stood behind the plate. "Nothing's been raked yet. We got here just in time."

I threw some easy tosses to him from the far side of the mound until I felt warm enough to throw with a full windup from the pitching rubber.

"Ahggg." Dad bent into a catcher's squat. "I hope I don't look as old as I feel."

I wanted to think of something funny to say back, but I was already getting into game mode. I am surprised when I recall how important I made that game. Whether it was just a buildup over the years of having to stand in the shadows of the twins' glory or what Debbie implied about me being a momma's boy or the night encounter with Billy, I don't know. But I had this feeling that if our team could beat their team, my whole life would turn around.

After a few pitches, I noticed how comfortable the mound felt and said, "It feels the same as at home."

Dad gave me that smile that exposed his gold crowns. I didn't know then what I know now that, in addition to all the measuring, he had gone to about a dozen sporting goods stores until he found exactly the same pitching mound rubber as the one at the Little League field. He also had a friend who pitched in semipro introduce him to the head groundskeeper for the old Pacific Coast League Padres for further pointers.

Even on the days I wasn't pitching, Dad and I were always the first on my team to arrive. Today most of the Elks were already driving up while I was on the mound. The twins came first. By the time we finished my warm-up, their whole team was there. I wondered if this was the reason they had not lost a game in three years. Two years ago they almost filled the whole all-star squad with their position players, so the league made a rule that each team must have at least one all-star, even if they weren't as good as the Elk at that position.

When I had finished throwing, Dad walked out to the mound and looked it over, nodding. This was the first time he'd seen it since drawing up the plans for the one at home. "Not bad. Not bad if I do say so myself."

We walked to the sidelines together, and he placed his hand on my shoulder. "Remember, one of the beauties of baseball is that on a given day, anyone can be beat." He winked as the twins walked by already with their polite but stern game faces on. We all nodded to each other.

In the dugout, I sat next to Stumpy, who had arrived a few minutes before and would be catching me. We watched the Elks warm up. You couldn't tell now because they all had caps on, but everyone had the same short haircut. No parts on the heads of these guys. And they carried themselves like winners with the crispness of their throws and the way they got themselves into position for groundballs and flies. Also, their uniforms always looked new because they were required to iron them before each game.

They had the same routine for the infield warm-up as most baseball teams, with one difference. Every time someone snagged a ball hit off the bat of the manager, all of them yelled, "Uh huh." Every time a ball was thrown to another player and caught, they yelled, "That's right." Even if you didn't already know how good they were, it would have been unnerving.

Terry was the shortstop, and Jerry played centerfield. While Jerry caught flies between second base and the fence, Terry was fearlessly short-hopping hard-hit grounders and firing to first base with his cannon of an arm.

Stumpy bumped me while still looking straight ahead. "I've got an idea."

I turned to him.

"Don't look at me. Just listen."

I had wanted an excuse to *not* watch how good the Elks looked but turned away from Stumpy and back on them, as he demanded.

"I've been doing some scouting on the chins." He always called them that because they had these Kirk Douglass jaws, and I thought it was funny every time. "I've been taking notes on what pitches they go for, which innings they're strongest in. Trying to find some weakness."

Excited, I turned to him and turned away again when he punched me.

"Listen. Jerry always follows Terry because Jerry's the homerun hitter and they hope Terry will be able to score, too, when his brother blasts one out. And it happens a lot. But I noticed that he usually grounds out after Terry doesn't get on base. In fact, if Terry not only doesn't get on base but strikes out, almost every time Jerry strikes out, too."

While Stumpy was talking, I watched Terry jump in the air to grab a bad hop and lob it perfectly to the second base-man so he could turn the pretend double play.

"So, the only problem is keeping Terry off the bases. Wow, Stumpy you're a genius."

Now *he* turned to me, but with his tongue stuck out. "Shut up, I'm not finished." He sat forward and leaned on his knees. "My point is that Terry," who was now running into left field chasing down a pop fly that he caught over his shoulder and then rocketed perfectly to the catcher, "is the one to concentrate on."

Stumpy paused while his mouth hung open in response to Terry's play. "He usually gets fastballs because most of the pitchers can't throw anything else that actually goes over the plate."

Nobody but Stumpy knew I used the tire in the back-yard to develop a pretty wicked curve after he showed me a few possible grips. Dad had advised against it and so had our manager, but conquering the twins might be worth the price of the torn shoulder they warned me about.

Stumpy went on. "As good as the chinsters are, they are so used to doing well they never have to deal with any adversity in these games."

I smiled then, and I'm smiling now as I recall the conversation because Stumpy actually thought all we lacked was a good strategy.

"If we can find a way to make them doubt themselves, just for a part of the game, even if we don't make the right pitches, they may just defeat themselves."

I liked Stumpy because he was Billy with a little more intensity and intelligence. Both were easy-going, liked to laugh, and hated the same people as me. But Stumpy had a competitive spirit and a little more physical talent than Billy, even though they resided pretty much in identical bodies. Also, he was good at arguing and almost as well read as Debbie.

Some of our teammates joined us on the bench and Stumpy stopped talking like we were spies worried about being overheard.

Finally the game began. The first few innings were uneventful. Jerry hit a foul ball that would have been a homerun if fair and then popped out to short. Terry hit a fierce line drive to our second baseman, who looked shocked to find it in his glove. As for the rest of the Elks, they got a few hits, but nobody made it past first base. It was more luck than good pitching. As for the Jets, we actually loaded the bases with one out in the second inning when Stumpy came to bat. He hit a dribbler back to the pitcher that became a double play.

In the fifth inning, Terry was leading off and the score still tied at 0–0. You could see the frustration in the Elks. I wasn't striking anybody out, but every ball stayed in the infield, which was fortunate because our outfielders were notorious for misjudging flies. When we were at bat, Stumpy had been begging me to start using my curve, but I was nervous about it for two reasons. First, because Dad and our manager had already talked about it ruining my arm. I laugh now at the idea I thought I had a future in baseball. Second, because I was also afraid I didn't quite have it under control enough to keep from hitting the batter. Still I had to admit that I was actually doing pretty well, throwing strikes almost every time to a team that always got a lot of bases on balls just by being patient.

So Terry walks to the plate and gives me his best look-right-through-you stare. I hoped he couldn't see how scared I was. By now he was surely expecting to get a hit, so Stumpy was hoping he might go after a few bad pitches. Stumpy set up a little outside and I hit the mitt perfectly, Terry swinging right through it. He looked at me as if to say that was just luck and took a few practice swings before getting back in the batter's box. The next pitch was way high and Terry smiled. The next he fouled off the top of the back-stop. I reminded myself that I was doing well just getting the ball over the plate. I'd seen Elks games in which they would bat around, half of them getting walks and the rest of them knocking the ball into the outfield, often on bad pitches, most over the heads of the infielders and the rest right through their legs.

The count reached three balls and two strikes. Since I had miraculously avoided walking anybody so far, I figured it wouldn't hurt to risk one walk by throwing my curve. I glanced at Dad in the stands, and he made fists at shoulder height and shook them at me. I couldn't tell if he was encouraging me to be strong or threatening to beat up someone if I didn't do well. Anyway, I wound up slowly and threw the ball toward the middle of the plate, but just before it got to Terry, it took a wicked turn and surprised me by dropping a little, too. Well, I wasn't the only one it surprised. Stumpy could barely block it and Terry spun around, almost losing his balance. Strike three.

Oh, Lord God Almighty. I was beside myself. I could already hear Dad yelling, "That's my boy. Mr. Strikeout. That's my boy." When I looked at him his mouth was wide open and he was, well, you'd have to call it dancing, in a way. His arms were waving like he was in the chorus of a musical and his hips were doing this funny jerking. I didn't recognize it as any of the popular dances like the twist or the watusi or some of the stranger ones Debbie would do. But I had to admit it I wasn't embarrassed over him looking goofy. I just enjoyed him enjoying me striking out the first twin.

Terry said something to Jerry on the way back to the dugout and then stared at me for a moment before going to his seat. When I looked back at Dad, Mom was talking to a woman next to her. She had apparently missed the whole thing because Dad said something to her and then she began to clap and smile. Even this far away it looked like the fake one she used with people she didn't know. I shook my head to get back in the game.

Jerry was up next and intimidated every pitcher because he had the biggest bat and because it seemed to have a personality of its own. Like it would come after you if Jerry didn't do well at the plate, which wasn't usually a problem. Jerry encouraged such thinking because he talked to it. I walked around the mound like I'd seen pitchers on TV do when they needed to concentrate. I was so giddy over striking out Terry, with my new curve ball no less, that I caught myself smiling as I looked at Stumpy. You really didn't give signals in Little League, at least not on our team. As I said earlier, it was almost a miracle to keep from hitting batters or walking most of them. We had played one team that walked the bases loaded without throwing one strike. That's right, sixteen straight balls not even close to the strike zone. But Stumpy gave me a signal anyway, a single finger down calling for a fastball. For some reason it gave me more confidence to have him giving signals like a major league catcher.

Jerry seemed more determined than usual, if that was possible. He kept adjusting his batting helmet and nodding every time his bat slapped home plate, like he was responding to what it was saying to him. I think he wanted to hit me as much as he wanted to hit the ball. The first pitch was over the plate, and he whacked it so hard I thought I heard the ball whimper: a rocket down the first base line, but ever so slightly foul. He stepped out of the box and adjusted his helmet again. Back in place he didn't tap the plate. He just swung real slowly, each time ending his swing by pointing his bat at me. I was mesmerized by it, and Stumpy had to yell at me to start my windup. Another fastball down the middle, and he was early because my fastball wasn't so fast. The ball almost hit the third base coach, but, mercifully, it was another foul ball.

I decided it was time for the curve again. I glanced over at Dad, who was just nodding as if to say, you're going to do this. Under my breath I asked Dad to forgive me for not telling him about my new pitch. I tried to do just what I had done to Terry, throw the ball down the middle of the plate, so that if it curved (I hoped it would drop again, too) he would have no chance of touching it just like his brother. It did drop, but I threw it off the plate and, anxious as he was for a hit, he wasn't even close to being tempted.

Stumpy was nodding with an exaggerated motion, so I knew he meant me to try the curve again. I thought I felt a pain in my elbow but decided Stumpy was right. He had done the research. Jerry actually looked rattled and maybe even angry. I had him where I wanted him if I could just get the stupid ball near the plate. I muttered a short prayer, promising I would never look in another window again and would do the dishes every night without being asked.

The pitch seemed to take forever to get to the plate. Jerry wasn't expecting it. It started for the middle of the plate just like the one to Terry and then moved to the left like Jerry's body was the magnetic opposite of the ball. He swung with so much effort he sounded like an Olympic weightlifter straining during the clean and jerk. I instinctively turned to see how far it had sailed over the fence only to see my teammates jumping up and down. I turned back to the plate, and Stumpy was running out to me like guys do when they've won the World Series. Jerry was shaking his head and dragging his bat behind him like it had betrayed him. I had struck him out. I had struck out both twins back to back. I was amazed. I was amazing.

Dad was jumping up and down. Mom was not next to him, but it was just as well because he might have jumped on her accidentally. He was so excited I started to cry. Everybody was crowded around me, pushing me and hugging me and screaming. Our manager had to remind us that there was one more out.

As it turned out the Elks came through in the end. I had already thrown a lot of pitches, so Scott came into pitch the last inning and proceeded to give up hit after hit. Both Terry and Jerry hit homeruns, and we lost ten to nothing.

But no one could take away the glory of striking out the twins. Stumpy kept smiling at me with a scrunched up face and his tongue sticking out as we gathered our stuff to leave.

I tried not to look too happy since we were beat so bad, but Dad has his hand out smiling as I came up to him. He winked and said softly, "We'll talk in the car." He kept shaking his head and running his hands down his sides and touching his nose and ear like he was a third base coach giving me a sign, and then laughing.

Mom walked over with a kind of puppy dog frown. She had on a sleeveless lavender blouse tucked into a tight-fitting black skirt that just touched her knees when standing. Along with her patent-leather heels, she looked like the wife of an executive or a politician, someone who had gotten married more for the impression she made with her looks than anything else. Not exactly a bimbo, but not a mother of two working for a low wage on the office staff of a school either.

"You are so smart. What does this game matter?" She hugged me like my best friend had died, and I would be able to cope just fine without him.

I didn't hug her back because I was so stunned. She didn't notice my standoffishness and asked me if I wanted to help her in the snack bar, I guess to get my mind off the disappointment of losing.

Dad interjected that we were going to talk over some things about the game. "Can you get along without him this time?"

He never suggested we do something else when Mom wanted help. I was ready for a little dustup between them, but Mom didn't seem fazed, acting like this was what fathers always did with sons after a game in which their butts had been kicked.

She said she would see us later and walked to the stand for which she scheduled the volunteer moms and ordered all the supplies. On the way over other fathers followed her with their eyes while they talked with the women and boys near them. I never thought of my mother as a flirt, but she wasn't discouraging anyone by the way she dressed and the way she walked, a bit reminiscent of Jayne Mansfield but not quite as pneumatic.

I was in turmoil. I didn't like Mom's response and couldn't blow it off as just someone who didn't understand baseball. I felt a little guilty because she didn't try to make me feel bad for going home with Dad, but why did I feel guilty when she had missed the significance of the whole game?

In the car, Dad went over every pitch I threw to the twins. He was like some radio sportscaster who could remember a play-by-play from years ago. "Did you and Stumpy have some kind of strategy going?"

I was pleased it seemed that way to him.

He was backing up out of the parking space on the dirt lot. He hit the accelerator a little hard and the back wheels spun, throwing up some dust.

"Yeah, Stumpy had been watching the twins and thought of a way to rattle them."

"Look, throwing a few curves in one game won't hurt, but your manager was right about what it can eventually do to a young arm." So he could tell. He pulled onto the road that paralleled the freeway. "But boy you made them look silly. They always say that is what separates the major leaguers from the rest, whether they can hit a curve ball."

He said that the twins would have new respect for me even though they won the game. But he said that the most important lesson was how practice made me better. "Most people never learn that. They think that someone is good at something—baseball, violin, acting, math—because they were born with the ability."

I started to say that the twins were already good in third grade. But I had to admit they worked hard. You got the feeling that they practiced plays just for our pick-up games in the street even though they were on opposite teams.

The Elks were doing their usual post-game discussion, which might lead to a short practice in a nearby park if the manager and coaches felt there was something that it didn't go well. I remember Jerry telling me that they spent an hour just bunting when two of their best hitters hit a foul ball for the third strike. They had won that game, too.

They must have had at least a short practice (maybe the twins demanded batting practice) because we beat them home by a long shot.

CHAPTER FOUR

DAD AND I WERE the first ones to bring news of the game to Chelsey Drive.

Billy was working on his jeep as usual. He stopped to yell, "So?" as if we were still pals. Or maybe he was just more interested in the game against the twins than what happened between us a week ago. "We lost," I shouted through the car window.

"Whoa, whoa, whoa," said Dad. He got out of the car and motioned Billy over. "Are you a baseball fan? I mean, if I talk to you about fastballs and curves, will you understand?"

"Sure," Billy said. That might be true, but he was certainly not an avid fan like Dad and me.

Dad went on to describe how I had pitched to the twins and how the twins had responded both with their bats and with their body language on the way back to the dugout.

"Back to back strikeouts?" Billy wiped his dirty hand on his already dirty T-shirt and shook mine heartily. I hoped he was implying that besting the twins made up for everything else. "Were they pissed off beyond belief?" He looked at Dad to see if he should have used another word, but Dad was already walking up the steps to the front door.

"Terry looked like he wanted to break his bat over something." I laughed a little uncomfortably. "Probably me."

Billy was nodding like he could easily imagine it. His hips did a wiggle of delight, his belly jiggling in sync.

The Carrolls drove up as Billy returned to his jeep. The manager and coaches must have been pleased with their performance. Billy looked up and waved. The twins were all smiles, conquering heroes and all. I thought I caught a look of pity on Mrs. Carroll's face when she noticed me.

"Football later?" Terry yelled.

Billy said, "Soon as I get this carburetor back in." He looked at me and winked.

I think I was as happy for that wink as I was for my pitching success.

Captain Carroll said something to the twins as they walked in the house, then looked back at Billy and me. I knew that meant they had chores to do and wouldn't be able to play until they were finished.

On our porch I heard, "Congratulations." Debbie was greeting me from inside. I looked at her closely to see if she was being sarcastic. Her pigtails hung over a sleeveless blouse that looked like one Mom might wear. She had on her usual weekend cutoff jeans and flip-flops. "Whaaat? I mean it. Dad told me about you striking out the twins."

This was turning into a very interesting day. We lost big, but my tiny moment of glory was what gets the press. I told her it was true and thanked her.

I went to my room and began to take off my uniform. I sat on the sofa and wondered if there were any girls in the stands who noticed. I looked out the window at the ice plant blooming purple and white on the hillside of the neighbor's yard above us. What should I do now as I basked in my glory? I could practice with the tire in the back and get Dad to catch me some. I could see if Billy was finished with the carburetor and ask him if he wanted to throw the football around until the twins were ready. I could think about Sandy.

"Where's Joey?" I heard the front door screen slam and then a knocking on my door.

As usual Mom didn't wait until I let her in. "Oh, honey." She sat on the sofa and put her arm around me pulling my head to her bosom. "You have nothing to be ashamed of."

I had the horrible feeling Billy had told his parents about Saturday night, and they had just told Mom.

"Who cares if you lose a Little League game? You've got so much more to be proud of." She got up and began to pace. "When I think about how well you're doing at Douglass. Did I tell you the principal said you have the highest grade point average in seventh grade?" She looked out the window with her hands on her hips. "God, I'll be dead before those oleanders do anything."

I stood up and threw my glove on the floor. "What are you talking about?"

Mom looked at the dust I stirred up. She had vacuumed in here just a few days ago. Though scraggly oleanders and a dirty carpet were beckoning her, she kept focused. "Pup, those twins aren't going to college. Unless they get there on some athletic thing. They're not in the youth symphony. They're not in advanced classes. They don't have a smidgen of the—"

She stopped when she saw a yellow stain on the collar of her blouse and began licking it. In spite of the mustard, she looked like she had just come from a play at the Old Globe, but being beautiful and well dressed didn't help her now.

"Mom, did you see me strike out the twins?" I looked at her to see if she was paying attention. "In the same inning?"

She looked at me like I had just asked if she knew the distance to the moon, in kilometers. "Sure. I mean, I was there for the whole game if that is what you're asking."

"Never mind. Just leave me alone." I said it quietly, but I was shaking, hoping she would get out before I lost it. When she touched my shoulder, I snapped. "You weren't even watching. The only reason you know anything of what happened is because Dad told you." She started to say something and reach for me again. I backpedalled to the other side of the room.

"Oh, baby. You're going to be okay."

"Just shut up. Just—" She pulled me into her before I realized what had happened. It was like someone who had just murdered my family was trying to make me feel better with a hug.

"AhhhhHHHH." I screamed and shook her off. "Don't touch me. Get out. GET OUT OF MY ROOM." I was jumping up and down. I felt I would strangle her if she came near me again.

Looking back on it all these years later, I want to cheer for that kid. At the time I just felt I was going crazy. Or having a nervous tizzy. That's what the doctor called it in Port Arthur when Dad was in Korea and I screamed every time someone touched me for a whole day.

"Sam, come quick." Mom was sobbing. Dad did come quickly, and it's funny because, for all her carping about Dad, she still depended on him in a crisis. And this was a crisis of momentous proportions to her. I, her beloved son, was telling her to leave me alone and, what was probably worse for her, not allowing her to comfort me.

Debbie, standing in the hallway, offered her two cents, like she was a color man for the regular play-by-play sports announcer. "I've read about something like this, where abused kids just freak out, but it was usually girls." Maw-Maw came out of her room and asked no one in particular what was wrong, but was ignored.

Dad put himself between Mom and me and demanded she calm down. I hoped he was going to slap her like James Cagney did in the old movies. Then, with his back to me and his face to her, he eased her out of the room.

I learned later that Debbie was right, even if I didn't want to hear it then. I was responding the way someone does after a traumatic event. Any touch just overwhelms the sensory circuits and, while the victim might want and need comfort, it can only be received as the precursor to another violation.

All I wanted then was to hide. I felt as ashamed as I felt angry because I believed I had caused Mom's reaction. I thought of opening up the sofa bed just so I could fold myself inside it.

Debbie told me later that Dad had gotten everyone out of my room and quietly closed the door, asking her to stay in the hall listening for anything weird while he dealt with Mom. I think he was afraid I might hurt myself or try to run away. As a matter of fact, I considered doing both.

I heard Mom insist that Dad call our doctor for advice. Maw-Maw, on the way back to her room, said she would pray. That may have been when she decided to take up her friend Ethyl's offer to join a Christian commune in the desert. I heard Dad tell Mom to take another pill.

Our family physician, part internist and part psychiatrist, was already giving Mom sleeping pills, which I had heard about, and tranquilizers, which I hadn't. The latter was Librium and was the go-to med just before Valium came on the market. I'm guessing that was the pill Dad was referring to after he talked to the doctor.

I calmed down enough that I convinced them I was going to take a nap. I did go to bed but not for sleep. I used Sandy again and took care of business pretty quickly. That helped take the edge off things, but I still had this weird aversion to Mom, the one person I felt closest to. It wasn't really because she didn't understand what was good about the game that day, but that is what I thought. I kept playing her response to the game over and over in my head: how she didn't understand, how she was just being a phony, something Debbie accused her of all the time, how I couldn't trust her, and how I hated her.

I changed into some shorts and an old Jets baseball shirt with the solid white body and long green sleeves. I slowly opened the door. Debbie was waiting there, still on guard.

"What's going on, buddy?"

"Where's Mom?"

"In bed. Dad made her take a pill. Two, actually." Debbie was barefoot and kept scratching her left leg with her right foot. "Bad day?"

"I don't know." I didn't want to talk about it. "I'm going to see if the twins want to play now. Did Dad call the doctor?"

"Dad pretended to and then told Mom the doctor suggested we wait to see how you are tomorrow morning. Dad said he told her to take the pills."

I pushed my sneakers into the carpet, wondering how long it would take to make a hole. I could hear Maw-Maw praying behind her closed door, not because I could understand the words but because of the tone. Debbie seemed less concerned about me than she was pleased that I had spoken out against Mom. Maybe she thought our talk the other night had contributed.

I'm not sure how I managed to get it together to go outside, but I knew I needed to do something. I thought of calling Mr. Bodenhamer, my Sunday School teacher. I even thought of going to his house. The fort in the canyon was a possibility, but if I went there without letting anyone know, it would be like running away, and Mom would really go berserk. If I told them I was going there, they were sure to stop me.

That night I was worrying about what I would do next when she came to tuck me in. What happened earlier wouldn't keep her from our evening ritual but would make her all the more adamant. I knew her well.

But I also knew that something wasn't right. Debbie had made me question things. The encounter with Billy was disturbing in another way. But I hadn't connected any of it to Mom until I had realized she completely missed the significance of today's game.

When I got outside, I could see the twins were busy washing their car. Watching them work was comforting because it was familiar, things going on as they usually did. Terry had the hose this time, which meant for the next washing Jerry would get to spray. I knew they traded off because I had seen them do their outdoor chores for years. When they were younger, their father showed them how to stand on the threshold of an open car door to reach the roof. To the Captain, that was the only hindrance to having them wash the car. They learned that about the same time they were starting fractions and decimals in school, which didn't go as well as reaching the top of the car. I know because they used to ask me for help. They didn't have to stand on anything now to wash the top, and they were still better at washing than math. Terry rinsed the whole car a few times, and then they got to work with the chamois.

You will not believe this. I still smile when I think about it. When they signaled they were finished, their father would come out with a glove, I guess an old one that he no longer used with his dress whites, and run it all over the car to check for anything they had missed. I don't think I ever saw him tell them to rewash it because they always knew the glove was coming and used a year's supply of water to make sure it was clean for his inspection.

Washing the car wasn't all they did. They took care of the yard, mowing and edging the lawn, and did it all by hand. Then power mowers were only used by professionals and people who had enormous yards and lived where it rained a lot. Indoors, the twins did the dishes after every meal, the dusting and vacuuming every week. Billy said they would make great housewives.

To top it all off, they had to be in bed by eight o'clock school nights and by nine o'clock on weekends. During the summer they got an extra hour. Year round they were allowed to stay up later on Friday nights, when there was something at church or when the family went to the drive-in. That meant during daylight saving time they were in bed before dark.

My schedule was entirely different. I had nothing to do regularly. I would help Mom in the kitchen and occasionally do some yard work or wash the car if I wanted some extra money, but as long as I was doing well in school, I didn't have to do anything else. I did make my bed, but that only involved folding it up.

It's funny, but I envied the twins for their strict discipline then even though I would never have chosen it. I thought it might have explained some of their success in sports. Also, I thought it made them more important to their family. They were depended on, like on the frontier where the family's survival required the children to pitch in. I was a kind of privileged prince in our family. With special access to the queen.

I had more fear than respect for Captain Carroll. At well over six feet, he never smiled except after telling a joke that usually wasn't funny. I don't know if he believed in spanking, but I knew that any infraction of the rules was dealt with harshly. Once the twins had snuck out of their rooms after bedtime to watch the eclipse of the moon for a school assignment for only fifteen minutes. For the next month, they were not allowed to watch TV. Not that they got to see much anyway since many of the good shows started after they were in bed.

Today, with the inspection complete, Captain Carroll waved in my direction and said, "They're all yours." He smiled, but it was creepy like Vincent Price's.

Billy heard and began wiping his hands on those blue towels all mechanics seem to have. Jerry went into their garage for the football and tossed it to me. Terry tried to intercept it and just missed tipping it away from me, but his attempt made me drop it anyway.

He rubbed his head and nodded. "Man, you were great on the mound today."

I looked at him waiting for him to say, "…but it didn't matter because we wiped you guys all over the field," but he didn't. He seemed to mean it. Was I supposed to reciprocate by saying they were great in the last inning? I was still pissed off about Mom, so I just said, "Yeah, some of the time."

Billy walked up as Jerry joined us. "So, Whitey Ford, Jr. was pitching for the Jets today." He was smiling and holding his hands over his belly the way a pregnant woman does unconsciously.

Jerry was nodding and turned to me. "When did you get a curve?"

I started to say that I developed it after hours in the backyard but changed my mind. "What curve? I just threw fastballs today. Some of them just did funny things now and then."

Both the twins looked at me to see if I believed what I said when they knew it couldn't be true. I smiled and admitted that I learned the curve from Stumpy.

"Yeah," Billy said, "we husky guys," he was referring to Stumpy and himself, "have to use our guile to make up for being a little slower." We all stared at him: the twins because I knew they had no idea what "guile" meant and me because I couldn't believe Billy knew what it meant either.

Billy laughed, and we started our game: Jerry and me on one team, Billy and Terry on the other. We played for about two hours, which meant the twins must have already done all their chores and that Mom was really knocked out by that pill. I wondered if Dad had given her a third. I was pleasantly worn out by the time we all went in.

Dad met me at the door. He took off his glasses and rubbed the dents on the sides of his nose. I had decided that I would never have glasses. For a while I had eaten an average of six carrots a day. I had doubled it to twelve when I met this kid my age that had Coke-bottle bottom glasses. If the flu hadn't made me throw up the carrots, I might still be consuming a pound of carrots daily.

Dad sat down on the porch and motioned for me to join him. "I heard what you said to your mother. About her not seeing you strike out the twins."

I was starting to get angry again, because I knew he was going to excuse her. He always did. The most common direction I remember getting from him was, "Don't upset your mother."

"No one can really know what it means without spending all the time we do watching baseball on TV and practicing." His pants were touching my leg. I moved away and started to stand up.

Dad pulled me down gently. "Look, your mother has problems, and I don't just mean the ones that make her get up at night."

I looked at him in surprise.

"You probably wonder why I don't get up."

As a matter of fact, I did.

"I used to before you were born, but your mother has these stomach problems because she won't do what the doctor suggests."

I rolled the cuff on my shorts and looked at Sandy getting into a car with someone old enough to be a parent and two other girls. She had on sandals and a dress with spaghetti straps. She waved to us as she got in.

"What does the doctor suggest?"

Dad put his glasses back on. "She is supposed to eat only small portions, but you know your mother. That's like asking Babe Ruth to bunt with the bases loaded."

I nodded, happy that he didn't let her off the hook. I got up, shook his hand like we were peers, and went inside.

Mom didn't even get up for dinner but stayed in bed until morning, so I didn't have to deal with her that night.

CHAPTER FIVE

Mom hadn't tucked me in since that Saturday a month ago. She would come to my door and say, "Goodnight, sweet dreams," but she never came in. I could tell she wanted to be asked, though in the past that never stopped her.

She only mentioned the situation once, while we were doing the dishes the night before we left on vacation. She had an apron over her work outfit and the scarf that she wore on her head when she dusted and vacuumed. She looked around to see if anyone else was in the kitchen. "I hope you don't mind that we haven't, uh, snuggled at night. I've just been so busy getting ready for tomorrow." She had this funny look in her eye, like she was thinking of saying something else and thought better of it.

"That's okay." I put a plate I had just dried in the cupboard. I tried not to sound too understanding because that would have meant I didn't miss her coming in at all.

Part of my confusion stemmed from both missing the special attention and yet getting all panicky when she got too close. She was like a beautiful vampire that looked attractive until you started losing blood. I felt a sickly fullness when she wasn't around, like I needed some leeches to drain the extra bodily fluids. Last night, it took a while to get to sleep, but I managed by doing what I usually did, which also involved bodily fluids.

I grabbed a glass and dried it on the way to the cupboard. That way I didn't have to stand next to her too long at the sink.

Except for the problems with Mom (I guess I'd have to say Sandy, too), I enjoyed this week before we left on vacation almost as much as the actual trip. While Debbie was growing out of our family vacations ("Why do we have to drag the whole thing out by driving?"), I loved the destination, the preparation, *and* the journey. Maw-Maw agreed with Debbie and flew whenever she went back, which was not often.

At 1,500 miles, Dayton is halfway across the United States. For the first twenty-four hours, we would go through desert after desert until we reached the New Mexico/Texas border. (Debbie could see no point in a landscape without beaches.) The second half of the trip, almost 800 miles and all in Texas, had that great expanse of sky and land that only Montana rivals. The interstate was mostly billboard-free, so there really was nothing to notice but the space. I loved it. I think the vastness made Debbie feel smaller, the opposite of what a budding actress wants. I felt enlarged by it, so I was surprised to find out that anyone felt the opposite.

On Friday, we were frantically trying to get ready before Dad arrived for dinner. He had been reminding us all week that we should be packed by Thursday night just in case something came up on the next day to hold us up. It was the kind of nagging that Mom was usually in charge of. But I didn't take it that way because it served as a constant reminder that our vacation was about to begin. Of course, neither Debbie nor I paid attention to the deadline. It was a week into summer. We had the whole day before Dad came home. But the reminders helped some because, as his arrival approached, we switched into full scurry mode.

A few years ago, I got so nervous that I left behind all my BVDs. Mom would only buy me one new pair because she didn't want to reward my oversight. In defiance of her, Dad bought me a few more once we had reached Dayton. Otherwise, he said, I would have to be washing every night. I think he was more understanding of me forgetting to pack them because it meant I had taken his timeline for leaving so seriously.

"Dad's coming," Debbie yelled from the kitchen window. He was walking down the street carrying his lunch box.

He didn't even say hello, but stood on the front porch and called out to us, "My fellow vacationers, bring out your luggage, for the final packing is about to begin."

Dad said the exact same words every time. Sometimes he waited until he changed clothes to make the announcement. It didn't matter much since he only took a couple minutes to dress anyway. Mom met him at the door, holding an outfit she had found on sale yesterday, a nice black polo shirt and a pair of khaki shorts with a soldier's crease down the front. She even got him some sandals. Normally, he never wore anything new within months of receiving it and still had shirts wrapped in their original packaging from Christmases past, but this time he went straight to the bedroom to change.

He was already standing next to the car by the time Debbie and I brought out our bags. "What do you think? Sharp looking, huh?" Both of us did a double take. At the most, when he received a gift of clothes, he just mumbled a thank-you in a tone that said he wished you hadn't bought him anything since the rest of his clothes weren't worn out yet.

"Uh, nice," Debbie said, looking confused.

"Just drop your stuff there." His legs didn't have enough hair to conceal their chalky whiteness. His toes looked like they were trying to hide. He hardly wore anything but suits and ties and the clothes that went with them. His work-around-the-house clothes were just old slacks and white shirts that were too worn and stained to wear to the office.

To fit everything in the car trunk, Dad limited our suitcases like we were on a plane flight. As per the packing ritual, Mom complained about being limited to one large piece and a vanity kit. Dad would then, playing his part in this dance, graciously offer a little space in his own suitcase as a compromise. Debbie was allowed a second small suitcase of books and magazines to keep her quiet. It was the same every trip, and I loved it.

One indication of how special these trips were to Dad was that he agreed to let Maw-Maw fix dinner. I never could decide if she was happier about having the house to herself or about being put in charge of the kitchen. Mom said once with a slight frown that Maw-Maw didn't seem particularly sad to see us go. While Debbie and I were watching Dad rearrange the trunk to get her personal entertainment bag in, Maw-Maw called through the kitchen window, "I'll have it on the table in a few minutes."

She never went with us because she didn't want a substitute to teach her Sunday school class. Besides, she was glad to be in California away from all her crazy relatives, especially her alcoholic brothers. One of her sisters had married a guy in the Ku Klux Klan (fortunately he wasn't active any longer), but he was a sweetie compared to her brothers under the influence. She said you took a vacation to California to get away from Texas, not the other way round.

"Okay. Are we ready?" Dad looked like a tourist from the Midwest getting off a bus in Hollywood. He had gotten everything in the trunk except for Debbie's extra bag that Dad allowed to be between us in the backseat if I was willing. I was too full of joyful anticipation to object. Besides, I liked having a barrier.

For dinner we ate macaroni and cheese, green peas, and lime Jell-O with canned pineapple tidbits. "To save time, I packed part of your supper for later." Maw-Maw felt it wasn't actually a meal without some meat, so the fried chicken in the Tupperware would take care of that. When Mom found out Debbie's and my toothbrushes were already in our suitcases, we had to promise to brush really well at the first motel.

Dad herded us into the car, yelled thanks to Maw-Maw for the dinner, and got behind the wheel. As soon as he sat down, Mom said, "Give me a minute, Sam," and got out of the car. "Anyone else need to use the bathroom?"

Dad looked into his lap like he was either trying to reign in his temper or to see if he had to go, too. He told her he was good, but, through clenched teeth, mumbled that he wouldn't be if we didn't leave soon. Mom took this as a cue to run. I prayed it didn't mean she was having stomach problems.

When Mom got back, Maw-Maw stood on the porch in her light blue housecoat that had about as much style as a hospital gown. Debbie said it looked like she got her hair colored to match her outfit, not the other way round.

Maw-Maw had told me she liked being by herself when the rest of us went to Texas because once her husband died

(I never met him), she was always staying in a room in someone else's house. One disadvantage to having us gone was that she had never learned to drive, but she got by just fine. Friends would give her all the transporting she needed: to church, out to eat, and any other place she wanted. She waved and smiled broadly. I waved back, matching my joy with hers.

It was 5:45 p.m. We were pulling out of the driveway, exactly one hour and fifteen minutes after Dad had stood on the porch asking for our luggage. You'd have to admit this was fast, but it wasn't even close to our record. That occurred two years before, when he called to tell us on the Friday we were leaving that he might get laid off by the end of the month. Mom decided to cheer him up by getting on the road as soon as possible. He arrived to find the car already packed, and our dinner wrapped up like a to-go order. He didn't even change clothes. Debbie timed it. We left exactly thirteen minutes after he walked in the door.

Tonight Dad was whistling by the time we turned east onto Highway 80 in Mission Valley. To show that she was in sync with the vacation attitude, Mom agreed to a rock and roll station. Dad always said that once we got out of California, we couldn't get anything but country-western, so Debbie and I made the most out of it now. "The Twist" played as we passed the turn off for La Mesa. At the edge of El Cajon, one of Debbie's favorites, "A Town Without Pity," whined out of the small speakers. When Dad went Johnny Cash and Patsy Cline on us later, she had her transistor radio to her ear, and I had my Hardy Boy books.

During the day, even with the A/C on, the desert was never that comfortable, so I think it was on our second trip to Texas that Dad had us doing most of our travelling at night. If we stayed in a motel before El Paso, in Tucson say, we would drive until early morning, get some sleep during the afternoon, and then leave again in the middle of the night. If we drove all the way to El Paso without stopping, thereby breaking our rule of avoiding the road during the day, we would get there about noon on Sunday and stay until a few hours after dark.

At night we had to share the road with trucks, but the overall traffic was light. It was cool enough that sometimes Dad had us roll the windows down so he could turn off the A/C. The Plymouth Fury with its V-8 engine got poor mileage, but, even adjusting for lower wages then, thirty cents a gallon was dirt-cheap. With the interstate system begun by Eisenhower almost complete, everybody was driving, especially families like us who couldn't afford to fly, even to domestic destinations, much less to the exotic places where Billy's family went. This year they were going to Australia to see the Great Barrier Reef, which I had never heard of before Billy showed me in *National Geographic*. But I didn't envy Billy, though their Hawaii trip last year sounded like fun. Our low-budget vacations—with the long stretches of highway, the restaurants, and the motel swimming pools (the Bradleys had a pool in their backyard)—were perfect for me.

Dad even managed to enjoy Mom's pickiness, like the way she inspected prospective restaurants. Our first stop was for breakfast since we had the fried chicken to carry us through the night. Dad wanted us to eat at the same time we stopped for gas, but that was always too soon, usually Casa Grande at about midnight. He had heard of short-bed trucks adding an extra gas tank and would have if Mom hadn't put the kibosh on it for safety reasons. Anyway breakfast was in

New Mexico, either Lordsburg or Deming, depending on how much we all wanted to eat and how early it was. Too early meant only the truck stops were open, and Mom was never keen on them. I think it was all the attention she got when she walked in. But she never seemed to think of wearing clothes that were less revealing. On this trip she had on a sundress that made it pretty obvious what kind of figure she had. Dad never seemed to mind that other guys stared. I think Mom would have preferred some jealousy now and then just to prove he was still interested.

I don't ever remember us eating any place that had not passed Mom's inspection. Ostensibly she would go in to look over the menu, but mostly to notice if the person taking money also handled the food and to check the fly population. She said that if a restaurant couldn't control flies, it certainly couldn't control germs you couldn't see.

We pulled into Lordsburg just as the sun rose above the distant mountains. A "Breakfast All Day" sign was almost better than an "A" to Mom. Even though it was still early enough to get breakfast at any place that was open, Mom felt that a restaurant that was known for breakfast during lunch and dinnertime was one that knew how to cook, but she returned from The Desert Hot Spot without even going in. "What could these people have done to get a "C?" she asked as she folded her wide, yellow, pleated skirt under her to get in. I thought she looked at Dad to see if he noticed what she was wearing. "I feel we're already risking our lives with a "B."

"Maybe they grade on the curve." It was the first time Dad had joked with Mom on the trip, and I knew her response would tell us whether she had calmed down since we left. She looked at him to see if he really was kidding and must have caught the twinkle in his eye because she smiled. Looking straight ahead, like she was directing our chauffeur, she said, "On, James." This meant at least that, even though she would still be conscientious about finding a clean place to eat, anyone who didn't take it as seriously as she would not have to risk her cold silence through the subsequent meal.

We finally ate at Mabel's, a diner that required shirt and shoes for service, a notice Mom thought was superfluous but hoped it helped to keep the riffraff away. She approved because it served grits, and because she heard The Glenn Miller Band playing "Begin the Beguine" when she did her initial reconnoitering.

We didn't need a full tank of gas, but since we were stopped already and Dad had finished his pancakes and sausage quickly, he wanted to fill up across the street at a Texaco while the rest of us were still eating. I had scrambled eggs and hash browns, turning down Mom's offer to have grits with my eggs, and finished just before Dad. "Can I come with you?" I tried to appear eager without sounding desperate.

Mom looked at Dad knowing that if he answered yes it meant I would get to "drive" as soon as we were on the interstate, a further test of her vacation spirit.

"Sure. You can do the pumping while I do the windows. These small towns never seem to have enough help."

His leaving early would mean Mom would have to pay the check, an affront to a Southern girl, but she was already reaching into her purse when I snuck a look back. I think she was smiling though it could have been a smirk.

With the tank full, Dad and I returned to the curb in front of the restaurant, with me next to him up front. He got out to let Mom in the back. She could have sat up front with the two of us, but it would have been a bit crowded. He mollified her by opening the back door. I swear she did a slight wiggle of her shoulders as she swung her legs into the car. As soon as we saw the "Now leaving Lordsburg" sign, I scooched next to Dad and reached over to grab the steering wheel with both hands.

"Try not to kill us." He bumped me with his shoulder good-naturedly and took his hand off the wheel.

He handled the accelerator (I could request a higher speed, but that was all) and the brakes. Now and then he would correct me by aiming the car closer to the middle of the lane, but most of the time I was the Steerer-in-Charge. When nothing happened for a half hour, like him having to jerk the car back into position, Mom settled down and went to sleep.

I don't know if it was his trust in me (even though he really was still in control) or his willingness to be inconvenienced (I've since done it with my own girls and it's rather nerve-wracking) or his recognition that I desperately wanted to be old enough to drive that felt so good. But it was just one more reason for me to love our vacations. Because the roads were straight for hundreds of miles at a time, I had about as much actual driving to do as I did in the midget cars of Disneyland's Autopia. But this was a real car on a real road, not some amusement park simulation, and accidents could happen. After I got tired of leaning over, Dad resumed full control. I traded places with Mom at the next gas stop.

We made it into El Paso about noon. That meant we had all afternoon to swim, or at least I did. Debbie would mostly lounge around in her two-piece bathing suit (Mom did not approve of the latest skimpy bikinis) and attract boys like our church hoped to attract sinners. Dad might go in if it was over a hundred degrees outside, but only briefly. Mom would swim a few laps and spend the rest of the time dozing in the sun.

I loved the El Camino Motor Hotel not just for the almost Olympic-size pool but also the rooms, which were actually separate cottages with tiny lawns. Each one looked like a miniature villa with a small rough timber fence setting off a private courtyard and an orange-tiled roof above whitewashed adobe walls. Blue tiles in patterns surrounded the door lintels, were placed indiscriminately in the walls, and checker-boarded the paving around the pool. I don't think I ever see blue ceramic without feeling a surge of nostalgia.

**

For the rest of the year, my family didn't quite measure up to the other families in the neighborhood.

Take the Carrolls. Sure they controlled the twins like they were running a boot camp, but the boys seemed to revel in the focused fierceness, the way an army does when it's mission is meaningful. Captain Carroll shipped out to sea for long stretches, so the twins' heavy chore load prepared them to take up the slack. I didn't notice until later that he never did much other than order them around, but you could tell the twins felt important and respected like they were taking his place as the man of the family.

Though they had a strict schedule during the week, after the weekend chores were done, their parents took them to a drive-in movie every Saturday night. And after church on

Sunday, they went out to eat on the way to the desert or the mountains or some small town up the coast. I know now that they put on a nice public face just like our family did to hide major fissures in their family structure, but I almost never heard the twins complain. Just once because their early bedtimes made them miss a *Leave It to Beaver* that everyone was talking about at school.

The Twambleys on the opposite side of us from the Bradleys had only girls and were Mormon, both of which made the family exotic. I didn't know much about the girls except that they were all beautiful and their father would get real angry about once every few months and yell about stuff that wasn't done. Once he tore the kitchen door that opened onto the driveway off its hinges and slammed it into the garage door. I heard the glass shattering from our backyard. But the girls and their mother doted on him the rest of the time. They acted like kids who had been rescued from foster care and were forever grateful to be back home. They went on weekend vacations almost every month, to Solano Beach or to the Cuyamaca mountains, sometimes to Disneyland. They never took long vacations in the summer like us but would just extend their monthly getaways to four or five days.

The Bradleys, the only non-churchgoing family on the block, seemed to be the most affectionate with each other. Their good-byes were "I love yous," and they hugged all the time. I don't know if they were atheists, but anyone who didn't attend church on the major religious holidays like they didn't was labeled something almost as bad, an agnostic. At my church doubting made you an unrepentant sinner, as heathen as the African cannibal.

Once Billy came with me to church. I don't remember how I convinced him to attend, but it was only one night and it was during a revival, which consisted of a worship service Monday through Friday nights for the sole purpose of bringing the lost to Christ, especially our neighbors. For a guy who read very little of anything that wasn't assigned in class, if he read that, he was quick to pick up on the inconsistencies in our theology. He particularly had trouble with the hell stuff. "Seems hard to jive with a God of love, don't ya think?" he said to me once in our canyon fort. I tried to explain to him about omnipotence and omniscience and free will and quoted a few verses about Jesus being the only way before we went back to talking about girls we wished would dance with us.

His parents were definitely the least strict on the block. Sandy and Billy were allowed to go to movies and do sleepovers, even on school nights. My parents never let us go anywhere during the week unless it was to a church or a school function, and only to the school event if we could prove we had done our homework.

CHAPTER SIX

WE ARRIVED IN DAYTON about an hour before dark and parked on the grassy area between the runoff ditch and the street. So different from San Diego: the sleepy mugginess of the air, the enormous canopies of the magnolias lining the streets, and a green lushness everywhere. Were people in the South slower, in action and speech, to take in this earthy opulence?

I ran from the car across the concrete culvert pipe that provided a bridge from the street to the grass-trampled walkway. In California we celebrate the new, the electronic, the manmade. Our model is Tomorrowland. Here everything feels older and more permanent, more solid, more reliable, yet more alive and present: insects buzzing just overhead, trees swaying in a gentle warm breeze, water dripping from roof to bush, and the air perfumed by the relentless search for nourishment. In his Vermont, Frost called this abundance of life an extravagance. How much more so here in the warmth of the South.

"You think you're gonna be first in?" Debbie pushed me aside and ran up the steps, letting the screen door slam behind her.

I wanted to get angry at her, but I couldn't. I felt dazzled, like I was in some Disney movie and pretty soon either Uncle Remus or Huckleberry Finn would step around the corner of the house to invite me on some adventure.

The porch itself was magical because of the two stubby brick columns topped with a square of concrete that flanked the wooden stairs. The concrete was wide enough for me and Bart, my Grandma's enormous tomcat, to sit without touching each other. The steps to the porch and the porch itself creaked, like the one in every scary movie set in a small backwater town. But to me it was a lovely embracing sound like the crackling of a campfire or the gurgling of water over pebbles in a stream.

I opened the screen door and heard Mom yell, "Don't let it slam like your sister did," just before I let it slam. I didn't care because I knew that here Mom was overruled. Everything changed under Grandma's roof, not because she demanded it but because, in her world, life was too slow for guilt. Maybe that's why Mom never stayed long with us in Dayton but hurried off to Beaumont. The official reason was that we only had a week in Texas and she needed to spend *some* time seeing relatives and friends there.

Grandma never came out to meet us. She was usually either napping in her small bedroom off the kitchen or sitting on the back steps petting Bartleby. It was always one of these two. Maybe that was because we always arrived about the same time, or maybe it was because those were her two main activities.

Inside the front door, the smell of camphor evoked her ancientness: white hair, wrinkled skin, and bent back. She had no carpets and only a few rugs on her hardwood floors. So unsuburban to Mom. Even more exotic was the living room that was missing that faux hearth, our TV, but I only knew that from past visits because the drapes were pulled now, so I could barely see well enough to avoid bumping into her furniture.

"Hi. We made it." I could hear Debbie yelling not because she was so far away from Grandma but because Grandma was as deaf as Maw-Maw, but without hearing aids.

"Lookee lookee here," Grandma yelled back. I could hear the smile in her voice. "Lord almighty, you're an Amazon girl."

Grandma was just a few inches over five feet and seemed to shrink a little between each visit. She had on the same housedress with buttons down the front she had on the last time we were here. Mom had bought her a few new ones, but Grandma was like Dad and kept them wrapped up until the old ones completely wore out. Her hair was supposed to be long enough to reach her waist, but we only saw it wrapped in braids on the top of her head like she was auditioning to be an extra in a Heidi movie.

"Well, look at you, too," she said to me.

I stood next to Debbie in Grandma's tiny bedroom. The house had three, the other two about twice the size of this one, but she chose to stay in what would have been converted into a laundry room by a young couple with kids. Now I wonder if she just lived for our visits and remained in the back of the house to make the rest of it accommodating for us. If she did it for anybody, it would be for her favorite son. Dad had three brothers, one of whom had died a drunk in New York, and one sister. They were last here when Grandpa died five years ago and seldom before that once they had left to raise their own families.

"Okay, now you two go get those Girl Scout cookies and pour yourself some milk."

The kitchen had speckled tan linoleum floors with the edges peeling up under the metal fascia at the intersection with the walls. The sink was separate from the counter and shaped like a small version of a claw-foot bathtub, which is what she had in the bathroom. There were four quart bottles of milk in what she called the icebox. I knew it was actually a refrigerator run by electricity, but I always hoped I would see a big block of ice in it whenever we opened the door.

Mom walked in while Debbie was pouring milk into our glasses. "Milk, madam?" she said turning and bowing to Mom.

Mom looked confused like she couldn't believe Debbie was asking her, or she couldn't believe Grandma had milk. She grabbed the bottle away from Debbie and sniffed it.

"Geez, Mom. Are you going to inspect Grandma's for roaches, too?"

Strands of Mom's hair clung to her forehead in sweaty loops. Her blouse had large, wet half-moons under her arms. Her Capri pants might have been wrinkled if they weren't so tight on her, the result of a few too many pieces of fried chicken and Maw-Maw's tasty desserts, but she was still gorgeous. Right now she was calculating whether to admonish us for eating dessert before dinner or to just go along with the craziness of this house (and town) until she could be on her way tomorrow morning.

"Now, don't spoil your appetite." She shook her head to Debbie's gesture of pouring her a glass of milk.

Dad walked by grinning, said he'd take two cookies but with buttermilk, and continued on to greet Grandma. "Howdy, howdy, howdy," Dad sang in an arpeggio as if he was warming up for a solo. "Tumbling Tumbleweeds" had been playing on the car radio before he turned off the motor. Entering his boyhood house seemed to seal his transformation from California professional into a good ole boy cowboy troubadour.

"Oh, Sammy. These kids are so beautiful." In a loud whisper she added, "And so big. What do you feed them in California, buffalo steaks?" Then she cackled until she began coughing and gasping for breath. She loved a joke, even if it was a silly one she just made up. Her laugh made us join in, which gave her a skewed evaluation of how funny she really was.

Mom went right for the linen closet to get fresh sheets and began to strip the beds. She walked back in the kitchen and motioned for me to follow her, but I pretended not to notice. We caught each other's eyes for a moment. I tried to look like I was oblivious, but my heart was pounding for defying her like this. She glanced at Debbie and then went back to making our beds safe from bugs and the general unsanitary conditions of Grandma's house.

Essentially, Mom treated Grandma's house like one more motel. To her the smell of mothballs evoked nothing nostalgic. The house was dusty, dark, and to Mom smelled of poverty, what she had worked so hard to leave behind. It had to be sanitized, if only temporarily and in small ways, with clean sheets and a recently scrubbed bathroom lavatory to make it acceptable for her children. They would never have to suffer what she had during those two wars and the economic devastation before them.

For dinner, Mom fashioned croquettes from canned salmon and cooked some collards I picked from Grandma's backyard garden. After we finished clearing the table, Dad told Debbie it was too late to go to the public swimming pool. Instead, we sat at the kitchen table, which had the best light in the house and played the Monopoly game we had given Grandma last Christmas. Mom went to bed before Debbie had finished buying up Boardwalk and Park Place and signaled me to go to bed, too, but I didn't budge. The four of us remaining had milk again, even Dad, but this time with graham crackers. I began dozing as Debbie was putting those ominous red hotels on her property.

Mom had Debbie in her room and me with Dad just like we did on the road. After Mom was in bed, I pulled my cot onto the screened-in back porch.

"What are you doing?" Dad stood in his pajama bottoms and a sleeveless undershirt.

"I wanted to see the stars."

He stepped through the door and breathed deeply. "Ah, those magnolias. Every time I see some in California I remember what it was like living here." He stepped outside the back door and looked up at the sky. "Won't be seeing any stars tonight, but you'll be the first to hear the rain. The car could use a shower."

He grabbed me and scratched my head before I could wiggle free. "Goodnight, pupper. Don't let the bed bugs bite."

I was real tired, in spite of dozing in the car, so I didn't need to do anything to get to sleep. In a dream, I was pitching a perfect game against the Elks and on my way to striking out the last batter to seal the victory when I heard Debbie yelling and realized it wasn't in my dream. I wondered if even Grandma would be wakened. I got up and almost fell over Bart. He meowed angrily, and pushed his way out the screen door.

"What are you talking about?" This was Mom, and she was crying. "What do you know? You never think of anyone but yourself."

"Oh, like you do?" I stood next to the door to Dad's bedroom. He was still snoring. Mom and Debbie were in the front bedroom, which was separated from Dad's by the bathroom.

"What were you going to do?" Debbie sounded in control, the prosecutor who was about to rattle the witness into a confession.

The hall smelled dusty and faintly of smoke, like the remains of a barbeque. I walked carefully to avoid making the floorboards creak.

"What do you know about being a parent? You have no idea what we have gone through to give you this life, the life your father and I never had."

I stopped just outside their door and listened, my heart thumping because I knew it had something to do with me.

"We're not theorizing about proper parenthood here. Joey should never be exposed to what you do with him." If you didn't see her, you would never know this was a high school student speaking.

I heard bedsprings groan, probably Mom's response to what Debbie had just said. I didn't know if this was the first time Debbie and Mom had discussed the bathroom stuff, but it sounded like it.

"He's a boy for crissakes. And he's almost grown. He notices stuff he didn't when you tucked him in as a baby."

"Don't use that kind of language with me, young lady. And keep your voice down."

"Why? Because Joey might hear us?"

I wanted to hear the rest of it, but I didn't want them to see me. I walked back to Dad's door and stayed until I could hear his heavy breathing. When I turned around, I forgot about the table with the telephone on it, and the corner speared my thigh.

I don't know if they heard my cry of pain or the receiver striking the floor.

"See," I heard Mom say, and she opened the door.

"Oh, baby, are you okay?"

I was seething, but I didn't know why. I just wanted Mom to leave me alone and assumed Debbie had questioned her about getting up to come to see me tonight, which had started the whole argument. I looked at Debbie, and, for the first time in my life, she seemed to look at me sympathetically, or at least not condescendingly. I was holding my leg and squeezing my jaw, determined not to cry.

"Come here, Puppy."

I froze, rigid and silent. Thank God, she noticed and stayed back because I would have slapped her or cussed her out. At that moment, Mom represented everything that was wrong with my life: my need for love, my impotence as a male, my general wimpiness. What I really wanted to do was squeeze her throat until she admitted she was fucking me up. I just wanted her or someone to take responsibility for the shitty way I felt about myself. That everything I was good at just made things worse with all the things I was lousy at. That being smart never makes up for not having the respect of the other boys. I didn't know why I felt this way about Mom, but I did. It was terrifying, and I had to get away.

I ran out the front door and stood in the street. It was just beginning to sprinkle, but it was still warm enough that I was okay in my thin cotton Superman pj's. I had seen some movie where the main character stands with his face to the heavens and just lets the rain mingle with his tears. If I was remembering right, his son had just died because he couldn't get back soon enough with the doctor. As he stood there, it began to pour so you couldn't tell whether he was still crying or not. His wife was standing on the porch out of the rain, her face drenched, too, but only with tears. She was calling for him to come back.

I realized part of this was not a movie now, but that someone was actually yelling my name. I looked toward the house and thought I saw Mom crying. A therapist later explained to me that I was her only truly satisfying relationship and to lose me was to lose her chance at love. I don't know if I buy that, but I do know she was taking it hard. She had not bothered to put on a robe and her negligee was so wet that she might as well have been nude. I stared at her for a while until I started to get aroused. I squeezed my legs together in anger and began to run down the street, with some vague idea I would go to the pool since I was already wet and try to wash off all I was feeling in the warm water. I heard Mom scream, and it was a scream of fear this time, but I didn't look back.

I ran past the junction with the state highway to the other side of town. The pool was in the area known as train town because years ago some part of Pullman cars were manufactured there. I waited for a truck to rush by and laughed when the spray from the tires was less drenching than the falling rain.

By now Mom would be in a panic and probably waking Dad to go look for me. I walked past an automotive repair shop and watched the rain glisten on a '57 Chevy. Even in the poor lighting, I could see it was candy apple red and looked like the featured special on a used car lot in San Diego.

I walked on the edge of the street because there were no sidewalks in this part of town either. A car's headlights blinded me for a moment as it passed by on the other side. I loved the smell of the rain mixed with the oil on the road and the faint sweetness of fruit tree blossoms that mingled with it. The car that passed had turned around, and I could tell now that it was a police car. The man on the passenger side rolled down his window as the car pulled up next to me.

"Nasty night to be out," the man in a hat with a badge in the middle said, "even if you are Superman."

I forgot what I was wearing and started to laugh until I thought it might make him think I was being a smart aleck. "Couldn't sleep. Just out for a walk." I tried to sound as reasonable and nonchalant as I could, considering my clothes were soaked and I had to blink regularly to avoid getting water in my eyes.

"Tell you what. I just happen to have a towel so you won't mess up my car seat. Why don't you jump in the back and we'll take you home?"

Debbie had told me about the freedom riders and how Texas Rangers and other police in the South viewed college students from California. I knew I wouldn't pass for one, but I also knew they could tell from my accent that I wasn't born in Texas. I find it hard to believe now that any of that went through my head at the time, but whatever Debbie said tended to find a place in my memory, especially regarding Texas.

He looked at me like riding with him might be my only choice. As I began to get in, Dad drove up. "Hey there, Sammy. When did you get in town?" the driver said to Dad.

Dad knew both of them, and they were happy to turn me over to him. He had a towel, too, and I began to dry off outside until Dad said I better get in the car first. He chatted for a few minutes with the officers and then got back in and drove me home. I mean, to Grandma's.

On the way back he didn't say anything or even ask a question. I didn't either. When I got out of the car, Mom was still standing on the porch. I hesitated at the bottom of the steps until she stepped aside and I walked in without saying anything to her either. Debbie was there, too, and I thought I saw her wink like we were co-conspirators in this whole thing. I wasn't so upset that I didn't notice what they were wearing. Mom had put on Dad's green plaid flannel robe and Debbie was sporting a red polka dot top with red shorts.

Someone, probably Mom, had laid out a towel, a pair of boxers, and a T-shirt on my cot. I took off my wet clothes, dried off, and fell into the sleep of a wanderer who had finally come home.

CHAPTER SEVEN

MOM LEFT EARLY IN the morning. I was planning not to see her off but decided that was cruel. I felt sorry for her because of last night. Whether Debbie was getting to Mom about me helping her in the bathroom as Debbie had been getting to me, I didn't know, but I felt I had an advantage over her in Dayton and that all her friends in Beaumont wouldn't make up for her trouble with me. Again how I was aware of such stuff at twelve, I don't know, but I remember it clearly.

I picked up Mom's suitcase in the hall and took it out to the car where Dad was cleaning the windshield. God, he looked happy. His T-shirt had a few smudges where he had leaned over the fender to dry the glass cleaner he had just sprayed on. He had on the black walking shorts Mom had bought for the trip. He was whistling until he heard the screen door close behind Mom when she had failed to catch it in time to avoid its slamming.

I looked back to see Debbie follow Mom out and make sure the door slammed even louder. Oh, my sister was good. I think she would have been a great interrogator, finding all the ways to get under people's skins until they broke.

I have to ask Debbie the next time I see her if I have remembered her outfits correctly. This time I think it was a long-sleeved lavender shirt under a tan, brushed leather vest over shorts that looked like cutoff chaps because they had leather fringe on the sides. If she could get Dad to pay for it, she would be wearing a cowboy hat soon.

"You two mind your father."

I don't think she was so concerned about us doing what Dad said as she was about making it clear that minding Grandma didn't matter. Mom couldn't respect a woman who cared so little about clothes and was too shy to provide the gregarious, food-laden hospitality Mom was known for. And Grandma would never have had Mom's style. This morning Mom had on a black summer dress with white polka dots, thin shoulder straps, and a billowy skirt. With a floppy ivory summer hat to match the polka dots, she looked like Faye Dunaway playing a Southern belle.

She motioned for me to come for a hug and I obliged, pulling away before she was finished. "Wish me a good time," she said to no one in particular.

Debbie said in voice that the whole block could hear, "Have a *damn* good time."

Mom's eyes flared. She said nothing while I looked at Dad as if to say, "See, this is what I have to put up with."

In a mellow voice, Dad said, "Tell Aunt Violet hello and don't have too good a time with all those ex-boyfriends."

Mom smiled, gave Dad a perfunctory peck on the cheek, and rode off.

Dad turned back to me and Debbie, nodded his head, and slapped his hands together as if to say that now was the time we could get down to having some fun. "Who's ready for some pancakes at Pete's?"

"I am. I am," I said jumping up and down.

"I'll keep Grandma company," Debbie said while jumping up and down to mock me before she went back in the house.

Dad hadn't let Mom, and certainly wasn't going to let Debbie, ruin his first day free. He smiled at me, looking me up and down like he was going to say I needed to change clothes. Apparently shorts, flip-flops, and my baseball undershirt were fine because he turned around without speaking and motioned for me to follow.

I looked up to an unclouded sky. It could rain with little warning, but now it was a sunny morning full of hope. The smell of wet dirt helped me pretend I could hear the grass growing. We walked in and out of the shade of pine trees and kicked a few cones back and forth until we came to the highway. Everything commercial, including the public swimming pool I didn't quite find last night, was on the other side, and everything residential on this side, the one exception being the mortuary that had been converted from a two-story home that was owned by the Samuelsons, the only Jewish family in town.

Dad greeted everyone we passed and seemed to actually know most of them. A guy on a mower yelled something unintelligible over the sound of the motor. A woman in high heels, shorts, and a halter-top called Dad, Sammy the Shammy, and blew him a kiss. After Dad turned down a ride in a truck, the driver drawled out, "See ya at Pete's."

After the first summer vacation to Texas, when we got back to San Diego, I told my friends how friendly everyone was, even the telephone operators, who sounded like neighbors concerned with how comfortable you felt. It made me wonder how the state ever got anything done. Dad said then that oil wells don't require a lot of hurrying.

Outside the diner, a horse was tied up next to a few trucks and a beat-up Model T. Dad said that the horse was probably Sharon's and the old Ford belonged to either Pete himself or to his son. Inside, a jukebox played Hank Williams while the customers, the only waitress, and Pete, who was also the cook, welcomed Dad home.

Dad winked at me and gestured to his right, "Want the counter," and to his left, "or a booth?" I picked the counter, surging with pride that Dad was so well known.

An old man with tobacco/coffee breath and whiskers like Gabby Hayes put his arm around me. "Your father is a winner. He's one of the few to make it out to the university and actually finish."

Dad grinned and nodded. "You mean except for you and all your kids."

The man laughed and spit into a blue paisley handkerchief he pulled from his back pocket. "Well, I guess we're one of the few, too." Then he laughed again until I thought he would choke and slapped me on the back each time he coughed.

I didn't understand all the jokes because some had to do with the high school football coach's strategies and some were dependent on obscure Southern slang. Most comments had plenty of sexual innuendo because Lucille, the waitress, told Fernal, the Gabby Hayes lookalike, to shut up frequently in a way that meant for him to keep talking. She looked like she had been involved in much more than innuendos. She had on an outfit that showed more than it hid. Her white rayon dress was tight enough to see the ribs of her girdle and managed to display plenty of thigh when she bent over to get silverware and cups. Her top buttons were unfastened so there was no doubt she could find a part-time job as a wet nurse if business slowed at the restaurant. She had this sensuality that perfumed the air above her lusty male customers.

Dad ordered pancakes with sausage, and so did I. He didn't say a thing when I ordered coffee, too, maybe because, to him, it was more of a vacation dessert once I added sugar and cream.

Sharon *was* the one on the horse and made some comment about Dad being the one who got away. Dad said, "I tried to stay, but couldn't." Fernal thought Dad was referring to World War II because he said that they all appreciated him for it. Later Dad told me Fernal had lost a son in Germany.

Outside I felt sleepy and wished we had a car for the few blocks to Grandma's, but Dad started walking in the opposite direction. "Let me show you something."

We went past the hardware store and a small market that advertised three loaves of bread for fifty cents. I didn't recognize the brand. A truck with hay passed us, wisps blowing around it like flies. Dad pointed ahead, and I could see a big grassy area that I assumed was the town park. When we got closer, I saw the metalwork arch that connected the tops of two brick pillars. "Cemetery" was spelled out in loopy letters like they had been formed by a sky writer who used molten metal. A sign just the other side of the pillars read, "Respect the dead. Don't walk on grave sites."

Dad went ahead and stopped. "Come here."

Before running to catch up to Dad, I paused to read a tombstone to my right of a child who was nine when he died last year. Dad was standing in front of a small stone building about the size of a garden shed with the name Norton on it. All around it in neat rows were tombstones with dates and first names only.

He pointed to one with Stewart on it. "Your great-grandfather owned the only mill for miles around, so almost every building constructed before 1940 used his lumber."

"Was he rich?"

"He would have been if he had been a business man. He always said his job was to help people realize their dreams. He believed that if he did a good job with that, he would make money, too."

I kicked a stone. "Was he right?"

"Nope. But your grandfather said he was respected by everybody in town, except the corporate lumber yard that drove him out of business."

Dad reached out for me to come to him, and when I did, he put his arm around my shoulder. "That's not why I brought you here. I'm going to tell you what my dad told me in this same place when I was about your age, give or take a few years." He looked up as if he was asking for permission to continue. "I don't mean to scare you, but this is important."

He let go of me and touched a particularly tall cedar that he was in the shadow of. "If this isn't exactly the spot, it's pretty close. 'Son,' my father had said to me, 'everyone ends up here, the president, your friends, your enemies, your parents, your children, everyone. We lose them all until we ourselves are gone. *Now* is your time. Make the most of it.' Then he quoted some play where a character was telling about what he had heard as he walked through the cemetery the night before: voices coming from the graves, and all of them were saying the same thing. 'Live. Live. LIVE.'"

Dad walked up to the tombstone for his father and ran his fingers over the year he died. "And here's the part I'm adding for you. Life is too short not to forgive the people closest to you."

I knew he was talking about Mom. I have thought about what he said a lot because of what would happen to him in a few weeks, but then it just seemed one more time he was giving into her.

"Your mother had some terrible shit happen to her."

I looked at him and stared.

"Yes, it's true."

I wasn't surprised by what might have happened to Mom but because I didn't ever remember him using that word before.

"She may tell you some time. Maybe I will myself, if she gives me permission. But believe me, once you find out about things that were done to her, before she was your age I might add, you will give her a lot more slack." He picked up some dead flowers in a vase and walked them over to a trashcan. He nodded like he was giving assent to what someone else said and started to walk back to the entrance.

During that time in Dayton, it seemed like I was in a movie from the past: when cars were less dominant, when people were friendlier, when time was not something to be outwitted but could just float on by. If acceptance and appreciation are the secrets to happiness, then that week in Dayton was a seminar on how to enjoy life.

We walked slowly back to Grandma's, holding hands until some kids rode by on bikes. I didn't know it then, but those days would be some of the happiest ever.

Dad, in this relaxed atmosphere, seemed to realize for the first time that Debbie and I could be trusted. Or that his town was so safe we could be given privileges we would never be allowed in California. It was like we had just come from some war zone and could now relax because all the danger had been neutralized.

The first evidence of this was when Dad gave Debbie permission to go to Galveston in a car driven by a college student home for his summer break. Now it's true Darin was someone Dad knew. He was our second cousin, and his parents took in Dad when his father almost died and Grandma had to stay at the hospital day and night. But I don't think Mom would have given permission to our own Pastor Bobby, even before the scandal. But here was Debbie, sitting in the front seat of this Ford convertible with another boy and two more girls in the back.

"Darin, make sure you have her back before dark."

"Sure, Mr. Norton." Darin had that goofy grin a guy gets when he's been given such a good deal that he will agree to anything. But he didn't look goofy to Debbie. He had the shoulders and chest of a surfer minus the tan. He was a philosophy major at Baylor, but he did a pretty good imitation of a happy-go-lucky California beach boy in his Hang Ten surf trunks and Hawaiian shirt.

I wondered what trouble Debbie might stir up with him since she always talked about Texans like they were ignorant hillbillies, but I guess even she can be influenced by a fine jaw line and muscular arms.

Before Debbie left, Grandma made sure she had Grandma's phone number memorized. While Debbie and Darin drove away, Grandma waved to her as enthusiastically as she could with her arthritic shoulders. If all you had seen were the car and the kids inside without any of the background, you would have sworn they were on the way to a beach in La Jolla. The only part missing were the boards. I had a bad feeling they would get in a car accident, but now I know that was just what I had absorbed from Mom, this feeling that anything good was liable to be taken away as soon as you felt good about it.

Dad sat down on the porch swing and pulled out the crossword puzzle he had not completed on the trip. "You going to the pool?"

"I don't know."

I wanted to go, but I was older this year, taller, which was good, but also skinnier and well short of the standard set by Darin and the twins. Think about it, which I did all the time, what's the first thing a girl notices at a swimming pool or on the beach? Your body. Not your face, your hair, or anything that you first notice in places where clothes cover most of you. I had begun doing pushups every day, but that was a few weeks ago, and the only difference I noticed was a bit of tightness in my chest.

"Well, you just let me know when you're going." He leaned forward squinting at the paper. "What's a five-letter word for delight that begins with a 'b'?" He began to rock, and the swing gave a squeak each time it hit the top of the arc. "Ah yes, bliss." He smiled the smile of the fortunate.

I went back inside and sat down at the kitchen table while Grandma ate. She never really consumed a full meal but kind of snacked all day. I thought I would eat that way when I moved out and got my own apartment. Now she was dipping saltine crackers into a glass of buttermilk. Her teeth were soaking in a fizzy solution, so her mouth was kind of caved in. It seemed a lot of people in this town resembled Gabby Hayes.

She looked at me as she gummed a soft cracker and smiled. "So how you doing out there in Cal-ee-FOR-nigh-ay."

I shook my head and shrugged, wondering if she had an idea what was going on. I knew Dad wouldn't tell her anything too personal. Besides, he didn't know that much to tell. Debbie could have, but I didn't think she had had an opportunity, and it would have been embarrassing enough to Grandma that even Debbie might get uncomfortable.

Grandma had put on a new housedress since she first got up, mostly gray with thousands of little roses. I think it was one of the ones Mom had given her. It still had the creases that the packaging caused. I wondered if she purposely waited until Mom left. Her arms were thin and fat at the same time because what little flesh she had kind of hung on her bones like it was tired. Her face and hands had dozens of dark brown spots like Maw-Maw had.

"I always wondered about Hollywood and all. I know your mother likes it, but I wondered about your daddy and you kids. Sometimes I think California's a better place to go after you're already grown up."

I was still surprised that she talked more like the guy in the diner than like Dad, who had lost his accent long ago. If Mom spent any time with people who had Southern accents, hers would come back like she'd never left the South. Debbie and I used to ask her to count because, even without others to influence her, she would say fo-wa instead of four. But otherwise she sounded just like Dad.

Grandma offered me a cracker, and I took it, but I shook my head when she offered her buttermilk for dipping.

"I don't know. I guess I like it out there. I'm kind of used to it." Yeah, and used to ridicule and self-consciousness and feeling like a wimp all the time, I could have said. And then there's that little window thing.

"Joey, you're a lot like your daddy. You're smart. You pay attention. You notice who's in pain." Was she referring to the puppy I tried to save? "And you're very hard on yourself. Just like him. Out there in California, it seems there's too much competition. Too much hurrying about to get things that ain't never enough to make anyone happy." She laughed. "Oh, maybe I've been watching *The Beverly Hillbillies* too much."

She caught my quizzical look.

"My niece has a TV set and right after prayer meetin' on Wednesday she takes me home with her. Almost enough to make me want to buy one."

I wanted to talk to her about the TV programs I liked, especially *The Dick Van Dyke Show*, but decided to go to the pool. Something about talking to her gave me more confidence. Besides, I remembered I had had a good time last year and certainly wasn't muscular then.

I stood up. "I'll see you later after I've thought more about how I like California." I pushed my chair in. "I like it *here*, too."

She smiled, and I gave her a peck on her wrinkly, dry cheek before going to change.

CHAPTER EIGHT

I WAS DETERMINED NOT to check myself out in the mirror, but when I had to pee, I glanced anyway. I had brought my surfer trunks, the same style as Darin's, and had a white T-shirt that I hoped by being loose would make me look a little bigger. I pondered whether wearing a smaller shirt whose sleeves my arms stretched out was a better strategy. I tried to focus on last year at the pool and the girls who were friendly to me. I remembered my cousin introducing me to some of his friends and playing baseball in the vacant lot near Grandma's every morning. We would cool off by swimming in the afternoons.

Grandma had one beach towel that advertised some local beer, so I folded it to keep Dad from seeing. But I'm not sure he would have cared because it was mostly Maw-Maw that was so anti-alcohol. He used to tell me stories about her brothers when we were by ourselves. I liked the one about her younger brother who stripped naked, peed into a public swimming pool, and then dove into the middle of the yellow.

As I walked down the steps, Dad was using some rusty clippers to trim the hedge beside the porch and wished me a good time. He had on those same black shorts from the trip, but I'd never seen his shirt. It was a bit too big, so I assumed it must have been something he found in grandfather's closet. The buttons were quartz encased in silver, and the cloth was red-and-white checkered. He looked about as fashion-challenged as the other people in town. I stopped to watch him saw on a thick branch until it finally broke free.

"Turn left on Primrose, right?"

"Right. I mean, correct. The pool usually opens at noon, but maybe it's hot enough they'll let people in earlier today." He wiped his forehead and neck with one of the handkerchiefs he carried. Mom always had Kleenex. She felt cloth was unsanitary. He thought using tissues was wasteful.

I tensed and released my arms in order to pump them up while I walked down Sycamore. I passed a house you could barely see from the street and, in their driveway, did as many pushups as I could, as quickly as I could. Which turned out to be thirty-one. Well, twenty-nine really, because on the last two I didn't go all the way down. Maybe twenty-three strictly regulation ones because I was bobbing my head and hiking up my hips for extra leverage on a few more. The only thing I accomplished was to make myself more self-conscious.

On Primrose, the high-class district, the houses were all two-story white clapboard with only differences in trim to distinguish them: green, gray, or black. The super-thick lawns were cut neatly and each driveway had a two-car garage at the end. I had seen some just like them in San Diego, but the vegetation made all the difference. You could tell it was rain not sprinklers that produced so much green. And there was no bare ground. Everything had something growing on or in it, even the smallest cracks in the asphalt.

I could hear splashing and screaming before I saw the pool. A hedge that smelled like orange trees hid it from the street. I came across the parking lot first, which only had a few cars near the pool area. A tall chain-link fence surrounded the pool and two buildings. A sign said $1.00 for adults and $.50 for children under twelve. I was proud to pay a dollar. The high dive was close to the entrance with the kiddie pool at the far end. That was the source of the screaming.

Grandma had said her grandnephew Hank had the first shift and there he was, sitting in the lifeguard station. He was a senior in high school and had the build of a swimmer—long sinewy lats, cut pecs, and a sleek muscularity to his legs. His silky tan made him look more Californian than I did, which explained why so many girls had placed their towels on each side of his elevated chair. His eyes darted back and forth across the pool and on one of his sweeps, he noticed me.

"Hey, Joey. You're back."

Every girl immediately turned my way, noticed I was nothing special, and went back to basking in his aura.

One girl was just getting out of the pool near me and ran up to give me a big hug. Only at the last minute did I recognize her as Hank's younger sister, Gloria, but I noticed immediately the difference in her from last year. She had on a modest one-piece swimsuit like Olympians wear that she filled out quite nicely. Her sizeable wet breasts were now pressing against me. When she backed off, I crossed my arms to hide the two round wet spots on my T-shirt. I thought of taking it off, but then she would just be reminded of how undeveloped I was in comparison.

It's not that she looked like some voluptuous movie star. It's just that I didn't remember her being so striking before. She had dark hair like Elizabeth Taylor and gray-green eyes. Her shoulders and arms were still pretty pale for this late in the summer, though a bit sunburned now, which made her seem wonderfully fragile. Her nose was a little crooked and narrow. Her feet were unusual because they were so long, like someone had made a clay mold for a foot and pulled on the toes too much. They almost gave her an amphibian look, and last year she told me she was ashamed to go bare foot. I could understand completely, not so much about her feet—they were fine to me—but about exposing body parts. I guessed her development above the waist took people's minds off her feet. Last year Mom said she had been cute and I agreed, but that always seemed a word you used for someone you thought was just average. Now she was a knockout, and she had run up to me in front of everyone to give me this wonderfully embarrassing, soggy hug. I stuttered a hello.

"When did you arrive?" She drawled out the long "i" sound. "You better not say before yesterday or I will be reeeeal angry."

I didn't remember being that important to her last year, but loved the assumption now.

"Sorry for getting you wet."

She ran to her towel and dried her hair as she walked back. Her hair came about halfway down her back. I knew then I would never see a shampoo commercial without recalling the way she dried her hair now. She rubbed her hands together with the towel on each side of her hair, first on one side of her head and then on the other. I think I could have watched her for hours: going in for a swim, getting out

and drying her hair, and then repeating the whole proce-
dure over again.

She said, "Are you here for long?" but I heard her say,
"Do you like my hair long?" because that had been a change
since last year, too.

"Yeah, you look great. I mean, it looks great."

She cocked her head and scrunched up her nose. I
wanted to apologize for saying anything that made her do
that to her face. I wanted to tell her that Grandma and Maw-
Maw looked like that all the time, and she must stop that at
once.

"What looks great?"

"Your hair."

"Thanks. So you like it long?" She fluffed it as she
turned her head like some coquettish ingénue.

"When do you leave?"

I wanted to say never. "Friday."

She took hold of my hand like she was my girlfriend
and pulled me over to where her stuff was and had me sit
beside her.

"I am so glad to see you. I was just thinking how much
fun we had bowling and playing baseball." She was a bit of
a tomboy and the only girl who played with us last year.
"Remember those Monopoly games?"

Between Sophia Loren and Brigitte Bardot, I was pretty
partial to Italian and French accents. And I wasn't alone
among my friends. But I now realized that a beautiful girl
giving me her full attention made a Texas drawl just as
attractive.

I had forgotten about Monopoly. It had been just her
and me. We were in the living room with her parents, who
watched TV without any lights on, so we had only the

glow from the set to see the board. Mom had not left for Beaumont yet, so the only reason I was allowed to stay up that late is because Mr. Longham had said he would take me home when they finished *The Tonight Show.*

Someone watching us might have thought we were whispering like lovers to keep from bothering her parents, but I never thought of her as anything other than a pal who happened to be a girl. Besides, she was my cousin. But now this absolutely gorgeous creature wanted to know what I was doing like we were long-lost friends at our own personal reunion. Something about the way she looked at me made me feel she really was interested.

I told her about the twins and Billy and me playing football in the street. I told her about how Dad had built a mound for me in the backyard. I mentioned striking out Jerry and Terry, without going into the final score. I told her about Greg the bully at school. I told her about the puppy I rescued who died. When she started to cry, I put my hand on her shoulder and she shivered at the thrill of my touch, or so I wanted to think. I was awash in feelings of love and lust and the simple pleasure of talking to a girl who seemed as interested in what I had to say as I was in being near her.

A couple of her friends came by, both budding young women, too.

"Hey, y'all. Wait a minute."

One was short and chubby with a wide freckly grin. The other had blond pigtails that bounced because she had this habit of jerking her head to the left when she talked. She was about as skinny as me, but it looked a lot better on her.

I imagined Gloria and me walking down the street together back home and the twins and Billy noticing. I imagined Sandy pouting because she realized she couldn't compete with my new love. I felt the glory that would accrue to me whenever anyone saw me with her. I imagined taking her to the prom in high school even though I had sworn not to go after our last school dance.

"I want you to meet Joey. He's my cousin from California."

As soon as she finished the last syllable of California, a change overcame them. They nodded, said wow, and started plying me with questions about Hollywood, Disneyland, and the Beach Boys. I listened to the radio a lot, but I was so excited by all the attention that I couldn't remember one of their songs. Then the short one, Betty, asked me the crucial question that I would pay for later. "Where do you surf?"

"I, uh, well."

The blond one, Sharon, jerked her head. "Oh, Betty, they go to more than one place," and punched her like she should know that.

I just nodded and hoped they would go away, so I could have Gloria all to myself. But they stayed long enough for me to exaggerate my surfing experience and for them to suggest we all go to Galveston so I could teach them. I agreed just to get them out of our hair.

"G-L-O-R-I-A. Gloria." The song wouldn't come out for a few years, but I have never heard it since, whether sung by Van Morrison or not, without thinking about that summer in Dayton. Oh, my God, I was in love. Best evidence? I actually forgot about Mom for a few days.

"Want to come over tonight?"

"Sure." When I noticed I was nodding vigorously, I stopped, hoping I had not been doing it too long.

"Just a minute." She walked around the pool at the kiddie end to say something to Hank. He looked over at me and gave me the AOK sign.

She came running back until Hank yelled at her to slow down.

"All right. All right," she called back and then turned to me. "Want to walk me home?"

Would I walk you home? Where? To your home? To Grandma's home? To my home in California?

"Yes," I said a little too loudly, and some parents looked up from helping their kids put on suntan lotion with a frown. I just smiled meekly. Gloria giggled.

She put her hand in mine like we had been dating for months. I pulled mine out, wiped the sweat off it, and gave it back to her. I gave her more than that. I gave her my undying love. Every poem and song I knew seemed to be the perfect one to describe how I felt. I didn't realize I knew that many songs until I was being flooded with them. "Bring your loving, your sweet loving, bring it on home to me" (Sam Cooke). "I Can't Stop Loving You" (Ray Charles). "Do You Love Me" by the Contours, and I couldn't even dance.

There were plenty of break-up songs, the ones Debbie liked the most, even though it was always her breaking up with guys not the other way around. But I put those out of my mind, just like I had put out of my mind my embarrassing skinniness. Could it be that even gawky, long-necked, puny-chinned guys like me could get beautiful girls?

And that was it. That was what was most important. I didn't feel like some pencil-necked geek. I didn't feel weird and less a male. I felt more. I didn't know if it was her beauty or her devoted attention or her happy demeanor, but I could barely breathe when she turned to me after we passed the pool gate and said, "I know boys are supposed to ask girls, but would you be my boyfriend, at least until the end of the week? I thought of you every day for months, hoping you might write back. Did you get my letters?"

In horror I remembered she had written, but I had dismissed her as too immature physically compared to Sandy next door or the actresses I pretended to kiss into my pillow at night. Now I felt I owed her an apology and wanted to call Maw-Maw long distance to have her read the letters to me over the phone so I could respond now.

We walked back to Primrose and then in the opposite direction I came. She grabbed a magnolia blossom and tried to put it in my hair. She had on a long white shirt, probably her father's, to serve as a robe over her swimsuit. Her walk was springy, like her calves had so much energy they forced her heels to pop up with each step. I watched her bounce and sway and found my mouth was dry because I was breathing with it open. But how else could I respond? In Dayton, 2,000 miles from our cul-de-sac, I'd found the girl of my dreams. Though I would ask Debbie later about the cousin thing, I had no thought of any impediment now.

I'd heard of kids moving to another state to live with their grandparents, usually ones who got in trouble, like boys getting caught stealing because they were hanging out with the wrong crowd or girls getting pregnant. Maybe I would have to do something like that to get Mom and Dad to agree to send me to Grandma. Just running over the possibilities in my mind made me dizzy with joy.

Gloria stopped suddenly. I almost knocked her over.

"Here we are."

CHAPTER NINE

I KNEW IT WAS only a Monopoly game and she was my cousin, but I took forever to decide what to wear. Not that I had that many choices. Mom made me pack a few nice shirts, including one that I could wear to church, but they seemed too fancy for playing a game. Finally I decided to go James Dean with Levis and a clean white T-shirt. I remembered that last year she said she watched *Giant* on late-night TV every time it was replayed and her older sister had taken her to Houston to see it in some retro movie house.

"Say, pardner, where's the boots." I had on some casual loafers that I would sometimes wear to school when I wasn't wearing white tennis shoes. "And no hat?" Debbie was standing in the doorway to her room, which she was not having to share with Mom. With her hair tied back into a ponytail, she had on a cowboy hat that I had to admit looked cool on her. She would have passed for an authentic Texas yellow rose two-stepping across a dance floor. I knew she would find a way to get some cowboy boots soon.

"So, found a girl already?" Debbie had not talked much about her trip to Galveston, but she did mention how much Darin and his friends were dying to hear anything about life in California, just like Gloria's friends at the pool. Did she assume I was getting the same attention?

"It's just Gloria." If ever "just" was used to tell an enormous lie it was now. My face must have reddened because Debbie raised her eyebrows.

"Oh, *just* Gloria. Be careful because she's at least a second cousin, so nothing legal to hold you back from having kids."

God, she could be so disgusting. I thought she had changed when she discovered me in the bathroom with Mom because she had seemed actually worried about what Mom was doing to me. But sarcasm always won out with Debbie no matter how much she might feel sorry for you. It was probably a way to keep people at a distance, the way she felt she had to keep Mom at a distance. But even if I had known that then, it wouldn't have made it less irritating. As adults, Debbie and I have talked about how desperately we wanted to be close to people but were afraid that they would take advantage of us like Mom because she was so insatiable. At least that's what I believe now.

"Thanks, Missy Prissy." She was actually the opposite of a priss, so it had no effect on her. It rhymed with Missy, that was all.

"Okay, Mr. and Mrs. Bickerson." Dad was standing at the end of the hall, next to the kitchen.

"Gloria's house is not far, right?"

"Yeah, just a block past the pool."

"Okay, if you don't stay too late, you can walk home by yourself."

I looked at him for a moment, waiting for him to say that he was kidding and to call when I was ready to come home, or that Mr. Langham, Gloria's father, could bring me home like last year. But he didn't. This wild, crazy, wonderful day was turning into a wonderful night, and I hadn't even got to Gloria's yet. I looked at Dad again just to make sure and said as nonchalantly as I could, "Okay, see you later."

He said, "Have a good time," and went back to a playing checkers with Grandma in the kitchen.

On the walk over, I thought of ways I could let her win since I had easily trounced her last time because she wasn't into competition. My God, soon I would be trying to think of ways to slump around her so she wouldn't feel too short. I kicked a can to the grass and looked at the setting sun, toward California, which now seemed more than a few thousand miles away.

Right before Grandma and I had had lunch, I came into the kitchen to continue our earlier conservation. "What did you mean about how did I like living in California?"

She was opening a tuna can to fix sandwiches. She had on a light cotton dress with a billowy skirt and thousands of little flowers. Compared to what she usually wore, it seemed rather festive. Must have been another present from Mom.

"So many of the people out there were born another place. Sammy said you had lived some places and hadn't even met your next-door neighbors."

"Where we live now, I know everybody." I thought of Sandy and found Gloria comparing to her just fine.

"But your momma is always talkin' about havin' so little time. Every time Sammy calls, she's gone somewhere or too busy to say more 'n a few words."

That had to do with Mom not respecting anyone who had time to spare. I think that was as big a reason for her going to Beaumont as the stated one of visiting relatives and friends. She couldn't stand to be in a house that had no time pressure tyrannizing it. Grandma didn't do the dishes as soon as a meal was finished, like Mom did. Grandma would even leave them until the next morning if a conversation had lasted long enough. And she never interrupted anyone to start a household chore.

But now I was on my way to Glory, I mean, Gloria's, and Grandma's worries about the West Coast and Mom's worries about Grandma's influences blew away like a gull in an offshore gale.

I saw a shiny oil tanker truck in the distance and made the pulling-a-rope-down sign. I didn't even know if that is the way a driver engages his horn, but the guy let out the blast and waved. I guessed I could get it to happen in San Diego, but you'd have to be on the freeway. The truck had slowed down to go through town, as if to say that here even the truck drivers weren't in a hurry.

I smelled something putrid and looked down to see a cat on its side, guts spilling out and maggots in constant motion. Crows were standing nearby, probably wondering if I was a competitor for this juicy meal. I shooed them away, like it would do the cat some good. It made me think about leaving in a few days and how I better make the most of what little time I had with Gloria.

Gloria, Gloria, Gloria. Gloria, who asked me to be her boyfriend, who acted more excited to see me than kids I'd known for years, who seemed to increase in beauty the more I saw of her. When I got back home, nobody would believe me, even with photos. They would think it was too convenient to get a girlfriend on vacation when I never had even the slightest prospect of one at school.

I ran after the crows again and then kept running to Gloria's house. She was out front playing catch with Hank, whose shirtless body shone in the day's last rays of sun. He seemed to look even more muscled when he was on the ground. They didn't see me at first, so I just watched them toss the baseball back and forth. She had on a NY Yankees cap, a pink knit top just tight enough to show off her breasts, and cut-off jeans like Debbie often wore. Her whole body helped her throw the ball like boys do, not that silly arm-only motion that girls or uncoordinated boys use when they've never been around anyone to correct them. I liked the shape of her mostly bare arms and the little sway of her butt when she released the ball.

"Hey, you're here." She came running over, hugged me, and pecked me on the cheek. It seemed like something from a movie, Elizabeth Taylor running up to James Dean, but she was a lot closer to Miss Taylor than I was to Mr. Dean. Maybe if I took up smoking.

Hank said hello as she led me into the front door. The Monopoly board was already on the floor. Her parents were at a special meeting to choose the next pastor at their church, so this time we had a few lamps and not just the TV tube for lights. One other strange thing about Dayton. I never seemed to miss TV here and that was mystifying because at home we watched it every night, and I sometimes would sneak into Maw-Maw's room past my bedtime to watch UCLA basketball and the occasional Tonight Show.

Gloria lay down with her head in her hands and her legs behind her and asked me which piece I wanted. I took the green one and she took the one that looked like an abstract human bust. She wiggled her toes in the air. "Do you want something to drink?"

"Do you have Dr. Pepper?"

She looked at me like I had asked if Texans have drawls. "Yeah, Mr. Pup."

I wonder who told her about my puppy or if it was just a coincidence. She didn't have a dog, but I knew she was trying to talk her parents into getting one last year. I watched her get up by rolling over on her back, throwing her legs over her head and down quickly to pull her upper body into a sitting position. I was fascinated by everything she did. I had had trouble hearing some of what she said at the pool because I was staring at how her lips moved, the upper one crinkling to one side whenever she would start a word with a "W." Even at twelve, I wondered if that was a little weird, not her lips but my obsessive observation.

I'm always hearing about stories, in books or on the screen, in which the main character never finds anyone to match the feelings he had for his first love. Somehow everyone after never quite measures up. Not that the girlfriends or wives to follow are necessarily less beautiful, less talented, less smart, less compassionate, or less funny. No, it's that the earlier one got the press that none of the rest can match. The one that got away becomes so idealized and reimagined that by definition everyone else is less than. It's as if every characteristic of the latest romance must be placed just a little below what once was. Never her equal nor as good as her, no matter what friends or relatives who knew both might say.

I've heard of men who marry the first woman who seemed to like them. I've heard women say that men never do the choosing, that even when they think they have, the women have done something to get the men to notice them. I don't know about all that, but I do know that any time someone outside my family paid attention to me and, as in Gloria's case, seemed to enjoy a deep affection for me that

I could in no way figure out how I had earned it, that is the most glorious feeling in the world.

She came back in with a small transistor radio and fumbled around until it picked up some superstation from Houston. I know I have kind of enshrined this evening with a romantic glow so that it might not have been exactly as I'm relating it to you now, but as best I can remember, it played all those songs I heard in my head at the pool. The first one was Sam Cooke singing "Bring It on Home to Me," as in "bring your loving home to me." She smiled kind of mischievously like she had called in the song just for me and sat down. I must have been staring at her because when "Do You Love Me (Now That I Can Dance)" started to play, she said, "It's your move."

Boy, what a pregnant statement. I guessed she was talking about me throwing the dice but, oh, the possibilities. I landed on Boardwalk and decided not to buy it. She looked at me with one of those I'll let you drown yourself in my eyes looks and gradually broke into a smile, not because she wasn't sure she wanted to smile, or was trying to force herself to be kind, but because she wanted to savor the joy she was feeling. She crawled right over the board, and just before I began to protest that she was knocking her piece aside and messing up the cards in the Chance square, she sat next to me. I always tear up when I remember this or the few times I've told other people. She took my face in her hands and said, "Joey, you are the sweetest, most intelligent, funny boy I've even known." Even then I wanted to make light of it and point out she managed to say nothing about my biceps or handsomeness, but I was too out of breath to reply. "I don't know why you think you're too skinny or too uncool to have a girlfriend." Oh God, why did I tell her that last year? "Will you let me kiss you?"

Would I let her kiss me? I know that's what she said, but I could think of nothing but how absurd the question was. That was like asking did I want Mom and Dad to get along or would I allow my muscles to match the twins or would I accept an invitation to play for the Yankees or would I be willing at some future indeterminate date to have sex with almost anyone.

I nodded so fiercely that my face slipped out of her hands, and she began to laugh. I could only think that I had destroyed the most perfect moment in my short life and would forever have to pay for being such an idiot. But she was laughing out of affection not derision. She gradually slowed the bobbing of my face and slowly, ever so slowly, like the most practiced Hollywood actress, moved toward my lips. They were soft and warm and sent a tingle that moved from my face to my groin and back again a few hundred times. She kissed me a few times because neither of us could hold our breaths too long and because we didn't want it to end. When she stopped, she leaned in my ear and said, "I love you, Joey, and I always will."

I couldn't take it. It was too much goodness and beauty and stimulation and joy and the fulfillment of every dream of what having a girlfriend might mean. I turned to the side and began to cry. First the tears rolled down slowly, like her lingering kiss, and then I began to sob like the women from other countries I'd seen on TV who would drape themselves over the coffin of their husband or their child. I sobbed and I wailed. I didn't know where Hank was and thank God her parents hadn't come home yet, but I cried out every dream that hadn't come true and every doubt I had about myself and every bit of inadequateness.

I knew deep down that I didn't deserve this. I was the murderer being forgiven by the daughter of the man I had killed. I was the rapist being forgiven by the father of the girl violated. I was the bully being loved by the victim. I was being offered innocence and beauty and love, and I was completely unworthy.

I collapsed to the floor and smelled the fruitiness of her shampoo when she lay next to me, saying over and over again, "It's okay, Joey. It's okay. You're a wonderful boy. I love you."

I wanted to turn around and kiss her hard, maybe enough to hurt her. Or to rip off her clothes and try to force myself on her though I didn't know exactly what to do. I wanted to be mean to her and tell her about Sandy and Mom and other things I thought of that made me such a horrible human being, but the more I thought of hurting her, the more it made me cry.

She lay behind me and just held on to me until my breathing slowed down and she could sense I was cried out. I remember taking in one long deep breath and pulling her hand away from me so I could sit up. I couldn't look at her and just heard the beginning of "Big Girls Don't Cry" playing over and over in my head until I finally said, "I'm sorry. I just…" but I couldn't continue without starting to cry again.

She took my hand and held it hers. "Joey, do you remember bringing me that peach from your Grandma's tree and telling me how when you smelled it, you thought of me?"

I didn't remember, but I nodded yes.

"Do you remember telling me that some of the best and most beautiful actresses are short when I was complaining about always having to be up front in every class photo?"

I did remember that.

"And do you remember saying that my feet looked elegant when you had asked me why I put them behind my legs and I said because they look like a lizard's?"

I nodded again and wiped my eyes.

"Joey, I have never known anybody who is so good at noticing things and making people feel good about what he notices, especially when they are things that we're ashamed of."

I knew these were compliments, but I was getting distracted by watching her breasts expand with each breath and her eyes blink shut on important words, as if she was purposely holding back the deep pool of green in them to make me appreciate them more. For the first time I understood how someone could say I could eat you alive. I just wanted to make her a part of me, consume her, like we were consuming Jesus's flesh made holy in the Lord's Supper.

I stood up and opened my arms to her. I don't know what made me do it. I probably had seen it in some movie. She struggled to stand up, and I helped her by grabbing her under her arms and thereby gently brushing her breasts. I tried to ignore the electric shock and pulled her into me. The radio was playing again "Do You Love Me Now That I Can Dance." I doubt it was referring to slow dancing, but that is what we did, swaying to the music and me breathing in the fresh smell of her hair, the slightly rank oily smell of her skin, and the salty taste of her neck as I kissed it ever so slightly, more like I was nibbling on it to see if a dish of her needed any more seasoning.

I don't know if I ever loved again, but I knew I loved then. I would have done anything for her, anything to protect her from harm, anything to make her realize how utterly glorious she was. G-L-O-R-I-A, Glo-ri-a.

CHAPTER TEN

I WANTED IT TO rain on the way home so I could pretend to be Gene Kelley, but there were no tall buildings, no lamp-posts, and, most disappointing of all, no rain. Not that I could dance—I didn't count slow dancing with Gloria—but I wanted to do something to show how everything had changed.

I didn't think about how it might affect my relationship with Mom, Debbie, or the guys back home. I just knew I was transformed. "Then He Kissed Me" played in my head, even though the Crystals were singing about a boy making the first move. Every love song, every musical, every romantic movie dialogue that I could remember seemed to apply. If I had read poetry, I would have been recalling that, too. I had been Gloria-fied.

I stood next to the trunk of a tree and stumbled through a medley of songs. I was Elvis Presley who couldn't help falling in love. I was the dream lover, Bobby Darin. I was on Broadway singing "On the Street Where You Live." I was Gene Pitney, Roy Orbison, and Brian Hyland. I was Nat King Cole and Bobby Vinton. I was even Connie Francis, Marcie Blane, and Brenda Lee. I didn't care if I was singing about love lost or love found or love only dreamed of; I just wanted to sing.

If this were a movie, our together days would be dramatized in a video montage: Gloria and me in the backseat of Darin's convertible as he drove near the beach with "Dream Baby" playing in the background and our hair flying behind us (well, Gloria's); both of us falling off surfboards laughing under a clear sky; Gloria sliding into home plate safe because I missed the tag; Gloria jumping, cheerleader fashion with feet to butt, to celebrate bowling a strike; and, finally, the two of us, backlit by the sun, holding hands on a park bench.

But this was not a movie, so what we really did was walk around Dayton hand in hand, swim at the pool, and play the same Monopoly game every night until I left. Of course, we made out: on the rug in her living room, on the swing in her backyard, and on the porch at Grandma's after Gloria walked *me* home. We almost made it to the Gulf because Dad let Debbie go again, and Debbie, miracle of miracles, invited Gloria and me to go along. But we both realized that would mean sharing our precious time with others.

Thursday night finally came. We were sitting on Grandma's porch with my knee touching hers. Every so often, I would move mine toward her, and she would return the pressure. I refused to make my good-bye official with conversation, even though we both knew Mom was coming back in the morning.

"You leave tomorrow."

I looked at her astonished, like she was saying she wanted me to go.

"Uh-huh." I tried to sound like it wouldn't be the worst thing that had ever happened to me. I had on a white shirt

Mom packed for church, some black cotton slacks, and my new black-and-brown leather dress shoes.

"You look like you're going to a wedding."

Or a funeral, I thought.

"You look so handsome."

I almost laughed. Anybody who saw us together would suppose I was rich or had magical powers because I was obviously trading way up in the love market. It was a wonderfully kind exaggeration to call me handsome. It would have been an insult to call her beautiful.

I choked out a "thanks" and looked her up and down very slowly while she gazed away from me. In this light I couldn't see the red streaks or even tell that her hair was brown, but the shape of it as it fell over her bare shoulders was stirring. I could see the outlines of her lips and nose and thought of the Greek statues I'd seen in *National Geographic*. Was she trying to remember what we had done these past few days? Was she looking into a future when we were back together? Was she forcing herself to forget about tomorrow?

"You are so beautiful. I sometimes think you've been given a potion that makes you believe I look like guy who would have someone like you." She started to protest, and I went on. "I don't mean I'm nothing. But, well, you're, you're, just amazing."

I wanted to paint her or star her in a movie or write a song about her that would play on the radio. I was about to cry, not because I was leaving but because she made me feel so special, so I got up and walked toward the street. She followed a few steps behind.

Without turning around, I said, "I don't know how I can get back here before next summer. I don't even know how I can stand to be traveling across Texas, but not in Dayton." I was crying now and realized I should promise to write often and to find some way to call every night, but I couldn't speak.

She was facing me now, with her hands behind her back, which made her breasts especially prominent. I did my best not to stare.

"Joey, I waited a year for you. I can wait again."

She looked so deeply into my eyes I had to look away. I wanted to press my lips to hers like I'd seen Steve McQueen do, but I froze.

"I love you, Joey."

She leaned into me, whispered, "Good-bye," in my ear, kissed me on the cheek, and walked away. I watched her in the moonlight. She swayed some, but her shoulders were straight. Soon she broke into a run and disappeared around the corner.

Once she was out of sight, I sat on the porch stunned, as if the week had not happened. I still remember that it felt more like I was overwhelmed with joy than with sadness. It felt unreal, too, because something this good couldn't happen to me. Certainly not with a girl.

A bird chirped in a bush nearby, and I remembered the argument that Romeo and Juliet had about whether he should leave. *It's the lark and you have to go. No, it's the nightingale and we still have time.* The chirping in the bush stopped for a few seconds and started again. The magnolia trees looked ink-black in front of the moon.

I walked up the porch steps and into the dark house, making sure the door did not slam behind me. Except for a groan when I bumped into the sofa and a scraping sound when I nudged a chair in the dining room, I made it to my room with little noise. I sank onto the bed with no intention of changing into my pajamas. I was too excited to cry and too happy to laugh. I resisted giving in to sleep because I feared the feeling would disappear with unconsciousness.

In the morning I felt a kiss on my cheek and wondered how long Gloria had been in my room. I didn't see what she was wearing, just that she smelled of onions and peppermint toothpaste. But it was Mom, who was asking me why I had slept in my good clothes. When she kissed me, I ran to the bathroom. I had the smarts to lock the bathroom door before puking up everything. I didn't think I had eaten that much.

Mom asked through the door how I was and I said I would be out in a few minutes. I stood before the mirror and looked at my long nose, high forehead, and what seemed like sunken cheeks. Billy might have a case for calling me emaciated now. Mom knocked again, and I unlocked the door. I squeezed past her and began packing. She walked in behind me and asked if I wanted something to drink.

"I'm okay now. I'll get something later."

She didn't say anything else. I was surprised she left me alone but, with all that happened before vacation, she was more cautious around me now. I was grateful because I didn't know what horrible things I might have said to her. I was trying to look as busy as I could to keep her at bay, folding my T-shirts and searching the room on my knees for any clothes I might have left behind.

"How you doing, Pup-man?" Dad was standing in the doorway, back in the black shorts Mom had bought and a blue-striped seersucker short sleeve shirt, clothes he never wore back home.

"Okay," I grunted, reaching under the bed.

Dad escorted a stunned Mom to the kitchen where he had fixed her favorite breakfast: an omelet with bell pepper, onion, and Monterey Jack cheese. I had heard him asking Grandma where he could find jalapenos yesterday.

I searched all over for the cross Gloria had given me until I remembered I put it in my jeans pocket. I put it around my neck and tucked it under my shirt. I knew wearing a cross was a Catholic thing, so I would only let it show after I had worked out some plausible rationale.

For the next hour, everything was about getting on the road. Surprisingly, Mom encountered resistance from Debbie. In the past Debbie complained about Dayton all the way here, all the time we were here, and all the way back, but this time she had a different experience. Darin, our movie star-looking cousin, her California girl celebrity, and her fully developed body gave her more attention than she usually got back home, even on stage.

"Why can't you just come back through here? It's not that far out of the way." Debbie had on jeans, a man's white dress shirt, and a blue paisley scarf around her neck. I had to admit she looked quite the Texan cowgirl ready for a little two-stepping at a local bar. She was right about the distance, but that wasn't the issue.

Mom was looking at Debbie like she was about to remind her of how much she has always hated Dayton. "You haven't talked to Louise, your godmother, in a year. And everyone at the church is looking forward to seeing how you've grown into a fine young lady."

I didn't know if Mom was referring to her breast development or to the character traits she wished Debbie had, but in either case it was pretty funny.

Debbie just looked at Mom, stunned into silence. Before she made a crack, Dad stepped in and escorted Debbie out the back door. "So what's going on, Mouse?"

"I just like it here, for the first time in my life. There are all our cousins, and we only get to see Grandma once a year. Why can't I stay? You know it's not that far out of the way."

"That's not the point."

I couldn't see them, so I didn't know if Dad was using his eyes and gestures to let her know he was on her side while his words would have said to Mom that he was supporting Mom's view. Debbie agreed to go to Beaumont after Dad said he would see if we could afford to fly her back during Christmas vacation.

I closed my door and sat on my bulging bag to connect the clasp. I thought of Gloria saying she loved me. I thought of her hands holding my face while she kissed me. I thought of how much I enjoyed losing to her in Monopoly. I wanted to be on the same flight next Christmas, but that might mean having to confirm what they suspected about Gloria. I had pretended I was spending time with her brother Hank when I went to see her.

I don't remember much about Beaumont or the trip home. Grandma had this jar she put change in every time she came back from shopping and always gave half to me and half to Debbie. Usually we couldn't wait to exchange the coins for bills, but this time I wanted to feel their weight, as if their heaviness would keep me from leaving. In Beaumont I was able to sneak out from a potluck at the Baptist church and call Gloria for the first time from a phone booth using some of Grandma's change. Fortunately, she had a lot to say because I cried most of time until at the end. I only said that I missed her and hung up.

The rest of the trip was one attempt after another to find a way to call her. In El Paso I used a phone in the lobby. When we stopped for lunch in Tucson, I used the one in the hallway on the way to the bathroom. In Yuma I wanted to call while Dad was getting gas, but it was in plain sight.

On the way back, he was in less of a hurry, so we stopped three nights at motels. Each night I cried myself to sleep, doing my best not to let anyone hear me. Mom still kept her distance and even Debbie let up on her usual mocking repartee.

We turned onto Clancey Street late Sunday night and were all too tired to say much to Maw-Maw before going to bed.

CHAPTER ELEVEN

OUR FAMILY WENT TO church a lot, even compared to the Mormon Twambleys and the noninstrumental Church of Christ Carrolls. (At least they were allowed to sing.) In the morning our church had Sunday school followed by a worship service. The evening service was basically a repeat of the morning, but a little more casual. Sometimes, during the summer, the pastor even wore a short-sleeved shirt. The Wednesday night prayer service was, not surprisingly, a lot like the two services on Sunday, but with, you guessed it, more praying. An hour before that weeknight service there were also activities for kids: Royal Ambassadors and Girls Auxiliary, for example. We Southern Baptists were dedicated but not ridiculous like the Catholics with daily mass. I enjoyed Wednesdays because Mr. Bodenhamer was our RA counselor and because we memorized a lot of Bible verses, which I was good at. The more verses you could recite and the more facts you knew about the Bible, the higher rank in RAs you reached, kind of like merit badges in the Boy Scouts. We also went on campouts.

We had arrived home from our vacation late Sunday night, but not too late for me to contact Gloria. On the trip back, when I had called from a telephone booth in Yuma, she and I had worked out a way to phone late at night without alerting our parents. She was to sneak out of bed at midnight, and I would call at exactly 12:05, letting it ring just once. If it was busy when I called a second time, I knew she was up and ready to answer on the first ring of the third call. If it was not busy when I called back, I was to assume she didn't wake up in time, hang up after one ring, and not call again that night. We figured one ring would easily be seen as a misdial, so no one in her family would suspect anything. Then she would initiate the calls the next night. To keep track of whose turn it was, I called on odd days and she took the even.

On Monday and Tuesday night, Mom came by my room but didn't come in, just saying goodnight from the door. I felt guilty and considered going into her bedroom to give her a goodnight kiss, but it seemed like a betrayal of Gloria.

By Wednesday night I had made it through six days and five nights without Gloria and had done my best to keep our relationship a secret, but I was having trouble keeping a check on my emotions. It was still easy for me to cry every time the radio played some breaking up song, even though Gloria and I were anything but broken up.

As I already said, the Royal Ambassadors met before the Wednesday prayer service, just like with Sunday school before morning worship. Usually the last year of eligibility for RAs is sixth grade, but I was younger than most in my class, so Mr. B let me stay on as a kind of assistant. Besides, because of all the verses I had memorized, I was a legend, though lately rock and roll lyrics were beginning to take their place.

Mr. Bodenhamer was sometimes called Mr. Body because he was built like Jack LaLanne. He worked as a lifeguard, and surfed to boot. He had a broad back with bulging pecs, which made him the envy of all the boys. He was hairy everywhere, which could have given him a caveman look, but he spent so much time in the sun that his light brown hair was bleached blond. It appeared to be merely peach fuzz like on kids who had not begun puberty.

He was wonderfully strange for an adult, especially at church, because he was so open. He talked about how much he loved his wife and how unkind he could be to her. He talked about why he hated his parents when he was our age and how he had changed when his daughter was born. He made us find things we appreciated about our parents, but only after we admitted what about them bugged us. He had no trouble criticizing anything, even God. He said self-honesty always trumped being nice to yourself when it came to the most important matters, like relationships. And that wasn't all. He taught us how to set up tents, build campfires, and bury our poop. Though I was looking at Dad differently since we returned from Dayton, Mr. B still represented everything my father wasn't.

We RAs met in the same room the high schoolers used for Sunday school, so that gave us a little more prestige. Mr. B had us sitting in a small circle tonight. He had just asked us to think about someone that we loved enough to be embarrassed for.

"You see, I find that embarrassment is the ultimate in thinking only about me. So if I am willing to become embarrassed for someone else, it must mean I am really concerned for them." He was sitting with one leg crossed over the other like a college professor. His short-sleeved white shirt with buttoned-down collar bulged like he had worn it while saving someone from drowning, and it had shrunk on him before he could change. In tan slacks and penny loafers, he looked more like the president of a corporation on vacation than a lifeguard who had dressed up.

"Joey, what do you think?"

I swallowed and choked on my spit. While coughing I motioned for someone else to go first.

Marvin talked about being teased at school when he had hairs on him from his cat, Twinkles, who slept with him. Craig said his mother had epilepsy and that he stayed with her during seizures in public. Mr. B said his daughter had cussed him out in front of her friends because he did not give her permission to go to a dance on short notice. In spite of her humiliating him in public, he managed to wait until they got home to discuss it. He found out her band had been chosen to play at the last minute when the original group had cancelled and that was why she had asked so close to the time for the dance. Once he had calmed down, he and his wife actually agreed to let her go.

While I knew I would do anything for Gloria, I couldn't think of anything embarrassing that might happen with her. Then I realized that I was worried that guys at school and in the neighborhood would tease me mercilessly if they saw tears in my eyes for any reason and even more so because I missed Gloria.

"I might be willing to cry over a girlfriend." Like a good politician, I did not admit to either having cried or having a girlfriend, partly because I still thought no one would believe I was capable of it.

Mr. B held up his hand to stop the crack he could see was about to come from Paulie. As it turned out, Paulie didn't plan to say anything. He was having too much fun pretending to be me, miming like a bad actor in a melodrama that he was heartbroken. His bottom lip pooched out and his eyes squinched shut. He held his head in his hands, tossing it back and forth. He just looked stupid to me, but already the younger kids were beginning to snicker.

I wanted to show him what Gloria looked like to convince him he would be broken up about leaving her, too, but I realized that I didn't have a photo. (I would have to take care of that with tonight's call.) If he saw her, I knew he would be jealous. Even though girls thought he was cute and pretty funny, you can only get so far when you're five feet tall.

It was close enough to the time for the prayer service that Mr. B headed off more ridicule by getting out his guitar. We ended class, like we always did, by singing "Just a Closer Walk with Thee." He had taught a few of us to sing harmony, and we actually sounded pretty good, even with the out-of-tune guys. Because of the person I was not getting to have a closer walk with, I asked permission to go to the bathroom before we finished the last verse. I wasn't ready to be embarrassed for her yet.

In the bathroom I washed a few tears away and wondered if I would have to be baptized to keep Gloria. Except for her willingness to make out, she was pretty devoted to her church and talked about Jesus like some girls talk about a friend they have sleepovers with. I had to admit I was jealous of her certainty about God in general, and His Son in particular, because she said that Jesus gave her the power to love me.

It's not like I hadn't ever thought about walking the aisle. That was what we called the action of responding to an altar call, which we had at every service and sometimes at funerals and weddings. I was religious in some ways. For

127

instance, I prayed every day, usually that Dad and Mom would get along, sometimes that Maw-Maw wouldn't be so left out, but mostly for a girlfriend. Now that I had one, I wondered if I should give God credit and take the next step of devotion.

It didn't take too long to compose myself in the restroom, so I was somewhat early to the service. I stood at the back, undecided about where to sit. Mom was by herself in her usual spot, left side, third row, on the aisle. It was the same side as the pulpit because Mom liked to be close to the pastor when he preached. I knew she would want me to join her, especially since we were on the outs.

Then something strange happened. I asked myself what Gloria would do just the way people ask what Jesus would do. (Gloria, like Juliet's Romeo, had become the god of my idolatry.) I knew she would want me to be kind, especially to my mother. It was then I decided that if Gloria said that I must give my life to Jesus to have her love, I would do it.

I sidled up to Mom and let her put her arm around me and pull me closer. It felt both horrible and satisfying, the way painful exercise can. This was for Gloria, a pledge of my love, so it was worth the discomfort. Since I had already decided I could be embarrassed for her, I could definitely put up with the creepy feelings I was now having as Mom touched me.

A few minutes later, Dad joined us and pushed hard into me on purpose. I pushed back, and he grinned. He still had some of the swagger of our week in Dayton, but it was already beginning to wear off under Mom's demands. He winked at Mom, but she acted irritated, like he was doing something lewd. I saw Debbie was with her usual friends, the pastor's daughter and a girl with a voice like Judy

Garland they had recruited for the choir. The singer was even more of a sensation because she wore skirts a little too short and way too much jewelry for parents who had survived the Depression. It looked like all three of them were chewing gum.

Having just accomplished a deed for Gloria, I wondered what she would think of our modern sanctuary. Would she think we were California cool or just weird? She went to a church with white clapboard walls and a steeple bell that rang on Sundays. It was elegant, in a Shaker furniture way. We had walked past it a couple of times, and she told me about when she had walked the aisle and what she felt when she knelt and gave her life to Jesus. I was plenty embarrassed while she was talking because I got a hard on.

Some called our church an upside down Jell-O mold. Others concentrated on the interior and said it resembled a theatre in the round. Those who liked it appreciated that it belonged in the twentieth century, not something stuck in the 1800s like most churches. From the outside it did resemble half of an enormous clamshell, for the roof rose about three stories and then sloped down to about five feet only to rise again and fall again around the building in enormous waves. Each arch held stained glass of geometrically shaped color that was teal, yellow, or magenta. The building was circular, so if it had not been for the baptistery, the choir area, and the offices in back, the pulpit could have been completely surrounded by the pews as the stage was completely surrounded by the audience in some modern theatres. The pews' upholstery was light blue wool that was flecked with gold and tucked into a wooden mold of blond ash. There were no armrests, to encourage contact with one's neighbors. The carpet was a deep ocean blue. The

129

whole sanctuary had a cheerfulness and friendliness that contrasted with the warnings from the pulpit on the danger of society outside. To some critics the décor suggested a lightness that offended because it clashed with the somberness of a crucified Savior.

In keeping with that lightness, about fifteen minutes into any service at Calvary, the pastor would ask for the names and hometowns of visitors. He would joke with them about their football team or their weather or their food. If he knew nothing about their state, then he would comment on how blessed they were to have found us. He had asked a young navy couple from Texas, the home state of the majority of the nonnative Californians in the congregation, if it still had the best barbeque in the country and then recommended they come to the church picnic to prove them wrong, which was a bogus challenge since the recipes he was touting from our congregation had come from Texas, too. The décor encouraged such informality.

We always sang a lot and usually had a choir member perform a solo right before the sermon (though we would never refer to it as a performance). Tonight "A Closer Walk with Thee," our RA theme song, was being sung by a husband and wife in harmonies to rival the Everly Brothers.

I didn't hear the words at all. Instead, I imagined Gloria's lips lightly touching mine as she reached for me over that Monopoly game. I felt the board bend under my weight and an apology form on my lips, but she pressed all the harder with her lips to keep me from speaking. I had had my eyes closed and when I opened them I hoped I hadn't been physically mimicking a kiss. When I looked around, thank God, everyone was focused on the singing duo.

When the song finished, the pastor began his sermon, really just a short meditation when compared to the ones on Sunday. He started by reading the story of the prodigal son. I hoped he wouldn't repeat the anecdote he often told with this Bible passage. Not because I had heard it so many times, which I had, but because it always got to me, and I didn't know how I would respond in my Gloria-sensitive condition.

I became aware of his words after he had talked for a few minutes. "That man, that father of the prodigal, he didn't wait," Pastor Bob enjoined, "no, no, no. He ran out to meet his son." The pastor looked from left to right as if to meet all challengers who wanted to dispute that that's the way it happened. His voice rose with each sentence. "He didn't see a bum who stunk from spending the night with pigs. He didn't see a wastrel who had squandered his father's inheritance. He didn't see an ungrateful profligate diseased from all his tom-catting around." At this point a few amens from the faithful punctuated his declarations. I wondered if some of them had survived such a disease.

"He was so happy to have his son back that even a hearty hug was not enough. He had to throw a party." Pastor Bob looked down and shook his head slowly, as if he was ashamed of what he had to say next.

His tanned face was beginning to sag with age, which may be why he smiled so much, a kind of anti-gravity cosmetic. He was tall enough that the extra weight collecting around his waist wasn't so noticeable. He looked like a man who had wanted to be a movie star or a famous politician or a success in business, but was forced to settle for a life of mediocrity and was putting as good a face on it as he could.

"This father, this son-welcoming father, is what our God is like." He looked up to heaven and then down at us, surveying the whole congregation slowly, even turning around to make eye contact with the choir. "But us, us sinners, yes, we sinners, pastors and unbelievers, presidents and hobos, movie stars and trash collectors, we aren't like that." Now his pursed lips widened into a grim, almost sarcastic smile. "At least on our own." A few uh-huhs and nodded heads followed, but not too many lest we sound much like our black sister congregation downtown.

"Some of you have heard this story before, but it's worth hearing again, like so much of what we declare in this holy place. It is worth hearing again because it's true, and truth never gets old or tired."

Mom touched my arm and looked at me adoringly, like I was the son from the story who had just come home.

"Brothers and sisters, please listen to me." He raised his hands as if appealing to God to make us pay attention. "Let me tell you a more recent story." He took in a deep breath, placed his hands on opposite sides of the pulpit, and leaned toward us. I thought he was looking at Mom.

"A boy had come back from the war. He had been beaten up pretty badly. A leg amputated. Only one good eye. The other just a socket with scar tissue. One arm was so badly burned that it was useless."

I knew the rest by heart, but I listened like a child hearing a bedtime story, pretending to wonder what would happen next.

"He stopped at a phone booth to make a call to his family. His father answered and this crippled son of his said, 'Dad, I'm back.'" We could hear the pastor's voice break.

"'Sonny? My God, where are you?'"

"'We just docked, Dad. I'm waiting for a taxi to bring me home.'"

"The Dad, choked up with tears, went on, 'We knew you were due in, but we didn't know on which ship. It is so good to hear you.' The father broke down and motioned for his wife to come to the phone." 'Here's your mother,' he said before beginning to cry.'"

"'Oh, Sonny.' the Mom says sniffling.'"

"'Hi, Mom.' He paused, choking up himself. 'I have a favor to ask.'"

"'Sonny. Anything.'"

"The son fidgets with the receiver and takes a deep breath. 'You see, I have this friend who fought with me. He's in pretty bad shape.' Then the boy describes his 'buddy.' 'He has only one leg, one good arm and one eye. I wondered if I could bring him home with me.'"

"'Why sure, bring him on. Any friend of yours—'"

"'No, Mom, I mean is it okay for him to stay with us? He has nowhere else to go.'"

"'You mean for good?'"

The boy takes a deep breath and can only squeak out, 'Uh, huh.'"

"'Well, uh, I don't know. Let me talk to your father.' There is silence on the line as the parents confer.'"

"His Dad picks up the receiver again, having resumed his composure. 'Son, he is welcome for a while, until he can sort out something for the long term, but those are some pretty serious injuries, so he's going to need the kind of care we can't afford. Oh, Sonny we are so glad to hear from you. Are you okay?'"

"'Sure, Dad, sure.'"

"That boy never went home. He was found facedown in the river at the edge of town. When his father came to identify the body, he wept like he had never wept before at his one-legged, one-eyed son." Pastor Bob let this sink in. "But our Father in Heaven has no requirement for his love. The lowest of the low, the maimest of the maimed, the least deserving of us is loved like we are royalty. When we come home to Him, He throws a party."

I always felt that it was unfair to the family, not to tell them the son was the severely injured one because they probably would have taken him even if they weren't willing to take in the friend in the same condition, but the story got to me anyway. Gloria was as close as I had gotten to God's kind of love. If I could have her by responding to this sermon, to this story, and walk the aisle, then I would do it.

It's not the first time I had thought seriously about asking Jesus into my life. At a youth conference in Yosemite the leader had us all lie on our backs on this enormous rock and think about how many stars there are and what kind of power created such a universe. If, he said, the person behind that power wanted to be in a relationship with us, could we turn Him down? I was moved by that but never as much as the story about the family rejecting their son.

The choir began to sing, "Just as I am, without one plea, but that Thy blood was shed for me." When Billy had visited one night during a revival week, he said they sounded like they were whining. Sometimes it sounded that way to me, but tonight it just seemed to be what my soul was feeling. "And that Thou bidst me come to Thee. O Lamb of God, I come, I come."

I'd seen one of Billy Graham's crusades on TV and made it to one in San Diego about four years ago. Rev. Graham used the same song and hundreds responded. It's hard not to. I was crying now for what I thought were my sexual sins but know as an adult that I was probably weeping for all the loss in my life: an absent father during the Korean War, the smothering love of a needy mother, the friends left behind at every move while my father was still in the service, and the two thousand miles that separated Gloria from me. I wanted relief, and this was what was promised by the pastor and what had obviously worked wonders on Gloria.

When I inched past Dad, he looked shocked more than pleased. I looked back at Mom to see tears running down her cheeks. I didn't know if she was crying because I was crying, because she hoped I would now come back to her, or because she wanted me to have a personal relationship with God.

Mr. Bodenhamer's wife happened to be one of the counselors and guided me to a seat. "Honey, we are so happy for you. What do you want to say to Jesus?"

That made me cry more.

She waited and then said, "May I ask you a few questions?"

I nodded.

"Do you know you are a sinner in need of grace?"

"Yes, ma'am."

"Do you realize that just by calling on Jesus's name you can have your sins washed away?"

"Yes, ma'am."

"Then let's kneel down."

Kneeling seemed like too much. I didn't dare look around to see who was watching. I hoped Debbie had snuck out like she sometimes did during services. As I stood there, I realized I hadn't come down here because I wanted Jesus. What I wanted was Gloria. I was doing this to get her love.

I shook my head at Mrs. B and walked up the aisle and out the door. I walked past our car and across the street toward the phone booth outside the Rexall Drug. I had a couple of dollar bills and got them changed inside. I tried Gloria's number about ten times but only got a busy signal.

The night was beginning to get cool and damp. I stepped on a piece of gum and felt the pull each time I lifted my shoe. I could see people coming out of the church across the street and decided I didn't want to walk home. Dad and Mom said nothing as I got in the backseat of our car. Debbie had this don't-you-do-the-most-interesting-things look on her face but said nothing, too. We sat in silence until Maw-Maw arrived.

"Your time will come," she said, as I moved to the middle between Debbie and her.

Was I going to hell? What if I died in a car crash on the way home? And, more importantly, would Gloria still love me after I had rejected Jesus? I was afraid I had just refused the only way I could relieve myself of the feeling I would never be loved. I couldn't have verbalized all those feelings then, but they were brewing inside. I wanted to be loved, but at this point, I could only see salvation in Gloria.

CHAPTER TWELVE

SUNDAY WAS HERE AGAIN. Another day at church. Before we left, Mom wanted us all next to the bougainvillea for the millionth photo in our front yard. Did she want the photo to reflect on for posterity, or so the neighbors could see her smiling family? In the house she had been scurrying around, half naked as usual, trying to get us to eat breakfast and to finish dressing ourselves. She had on a bra and a half-slip over a girdle. The ripples above her waist would be hidden once she finished dressing. As a child I found them disgusting, but today, when I see them on other women, they arouse me.

"Who wants pancakes?" she yelled from the kitchen without a response. Since Dad had eaten hours ago and was now sitting in the car doing the Sunday crossword, she could not have been expecting a response from him. Debbie had Sam Cooke on in her room, so she was effectively as deaf as Maw-Maw. Mom was pretending to ask everyone but was really only talking to me.

"I'll have some," I said.

"What?" she yelled again, apparently never thinking that she should be closer for a conversation.

"I'll have some," I screamed from just outside my door, and in that effort realized I didn't. Or to be more precise, I didn't want all the attention that would come with them.

I walked across the hall to look in the bathroom mirror, hoping this would be the day hair appeared on my lip, and heard Maw-Maw talking in her room. Now, I said to myself with Sherlockian logic, Mom was in the kitchen, Dad was already in the car, and Debbie was in her room, so that meant Maw-Maw could only be talking to someone on the phone or praying. I stepped closer to listen.

"I don't know. Dodo is fussing round 'cause Joey's bin actin' strange, like he's about to have a tizzy again." Silence. "I know, Ethyl. I got to submit, and I'm real clear I'll come eventually. But I don't know about right now."

I could hear some "uh-huhs" and "that's right," and then a final, "The Lord bless you, too."

I waited for a few seconds to knock on Maw-Maw's door. I tried to make it loud enough for her to hear but not loud enough for Mom to notice. Not really possible, but I tried. Maw-Maw always opened her door slowly, either because so few of us ever knocked on it or because she never could be sure of what she had heard.

Almost ready for church, she had on a lavender rayon blouse and a darker lavender skirt made of some thick material but still shiny like the blouse. A matching jacket hung over a straight chair. She was still in her pink fuzzy mules that Mom nagged her about not wearing since they had no arch support.

"Maw-Maw, are you thinking of leaving?"

She looked at me askance the way you look at someone who had just revealed a secret about yourself but you can't quite believe they knew enough to figure it out. "Did you think I was talking to Ethyl?"

"Uh huh."

"Well you're right." She sat on the bed and made like she was shaping her hair all over without actually touching it.

"That commune?"

She smiled. "Yes, sir. Sounds all communist, doesn't it?" She patted the bed next to her. "Close the door and sit down."

"Pancakes ready," Mom yelled.

Even Maw-Maw must have heard that because she said, "I'll make this short." She smoothed the covers on the opposite side of me. "I'm just not needed like I was when you and your sister were small. And your father, well, he still acts funny when I want to help around the house."

It was a little surprising that she was so open with me, but maybe she could see me becoming the outcast she had been. I surveyed the small room. Her TV with rabbit ears was in a corner. A small desk where she prepared her Sunday school lessons and read her Bible every morning sat under the window. A worn, overstuffed leather chair barely fit between the closet doors and the TV. In many ways it was about the size of a room in a convalescent home.

"Do they really share all their money?"

She smiled. "Just like in Acts. That's what appeals to me, living like that, so close to the Scriptures."

"Mam-Maw, I just couldn't do it last Wednesday."

"I know. You got to decide on your own." She hugged me and I flinched, but she held me firmly until I relaxed into it. "You'll be fine. The Lord is very patient."

I wanted to tell her about Gloria, but I didn't think she would approve of my putting Gloria ahead of Jesus. Mom called again, and I yelled back that I was coming. I hugged Maw-Maw and left before I started to cry, but not about her leaving.

Mom got her photo in the front yard just before we all piled into the car. She and Dad sat in the front with me in the back between Debbie and Maw-Maw as usual. We were early to church, but late according to Dad. He felt if you arrived less than thirty minutes before things started, then you were not allowing for an emergency, which was another way of saying that you didn't really care about being on time.

I still felt funny about what people might say if they were here when I walked out of the church last Wednesday or, what would be worse, what they might think without saying it. I hoped that those were there weren't coming this morning, which was ridiculous because it was the most dedicated members who came during the week. Fortunately, none of the RA guys said anything, no matter what they were thinking.

Mr. B was also the Sunday school teacher for the junior high boys, and he decided to do the Prodigal Son, too, but he talked more about the Prodigal's older brother. He said that the brother was pissed off that he never got a party thrown for him even though he was the good kid that always did what his father wanted.

"You see," he said as he took off his blue suit coat and revealed his brawny upper body, "some people think this story is not as much about the Father and how he is like God, but mostly meant for people who act like the jealous brother. He had been obedient, but not freely out of love and gratitude. He'd been doing what his father wanted because he was afraid not to and therefore always resented it."

Mr. B stretched his neck by rocking his head to the left and right. "Maybe the Prodigal actually got it right. Sure, he screwed up, but at least he had made an attempt to do things he wanted. Besides, sometimes families screw us up."

Except for people who ended up in prison, I had no idea what he was talking about. I looked out the window at the cars passing by. Where were they all going? It's a question that still haunts me.

At the service, a couple and their daughter were visiting from Liberty, Texas, which, of all places, is only a few miles from Dayton. The girl was about my age but had a smirk that reminded me of Debbie. I wanted to ask her if she knew Gloria but realized that I hadn't told anybody in San Diego yet. Dad might have sensed how I felt, but he never said anything.

When the offering plate was passed, I watched Debbie, who for some reason was sitting near the front. She held on to the plate just long enough to get the usher's attention. His neck was red, and I couldn't tell if he was sunburned or if he was flushed with embarrassment. She turned her shoulders ever so slightly, like she was trying to give him a better view of what she had inherited from Mom, her ample breasts.

She often would badmouth the men at church because they couldn't seem to keep from staring at her. I had seen her go Marilyn Monroe on them, pouting her lips and making her eyes wide, like she didn't have anything to do with how they reacted to her. I heard her tell her best friend Tamara that she called them Dali men because their eyes melted down the front of women like the clocks that drooped over the edge of a table in one of the painter's famous works.

I had many models for being a man and admired very few of them. There were the deacons lusting after Debbie.

There was Pastor Bob, who paid a little too much attention to Mom. Male teachers didn't inspire because they were too bookish. Movie stars and professional athletes were way out of reach. Some of our neighbors were in the running, but then I felt disloyal to Dad.

I might have looked up to him if I had not been hearing Mom complain about him for so long. She told me everything he didn't do that he could have and used that to either compliment me on what I had accomplished so far (especially in school) or to predict how wonderful I would be in the future (in everything). It didn't make me feel better since I was being elevated at Dad's expense, but I didn't know it at the time.

I think Sandy and Mom did more to influence how I felt about becoming a man than any of the men, even more than Gloria, because Sandy was so desirable but out of reach and Mom was undesirable but so close. I was just doing my best to navigate the strait between lust and the mainland, smother love. Now that I was away from Gloria for so long (at least in twelve-year-old time), I could only hope that our late-night phone calls would keep us together.

What makes a man a man? Someone who gets women to love him? And can that only be proved by her having sex with him? Are all the sought-after women divided between the suave James Bonds and the macho John Waynes? There are the fathers on TV—Ozzie Nelson, Jim Anderson, and Ward Cleaver, models of patience and occasional wisdom— but what kid wants their wives?

That night I was feeling especially anxious and lonely because I hadn't been able to get through to Gloria for a couple of nights. I felt just a peek in the window of the Twambleys (and what I would do later in bed) would make it possible for me to sleep. Dad had gone to bed early, anticipating a tough day at work. Mom was still wary of me and just wished me goodnight before joining Dad. Everybody else was in their own room and, unless they decided to get some water or a late-night snack, no one would notice me leaving.

I went out the garage door into the backyard and glanced at Sandy's bedroom as I walked in the opposite direction. On the other side of the house, in the corner of our yard, the gate would have opened into the Twambley's if it weren't always locked. In my current state of excitement, I hopped over it easily.

At first I thought I saw something near the swing set, but I was distracted by hitting my knee on the corner of the garage and when I looked again, nothing was there. I stood behind the garage, trying to decide which window to approach first. It didn't really matter, unless it was the parents, although Mrs. Twambley was pretty good looking, too. I smelled dog poop nearby and hoped their Irish setter, Darby, was kept inside at night.

After all the years of therapy and my own extensive reading, I'm still not that clear why I wanted to look. At times it seemed no different than watching someone on TV or in a movie. Of course, one difference is that the performers know people are watching, but isn't it intrusive too since they are either experiencing very private emotions or involved in just as private activities as one is in their bedroom? I'm not trying to blame my voyeuring on the film and TV industry, but I wonder if part of the thrill of being a viewer in the audience is that we are watching something that would normally be off limits.

The Twambley's had had a house warming party when they first moved in, and I had played Ping-Pong with the next oldest girt, Esther. She had this way of looking at you that made me both uncomfortable and excited. It was as if she was giving you the come-on while making clear you had no chance with her.

I heard a cat screech and saw something much larger than a cat walk across the yard that, for a second, was illuminated by light from the window closest to the patio.

"Shit."

I jumped back behind the garage and listened. Even with only one word I could tell it was a guy, but not big enough to be Mr. Twambley, him being the only male in the house. I peeked around the corner like I'd seen countless detectives and cowboys do. This trespasser said "shit" over and over again in a harsh, angry whisper so that I was able to tell who it was. I almost laughed out loud. He had enough light on the concrete edge of the patio to scrape off his shoe. Apparently he had come upon a deposit in Darby's yard bank.

I decided to watch for a while. I've done that before in more public circumstances, just watching someone's response to a girl that is beautiful or sexy or unusually attractive in some way. I still do it and wonder if it is again related to the experience of watching a film, like the director who said that it's much scarier to watch someone who is afraid of a monster than to see the monster itself. Likewise, at times, I can get more of a thrill out of watching the lust in the eye of the beholder than the object of that lust.

I didn't know then that people are often the hardest on those that do exactly what they do themselves or at least what they want to do. I just saw the usual unfairness, regarding which every kid is an expert because I was pretty sure Billy was here to do exactly what I did to his sister.

Like any good detective, I waited for the incriminating evidence. Later I would tell him that even his usually soiled T-shirt stood out, and the moon was only a thin crescent. I could see him hug the wall until he got close enough to a window. I had no idea whose window because this is the first time I had tried this on the Twambleys. The smell of damp grass made me think of camping and the lurking fear I always experienced in the wild.

Billy slowly pushed his head high enough that his eyes just barely cleared the bottom of the window. Just like Sandy's room, there was a curtain and, also like hers, it was sheer enough to get a pretty good view. It looked like Rachel, and she was trying on blouses. Each time she took one off to try on another, it was like a strip tease without the music. I was so absorbed with her that I didn't see a possum until it was almost next to me. I didn't exactly scream, but the sound I made was certainly loud enough for Billy and Rachel to hear. She came to the window and blocked out the light from her room by framing her hands around her head. Billy had dropped to the ground so I couldn't see if he was looking my way, too. I froze, just like any good prey, hoping the predator would not see him and go about his business looking for food elsewhere.

"Who's there?" I heard Billy whisper. "I may have to call the police if you don't get out of here right now."

I was not sure what to do. Part of me wanted laugh at Billy's hypocrisy, another part wanted to scare him, but the part of me that remembered Mr. Twambley kept me quiet. I figured since Billy had beaten me up, Mr. Twambley might break my legs. "Shut up, Billy, it's me," I finally hissed. I was getting pretty indignant the more I thought about why he had thrashed me.

"Joey?" He was still whispering but when Rachel turned out her light, probably to get a better view of what was going on outside, he fell silent.

I could imagine her as if she were standing in front of me in full sun. She had short reddish brown hair and exactly three freckles on her nose though with exposure to the sun more would come out temporarily. She had just begun to develop breasts and had that sexy/innocent look that young girls have when they are beginning puberty. She laughed easily though I seldom talked to her. I would hear her when they were loading up their car to leave or pulling into the driveway when they came home. She had lips that were almost too plump but stretched into a more normal shape when she smiled, which she had done to me a few times, or so I wanted to believe.

By now Billy was crawling across the lawn like some commando on a mission. I was getting cold in my sweatshirt and jeans and almost felt sympathy for him in his shorts.

"Heh, what are you doing here?" he said, pretending to be nonchalant, like we had just surprised each other while doing something mildly embarrassing like trying out perfume in a department store.

"Shut up. You are such a phony. I actually felt I deserved what you did to me."

I could smell peanuts on his breath. He had said that the only reason he ever liked going to baseball games were for the hot dogs and peanuts. He always had a small Mr. Peanut package in his pocket just in case, according to him, he was abducted or forced to stay after school for detention.

"I meant to apologize to you."

"Bullshit." I couldn't believe what I had just said, even if it was appropriate. I was called virgin ears at school because

I never cussed and acted way too self-righteous when others did.

Billy started to laugh. "I've never heard you say 'shit' before." He continued on his knees until he could stand up unnoticed behind the garage. "I'm not doing what you're thinking."

"Oh yeah, what am I thinking?"

"Look, it was my sister. Even a younger brother has to protect his sister."

I did not quite understand how beating me up for standing outside her window was protecting her, but I had to admit I wasn't there tonight and hadn't been since he let me have it. I was doing the Twambleys instead, along with Sandy's protector.

"Yeah, well, just don't be hitting me over something you do, too."

I kind of wanted to ask if he had done this anywhere else or had had ideas like trying bathroom windows, but just seeing him looking in Rachel's window was enough for now.

When I have thought about this recently, I realize that the normal response from him would have been to keep blaming me or at least to be angry about his own duplicity and want to deny he had a problem even with such obvious evidence. In fact, it could have led him to beat me up again for even suggesting that he might be called a pervert, too. He didn't, and I am grateful for that to this day.

CHAPTER THIRTEEN

MOM WAS STILL ACTING standoffish during the ride to school on Friday morning. I didn't linger when I got out of the car because I was afraid she might want me to help her in the library before my first class.

The sky was obscured by the usual morning low clouds we heard about so often on the radio weather forecast. I had "polished" my tennis shoes last night and hoped they were dry enough not to bleed white if it rained, which it hardly ever did. But I worried more about them getting dirty. Once, during a recess, I tried to clean them in a toilet stall after Greg the bully scuffed them.

All day at school, I kept thinking that Mom and Dad were going to get a divorce. I didn't have any special reason, but it didn't help that we ended up with a rainy day schedule (just a drizzle, but enough to keep us from going outside for PE), and we had to watch a film on how to have a healthy marriage. When the wife in the movie bemoaned her husband's inability to converse after work, I tried to remember if Mom and Dad *ever* talked for any length of time without it leading to an argument. I felt some responsibility since Dad would often go to the backyard with me to practice pitching immediately after coming home. The father in the film seemed more like the ones we all knew on TV, Ward Cleaver and Jim Anderson, than anyone I knew, except maybe Mr. Bodenhamer. I used to think that if we had had a two-story house like the Beaver, we would have a happy family.

That afternoon, on the way to my room, just after I grabbed a couple packages of potato chips and a bottle of Coke, I noticed the door to Maw-Maw's bedroom was open. As I walked closer, I could see she was putting clothes into a suitcase.

Without looking up, she asked, "Do you want something to eat?"

She turned toward me, and I held up the chips as an answer.

"You going on a trip?"

"What?" This was a typical response from her whether she had heard or not, but it still was irritating. She was wearing church clothes. Actually, except for what she had on around the house, they were the clothes she wore all the time: whether shopping downtown, travelling on a plane, or going to church. Black granny shoes with a small heel and laces supported her ample weight. Her favorite color was blue and its cousins because she felt they were slimming, so never red or yellow. Today she had on a plain mauve blouse and a long navy skirt with no pleats, the kind you might associate with strict religious groups like the Amish. I suppose the color was slimming in a way because she didn't look fat, just big.

"I'm going to the desert."

"For a retreat?" I had heard of Catholics doing it but not Southern Baptists, but I knew it was the commune with her friend Ethyl.

She looked at me for a moment, like she was going to be forced to say "no" to something I had requested and was regretting it in advance. "I'm going away for a while, to live with some believers, like we talked about." She put in a stack of handkerchiefs. "Ethyl wants me to be in charge of their Bible education."

"You mean, like at Calvary?" She had been Sunday school superintendent for years. She said it was what kept her from going senile.

"No, more like what I've done in the summer with vacation Bible school, but this will be year round. Like a class you would take in school."

I could smell mothballs and realized Maw-Maw was taking even the stuff she kept stored in her cedar chest. I wanted to claim dibs on her TV but decided that this wasn't the right time.

"Does Mom know?"

"Yes," she said, frowning her eyebrows until her eyes were slits.

I rubbed the oil from the chips onto my pants when she looked away. What I was really asking was if Mom approved. Mom seemed troubled since we returned from Dayton. She had tried once to resume our thing at night before bed, but I said I was too tired. Dad was different, too. He didn't kowtow to her as much. It was like she was losing control, and Maw-Maw's leaving, especially if it was without Mom's blessing, might be a serious blow to her kingdom.

She snapped the clasps on the larger suitcase and pulled it onto the floor. "Look, honey, you'll be fine." She rested a hand on my shoulder. "Soon you'll have to make some decisions yourself that everyone may not understand."

Was she talking about becoming a Christian? Getting married? What my career would be? All seemed imminent, especially the marriage part. I had been trying to figure out how to get back to Texas for weeks and only came up with an idea that made me feel guilty—getting to go back for Grandma's funeral.

The doorbell rang. Maw-Maw looked at the clock. "That must be the boys."

Billy and the twins? At the door I saw, instead of my pals, two blond guys with short hair like mine in T-shirts that had a one-way sign pointing to the word Jesus in large block letters. The guy on the left had on a gray one with black lettering and the other a black one with white lettering. They weren't twins, but their noses were similar and they looked equally eager. It was like their attitude gave them the same nose, thin and pointed.

"Is Mrs. Garrison ready?"

"Yes," Maw-Maw said right behind me.

Both of the boys looked barely old enough to drive and so skinny that together they would make a normal-size kid. But they were tall, real tall, basketball center tall. That could overcome a lot in my book. She motioned for them to follow her down the hall, and both had to duck to enter the house. That seemed to please them, for they smiled at each other on the other side of the threshold.

I wondered if it would take the two of them to carry a single suitcase, but the guy in gray picked up both, one in each hand, while the other lifted a large box of Maw-Maw's books: her ancient leather Bible, the humongous concordance, a Bible encyclopedia she referenced all the time, and her set of *Reader's Digest* condensed books. That had to be even heavier than the two suitcases, but it did not stop him from smiling. They said "Praise the Lord" a lot, like I might say "uh-huh" or "okay." I wondered if Billy was right about never trusting people who are too happy.

"Are you leaving now before Debbie and Mom get home?" I didn't say anything about Dad because I couldn't imagine him or Maw-Maw losing sleep over not saying good-bye to each other.

"I've already talked to both of them."

I guessed that was a yes. I watched as the two bean-poles came back for the last load. Maw-Maw was standing in the kitchen drinking some iced tea while I finished off my second bag of chips. We didn't say much. I felt a little sad but also confused. She had been supportive when Mom was too demanding, but was also pretty strict herself, especially when it came to four-letter words, movies, and clothes. Still, all in all, I felt simpatico with her because she had gotten a rotten deal in our family, too.

She hugged and kissed me and told me to be good. I watched the van drive away and felt like all I was doing lately was saying good-bye.

Debbie was walking around the corner just in time to see Maw-Maw wave from the front seat. Only one of the stick boys was next to her, so the other one had to be riding in the back. Debbie's arm waved slowly, like you might on a parade float. When she passed me on the porch, I could tell her eyes were moist.

I waited until I heard her bedroom door close before I went back in the house. I had only seen her cry once before but that was years ago when she was about my age. Her best friend then (and now) was Tamara, and she had called to tell Debbie that Tamara's tomcat Ivan had been run over by a car. Of course, she could have cried countless times since

153

then when I wasn't around, but I doubted it. She didn't even cry when Puppy died a few years ago, and I know she was sad.

She often had iced tea just like Maw-Maw when she got home and sometimes yogurt. I grabbed a small carton of the vanilla-flavored one and poured the tea Maw-Maw had already fixed over ice in a tall glass. At her door, since my hands were full, I knocked with my foot, a little louder than I intended.

"What are you trying to do, break the door down?" She yanked open the door in anger, accidentally knocking the yogurt out of my hand. When she could see I had been carrying her usual after-school snack combo, she picked up the yogurt and grabbed the glass, said "Thanks," but still closed the door without saying anything else.

I didn't expect her to gush with gratitude, but I was pretty pissed, probably for the same reason she was crying. I stood facing the door for a few moments and pulled my leg back to kick it through its hollow core that Dad was always complaining about as evidence of shoddy home construction. Just as my foot was about to make contact, Debbie opened the door and I completely lost my balance, landing on my back. I hit the ground hard enough to knock the breath out of me and lay there stunned for a few seconds.

Debbie was doing a lousy job of trying not to laugh and when I realized I had knocked the cup of yogurt out of her hand and it had landed upside down right in my crotch, I started to laugh, too, except I couldn't get enough air to do more than wheeze.

We heard a car pull up in our driveway, and Debbie went to her window. "It's Mom."

I figured she must be sick, and I panicked that it would set off another shouting match between Debbie and her. Debbie went to the kitchen and came back with some paper towels. She started to clean the yogurt off my pants, looked at me, and then left me to do it.

I was desperate to get cleaned off before Mom came in. It's not that I expected her to be upset about the mess on the carpet but just that she would ask questions about how it all happened and we would have to talk about Maw-Maw leaving and maybe how Debbie was upset. Mom seemed to be good at giving sympathy, but it was usually about making herself feel better not the one who was supposed to be receiving it.

She didn't even notice us cleaning up because she flew by, hell-bent on finding Maw-Maw. She had started calling for her as soon as she walked in the front door and continued as she hurried down the hall to her room. We could hear her open the closet door. She came back into the hallway and looked at us. We were staring at her from outside Debbie's room.

"Where is she? I mean, when did she leave?" Mom was now out of breath and seemed to need to exhale separately for each word.

"She's gone." Debbie seldom said the obvious unless it was to be facetious or to inflict some pain. Here it could have been either.

Mom was so upset she didn't notice what Debbie was wearing. I wondered how Debbie had changed before coming home because no way her high school would have let her attend in this outfit. She had on a T-shirt with one sleeve rolled up and no bra, plus tight Capri pants that stopped about midcalf and hung ominously low on her hips. Her mascara seemed Halloweenesque it was so dark and thick. But now Mom was too focused on Maw-Maw's leaving to say anything.

Mom stared at us, as if Debbie's words were the first she had heard about Maw-Maw's situation. "I tried to get her to stay. I tried to get your father to realize she wasn't a threat to him."

"Oh, for Chrissakes."

Mom looked shocked that Debbie was angry. Apparently she still expected Debbie to be sympathetic some of the time.

"Maw-Maw has been treated like a leper ever since she came to babysit. For free."

Mom leaned against the wall. I looked at Debbie to show my disapproval and stood next to Mom. She reached for me and sobbed onto my head. I thought of Gloria and didn't move.

"What, we're supposed to feel sorry for you? Jesus Christ, you're something else."

Mom caught her breath and took the last comment as a direct hit at Maw-Maw's values, around whom saying even the euphemism "geez" was avoided.

"Shut up." Mom pushed away from me and the wall. "You think that because you read a lot and make good grades and have boys after you, you're the queen of the ball and everything you think is worth saying."

Debbie actually looked at me for support. I couldn't say Mom was wrong, but we were getting off the point. This was supposed to be about Maw-Maw.

Mom struggled for words. "I suppose none of us have really appreciated what she's done for the family." She looked down the hall. "She has had to struggle so much that she deserves a few breaks at this time in her life." She looked at Debbie and then back toward Maw-Maw's room. "Ones she didn't get here."

Debbie had turned to go back into her bedroom. I didn't want to know what might happen if she decided to close her door while Mom was talking, so I stepped back just enough that my foot rested against the open door. Sometimes I wonder how I could have done all this at my age, but in a crazy household, you can get pretty clever about doing what you think will keep the peace.

Mom smoothed her dress even though it wasn't wrinkled and pulled her hair back behind her ears. "You think your father is the bee's knees, but he has made it hell for your grandmother."

Debbie raised her hands. "You're gonna blame Dad for Maw-Maw leaving? She left because she had nothing to do. And maybe because we are so un-Jesusy to her."

I could think of nothing but getting to the fort. Mom had already given me permission to spend the night there with the twins and Billy. She had probably forgotten, but I could tell this conversation would either end quickly in some super nastiness or build to some worse ending in the back and forth of accusations.

I motioned that I needed to go to the bathroom. In there I ran water from the faucet into a plastic cup and poured it into the toilet bowl to sound like I was peeing. Then I flushed it and sat down. In the magazine basket was a *Women's Day* with Caroline Kennedy and her dog on the cover. I started to think of Puppy to purposely put Mom and Debbie out of my mind. I could hear them talking, but it hadn't escalated to a shouting match yet. I sat for a while until I was beginning to get too sad. I washed my hands and opened the door. Fortunately Mom was not in a direct line between me and my bedroom. I walked into my room and closed the door.

I had not made up my bed, so I began smoothing the covers to make it fold up easily. Once I had replaced the sofa cushions, I sat down and looked at the window. It was flecked with dirt and had water spots.

In the hallway I said, "Excuse me," and walked between Mom and Debbie.

Mom asked where I was going.

"Outside."

I didn't wait for more questioning. In the garage I found some Windex and a few old washcloths. The ladder was too heavy to carry at the same time, so I put the cleaning materials just outside my window and came back for the ladder. I don't think anyone had ever offered to clean the windows on their own. I wondered what Mom or Debbie would think once they found out. I sprayed the whole window and wiped the part I needed the ladder for first. By the time I got to the part I could reach near the bottom, it had dried and I had to spray it again.

I thought about the night outside Sandy's window and the time I saw Billy at the Twambley's. I wondered if anyone had ever tried to look into my window. Mom and Debbie were getting pretty loud, so even though the louvered panes were shut I could hear voices. I smiled because I couldn't make out what they were saying. I thought of doing the rest of the windows on the backside of the house and began on Mom and Dad's bedroom, but looking into their room felt too creepy, so I only did the part closest to the ground.

Dinner was quiet, like everyone was getting ready to start an argument, but no one had the energy. Dad remembered I had gotten permission to go to the fort, so I packed my stuff quickly before Mom thought more about it. I don't know if Mom and Debbie came to any conclusions about Maw-Maw because Dad did the talking, mostly about some guys who wanted special help and hinted that they would give Dad a bribe. I didn't ever remember Dad talking this much.

Without asking, I took a large bag of Fritos from a storage cabinet in the garage. I already had an old sleeping bag and my pillow. Billy was bringing the drinks and the twins something sweet. I remembered I had forgotten my flashlight when I got to the back gate, but didn't want to go back for it and take a chance on them changing their minds about me going. Besides there was still plenty of light left.

The field behind our backyard was fill-dirt that had lots of rocks and had never been graded smooth so I had to be careful to avoid tripping. Once I was at the edge of the canyon, I followed one of the well-worn trails rather than just run down anywhere as I did when I wasn't loaded down. At the bottom I followed the dry streambed to a tree-size manzanita bush. The blond plywood walls of the fort were camouflaged by the bush so you wouldn't notice it until you were already past it. From the other direction, it was hidden by the fans of a stubby palm and us having used darker wood on that one wall.

Someone was already there because I heard music. By using a boulder and a complicated system of scaffolding devised by Billy, our fort perched about six feet above the canyon floor. The only entry was through a trap door in one corner. If you were the first there, you had to boost yourself up like a gymnast. If another guy was there, you would lock arms by grabbing his forearm as he grabbed yours and use his strength and your other arm to pull yourself up.

"It's about time." It was Jerry, and he had already extended his arm.

"Where's Terry?"

"He's waiting for the pie to cool."

I didn't ask if he had cooked it himself, or if they had gotten their mother to cook it like in most families.

A loud bang on the door and we heard Billy yell, "Open up, sez me." He threw up a package and asked for the pulley. We lowered the platform, and he put a case of soda pop on it. He had fixed the whole assembly like a kind of dumb waiter. Jerry pulled a rope on one side and I pulled on the other. It wasn't fast, but it was wonderfully mechanical and none of us had anything like this at home. It felt like the *Swiss Family Robinson*, which I loved. Whenever I talked about the fort, that was what I mentioned first, even before the trap door.

Once we got the drinks in, Jerry pulled on one of Billy's arms and I pulled on the other. When we got him high enough, Jerry grabbed the back of Billy's pants and pulled again, just enough to get Billy's belly over the edge. One time Billy's waistband ripped and he fell back down. That time we still had a stool from the construction period, so he could almost boost himself up from the top of it. Over Billy's protest, we kept the stool, but Billy always wanted to get in like the rest of us, and we usually obliged even though it took a lot of effort. Of course, that meant he always had to wait for at least two of us to arrive before coming up. Billy was sweating with all the effort and just lay on his back for a few minutes to catch his breath.

"So you brought it." Jerry was taking out the magazines from the paper bag and looking at the covers. Billy's father kept a stash of *Playboys* in the garage, and Billy would sneak out old issues. His dad kept them in cardboard magazine boxes just like in the library and regularly checked them so Billy couldn't keep them for long without his father noticing. Billy was pretty sure his father knew he took them now and then, but his dad never said anything.

As soon as I saw the first cover, my heart started to pound.

"This is almost as good as looking in windows." Billy winked at me, so I assumed he was thinking of the night in the Twambley's back yard and not the night in his. I could feel myself turn red and wanted to clobber Billy, but I nodded after Jerry did. Did Jerry look in windows, too?

Billy brought four so we could each have our own, though we would soon be trading back and forth. I got a December issue with a Playmate dressed like one of Santa's helpers.

Bang, bang, bang. We all jumped and looked down to see Terry reaching up a glass pan of peach pie. I thought it was the police or Billy's dad, both of which were ridiculous. The pie pan was surrounded by dishtowels. "It's hot."

Billy grabbed it carefully and let it linger under his nose before he placed it on the trunk that served as storage and table.

Terry pulled himself up effortlessly like some Olympian on the horizontal bar. Billy might have been awed if he weren't distracted by the aroma of our dessert. It made me hungry, too, and I'd already had chips plus dinner. The rest had had dinner, too, so a fourth of a pie plus the Fritos should get us through the night.

"There are usually some great cartoons, so make sure you don't just slobber over the foldout the whole time." Billy was a connoisseur, of sorts, in three categories: cars, food, and nudie magazines. He was always complaining about the *Playboys* not showing everything, so we used to joke that he would start his own magazine. I don't think he was ever involved with *Penthouse* when he grew up, but I wish I had kept in touch with him to see if he had ever tried something like it.

The next half hour we were silent except for when someone wanted to trade or to show the others something he couldn't believe. We munched on the Fritos but were not allowed by Billy to use our Frito hand to touch the magazine. I felt a little ashamed, whether because of Gloria or church, and found myself looking quickly at the foldout and putting it back to actually read a few articles. One was an interview with Miles Davis, whom I'd never heard of.

Terry and Jerry were lying on their stomachs on opposite sides of the fort. Billy was nearest the pie. I'm not sure he even cared about the photos. Of course, he had probably already spent hours with the ones he brought us and just considered the risk of messing up his father's magazine worth the tradeoff for food. And the twins always came through with good food.

"Time to eat, huh?"

Jerry said nothing and Terry said, "In a few minutes."

I wondered if what they all wanted was to use the magazines for another activity, but I certainly wasn't about to bring it up.

We knew each other about as well as you could expect boys to, considering we lived next door to each other but never did anything together as families. Which meant we didn't know much. I wondered if the twins ever did what Billy and I did or even wanted to. I wondered what they thought about girls in general. They sure got enough attention from them. I wondered if Billy felt as bad about being fat as I did about being skinny. I wondered whom all three of them admired besides the movie stars and pro athletes they would mention now and then.

"My God, she looks just like this girl at church."

"Who?" Billy and I said in unison.

"Cheryl." Jerry thought we were asking who the girl was at his church when we wanted him to show us the magazine babe.

Terry cocked his head. "Cheryl who?"

"Patterson. You know the one..."

"Oh, yeah."

Now Billy and I wanted to see her, too, but settled for the photo look-alike.

"God, I miss her." I didn't realize I had just spoken out loud.

"You know Cheryl?"

I realized that Gloria styled her hair the same way as the one in the magazine, pulled back straight from her face so her eyebrows and lips were what you noticed most. I started to imagine what Gloria might look like in a *Playboy* and wondered if she would be insulted or complimented.

"I was thinking of some girl."

"From school?"

"From vacation."

Now it was out, and I wasn't sure what to do about it. I wanted them to realize that a girl could want me, but I didn't want to share Gloria with them.

"What's her name?" Billy seemed to have forgotten about the pie.

I didn't want Gloria sullied by association with *Playboy*, but I had my reputation to consider. If I said she was a cousin, it would lessen the impact. If I said anything else about her, they would keep asking questions.

"Let's eat first."

Billy lost interest in my love life immediately. Terry got out a knife and cut the pie in fourths. He didn't ask if we wanted this much. First, Billy would want more and second, nobody would want less because we all knew that the Carroll pies, whoever made them, were better than any restaurant. I could attest they were as good as Maw-Maw's, and that was saying something.

Billy always got talkative when he was eating, especially dessert, and the privacy of the fort gave him permission to mention things he never would have broached during our games in the street. "So, are Christians allowed to whack off since you have to wait until marriage for the real thing?"

I could feel myself turn red again. My ears and neck were burning. I kept quiet hoping they wouldn't look at me and conclude from my embarrassment that mentioning it bothered me or that I never did it or that I did it all the time. Besides, the twins could answer.

Billy was busy finishing his pie, so he didn't push for a response. I saw Terry look at Jerry and thought they were conferring silently about whether it would be okay to spill the beans. I had had a hard-on ever since Billy handed me my magazine and hoped I wouldn't humiliate myself by shooting off so it could show through my pants.

"Well," Jerry said, "what makes you bring up such a subject?" He and Terry began to giggle as soon as he said "bring up."

"I heard," Billy said between bites, "that Christians believe that it blinds you."

"That's Catholics," I said and immediately wished I had not drawn any attention to myself.

The conversation lost all religious tenor and devolved immediately into which Playmate would be the best to masturbate to. We agreed that any would do, finished off a soda apiece, and got ready for bed, which basically involved choosing a spot to spread out our bags, taking off our shoes, and climbing in.

I was too excited to not try in experience what we were talking about in theory, and from the sounds I heard, I figured the others were doing the same. I wished we had talked about it some, even though I didn't want to tell them how often I did it or how my mother was involved at times.

Billy began snoring, but it didn't bother me because I got to sleep almost immediately after I finished what the photo started.

CHAPTER FOURTEEN

When I got home the next morning, all I cared about was getting some sleep. Dad was eating breakfast when I walked in. He said that I could do some pitching later off the mound in the back. I nodded and continued to my room. I didn't even open up my bed but just used my sleeping bag right on the sofa.

I got up about eleven o'clock to see Dad was pushing the lawnmower in the front yard. I didn't hear music from Debbie's room, so I assumed she was gone already. I paused to look in Maw-Maw's room. The door was open, which almost never happened when she was living here. I ate some cereal quickly in the kitchen before Mom thought to offer something more elaborate. Dad was almost finished mowing when I went out front.

"Ready, Whitey."

Last year had been the Yankee pitcher's best ever, so this was a double compliment. I immediately got the catcher's mitt, my glove, and a few baseballs before heading for the back yard.

Normally I hate presents that aren't wrapped, like the ones set under the tree that are supposed to be from Santa. But the pitcher's mound out back didn't need any wrapping to be the best present ever. It stood there under the sky sur-rounded by ice plant, and the pepper tree just waiting for some future major league baseball star to develop his skills. This was a present I had watched being made. Many times I wanted to tell Dad that it didn't have to so perfectly match the mound we used at Little League games, that what I needed most was someone to catch me, which, even on level ground, would help immensely. But he was so eager to get it right for me that I kept quiet, especially once Mom started saying what I had been thinking.

I put the catcher's mitt behind the home plate and went to the mound. I practiced a few full windups and then the abbreviated one that major league pitchers use when run-ners are on base. In Little League a runner couldn't leave the base until the ball crossed the plate, so no change in windup could either limit the runner's lead or minimize the time the ball took to get from the pitcher to the catcher. So my windup was definitely for future glory only.

"Which base has a runner? I'm talking about in the majors."

"First." I loved it when Dad would make up pro game situations.

"It's all decided by his lead and the time it takes you to get the ball to the plate."

He kneeled in position behind the plate and punched the pocket of his mitt with his right hand a few times. His pants were torn at the knee, and his shirt looked like it had been kept in the dirty clothes hamper for a week before he put it on. These were far-gone for the office, so they became yard clothes. Dad never gave away any clothes, even if they were out of fashion or he had other newer outfits he could wear. They were worn until ready for the trash.

"People who don't know baseball think it's all in the catcher's arm to throw out a runner, but the guy behind the plate has no chance if the pitcher is not doing his part."

Dad only played baseball as a kid, but he watched a lot and read extensively, both stories and coaching texts. He often said his biggest regret was not keeping at it until he made the high school team.

"Let's warm up first. Don't want to hurt that arm."

We tossed the ball back and forth in that easy swing of body and arm. Girls looked sissy when they threw because they thought it was just your arm involved, not your shoulder, hip, and leg in a coordinated follow-through. Essentially your whole body was involved, which Gloria understood fully. I loved that motion, and not just by her. Dad, mirroring my motion, made me feel we belonged together, doing what sons and fathers had been doing with each other for generations.

I was anxious to start pitching, but Dad reminded me that the damage from not warming up enough was not the kind of thing that shows up immediately. "One day your arms pops, and you either have to give up pitching or have an operation and maybe still have to give it up." We warmed up another ten minutes and then I began to throw hard.

"Yow." He stood up, pulled his hand out of the mitt, and shook it. "Give an old guy a break."

I didn't know if he really was hurting or just trying to make me feel good, but I didn't care. I knew I could throw harder than I used to, and Stumpy had commented recently on how I had an honest-to-God "heater" now, so I really could have hurt Dad. I thought of trying my curve on Dad, too, the one that worked so well on the twins, but, after what he said about warming up to protect my arm, I knew I would just be asking for a lecture.

"I'll put the target in a few different places and let's see how close you can come."

Before I could finish my full wind-up, Mom came out back and said Dad had a phone call. Dad seldom called anyone or got calls, so we always assumed it was someone in his family that was dying or already dead, but Mom looked irritated, not worried.

"It's a woman, but I don't recognize her voice," Mom said with obvious suspicion.

He looked at me, shrugged his shoulders, and said he'd be right back.

I watched Mom watch him. She had her housework scarf on, worn tan pedal pushers, and a blue work shirt with the collar turned up. She looked good in almost anything. She kept her eyes on Dad as he walked by, the way a police officer might watch a criminal in custody. When he was gone, she turned to me and gestured, as if to say, "What can you do with a husband like this?" before walking back inside.

I didn't think Dad would be gone long because he hated to talk on the phone, but I was too antsy to just wait on the mound. I went to the far corner of our yard, where the tire was hanging, and began throwing through it. Not much of a challenge any more, but that was why I enjoyed it. I could get a ball through without touching the rubber every time.

Dad came back, and I could tell by the look on his face that our time was up. His lips formed a thin line, and he squinted his eyes like he was in pain.

"Buddy boy, I've got to go. A lady from work needs some help, but it won't take long."

He didn't notice Mom standing behind him. "What lady?"

He handed the catcher's mitt to me. "She's the widow of a guy whose plans I checked." He looked at his pants like he was thinking of changing them. "When he was dying, I told him to have her or his kids call if they needed anything."

Mom's hands were on her hips in that skeptical pose Debbie and she had perfected.

"I don't remember you going to a funeral."

Dad looked flummoxed, but his back was to her so she didn't see. He turned around without responding to the funeral comment and said he wouldn't be long. When he got to the back door, he stopped with the doorknob in his hand and said over his shoulder, "It was a small ceremony for family only."

Mom looked at me with the same expression as earlier but with a slight lean forward as if this finished the argument on how hopeless Dad was.

I walked after him into the garage. He noticed me as he was getting in the old Plymouth. He waved and drove off.

What happened next I heard from Laura years later. Not the part about the ride to her house but what happened after he got there. The rest I imagined as best I could from talking to my sister and from what I knew of Dad myself.

Dad, I assume, headed straight for 395. He loved it because it represented everything good about freeways, which means it looked nothing like the ones in LA. Dad hated them because it seemed that all Angelinos cared about was getting somewhere fast, not about what was experienced along the way. The pathetic little plots of landscaping near the overpasses did little to mitigate the feeling of being encapsulated by concrete. To make it worse, everyone seemed to drive within one or two car lengths of the next car, no matter how fast they were going. Whenever we went to Disneyland, we would come back thankful for the relative sanity of San Diego drivers. And every time local politicians suggested a transportation "improvement," Dad would grumble that they were just trying to make San Diego another LA.

I am fairly certain that once he got in that old Plymouth, he could let everything go. Sometimes he would just sit in the car while it was parked next to the curb at home. He loved the rounded top, the feel of the fuzzy seats and its weight, a ton and a half. Even the year, 1949, pleased him because it was manufactured in that post-war period when cars were built with pride, solid enough to last through a few engines and therefore a few generations. It was made when people weren't encouraged to throw something away the first time it caused a problem, he would say.

The stretch of 395 from Mission Valley to downtown San Diego was called the park freeway by the locals because it seemed to have been created to go with the trees, not the other way round. The hillsides flanking it were covered with juicy, fast-growing ice plant to slow erosion during the occasional rain and to offer bright lavender and white flowers for much of the year. Above this ground cover, so prevalent they're often called freeway flowers, the spicy eucalyptus trees reached up to what, even if overcast in the morning, by afternoon became a clear blue sky.

This freeway was designed for older cars and slower speeds, not for, as one local columnist put it, "all those testosterone-saturated teenagers in hopped-up Chevys, testing the centrifugal force of its curves against the friction of their lives." (It was the first time I saw the word "testosterone" and couldn't wait to be saturated with it.) Dad used to talk about a car with Nebraska plates he had been behind that did the opposite. He joked that they were going slowly because they thought they'd spotted a koala bear that had escaped from our famous zoo.

Long-time San Diego residents knew that all of us— tourists, natives, and immigrants, whether from Mexico, the Midwest, or the South, like us—were here because this was a city with a promise of work and fun and family security that it usually kept, at least for those aspiring to the middle class. A city as unlike LA as this freeway was unlike those concrete monoliths to the north. They believed San Diego deserved our loyalty for its small hometown atmosphere and for its military service personnel, active and retired.

For the rest of this chapter, I am relying on a lengthy conversation Laura and I had some twenty years after all the events took place. Debbie had kept her number, so I had called her to join me for lunch at a fish place near the San Diego Bay. She did not hesitate to meet me and spent most of the afternoon telling me as much as she could remember.

We arrived well past the lunch hour so there was no demand for our table. She said that when I identified myself on the phone, she instantly remembered me jumping into Dad's grave because it was like a reenactment of that scene in *Hamlet* following the death of Ophelia. (More about that later. Me, not Hamlet.) I told her Debbie would appreciate that connection, her being a working actress now.

Laura smiled and pushed her red hair back over her ears. Though it was the end of the summer and starting to turn cool, she wore a spaghetti-strap tie-dyed dress that flowed to her ankles, like she had just left some artist's commune in Big Sur. She had slimmed down considerably and apparently was working at keeping the pounds off because she just picked at a salad.

She took a bite and looked at me intently for a moment. "I've always wanted to tell you what your father said to me during the months we were together. About what was going on with him and your mother. Is it okay to talk about her, too?"

I nodded.

She said he often talked about how he should explain her to me because he didn't want me to think that being a man meant having affairs. But he also wanted me to understand that a man could only endure so many disappointed sighs, slow condescending head wags, and incessant "friendly" reminders in his own home and still feel like a man. Only so many times could a man listen to his wife claim that she did everything. I told Laura how Mom would mow the lawn if Dad didn't get to it soon enough. Laura shook her head in sympathy.

She said Dad was most bothered by Mom always wanting everything done sooner than seemed realistic just because it was when she happened to think of it. I nodded in agreement. I said that Dad, in an angry outburst, once said that even God Almighty took a whole day to create the sun and the moon. We both laughed, enjoying the memory of his humor.

I felt comfortable enough with Laura that I told her some of what had come out in one of my therapy sessions. "As long as it took me to forgive my father for dying," which for a long time I considered our punishment for his having Laura, but I did not tell her this, "I never felt he was with you out of selfishness or disregard for Debbie and me."

Laura teared up and nodded slowly. She said that my father could never choose her over us, but he had finally accepted that he would never be able to make my mother happy. Laura said that he continually felt Mom's disgust for him, whether voiced or not. "He didn't use the word 'emasculate,' but that was the feeling I got." She ate a few more romaine lettuce strips and went on.

"The extra time on the bus and the extra meetings at church," I smiled and she blushed because we now know where he really was, "were the space he needed to put up with Mom." I turned my glass of water and nodded. "Boy, do I understand that now."

She said he used to assure her that once he made it through downtown and turned north on I-5, he could smell the ocean and immediately began to relax. She figured it was really the bay, but she never said so. Surfers could tell the difference, but of course he wasn't headed for the waves.

In Mission Beach, Laura had lived cheek by jowl with dozens of houses. She said they always seemed to her like a cartoon version of a neighborhood—they had roofs, yards, sidewalks, and garages just like anywhere, but everything was three-fourths the size, like those railroads built for going around sharp mountain curves. Her place stood out, but not because it was a different size or painted some garish orange or yellow that recent immigrants preferred. It was noticeable because it appeared to be mostly a garden with a shed in back, like a nursery whose sign had been obscured by all its plants. Even her friends had difficulty believing someone actually lived there.

Her front yard had a sycamore, only a few years old then so the neighbors couldn't complain yet, two ficuses, a miniature palm, and clay pots full of every conceivable blooming Southern California native. She had sages—salvias to the knowledgeable—and bougainvilleas with the most exotic names: Scarlet O'Hara, Raspberry Ice, Texas Dawn, White Madonna, and California Gold. Laura told me all this with some pride and, I suspect, a little embellishment.

She said Dad loved walking across the front yard, from the redwood fence near the side street to the brick wall of the neighbors. He sauntered through it like he was in a museum, and Laura was the docent. She'd pronounce the names and tell a story about who gave it to her or where she bought it or why this one made it while the others of the same species had died.

When he drove up that Saturday, she was standing in the doorway, wearing a kimono bathrobe that was so short she was hardly decent. At least that was what he said then. Her frizzy hair jutted out in every direction though she'd tried to contain it in a ponytail. He told her that her eyes, mostly gray like his, had just enough turquoise to make them wonderfully inviting, especially when framed by the blaze of red.

"Sam! I'm so sorry for getting Dorothy into this, but I couldn't wait for you to call."

She claimed he had never stopped feeling guilty about seeing her, and I believe that. It was not so much because he was cheating on Mom or Debbie or me, though I sensed some embarrassment (was it really shame?) when he waved good-bye to me in the garage. She said he didn't worry either about his Baptist brethren condemning him, and they certainly would. It was more that he was enjoying something that he couldn't possibly deserve. Laura blushed again when she said this. One time Dad told her that Mom was the one who should have had someone else because she kept after us kids, fixed four-course dinners every night, and plied every department store sale for the latest fashions at the cheapest prices. She was the one that kept everything going. She deserved a family *and* a lover. He felt he didn't deserve either. The more I listened to Laura the more I wished I could have found this out sooner, but then I probably wouldn't have understood until I'd had similar troubles of my own.

I wonder if he went so far as to say that it wasn't just the sex. Anytime I hear someone say that now I only laugh because it seems to start with sex even if it matures into a deep companionship. And sex was an integral part of this world Laura created for him, a world as colorful and fertile as her garden. Ironically she was not as attractive as Mom, at least in a purely physical sense. Chunky back then and less sophisticated, she would never have been able to hold forth as a hostess to the scores of people who came through our home. But I came to see in her a certain *joie de vivre*, untainted by the phoniness that crept into Mom and completely devoid of the continual complaining about everything from the price of tomatoes to the mechanic who kept Mom's car a day longer than initially promised. I may be exaggerating the difference between them, but I don't think so.

Her house sounded magical. She said that in the rooms and the passageways narrowed by furniture, books, and her sculptures—which she created when she was not busting her butt at the restaurant where she met Dad—he felt alive, like every time he saw the Big Sur coastline or the towering monuments at Zion National Park or the vastness of the Texas plains. In her living room were starkly wrenching Depression-era black-and-white photographs, her own abstract figure of a mother holding her child, a Diego Rivera with its thick primary colors, a small male-female figurine from Ghana, and a bloody Remington landscape. Intricate, precisely patterned Navajo rugs hung in the hallway. A Dorothea Lange print of a poor family watched over her bed while an erotic Georgia O'Keefe flower adorned the bathroom. I wonder if her creations, both made and bought, were their foreplay since I was aroused just by her description.

That last day of his life, he had stood at her gate. He had held his arms out to her, and she had jumped at him like she had so many times, wrapping her legs around his waist. I know now how women can bring things out in a man that their family has never seen, but the first time I heard this it seemed pure fantasy. She said he had just begun to touch her lips when a pain engulfed his left arm and moved to his shoulder, a pressing pain he had described as someone having just dropped a truckload of mulch on his chest. If she hadn't been so frightened, she might have laughed at the metaphor. He slowly sank to the ground with her still in his arms. Once she realized what was happening, she ran inside to call for an ambulance.

"Where am I? I'm at home for chrissakes," she had yelled into the phone. "Where do you think I am?" She giggled a little when she remembered this. She said she was angry then because Dad looked so pale that she thought he was dying.

"Oh God, I'm sorry," she had said into the phone. "Yes. Sorry. It's—seven—five—I mean, seventy-five. No, just a minute." She looked away from Dad and concentrated. It's seventy-two, twenty-five." She looked at him again, and he didn't seem any worse. Thank God, she said to herself. "Oh, sure. Mission Beach Drive. Yes, seventy-two, twenty-five Mission Beach Drive." She said she imagined the next day's headline: MAN DIES WHEN MISTRESS FORGETS ADDRESS. WIDOW SUES.

She shook her head and laughed again. "I remember all these details because I went over and over them for months after he died." She touched my hand before she continued.

She then had bent down and slipped her hand under Dad's head. "You've got to hold on, Sam. Okay? Okay?... Sam? Sammy?" When she pulled up his head, his eyes opened, but they didn't seem to register anything.

She looked at me for a few moments. I suppose deciding if I would want such details about my father. When I said nothing, she went on. She said he always kidded that she was too rough on him in bed and that he wasn't sure his ticker was up to it. She had hoped it wasn't anything serious like a heart attack, and then she scolded herself for being so naïve since his lips were beginning to turn blue. She placed a pillow under his head and crazily wondered if she had time to tidy up the living room before the ambulance arrived.

She said they often talked of how they could make it together. He had said he would hate to leave Debbie and me, but leaving Mom wasn't as much of a problem. I'm not sure I agree with that, but this is Laura's part of the story. They even talked of adding a second story to her place with enough room for Debbie and me and for her son, Will. But Will began to take his problems out on Dad, or at least on her relationship with Dad. Will called her a whore when Dad helped to bail him out of jail. I remember Dad being gone for a few hours on a Christmas Eve and Mom going crazy over it. He had said he was delivering presents to some poor family in Logan Heights and had forgotten about it until he got a call. I don't remember if Dad had covered himself by actually taking some presents that night.

So Dad bails out Will, but Will only notices that Laura did not bring his own father. She sneered, "Not that his father would have come even if I had asked." She couldn't believe that Will didn't know that.

That Saturday Will had taken her car God knows where. My father had come over because she had panicked, and before he could help her figure out what to do, he had a heart attack.

Concentrating on a crumpled Dad at her feet, she screamed when the doorbell rang, realizing she hadn't heard the siren. She went to the door and let in two beefy men. One, no taller than her, had a grin that suggested he'd either come to pick up some Christmas toys for children or this was his last call before a month-long vacation in the Bahamas. The other, looking like a football lineman with an enormous head, stood over Dad with a sad face, as if Dad were already dead. She thought that they could have sent some guys who could at least pretend they were doing something urgent. As they slid Dad onto the stretcher and pulled it up to waist height, she could only think about how hard it must be for the taller one to find caps large enough for his head.

She hoped they wouldn't ask her about her relationship to Dad, but she was ready to say she was just his friend, realizing that she might as well use Will's word if she couldn't come up with something a little more convincing. She knew she would have to call Mom unless he recovered quickly enough to call himself.

After the ambulance had arrived at the hospital, Dad was rolled into a room of sorts. Its walls were curtains hanging from metal frames. It reminded her of the shower scene in *Psycho*. Inside, it had lots of equipment including that heartbeat-monitoring machine that we all had seen on TV. Without even asking her what happened to him, a nurse peeled back his shirt and hooked him up to it. When she motioned for Laura to leave, Laura wanted to tell her that she had as much right to be here as any wife. In fact, she knew him better than his wife did because he talked to Laura about her, but he never talked to her about Laura.

The nurse attending Dad was young—Laura could tell by the firmness of her upper arms—with an old face, not because it was wrinkled but because, with her small mouth, her hair under her cap, and her sunken cheeks, she looked like someone who had seen a lot and wouldn't take any guff from Laura about wanting to stay with Dad. Not that the nurse had brought any of this up.

I took a drink of my water and looked around the dining room. There was one couple in a booth and a woman eating by herself. I wondered if they would be surprised to know that my dead father's mistress was giving a blow-by-blow account of my father's last hours.

In the waiting room, she got a cup of coffee she didn't really want from the machine next to the entrance. A bald old man, hunched over and drooling, sat next to a white-haired woman who was reading a *Ladies Home Journal* with summer desserts on the cover. The woman turned a page and wiped his chin every few minutes without even looking at him. God, the indignities, she had thought.

A boy with a badly fractured leg—Laura had gagged when she saw the bloody bone—looked angry. Did he have to miss the rest of the football game he could have helped win? Did he think his bones weren't supposed to break and was furious at this outrage to his indestructibility?

With a smile that was both condescending and earnest, the old young nurse walked up to Laura. "You were with Mr. Norton?" she asked knowing the answer. "Are you Mrs. Norton?" Laura felt the nurse knew that answer, too. Laura looked over her shoulder to glance through a slit in the curtain to see whether Dad was awake or not.

"Is he okay?"

"The doctor will be with you in a moment."

Laura wanted the nurse to talk to her as one woman to another, as someone who must have had men in her life that she was concerned about and with whom she had no legal connection. But Laura knew the nurse was more concerned with finding out who needed to be told than with being of any comfort. The nurse finally got more direct. "Are you his next of kin or should we call someone else to let them know he's here?"

Laura started to give her our phone number and then decided to call us herself. She was not sure if this was out of some wish to punish herself or some overblown sense of responsibility for my father—he had come to help her deal with Will—or just that she felt she owed Mom this courtesy for all the good stuff Sam had given her, even though Laura believed my mother deserved to lose him. At this point in time, I had to agree. But then she admitted that she was not sure anyone deserved to lose someone they love.

Laura looked at the nurse with as much fierceness as she could muster. "I'll call as soon as you tell me what's happened to him."

Laura smiled when she remembered how the nurse summoned her most patronizing look yet—the one she probably reserved for relatives who thought their loved ones would leave the hospital alive when the all-knowing nurse knew full well the guy would be lucky to survive the night—and said the doctor would talk to her soon. Then the nurse returned to the roomette where Dad was.

I was getting impatient because I felt this was more about Laura needing to get this stuff off her chest than to give me what I needed in order to see Dad more clearly, but I didn't know how to ask her to be more concise without the risk of her leaving out information I did want.

In the waiting room, the woman next to the drooler had put down her 100 best recipes and actually looked like she might care about more than just keeping saliva from drenching the guy's shirt, the one she had probably washed and ironed earlier in the week. The athlete was still angry but said nothing because his father, who looked even angrier, had just arrived. Maybe he wasn't injured in a game. It was the wrong season for football anyway, Laura realized. She wondered if the kid took their car without permission like Will had.

The background moaning had stopped. Laura hoped it meant a sedative had kicked in for the poor soul. A young doctor—apparently nobody over thirty was allowed to work here, Laura had thought—with something red on his sleeve and piercing button eyes devoid of any emotion that could cloud his judgment. As Laura had suspected, Dad had had a heart attack. No, the doctor said, a severe back strain could not be the cause.

Though she was in a daze, Laura knew what she had to do. She walked to the front desk and asked the receptionist, who looked like a twin of the shorter ambulance attendant, only with longer hair and earrings, to direct her to the pay phones to call Mom. Now that she had finished her part of the story, I asked her if she wanted any dessert, but she declined and confirmed what I thought earlier as she ate her salad.

"Finally got a lot of this extra weight off and want to keep it that way."

I walked her out to her car. Before she got in, she pecked me lightly on the cheek. "He would be proud, your father." She closed the door and lowered the window. "Thanks for listening."

I said thanks, too, and watched her drive off.

A few seagulls were fighting over a paper tray of french fries. One would swoop in and grab a fry and then drop it to squawk at the interloper. While they were fighting, a squirrel grabbed what the first seagull had dropped and scampered away.

CHAPTER FIFTEEN

I HEARD THE TELEPHONE ring and Mom saying, "Let me get some paper."

I stayed in the hallway as she came near the doorway, but I was still close enough to see her open a drawer. She fumbled around in it without finding anything to write on and finally just tore a page from the telephone book. Back at the phone, she said, "Yes. Mercy Hospital." Then, "Okay."

I did not need to see Mom because I had learned long ago to read her moods from the tone of her voice. But, after she was silent for a while, I couldn't stand it any longer and looked around the corner. She was nodding without writing. Then she said, "And what was your name again? Laura. I see." I could tell Mom thought of saying something else. I can guess now it could have been, "Who the hell do you think you are because I know you're the one that called just before my husband left without any explanation?" But she just kept nodding until she said that she would be there as soon as she could and hung up.

I had inched into her line of vision by the time she finished and, when she saw me standing there, she burst into tears. Holding her arms open, I took the cue and walked over to let her hug me. Her apron was made of terry cloth so I felt like I was being wrapped in a towel after a bath. I didn't hug back, but she didn't notice, so she held on to me for a long time, until she finally reached for a tissue to blow her nose. She stepped back and looked at me. With her hands on my shoulders, she bent down so her eyes were level with mine. She smelled of onions and perfume. I tried not to cringe. "We're going to be okay. You hear me?"

I nodded, but I wasn't comforted because I knew what she really meant. She didn't feel okay, and I was going to have to help her get better. "Your father—" She never used "your father" unless Dad was doing something she didn't like. "Your father is in the hospital, and I'm going to see how he is."

Was she planning to go by herself? Or was she so flustered that she had forgotten to ask us to go? I surprised myself by blurting out, "I'm coming, too."

"Where?" Debbie was standing in the doorway where I wished I were at this point.

Mom made a face like she was about to be pushed into cold water. "Your daddy"—she never used this word for anyone but her own father—"I mean, your father is having some tests in a hospital near Mission Beach."

Debbie couldn't have looked more skeptical. "That's what the phone call was about? You're rushing to see him because he's having some tests?"

Mom was in a pinch now. If she said it wasn't just tests, then she would have to explain how she hadn't been lying. If she stayed with the tests story, then Debbie would pursue the illogic of a nurse calling Dad to have them on the spur of the moment.

"I don't know. Joey wants to go." She smiled at me and turned back to Debbie. "I suppose you do, too."

"For what? What's wrong?"

Mom took in a deep breath and bit her lip like she does when she wants to avoid crying.

Debbie gave Mom her crying-ain't-going-to-get-my-sympathy pose.

"All right," Mom said and wiped her eyes. "He's had a heart attack." She didn't pause long enough for a reply. "I'm going to change quickly. We'll leave in just a few minutes. You two look fine."

She hurried down the hall while Debbie and I stared at each other. I knew Debbie would change clothes because she never went in public without something that emphasized her figure and an old oversize sweatshirt and cutoff jeans wouldn't quite do it.

As we walked down the hall to our rooms, the doorbell rang. I was still stunned by the news about Dad, so Debbie answered it.

"Are you ready?"

I knew the voice. It was Debbie's beautiful friend, Tamara. Not that Debbie wasn't beautiful too, but she was my sister. Tamara was a bit taller than Debbie, so she was almost six inches taller than me. Long, straight black hair, a thin, slightly crooked nose, and tanned skin gave her an exotic look, like some girl in *National Geographic*. I knew her parents were Jewish, so she must be, too, but she never talked about it around me. I knew Jesus was Jewish, also, but that was seldom emphasized in our church. Debbie had said some of her favorite authors were Jewish, and she didn't mean Biblical ones. I had no idea which ones she was talking about or why it mattered. But for Tamara I would have read every Jewish author who ever lived. At least before I met Gloria. I had already read most of the Old Testament and all of the New, but I didn't know then that almost all of the New Testament authors were Jewish, too. Anyway, Princess Tamara, with her long thin creamy arms and just enough bosom to be sexy but not gross like Debbie, was being invited to go with us to the hospital.

Mom must have been starting to think the worst about Dad because she decided not to change. Instead, she came back to the kitchen with her work clothes still on. Apparently she had started to take them off to try on something else because she was pulling on the same puffy white blouse when Debbie asked to let Tamara go with us. You could see her bra while she was buttoning up. She immediately covered herself when she saw Tamara.

One Christmas, long after I had left home, when Maw-Maw was staying with my wife and me for a few days, I asked her what Mom and Dad had liked in each other. This was just before Maw-Maw finally succumbed to diabetes-related problems and could still walk enough to take the train to Pasadena.

She sat at my kitchen table and told me a little about Mom and Dad in Beaumont, Texas, after WWII and before Dad went to Korea. She said Mom would have been the belle of every ball if they could have afforded to buy her a gown. There was always someone new asking her out or cozying up to Maw-Maw to get to Mom. She said Mom's potential boyfriends were the most successful bachelors in town.

Once Mom and Dad started sparking, as Maw-Maw put it, Mom would come home from work just after Dad would be driving away for the night shift at the refinery. Sometimes Dad could wait long enough to see her, and sometimes he'd just come to their house and talk to Maw-Maw until he had to leave. He told Maw-Maw that by talking to her he could at least be close to someone who was close to Mom.

Maw-Maw said she loved hearing that, but, she had to admit, she loved hearing anything he said. Mom felt the same. She told Maw-Maw that just the sound of his voice would make her feel hopeful at a time when everyone was trying to put the pain of the Depression and the War behind them. It was partly the quality of his voice because he sounded like a radio announcer and partly that he had such a positive outlook, like a salesman who convinces you he only wants to help you whether he makes a sale or not. He was confident that the country would soon be fighting in Korea and that things would be better once we stopped the communists there, so even when he was predicting another war, he made you feel optimistic, she said.

Once, on Dad's night off, Maw-Maw and he spent a whole evening looking at Mom's high school graduation photos while Mom was on a date with a cousin. Maw-Maw said that Dad liked one photo in particular, the one of Mom swinging under the old magnolia where she was so high all you could see were her legs. It was the largest tree on their block, and Maw-Maw said it gave them all a solid feeling, that if it could survive the occasional tornado and the less frequent hurricane so could they. This was the tree that was supporting Mom.

Maw-Maw said Dad talked about Mom's legs a lot. Maw-Maw seemed to blush a little while she was remembering. He had told Maw-Maw that Betty Grable had nothing on Mom. Maw-Maw was quick to point out that he said it in a romantic way that didn't sound dirty. I've seen some of those early photographs, and Mom really had the looks of an actress.

Maw-Maw said she was surprised at how much Dad changed toward her by the time she came to live with us in San Diego. She knew she shouldn't have been because many men feel threatened by their mothers-in-law, but they had gotten along so well back home she didn't expect it. She knew she had to come to San Diego even if she had known ahead of time how Dad would come to feel because Mom had made it clear that they would have to get a baby sitter otherwise. Maw-Maw said she wouldn't have her grandchildren left every day with some stranger. That was why she was willing to leave her beloved Texas for this heathen land, as she called it.

"What was Mom like before she met Dad?"

Maw-Maw smiled and asked for a glass of water. "Fill it to the top with ice. You have one of those icemakers, don't you?"

I nodded.

"Did your mother ever tell you she was valedictorian?" Maw-Maw's eyes were shining.

"No."

"She should have told your sister." Maw-maw was nodding and rocking back and forth slightly. "Your mother was no nincompoop, like Debbie thought, just because she didn't read *Time Magazine* and all that psychology stuff." Maw-Maw shifted in her chair and glanced toward the chirping of a few birds that were snacking at the feeder hanging from the backyard oak. "Your mother was such a smart girl. How she got A's, learned French, and spent all afternoon helping at the café, I'll never know. But you can guess from the way she works herself to death now. And, like I said, she had more boys after her than you could shake a stick at." She took a sip of tea and continued. "Sure, her graduating class was only twenty-five, but good grades were harder to come by then." Shaking her head, she continued, "And your sister always thought all her brains had come from her father."

But neither Debbie nor I knew about all that when we got into our 1962 green Plymouth Fury with Mom and Tamara and made our way to Mercy Hospital. In the backseat, when I wasn't distracted by Tamara, I was praying not only that Dad was okay but that Mom would drive carefully—she had had accidents before when she was upset.

I hoped that this emergency might be just the thing to bring Mom and Dad together. It sure happened often enough on TV, though I had to admit it was usually a child about to die that caused the parents to make peace. So I prayed a little harder, asking God to make sure Dad was okay while scaring everyone enough with the possibility of something terrible happening that they would change.

Debbie sat in the front with Mom. I sat in the back with Tamara. I had never been in the backseat with Gloria, and wondered what she would think of me being with another beautiful girl. I liked the idea of checking what I did against what Gloria would think. It was a recognition that what was going on between us mattered.

As irritating as Debbie can be about her superior abilities, she was a much better driver than Mom, even with only a learner's permit. When we left our tract house and came to the boulevard that connects to the freeway, Debbie had to remind Mom to go when the light turned green.

"I know," Mom said, and then she hit the accelerator so hard that the car jerked forward. Thank God no one screamed, or Mom might have run the car off the road. Debbie stared back at Tamara who made it clear by her gestures that Debbie should concentrate on keeping Mom from killing us.

Mom let us out while she parked, and Debbie strode through the front doors like she was at the head of an entourage, practicing for her future glory as an actress. She stood for a few moments in front of a woman with a headset who was busy answering and connecting calls at the switchboard. She had tiny eyes that were made even stranger by being so wide apart. She blinked a lot like someone was continually spraying water in her face.

"Ahem," Debbie cleared her throat as loudly as she could. No response from Miss Beady Eyes.

"Sorry to interrupt, but our father may be dying." Then she leaned in so close to the woman I thought Debbie might yank off her headset if she didn't respond soon enough, "so could you find out where he is right now?" She almost yelled the last few words. "Sam Norton," Debbie hissed before the woman asked.

She rifled through a few pages, finding nothing, when Tamara suggested he was probably in the emergency room and not written down anywhere yet. Debbie looked at Tamara and put her hands on her head in recognition of the obvious and that she could have skipped this whole encounter with Miss Beady Eyes altogether. "Emergency," Debbie shouted.

The receptionist at first thought Debbie was having an emergency and told her to calm down, and she would get someone to help her.

"Where the fuck is it?"

Mom arrived just in time to hear her daughter use the F-word and to see Debbie hurry off in the direction of the receptionist's pointing finger. When I saw that Mom was following us, I hurried to catch up with Debbie and Tamara. I wished Gloria had been there instead of Tamara, but she was a pretty good second choice. She reached back for me to take her hand, and I ran to take her up on it.

The receptionist in the emergency room looked much more formidable than the one at the front desk of the lobby. She was bigger in every way: large arms, more than ample bosom, broad shoulders, and a head that looked like it had been inflated by a tire pump. She put her hand up to stop Debbie from interrupting while she finished a conversation on the phone. Debbie had just read *One Flew Over the Cuckoo's Nest* and had called any bossy woman Nurse Ratched ever since, so I prayed she would not call this woman anything other than her given name. Debbie doesn't often get intimidated, but she used an entirely different approach with this staffer.

Debbie leaned in just enough to see the woman's nametag and made Mom proud with her sweet voice. "Mrs. Bellow, I know you must be busy, but our father had a heart attack…"

Before she could finish, a red-haired woman in a bright green dress with large white lilies on it came running up. "He's over here. I mean, you're Debbie and Joey, right?"

We nodded as she turned and motioned for us to follow. I didn't look around to see if Mom was following us.

While the woman looked pleased to see us, she was obviously distraught. She took us down a hall and into an area filled with curtained-off beds. People were scurrying in and out of the little rooms that looked like large, portable shower stalls.

Dr. Kildare and *Ben Casey* had been on long enough that we all recognized the gadgets of emergency rooms: the heart monitor, the tubes for breathing, the IV drips. That familiarity didn't make me feel better about Dad, but rather how serious this could be.

The woman in green led us to Dad, who had wires connected to his chest and a nurse watching over him. The nurse looked confused when she saw us and stared at me as if she was determining whether I was old enough to be there. Except for the time I found out I wasn't tall enough to drive a car in Autopia at Disneyland, never in my life did I hate being short so much. "He's been unconscious the whole time," the woman said to no one in particular.

The nurse nodded in agreement and shepherded us out by walking toward us. "We'll call you if there is any change."

"Couldn't a change be death?"

"Debbie!" I couldn't tell if Mom was more embarrassed about Debbie being rude to the nurse or with her being so blunt about Dad's chances of surviving. The nurse looked flustered, like this was a scenario they hadn't covered in nursing school, and was obviously relieved when a doctor arrived.

"Mr., ah, Norton," he said as he looked at a clip board, "has had a serious cardiac event."

Debbie started to say something, but Tamara grabbed her arm while the doctor went on.

"I'm afraid I'm not too optimistic at this point."

"He's going to die?" I said.

The doctor pulled off his glasses and rubbed his eyes. They were red like he'd been up all night. His hair was kind of long but neatly trimmed to just above his collar. When he put his glasses back on, he scratched his neck and breathed deeply. I thought that if he engaged in one more gesture before answering my question I would do what I could to give *him* a heart attack.

The doctor was younger than our family doctor but old enough to be careful about what he said next. "Your father…He is your father?" he asked me.

I nodded fiercely, hoping that would get an answer out of him faster.

"I don't know how much oxygen was cut off to the brain." He turned to look at the monitor. "His pulse is steady but weak."

Mom seemed to wake up to the whole situation. She rushed to Dad, put her head on his arm, and began to bawl. The shock of her response kept me from crying in front of Debbie and Tamara.

The doctor motioned to the nurse to pull Mom off Dad, which she did reluctantly but successfully. "Miss Riley, would you stay with Mr. Norton and report any change to me immediately?"

I remember her curtseying but, in retrospect, that seems unlikely. The doctor guided Mom to his office and everyone but the woman who showed us where Dad was followed. Debbie acted like she didn't trust the nurse enough to leave, but Tamara put her arm inside Debbie's and walked her along with us.

The office had a large walnut colored desk, photos of nature and one of a young couple with skis, a copy of his medical school degree (I couldn't read the name of the school), a large leather couch, and two overstuffed arm-chairs. He motioned Mom to sit closest to him in one of the chairs. I sat between Debbie and Tamara on the couch.

The doctor folded his rather large hands with his elbows resting on the desk. He pursed his already overly thin lips and shook his head. I wanted to scream at him, but he began speaking before I did.

"I don't want to give you any false hope. Mr. Norton is only alive because the paramedics got to him so soon." At this he looked at the doorway where the woman with the lilacs was standing. "I understand you rode in with him?"

"Yes," she said, looking guilty.

He looked at us. "You know each other?"

He said this because it was rather obvious we were all acting like we had no connection to her.

"No," Mom shouted. "Who the hell are you?"

"I'm Laura. Laura Masters. Sammy, I mean, Mr. Norton was with me when he had the heart attack."

Mom definitely connected the voice on the phone with this woman now if she didn't earlier.

"So what was your emergency that gave my husband a heart attack?"

"My son was…" she stopped because she must have realized that was not Mom's real question.

"Oh my God," Debbie said, grasping that this woman, who was dumpier and scruffier and generally much less attractive than Mom, was Dad's something on the side. Debbie smiled, and I hoped she wasn't going to laugh. She looked at Tamara and shook her head. Years later she told me that she was so fed up with Mom's hypocrisy and constant nagging that she thought it was the perfect comeuppance for Mom. Mom looked at Debbie and seemed to read Debbie's thoughts, but I had no idea at the time what was going on.

The doctor gestured for Laura to take a seat, but before she could take a step, Mom shot out of her chair screaming,

"Get that bitch out of here. You're the one who called, aren't you? You've been sleeping with my husband."

The doctor picked up the phone while Debbie held Mom back, or I think Mom might have punched Laura out or wrestled her to the ground like a scene from a prison movie.

Laura was nodding as she backed out of the room. "I'm sorry."

Her apology made Mom all the angrier. "What?! You think that's going to make up for killing him?"

Mom looked confused like someone else had just mentioned that Dad had died, and she just heard it. Tamara was on the other side of Mom from Debbie, helping to hold Mom back. Apparently in response to the doctor's call, two men in white took over for Debbie and Tamara. They placed her on the sofa and in a few more minutes, a nurse came in with a needle and looked at the doctor.

"Mrs. Norton, the nurse is going to give you something to feel better. You're going to be okay."

"But what about Sam?" She didn't notice that the nurse had edged close enough to inject her. "Ouch."

I squeezed my eyes shut to concentrate, but all I could hear was Mom calling the woman a "dirty, stinking bitch" over and over again until she got drowsy and went limp.

CHAPTER SIXTEEN

WHEN THE INJECTION HAD calmed Mom down enough that Laura felt safe to come back into the room, the doctor began explaining to us how Dad had a chance, but not much of one.

"Will he make it beyond today?" Debbie was talking to the doctor but looking at Tamara. We were all on the sofa: Mom at the end farthest from the door, Debbie next to her, then Tamara with me on the other end.

The doctor's cheeks sagged while his shoulders rose. It seemed almost a clown trick that he would have had to practice for months to pull off. He had a square jaw and flat nose, like he had been a professional boxer before studying medicine. His eyes were just slightly off so one would look at you while the other was checking something out on the wall behind you. It made him look reptilian, or like he had been taken over by an alien. Over the PA system, we heard a call for a Dr. Carrion. Just as he was saying he had to go, a nurse came in and gestured for him to follow her.

We looked at each other, wondering if this had to do with Dad. Laura had moved out of the doorway for the nurse and now was quietly weeping behind us in a corner of the room. Debbie walked over to her and asked if she was the one who had called our house.

She nodded while she dabbed her eyes. "My son had run off in my car, and I asked Sammy, uh, your father, to see what he could do." As if Debbie had asked why this would be a reason to call Dad, she continued, "He had helped me when Drew was arrested a few years ago." Debbie looked at Tamara with her eyes wide.

Laura blew her nose and looked at me. "I'm divorced."

Mom was leaning forward, holding her forehead with one hand. Whatever they gave her was something I hoped our family doctor could prescribe for her regularly.

"I would know you anywhere," Laura said to Debbie. "He talked about you all the time. You too," she said turning to me. "It's funny, but he never showed me a photograph. He was just very good at descriptions, like a writer almost."

In that awkward moment, the doctor returned and said we should follow him. Debbie and Tamara helped Mom up, and we walked down the hall, a funeral procession in the making. A different nurse parted the curtains around Dad's bed. Nothing was connected to him. All the wires and tubes were hanging from an apparatus on a stand next to him. The screen on the heart monitor was blank. Mom looked at Debbie.

"He experienced no pain," the doctor behind us said.

I wanted Debbie to ask how he knew Dad had no pain, or why he didn't say the most important thing first, that Dad was dead. But then I realized no words were needed to confirm what we were seeing. I was searching my memory desperately for a TV show in which a man was brought back to life. I thought I remembered an episode called "Lazarus," but it was probably on *Twilight Zone* and therefore even less likely to offer hope for real life, and the original Lazarus didn't seem to pertain.

Everyone was quiet and still, like we were in a sacred place.

Laura was the first to move. Slowly she approached his body, as if doing anything fast would have been disrespectful. She laid her hand on his arm very lightly, like she was afraid it might hurt him. I wondered if she would have thrown herself on him sobbing if we hadn't been there. Debbie and I walked to the other side and mimicked her by touching his right arm.

Mom began crying and probably would have begun to wail if she hadn't already been sedated. Her mascara was running down her cheeks. She had that African mask look women get when they don't dry their tears before they fall. She was catching her breath in sudden sucks of air, like a child who had been crying for hours and was continuing out of a perverse willfulness.

Debbie shocked me by doing what I now see as the height of kindness to Mom. She escorted her to Dad by gently cupping her arm and walking her to the bed. Mom looked at Dad and then at Laura, who was not paying attention to us but gently weeping into a tissue she had over her face.

Later Debbie would have some harsh, but accurate, words for Mom. Now she was giving her a chance to take in the horror of losing her husband so suddenly. Debbie took Mom's hand and had her stroke Dad's arm like you might guide a toddler to gently pet a dog.

"I loved him," she said to Debbie as if we had doubted it.

Most of this time Tamara had been standing next to the doctor, who had just left after his name was announced again. When Mom and Debbie had approached, I stood next to Tamara, and she put her arm around me. I had sobbed for days over Gloria and got teary-eyed when Maw-Maw left but couldn't feel much of anything now. I think I was expecting this scene to go to commercial and then show us previews of the next show.

My memory about what happened next is vague. I remember Mom telling Debbie they had to call Maw-Maw. I know now that Debbie talked to Laura long enough to get Laura's number so we could tell her about the funeral arrangements. I also remember Tamara taking care of me like Debbie was taking care of Mom. I think Debbie drove home. I know Debbie helped Mom into bed even though she was beginning to go crazy over all the people to notify. I also remember Maw-Maw coming back, but I don't remember if that was the same day or the next.

Once Debbie got Mom to lie down, I walked out back and looked at the pitcher's mound. A squirrel was sitting on the rubber fussing over something in its paws. I ran after it like it had just desecrated my father's grave and tried to get close enough to kick it into the next world, too. Whatever sad emotions I couldn't muster over Dad, I made up for with anger. I stomped on the pitching rubber, trying to push it underground and out of sight. Not making much progress, I went for the tire hanging from the tree and punched it like I'd seen Sugar Ray Robinson do in a newsreel, just pounding into the tire, one fist after the other, arms pumping, head bent over, eyes closed, every blow sending a message to whoever was listening that what happened was completely without justification, even in this shitty world.

When I started to cry, I thought it was because my hands were hurting. I don't know how long I had been hitting the tire, but it seemed to be none the worse for it while my knuckles were bloody. I couldn't figure out how to put everything together: Gloria, pitching, the twins, school, Mom, Mr. Bodenhamer, Sandy, Billy, and my skinny body. I was crying and kicking anything in my way. The ice plant and a stubby evergreen took a few good hits before I ran out the back gate. I thought of going to Maw-Maw's desert commune and then about asking Mr. Bodenhamer to adopt me. I thought of hitchhiking back to Dayton and living with Grandma. That seemed like the best idea even if the most difficult to pull off. I ran to the fort to think.

When I pushed up the trap door, I did it with such force that you could probably hear it back on our street. I pulled myself up with surprising ease and looked into the chest for food. I wasn't hungry, but I was thinking that any long-term strategy would have to involve a food supply. There were still some Fritos and a small bag of cookies. The sodas were not cold but would do for liquid. Someone had left a sleeping bag behind so I could use that if I decided to stay overnight.

"Joey."

I could hear my name clearly but did not recognize the voice except that it was obviously not Billy's or the twins'.

"Joey, are you in there?"

My God, it was Tamara. I didn't want to lie, but I didn't want to see anyone either.

"Joey, it's Tamara. Debbie told me you come down here sometimes."

As good as Tamara was to me at the hospital, I didn't want to see her now.

"Debbie's not with me." She paused and then in a somewhat cheery tone, "Your fort is closer to my house than your house is."

I heard her begin to walk away, so poked my head down the doorway as quietly as I could because I wanted to see what she was wearing. The floorboards creaked a little and she turned around. I pulled back and plastered myself against the opposite wall.

"Joey. It's okay if you don't want to talk. I just want to tell you that I know what it's like. My grandfather died last year and our dog, Perro, who used to sleep with me, was put to sleep last month."

I wanted to say that my father dying was much bigger than losing a grandparent or some dog with a stupid Spanish name.

"I know it's not the same, but I have some idea of how you must feel. And Debbie's told me enough about your mother—"

"What did she tell you?"

"Oh, I don't know. Just that she can be difficult."

She was standing right below the trap door. I looked at her bare shoulders and then what was in between. The top button of her blouse was about to pop.

"Joey, can I come up?"

I didn't say anything as she pulled herself up about as easily as one of the twins. She stood up, brushed off her pants, and looked at me with her arms open. I knew the cue. My heart was pounding in my chest like a cattle stampede. I swallowed and put my arms around her. My head fit perfectly between her breasts. She stroked the back of my head like mothers do to children who have had something sad or terrifying happen to them.

I was not going to cry, and I was going to stay true to Gloria in spite of what was racing through my head. Crazily I imagined myself outside her bedroom window. There she had just finished buttoning the very same blouse she had on now and the button on which my head now rested flew across her room and her boobs fell out. I was trying to tell her where her button went when she saw me in the window, and, instead of screaming, she gestured for me to come in.

Except for Mom and Gloria, this is the closest I had ever been to a female. Fantasy aside, it was pretty wonderful. I held on to her tightly and wondered what it would be like to nurse.

Then she bent down and whispered in my ear. "Do you want to touch me?"

Since I was already holding her, she had to mean some part I wasn't already touching. I had no idea. No, I had an idea, but I knew she couldn't mean that place. She leaned down and gently stroked the part of me that was in control now.

"Wow. What's going on here?" She laughed.

I felt like I was in some silly movie where the geekiest guy gets to have the sexiest girl. She pulled me down and unbuttoned her blouse. "Unhook me, will you?" She was talking about her bra. I followed orders just like I would at home.

They were small, soft beach balls with a dot not quite in the middle. She took my hand and placed it on top of one like I was about to say the pledge of allegiance for her. It was warm and smooth. I think I expected it to make a squeaky sound and recoil like an anemone. I knew I was doing something forbidden, and the thrill of it made me dizzy.

My next conscious thought was, "Why am I lying on the floor with a whopping headache?"

"Joey, Joey. For God's sake, answer me."

"Yeah. What?" Why was she yelling at me? Who is this person? Tamara? Is it Tamara? So I wasn't dreaming.

"My head hurts."

"No wonder. You took a header, and before I knew it, you were out."

"I wonder if this is what it feels like to be knocked out. You know, in the ring."

Tamara was smiling like you do at some child who says something cute. She stroked my forehead. She had put her blouse back on, but I could tell she had left off her bra. God, she looked beautiful. Her skin is the kind Mom is always going ga-ga over as she bemoans the few wrinkles around her eyes. Tamara's seemed to have no bumps or holes, like it had just been poured molten into a mask and set on her face. Her eyes were dark brown and stood out all the more because she had very thin eyebrows. But they were dark enough to keep her from looking creepy the way blond ones can.

"Is this where you go when things get rough at home?"

"Yeah. And I'm not going back."

"Do you want to come home with me?"

"You mean, to your room?" My face turned red and I couldn't believe what I just said. "No, I mean. What do you mean?" God, I felt like I'd just asked her if she wanted me to go to bed with her.

"Yeah, I suppose. I just mean another place to stay."

I wanted to ask if we would continue with the breast acquaintance program we had started.

"My parents aren't home right now, but I'm sure they wouldn't mind even if they were."

Oh, so I'm not the first. I don't know what made me think that. Maybe I was just feeling guilty about the whole thing and was doing a good evangelical job of blaming the other person for something I was more than willing to do to them even though I knew it was wrong and hated myself for it. I had just summed up the Southern Baptist take on illicit sex.

What I really wanted now was for us to take up where we left off before I was knocked out, which sounded much better than saying I fainted. Besides, anyone seeing Tamara would call her a knockout for sure. I held my head like it had started to hurt again.

"Oooh. Is the pain coming back?"

I nodded with the most pitiful face I could muster. Oliver Twist couldn't have done a better job.

She sat down next to me and pulled me to her like Mom would. I wondered if Gloria would have done the same. I don't mean the bra part, but the showing sympathy part.

I didn't really know what to do, but I wanted to have sex with Tamara. Something in my brain told me that was all I needed to feel better and until that happened with her or someone, I would never feel good.

"You can touch me if you want. It should be okay for you this time because we're already on the floor."

I didn't know whether to be grateful or to be insulted. I tried to think of something else. Of Gloria. Of Tamara being Debbie's best friend. I did my best to put out of my mind that what I was feeling now, what I was feeling an urge to do was what I had felt sometimes when Mom was tucking me in. I just wanted her to want me and to allow me to get as close to her as I physically could. I'm talking about Tamara, but I probably wanted it from Mom and definitely had been fantasizing about it with Gloria for weeks. Thinking of Gloria gave me a slight nudge in my conscience, but a nudge is a feather next to the hammer of the urge I was feeling now.

I think that is the first time I could sympathize with rapists even though I know now it has little to do with sex, if at all, but is all about rage and domination. All I could hear in my mind was that this is what I've always wanted. I guess it's a version of what people believe about winning the lottery. That it will solve everything. Having this thing was what I wanted, but, apart from the feeling you get in masturbation, I really had no idea what it was exactly I wanted. Maybe that's the way with deep unconscious desires. You experience the desire with so much force that the fulfillment of the desire is almost inconsequential. It helped that Tamara was a Venus, a girl that would never have been even close to wanting me without lots of money changing hands.

"It's okay." She took my hand and pulled it under her blouse and then guided it over her nipple and around it. She shivered slightly. I was greedy and wanted to see if I could head for the nether regions, what someone called the golden triangle or some such precious name. I started to stray and she pulled my hand up, but only to adjust herself. Then she opened her legs and pushed my hand below from my wrist because her pants were too tight for both her hand and mine.

She rubbed my hand over her hair and into a moist crevice. I had begun to lose interest because I had already fired off in my pants.

She seemed intent on something, and I began to feel a little weird, like she could have used anything to do what she was having my hand do. On the other hand, I didn't want to seem ungrateful for her being the first to allow me to touch her on (or in) her special places.

She groaned a bit and then seemed to notice that it was my hand and began to apologize. I think I then began to formulate my ecumenical view of religions, that we are all taught to be guilty as an indication of our devotion. She began to cry like she had just molested me and was sick with herself.

Years later Debbie would tell me about an uncle that had violated Tamara every Christmas season when their families got together, I guess she'd say Hanukkah season, until the slightest mention of Santa or the humming of a Christmas carol would cause her to leave the room.

At the moment all I could think was that God, or whoever was in control of the universe, had a strange sense of balance. A father is taken away only to have the one thing I thought about day and night given me without asking. Santa came early this year.

CHAPTER SEVENTEEN

EVEN NOW, A FEW decades later, I still don't know what affected me more: Dad dying or Tamara coming into the fort. Of course, there was the Gloria surprise. In the running could be Debbie's take on Mom and me in the bathroom. Soon there would be Mr. Bodenhamer's family. But next to Dad's death, Tamara's response seemed to be more pivotal than anything else.

On Sunday, I woke up from a dream in which Sandy, Tamara, and Gloria were dressed up as knights on horseback, jousting for me as the prize. Mom and Dad were with me in the stands. Dad kept grinning and patting me on the back, saying that no matter who won I would win, too. He winked at Mom, who muttered with a curled lip, "Sluts." Then she turned to me with her sweetest smile. "None of them are good enough for you, baby." Her blouse was open to the waist and she was holding her bra in her hand. No one else in the crowd even noticed.

After folding up my bed, I stood at my window looking toward the canyon and recalling as much as I could of the time with Tamara. I worried she would tell Debbie and thought I better have a comeback ready. I didn't know why Tamara acted like that but suspect now that her treatment of me had little to do with how much she was concerned about me but mostly with her own needs. However, at the time all I felt was love. Or at least I felt cared for by someone who wasn't obligated to like me as my family was. It was like what happened with Gloria except it had this illicit part. I comforted myself with the knowledge that what we had done would not produce a baby, so my soul was not in any immediate danger.

I hoped that the next time I saw Gloria or even talked to her on the phone, I wouldn't reveal in the tone of my voice that I had been untrue to her. For days it seemed every rock and roll love song I heard was about cheating.

I put on some shorts and a T-shirt and went to the kitchen for breakfast. I decided to have Grape-Nuts in honor of Dad. Even on the tranquilizers that Mom got from our doctor, she was in high gear, notifying everyone of Dad's death, planning the service at the church, and arranging the ceremony at the grave. My cereal was already soaking in a bowl, but Mom said, "Honey, would you get yourself something to eat? I'm just swamped."

I nodded, but she didn't notice that either. She was poring over the address book, talking to herself about who should be called and who could wait for a letter. She didn't seem any different now than when she was planning a home party or a celebration for church. I watched her for signs of sadness and wondered with horror if she was relieved that Dad was dead. After finding out about Laura, I could see that things between Mom and Dad must have been as bad as I had suspected all along.

I took my cereal to Maw-Maw's almost empty room, closed the door, and turned on the TV. Some old movie with Jimmy Cagney was showing. He was talking tough to some guy taller and heavier than him, but the bigger guy was obviously intimidated. We short guys loved stuff like that.

I heard a knock on the door and thought it was Maw-Maw since Mom had had Debbie call her as soon as we got home from the hospital yesterday and Maw-Maw had told Debbie she would be back sometime today. But before I could get up to open the door, Debbie walked in. Her eyes were red, and she looked like she had gotten at most a few hours of sleep. She glanced at the movie, mumbled something about having seen it before, and plopped down on the bed. She looked like she was dressed for mourning because everything she had on was black, including her socks.

"Fuck them all."

It seemed particularly blasphemous to say that in this room and pissed me off, but I had not slept much myself and just didn't want to get into it with her. Still, I did want to hear what she thought about it all: Dad dying, Mom's response, and maybe Laura.

"I can't believe she's acting like she even cared about him. When was the last time she ever got through a day without ragging on him?" She threw her legs over the side of the bed and swung up to a seated position.

James Cagney was now talking to some "dame" who was crying, and he was looking past her like he was expecting someone to come in the door.

"Can you believe it?" She was now standing in front of the TV.

"Believe what? That Maw-Maw left?" Or I thought to myself: that you're keeping me from watching this movie, that Gloria kissed me and pledged herself to me forever, that Billy seemed to be friends with me again after beating me up, that Tamara came on to me like a prostitute? Then out loud again: "That Mom is organizing the funeral or that Dad died?"

She looked at me like I had spoken some esoteric wisdom and that if she stared at me long enough, she would understand, too.

I stood up and turned down the volume on the TV and paced back and forth. "It's unfair. This woman had no right to be there, even if Mom and Dad were going to get divorced anyway. People should just leave us alone."

Debbie opened Maw-Maw's closet and started rifling through the clothes Maw-Maw had left on hangars. "Boy, she's just like Dad. Never gives away anything.

The phone rang, and we looked at each other. "Maybe it's Maw-Maw," Debbie said.

A few moments later, knock on the door and Mom said, "May I come in?" as she entered the room. She noticed Debbie in the closet. "What are you doing?"

Debbie didn't turn around. "Seeing what might fit me."

Mom looked puzzled and then remembered why she had come back here. "It's for you, Joey. Some girl named Gloria."

I had never told Mom about her, so Mom looked at me like she was expecting me to explain now who she was.

"Ooooo. Dayton calling." Apparently Debbie wasn't so upset about Dad that it stifled her sarcasm.

I wanted to choke her, but I wanted more not to waste any more of Gloria's money. I walked out the door slowly, then tore down the hall to the kitchen. I could have used the phone in Mom and Dad's bedroom but wouldn't have wanted to be there even if Dad were still alive.

Lists were spread all over the kitchen table. The receiver was dangling from its cord on the wall and it took a couple of tries before I was able to keep hold of it.

"Hi."

She couldn't have heard about Dad since Mom had only just begun calling people, and Mom hadn't even finished with the local calls yet. "You haven't called in a few days so I wanted to make sure you're okay." I had forgotten that her voice, while still sounding like a young girl's, had a slight husky tone to it like she was a smoker.

I started to say I was fine, and that was true until yesterday. Of course, lots had happened since we last talked, and I wanted to tell her everything: to apologize for Tamara and to get her comfort for Dad, but I said nothing.

"Joey, are you there?"

"Yeah."

"Joey, before I forget, my dad is coming out to Los Angeles in a week to see about a job. We could be moving." She sounded excited. "But he's also said I could take off from school and come with him. He knows I would want to see you, so he said we could squeeze in a day in San Diego. He's always wanted to go to the San Diego Zoo anyway."

I was excited, too, but in a distant, vague way. I wanted to be happy and already was thinking about what Billy and the twins would say when they found out my girlfriend was flying out to see me, a beautiful girl no less.

"Joey, isn't that great?" I could tell she was a little disappointed that she would have to ask me, and I wanted to tell her how great it would be, but all I could think was that she had a father and I didn't.

"He's dead."

I wanted to say passed away or gone on or one of the other euphemisms people used, but they seemed like lies now. He *was* dead. Dead as a doornail, as Dickens said about Marley. And he wouldn't be coming back as some ghost, either. He was really dead.

"What?"

I couldn't talk now.

"Who's dead?" I heard her take in a breath like someone does who's been knocked around by a wave and is just resurfacing for air. "Your daddy?"

I couldn't say yes or uh huh or how'd you guess or why not. I just nodded as if she were in the kitchen with me. I turned around because it felt like someone was watching me. Debbie and Mom were standing in the doorway to the kitchen. I didn't know what to do. I wanted to talk to Gloria, but only in private. I whispered, "I'll call you tonight" and hung up. "I'm going to get ready for church," I said loudly to avoid any questions about who I was talking to.

I went out the kitchen doorway that led to the living room to avoid Mom and Debbie and down the hall to my room. I thought I could hear Mom and Debbie talking. Maybe she was telling Mom what she knew or guessed about Gloria. At this point I didn't care whether Debbie had it straight or not.

I didn't want to go back to the fort for fear that Tamara might come back. I didn't want to go outside to play. I didn't want to be in this house. I didn't want to do anything but be left alone. I pulled the cushions off my sofa bed and lay down, pulling one of them on top of me. I just kept saying Glor-i-a slowly and softly, one syllable at a time. Every garage band in the United States would be playing the Van Morrison version in a few years, but now I had no tune to go with it. It was a mantra that soothed me some while I figured out what to do next.

I opened my door and listened. Mom and Debbie were still talking, so I went back to Maw-Maw's room. I turned on the TV to the old movie again. I don't remember the name of the movie I watched after the Cagney film, but I stayed there until I was ready to go to bed. Mom brought me a chicken TV dinner, but otherwise left me to myself. Debbie went to stay with Tamara for a while, and I worried about what she would say to Debbie but got into making fun of some really old Western until I felt sleepy.

Before going to bed, Mom said we would have a service for Dad on Wednesday afternoon and bury him just after. I called Gloria using our call-once-hang-up-and-call-again method. She started crying when I told her, and I lied that I had to get off the phone.

On Sunday I had no problem getting Mom to let me stay home. I did and didn't want to call Gloria. Didn't won out.

I watched more movies and read in bed. I didn't eat until dinner and then just had a few pieces of pie. Mom was accommodating in ways she never had been. I think if I had said I was flying to Hawaii to surf, she would have let me go, provided I could be back in time for the funeral.

School was unreal but survivable. I did a pretty good job of pretending everything was okay, even to those who had heard about Dad. I smiled a lot so that I actually forgot at times how sad and angry I was, but the afternoons and evenings were dizzying, like I had just gotten off a wild amusement park ride and couldn't get my balance. Everyone kept telling me I'd feel better after Wednesday, and I believed them. We just have to make it to Wednesday night, I kept saying to myself, not knowing if the other part of the we was Gloria, or Tamara, or my family.

CHAPTER EIGHTEEN

WE SAT IN THE front row with Dad in a casket at the end of the middle aisle. I sat next to Maw-Maw, and Debbie was next to her. Mom, on my other side, kept stroking my hand. There was a sweet smell, a combination of the perfume of the flowers and the scent of the women. Mom had asked us a thousand times before we left if she had on too much. She did, but all of us lied. She had already said she could shower fast if we thought she would offend anyone. Debbie kept her mouth shut for a change and gave me a painful look, probably because she had not responded to a great straight line.

Mom was so nervous as we walked into the church that she introduced us to people we already knew. I still don't know if the turnout was a tribute to my father's popularity or to Mom working the phone. People that Dad used to ride the bus with showed up. Almost the whole church was there. All the staff from my junior high school was there, including some of the teachers and most of the administrators. My violin teacher and his family were there. Some of the men Dad knew in the army came. Debbie's drama teacher and some of her fellow thespians showed up. And so did Laura.

The top of the casket was open so when you walked by, you could see Dad's face and torso. We would form a line to walk past him at the end of the service. Mom had decided against having viewing days at the mortuary, but she was adamant everyone got to see him one final time. Did she want confirmation that he really was dead?

"We'll begin with a hymn." Pastor Bob was standing just above the casket on the steps that led to the choir area and the pulpit. "Turn to page three ninety-five in your hymnals."

I didn't reach for the one in front of me. Maw-Maw opened one and offered to share with Debbie, who waved her off. Mom motioned to share one with me, and I grudgingly held a corner. The piano played a short prelude to "The Old Rugged Cross" before everyone whined and moaned their way through the hymn, all four verses. I felt Mom look at me now and then, but I kept my eyes on the casket.

In either a brazen act of sluthood, as Mom would later call it, or an act of courageous devotion, as Debbie saw it, Laura sat just behind us. She did not sob but was audibly crying through the whole service. I found her whimpering a comfort and an antidote to the crackling soprano of Maw-Maw and the overly sincere alto of Mom during the hymn.

"We could always count on Sam. In his capacity as a deacon or helping Dorothy with her ever-lengthening list of navy families they took in for Sunday dinners." The pastor smiled grimly at Mom, who patted me on the knee in response.

I had to use every bit of strength to keep from yelling loud enough that even Dad could hear, "Shut the fuck up. He's dead, you sanctimonious asshole." I almost smiled because I'd gotten that phrase from Debbie when we had accidentally turned to a TV station with an evangelist on. I didn't even know what "sanctimonious" meant, but I knew it was far short of a compliment, and I knew the "sanct" root had something to do with religion.

But I was still angry. I was angry that Dad was gone. I was angry that he interrupted my pitching to go to this Laura. I was angry that she was not even a member of our family, though probably knew Dad better than the rest of us, apparently more in the Biblical sense than Mom, and had been the one with Dad when he first had the heart attack. I was angry because Dad would certainly still be alive if he had stayed with me in the backyard.

The pastor invited those of us in the family to say a few words and Mom, waiting for Pastor Bob to say something to her directly, caught his eye and he responded. "Dorothy?" She shook her head weakly in a false protest and let him encourage her until she came up.

Both Mom and Pastor Bob made it worse because they didn't talk about Dad being gone. They were talking about all the things they admired him for, like this was Dad's retirement dinner. After Mom finished and Pastor Bob offered a short bio of Dad, he launched into a full-scale altar call with "Just as I Am, Without One Plea," the standard closing hymn for most of our services. Making this into a time to decide for or against Jesus left Dad in the dust. No one came down the aisle in response to the "invitation," but I considered going just to be closer to Dad.

Finally it was all over. Pastor Bob closed his eyes and lifted his arms with his palms facing us for the benediction. "The Lord bless thee, and keep thee. The Lord make his face shine upon thee, and be gracious unto thee. The Lord lift up his countenance upon thee, and give thee peace."

The congregation responded in unison, "Amen." Nothing from me or Debbie.

"The grace of the Lord Jesus Christ, and the love of God, and the communion of the Holy Ghost, be with you all." This time Pastor Bob said, "Amen," before anyone else could. I thought he was going for a few more benedictions, but he motioned for us to come by the coffin now. He suggested that as we did, we could also thank the Lord for the life of this godly man.

We, the family, were given the first shot at seeing Dad. The rest of the congregation lined up behind us. I followed Maw-Maw, who was first because Debbie stayed seated. Dozens of gladiolas surrounded Dad: in large sprays at the head of the casket, draped over the part still closed, and behind him, between the casket and the steps to the stage. The smell, though faint, was nauseating.

His face really did look like him. I knew that sometimes morticians had to be creative, like movie makeup artists, to get people with gunshot wounds or those in traffic accidents to look halfway recognizable, but apparently dying of a heart attack didn't change you much. Not that he didn't look dead. His skin was a waxy version of the real thing and, even though his eyes were closed, he didn't look asleep. I stood still for a moment to see if his chest was rising and falling. Dad had told me about people who had phones put in their coffins just in case a terrible mistake had been made. I wanted to touch his skin like we did in the hospital but was afraid of what people might say. I wasn't looking at anyone, but I could feel they were watching me.

Mom started crying again when she walked by, and the pastor held her for a while. His wife, Caroline, put an arm around me, but I didn't want to cry, so I squirmed away.

Debbie was talking to Laura, both of whom had still not joined the line to view Dad. From a distance it might have appeared that Debbie was angry at Laura because Debbie was talking in her loud stage whisper. Within a few rows, it was obvious who the source of her anger was.

"She used to rag on him all the time. I wonder if there was ever a day she didn't tell him how incompetent he was." Debbie glanced at Dad over her shoulder. "To buy the right groceries or to remember some place Joey or I needed to go or to ridicule what he was wearing in the yard or to nag him about those damn oleanders or to bemoan how much work she had to do to find bargains because he wasn't making enough money." Debbie shook her head at the unbelievability of it.

Mom must have heard but kept busy by acting like a hostess to the people who had just passed the casket. The pastor stayed next to her.

If it had been your first time to attend our church, you might have thought they were husband and wife and they made quite a couple: Mom in her gathered gray dress with black buttons that hugged her waist, he in a pinstriped suit that hid his love handles and emphasized his broad, sympathetic shoulders.

Apparently Debbie continued to blast Mom, but Laura had gotten her to talk quietly enough that no one was staring at them anymore. Laura did such a good job of listening that Debbie would forever treat Laura like she was a long-lost relative (which she was on her way to becoming). The more we learned about their relationship, the more she seemed to be Dad's main course, with our Mom on the side.

The mortician ushered the four of us into a black Lincoln Continental, just behind the hearse, which was being led by a motorcycle cop. The rest of the cars had been given yellow cards with the word funeral on them. Everyone turned on their lights, which you could barely see since the sun was so bright.

Behind the driver, the Lincoln had two rows of seats facing each other. Debbie and I sat with our backs to the driver. Mom and Maw-Maw sat across from us. Mom kept dabbing her eyes while Maw-Maw looked out the window, her lips moving without a sound. I assumed she was praying but wondered what she could be saying since the decision had already been made. It never occurred to me she could be praying for those of us who were left.

Many of the church people had said Dad was in a better place. When the pastor's wife whispered in my ear that he was with the Lord now, as if Dad had gotten a good deal by having a heart attack and leaving the earth before his children grew up, I clenched my fist, ready to punch the next person who made it sound like *not dying* would have been a worse deal.

It took me years to stop hating God, who seemed to relish destroying what he had created. A view of the divine in *King Lear*—"as wanton flies are to boys are we to the gods"—seemed less mean because at least those gods were indifferent.

My church taught that God was both all-good and all-powerful. So if anything happened that seemed mean or horrible, one, it was none of my business ("Where were you when I laid the foundations of the earth?") and two, it was for the best in the long run. You see, the explanation goes, we're just too limited to see the big picture, and everything always redounded to the glory of God. I was beginning to wonder if such a God could be redounded.

At the cemetery, uniformed soldiers were milling around Dad's gravesite. Dad had been an officer in the army, so he was being given a military funeral with the hallowed twenty-one-gun salute. Their rifles made me think they were here to protect Dad's body from being stolen the way his life had been. Dad survived two wars and countless hours on our lethal highways only to die in the arms of his mistress. Tragic irony or good fortune?

While people were parking their cars and those who arrived first were walking to the grave, I made my way up the hill to a large cedar that a few crows were using temporarily for a pulpit. Hitchcock's *The Birds* wouldn't come out for a year, but I knew the common term for a group of crows, so their presence seemed ominous, like one of us was soon to be joining Dad. I waved my arms at them, but they were too high up to be bothered by me. I wondered how difficult it would be to reach them by climbing. I wanted to be strong enough to shake the tree loose of them because they were too noisy and imperious to be allowed such a clear view of my father's burial.

My English teacher was a Shakespeare nut and, even though he couldn't quite justify giving seventh graders a complete play to study, he did like to show us scenes from movie versions as a way to get us interested in studying them in future classes. He had showed us the part of *Hamlet* where Hamlet jumps into his girlfriend's grave. I didn't understand why Hamlet did it, but I was impressed with his devotion. I thought that Dad might be better served by some heartfelt theatrics than the service in the church and here.

The stream of people had subsided, and Pastor Bob had taken his place at one end of the big hole. A backhoe rested a few yards away. The dirt looked fresh, like it had just been dug up a few minutes ago. It felt like Dad had just *died* a few minutes ago. It also felt like it had been years since he was alive. Maybe this is the way we avoid thinking about our own deaths, by making painful experiences seem like ancient history and therefore having little to do with our present lives.

I walked down from the tree, and its murder of crows to stand next to Debbie. I let her put her arm around my shoulder. She had invited Laura to stand on the other side of her. Pastor Bob was saying "ashes to ashes and dust to dust," even though usually such higher church phrases were assiduously avoided by the spontaneity-oriented, nonscripted-prayer Baptists. Maybe he had High Church aspirations.

The twenty-one-gun salute was impressive, but it was "Taps" that got to everyone. Dad never talked about his experience in Germany or Korea, so I learned more about what happened over there in movies until we found his diary. I wonder how many times he listened to "Taps" played for his friends and how much of what he experienced he kept from us to protect our innocence.

A hawk began circling in the distance over a canyon. I watched it as Dad was lowered into the ground. It disappeared as soon as they started to throw in the dirt. Dad once said that birds of prey soar over human remains, waiting to absorb their released spirit. Grievers in movies sometimes take a handful of dirt and/or a nosegay to toss on the coffin. My favorite mourners are the women who throw themselves on the casket of their relative, bawling as if this was the worst thing that could possibly happen.

Wasn't it? What could be worse? Watching someone be tortured? Being tortured yourself? Witnessing your lover being humiliated and then killed? I don't know. The wise ones say that death is a part of life. Well, that's like God being both omnipotent and benevolent. It's a theology that is way beyond me.

After most of the people had left, Debbie was in earnest conversation with Laura again. Mom was being consoled and escorted back to our funeral Lincoln by the pastor, so she didn't seem to notice. Maw-Maw had stayed in her chair and was bobbing back and forth like a Jew at the Wailing Wall.

Debbie stayed with Laura as she walked to her car. "The reception's for Dad, not for her," I could hear Debbie say.

Laura nodded and said she had had enough with the church service and burial, so it wasn't about Mom. "Let me see if I have something to write on? I want to give you my number."

"I want yours, too."

As critical as Debbie was and as difficult as it was for her to suffer fools, she made friends fairly easily. If this had been her funeral, I doubt our church would have been big enough to hold everyone she knew. But her acceptance of Laura was fueled mostly by antagonism for Mom, especially because Mom acted so heartbroken over Dad dying when Debbie saw little evidence Mom gave a hang about him when he was alive.

Anyway, Laura prevented further fireworks by not accepting Debbie's invitation to come back to our house. While it was weird to think of my father having sex with my mother, it was kind of exciting to think of Dad and Laura. It gave him a special cachet, this secret relationship. If it hadn't been part of what led to his death, I might want the guys in the neighborhood to have found out. Of course, it was also terribly shameful, and I figured the only one who would actually see Dad's affair as something to brag about would be Billy.

When we got back to the house, Mom was directing women from the church to assemble all the food.

Billy had seen me on the way in and gave me a sad face and a shake or two of his head. I appreciated the gesture, especially since he seemed to recognize that I didn't want to talk. Tamara had been waiting on our doorstep, and I hadn't realized she wasn't at the funeral until I saw her there. She hugged me a bit long like Mom would sometimes do and then said how sorry she was.

Debbie came up behind me. "Wow, you look great." She was happy to see Tamara and, after Debbie commented in more detail on Tamara's dark gray rayon skirt and matching jacket, which made her look like a beautiful actress playing a real estate agent, they went in to help get things ready. Debbie could be quite mature when she wasn't complaining about being treated like a kid.

I had turned red upon seeing Tamara and wondered if she was pleased or embarrassed to see my response. There was nothing in her demeanor that would ever have given away what we had done in the fort. I was beginning to doubt it had happened until she whispered, "Call me before you go in the canyon the next time."

Her breath tickled my ear and sent shivers to my crotch. I was glad I had on a jacket that covered me down there. Gloria, Tamara, Sandy, Laura, Mom, and Dad produced these dizzyingly confusing emotions in me. Maybe some of the Twambley girls would want to help like Tamara did. I went to my room to beat off and change clothes before I would have to put up with all the people trying to comfort me again.

Mom had called a few of our relatives in Texas and sent the rest a form letter. I hoped some of them, not just Gloria and her family, would come. I had to give Mom credit for something which Dad gave her credit all the time: she was a very good hostess. Today she would get special kudos because she was doing it under such duress. No matter how difficult she could be with us, she had a gift for making people, both strangers and friends, comfortable in public gatherings. Dozens of the navy families that the pastor had referred to in the service sent us Christmas cards, some even presents, because Mom had been their personal USO while they had been stationed in San Diego. That is what made Debbie, and now me, all the more unforgiving of the way she treated us.

Before someone could miss me and start asking where I was, I left my room and began milling among the crowd that had formed in our living room. Maw-Maw hugged me a few times as she roamed the room, and both Debbie and Tamara were overly solicitous of how I was doing. Most of the time I was trying to figure out a way to call Gloria before our money-saving late hour. Tamara kept looking at me and smiling, so I forgot about Gloria some of the time.

Billy and the twins came by. So did their parents, and so did the Twambleys. I don't remember any time that our neighbors had been in our house at the same time. I walked onto the patio where someone had set up a snack station on a card table. Billy was walking toward the back fence, and I started walking toward him through the ice plant when I heard my name called.

Mr. Bodenhamer was standing on the edge of the concrete, seemingly trying to decide if his dress shoes would be damaged by following me. He clasped his hands in front of him and rocked them back and forth. I didn't know what it meant, but it was soothing nonetheless. I had forgotten that he was shorter than Pastor Bob even though he was a million times more athletic.

"How are you doing?"

I shrugged my shoulders, which seemed like the most honest thing I had done all day.

"I liked your daddy. I never told you, but he and I had a long talk about our experiences during Korea." Mr. B was in the Marines. "When we talked, we had a lot of silences in between. That was true for everyone I knew who went. We had both lost a lot of brothers, and we could just look at each other and communicate. Did he tell you how he got that slight limp?"

"Something about shrapnel, I think."

Mr. B smiled. "Shrapnel? He was trying to pull a buddy back to safety and a grenade went off near him. He was a brave man."

He put his arm around me and noticed the pitcher's mound. "So this is where you practiced with him. He told me about the mound and how you had struck out a few of the neighborhood kids who are pretty good athletes."

I looked to see if the twins could hear us, but they were still inside. "Yeah. We worked pretty hard on it." I could still see Dad struggling to get out of his catcher's crouch after Mom had called him to the telephone, remembering now how he favored his right leg. "This was the last place I talked to Dad."

CHAPTER NINETEEN

MR. B. AND I were standing just out of the sun under the patio roof. Mom asked from the door if he wanted anything to drink, and he said he'd come get it.

"Thirsty?" he said to me.

I looked at the pitcher's mound and nodded. "A Coke. Please."

I was standing just enough beyond the house that I could see Sandy's window. She wasn't in her room because she came with Billy to the reception. If I turned further to the left, I could see through our chain link fence to the edge of the canyon where Tamara and I had met. With a little more turning, I could look east, toward Grandma and Gloria.

"Here." Mr. B was back with that grim smile on his face, like he'd just tried to catch a wave on his surfboard and was embarrassed about being unsuccessful.

I wanted to ask him why people died. I wanted to ask him if he believed that everything always worked out fine in the end. Or was that just for Christians? And if it was, was it only for the devoted ones? I mostly wanted to know why Dad had died just when he and I were doing so well.

Debbie came out on the patio and asked if I had seen Mom.

"I saw her go into the garage."

Debbie walked on without responding to Mr. B when he offered his condolences. I followed Debbie because I thought she might make a scene and, even as angry as I was at Mom, I didn't want anything to happen in front of so many people, especially our neighbors. Debbie had left the back door to the garage open, so I could step inside without much notice. What I saw was the pastor holding Mom on a ladder. She was trying to reach some paper cups that had been stored on two-by-fours that rested on the joists. Even in the poor lighting, I could tell she was blushing.

"Oh, honey. Will you take these in to Ethyl?" Mom was reaching out to Debbie. Pastor Bob had backed away and was standing to the side awkwardly. Debbie alternated staring at Mom and the pastor.

In a lame effort to get her out of there, I said, "Debbie, I need to talk to you."

She looked at me like I was a gnat that was buzzing her ear and waved me away with the flick of a hand. Then she shook her head to refocus. "So, let me see if I have this right. Dad has, I mean *had*, Laura, and so you have the pastor?"

Pastor Bob was acting like he had no idea what Debbie was implying by raising his shoulders in a mock gesture of confusion. Fortunately for him, he had taken the package of cups instead of Debbie and before Ethyl, who had decided Mom might need some help, could take them from him, he held on to them and followed her back, as if the cups were too heavy for her.

"Debbie, now don't you start. You don't know what you're saying." Mom smoothed her dress and put her heels back on.

"What am I saying? Or, more precisely, what is going on?" She didn't let Mom answer. "I see the looks on you when he's around, but I wouldn't let myself believe it. What about Caroline?" Caroline was the pastor's wife, and I prayed she didn't come out here.

"He was just making sure I didn't fall. He—"

"Oh, pleeeeeease. Joey may be fooled by your fictions but not me."

Fictions? I wondered if Debbie even knew what she was talking about sometimes. Novels? Short stories? Geez.

She went on. "Dad is dead, he's not coming back, and you can't even wait until the grass grows over his grave before you're messing around. With a married man! Our PASTOR for Chrissakes?"

"Now, just wait a minute, young lady."

Mom was whispering, but as loudly as she could, because Debbie had been screaming. She would have attracted an audience if Ethyl had not effectively blocked the door to the kitchen once she sensed trouble. I saw her look back into the garage just after she took the cups and quickly close the door. She was a stout woman. That is, she was overweight, hardworking, and stronger than many men, the epitome of the self-effacing Christian mother workhorse at our church, and she knew how to protect her own.

I had closed the back garage door after me when I came in, so I hoped no one in the backyard had heard. When I walked out again, Mr. B was talking to Billy, and neither noticed me. Everybody else seemed more interested in eating than in what was going on in the garage.

I looked wistfully at the canyon and saw Leslie Twambley walking near the oleanders, brushing their poisonous leaves as she went by. I wondered if I could get by her and out the back gate before she noticed.

"Oh, Joey." Too late. She was coming toward me with her arms open. She was only a year ahead of Debbie but was one of the tallest girls in the high school, taller than Tamara. A hug from her would mean my head would not quite be breast high. I stood still and let her come to me. When she closed in, I kept saying to myself, "I still love you, Gloria. I still love only you," but it was hard to concentrate with the top of my head touching one breast. It felt so warm, soft, and secure there that she finally had to push me away.

I was totally embarrassed, but Leslie was not paying attention to me as people had begun to gather at the back of the garage. The door was closed, but even from here, we could hear voices. As I got closer, Maw-Maw grabbed me and shook her head. "More people just makes it worse."

We all heard "shut up" because Debbie said it over her shoulder before she slammed the door behind her. She looked at all of us, who were staring at her, called out for Tamara, and, without waiting for her to respond, walked around the garage, through the side gate, and out front. When Tamara came by, I told her where Debbie went. I wanted to ask her what would be a good time to return the fort, but I had some sense of timing.

When I turned around, I bumped into Maw-Maw. "This kind of thing upsets everybody. We all say and do things we don't really mean." She was taller than usual in her sensible low heels. She had to be talking about Dad's dying because she didn't ask what had gotten Debbie so angry that she told Mom to shut up in front of dozens of people at the reception following his funeral. I nodded like I understood.

Back on the patio, I was grateful that people were at least pretending to be more interested in their own conversations than what had just happened. Mr. B walked over and said something similar to what Maw-Maw said and then asked if I'd like to go with his family to the beach sometime.

I said, "Sure," and thought of asking if I could move in with them, too.

I went out front because I wanted to know what made Debbie so angry but got there just in time to see Tamara climb in our car with her. Miss Learning Permit drove away like she did it every day. I hated her for leaving me behind.

When I turned back, I stayed on the sidewalk just surveying our house, like someone thinking of buying some investment property. The teal trim was flaking at the edge of the fascia and on the garage door. The bougainvillea had reached back so far over the roof that it almost touched the peak, like it wanted to escape over it into the backyard. In the front the vine formed a shape you find on anatomy charts in sex ed, the fallopian tubes reaching out to the right and left on the roof and the body of vine a riot of red where the main sexual organ would be.

Mom came out the front door. At first I thought she was looking for Debbie. The pastor was standing behind her on the porch. Instinctively I looked behind me to see if Debbie and Tamara were already around the corner.

"You okay, sweetie?"

Mom could turn on this sticky, sugary voice that seemed to charm people she had first met but drove Debbie nuts. I was beginning to see why.

"Yeah." I hoped she wouldn't ask where Debbie was because I would have to lie.

"Pastor Bob has something for you." She motioned for him to come over.

I always forgot how fat he was up close. Not grossly fat, but he was months, if not years, of dieting and exercise away from Mr. B He looked like a guy who used to play football and to eat big portions just to match his calorie output, but stopped playing and kept up the eating. Still I admired him just for being big, no matter what Debbie thought he was doing with Mom. He reached for my hand and engulfed it like a hamburger bun might do to a shrunken, overcooked patty. His mouth seemed big enough to swallow my head. He was giving me the same grim smile that everybody seemed to offer today.

"Joey, this is a rough time."

I didn't say, "Because Debbie caught you and Mom?" I just nodded.

"Sometimes we need things to help us remember those people who have gone on to be with the Lord."

He just died, you fat blowhard. Why would I need anything to remind me of him? What I really need is to be left alone for a while. "Yeah," I said, nodding.

"Your daddy said I was to give this to you if something happened to him." He handed me a small gold plate with the name Sam on it and a smaller cross in a circle embossed above the name. The church gave it to all the deacons. "Now, you let me know if you need anything else."

I wanted to ask, "How I could possibly want anything else?" He reached down to pin it on my shirt, but I took it in my hand instead. He had the same oniony and peppermint breath that Mom had right after she brushed her teeth. I looked at Mom who was smiling at me and raising her eyebrows. I guess to convey her appreciation for the pastor. I think she was the one who needed the reminder. Their mission accomplished, they both walked back into the house.

I was stunned, feeling a little like I had felt after striking out the twins and a little like I had felt after Gloria leaned over the Monopoly board to kiss me and a little like I felt after being with Tamara.

I looked at the Twambley's house to the left and wondered if they had room for another kid. Across the street the Carroll's had plenty of room, but I didn't think I could take living under the captain's regime. Billy's family had an enclosed patio next to the pool and probably would let me sleep there, though I didn't know how Billy would feel about me being closer to Sandy's window.

I wanted to get away from Mom and the pastor and Debbie and everyone except Gloria. Maybe I had enough money saved for the Greyhound. I had cousins that lived in West Texas, not far from El Paso. I could hitchhike to them and take the bus from there to Dayton. I must have enough money for that.

I had always wished they lived closer. They were like brothers and even looked like me, with their long noses, flat chests, and skinny arms. With them I saw my first dead body. Dad was the second.

They lived in a trailer park in Fort Stockton. There were four boys, but one had already left home to get married at only seventeen, and the youngest was still in preschool. Willie and Waylon (yes, their parents were country-western fans) were close to my age, with Willie six months younger and Waylon about a year older.

We had had a great time when they stopped by to see us on the way to Disneyland last winter. I wondered if Mom had already written them about Dad. Uncle Carson would be heartbroken because he and Dad were the closest of all the siblings.

Ethyl came out to offer me a sandwich, but I wasn't hungry. She said to come in when I was. God, did she forget I lived here?

I walked to Dad's old Plymouth, which someone had brought back from Laura's house. Inside it smelled of him: tobacco smoke and the faint odor of a sweaty T-shirt. Dad had loaned the car to Uncle Carson to take his sons and me to Tijuana. In all their years so close to El Paso, they had never gone to Juarez, and had been taking Spanish for years, dying to try it out on someone besides recent immigrants. They would call in to Spanish radio stations to make song requests and talk Spanish when ordering at Mexican restaurants but that was about all.

Dad had told Uncle Carson where to get temporary auto insurance, which would be necessary if we wanted to go further down Baja. Mom did not find out we had gone until they had already left San Diego for Disneyland, or I never would have been allowed to go. We had a great time in Tijuana partly because they really did know a lot of Spanish and could read all the signs and because almost everyone they tried to engage in Spanish always answered in English. It was a hoot.

As I said, that was the first time I saw a dead body, at least a human body. I had seen a dog whose abdomen was split open and millions of maggots were crawling around, but in Tijuana I saw a man's corpse for the first time, and he didn't have some funeral director to make him look good.

We had been walking around and Uncle Carson was feeling tired so he went back to the car and told us we could go into this one shop but not to go anywhere else. We went in the shop and were looking at these silver belt buckles, when Willie said, "I'll be right back."

He came running back in a few minutes and grabbed Waylon by the shoulders. "He's gone."

"What?" I panicked. "Gone where?"

They started laughing, "Asleep. He's asleep. He does this all the time with Mom. He naps in the car, and she can take as long as she wants while she shops."

I was beginning to worry about what they had in mind.

"It's just around the corner." Willie was already walking out the door.

Waylon seemed to know what he was talking about. "Are you sure? Daddy'll kill us and then tan our hides and sell us for leather belts."

I stood next to the car confirming for myself that Uncle Carson was really asleep. "How do you know how long he'll sleep?"

They laughed again. "Daddy slept for two hours when Mom was Christmas shopping. He slept through a fire engine and a thunderstorm. Come on."

Apparently Willie had talked to some kid who told him where this strip joint was and how to sneak into it. It seemed hard to believe, and I wondered if someone was setting us up to be robbed, or maybe worse.

Just before we turned the corner, I could tell that their father was still in the same position, head against the door window and mouth open. Ahead we could see the neon sign flashing "Les Girls" and some guy out front talking in English with an accent that made him sound a lot like the Cisco Kid's sidekick, Poncho. He was making gestures that could only charitably be called lewd.

Just the other side of the bar a crowd had gathered. We thought it was a competitor trying to get people to come in to see *his* girls and wanted to hear what he had to say. Willie squeezed his way to the front of the crowd, saw what the commotion was about, and came back for us.

"Wow," he kept saying and shaking his head with his eyes closed. He rubbed his head a few times, which seemed to make it easier for him to open his eyes, and looked at us fiercely and slowly. "You got to see this."

We squeezed through the sweaty and boozy men to the front. On the ground was a man in a cowboy outfit: boots, jeans, leather jacket, and a wide-brimmed hat beside him. His mouth was open and so were his eyes. His legs were folded back toward his upper body in what would have been an uncomfortable position if he had been alive. He was holding the handle of what must have been a knife. It wasn't obvious whether he was trying to get it out of his chest or he had just put it in. A pool of pomegranate red had formed in the space on the ground created by his chest and legs.

Willie translated some of the conversation. "He's dead." "Oh, you're so brilliant. Maybe La Migra won't find you next time." "Is it Juan?" "*Was* it Juan?" They said other things he couldn't quite understand, but they sounded a lot like some of the nasty words he knew.

It must have just happened because the pool of blood was slowly expanding. A man bumped me with his knee and said, "Perdona me."

I was beginning to worry that Uncle Carson might already be awake and going into the store to look for us and said so. Both of them agreed.

We weren't interested in the strip club anymore. We began thinking up scenarios that led to the knifed man on

240

the ground. Waylon said he had come to take a girl in one of the shows away with him and the manager killed him. Willie said he had been cheating in some poker game, got in a fight with one of the players, and he was stabbed during the fight. I said he had killed somebody's father and that after being searched for all night, he was recognized by his hat and a slight hitch in his walk and stabbed by the murdered father's son.

We wanted to come up with more ideas so we could laugh about it, but we couldn't. When Uncle Carson asked us if we had a good time, we smiled that same grim smile I was seeing the day of my father's burial.

CHAPTER TWENTY

I MADE IT THROUGH the rest of the week. Everyone knew about Dad at school because the girls' vice principal was a close friend of Mom's. She had placed a photo of Dad with a short bio and mentioned both Mom and me. I had to pass it on the way to math class every day. I could tell kids were talking about me at times but did my best to think of something else, usually Gloria. My teachers were very sympathetic, which made it worse because that brought me more attention. My favorite bully, Greg, must have had something similar happen to him because he made a point of telling me, like the police do on TV, that he was sorry for my loss. Next to Mr. B's response, I think I appreciated Greg's the most.

Bad news and death, according to Maw-Maw, always come in threes. If Dad was number one in the bad news category, then not making the Little League All-Star team was number two. Yes, the twins made it, even with the rule that every team gets at least one player, a rule originally instituted to keep the Elks from dominating the whole roster. Stumpy was chosen for our team, and I agreed. I also had to agree that all the other pitchers chosen were at least as good as me, and most were better. Still none of them had struck out the twins. In the same inning. With them swinging at the third strike, not due to some controversial call by the umpire. Maw-Maw pointed out that I was an alternate, and I had to admit that was some consolation. I determined to work hard between now and next season to make the actual team, but who was I going to pitch to?

My manager called me with the all-star news Saturday morning, and he emphasized the almost-being-on-the-team part. "Lots of guys were pretty good at pitching, so you're part of an elite group. Keep practicing." Which I translated into, *You didn't practice hard enough this year.*

I kept thinking about Mr. Bodenhamer's offer to go with his family to the beach and hoped he would invite me tomorrow. I wasn't sure I wanted to go, but I wanted to know that he still wanted me. Seeing him was the only reason I was planning to keep going to church.

The twins and Billy didn't ask me to come out to play, and I was just as happy to spend the day in my room reading Tom Swift. Mom kept asking me how I was doing, so I put on a convincing fake smile to get her to leave alone.

On Sunday Mr. Bodenhamer invited all the Royal Ambassadors who were at church to the beach. Since I wouldn't be the only one outside his family, I decided to go. It was almost a hundred degrees inland and still pretty warm at La Jolla Shores, as it was often in the early fall. The twins always complained that football practices after the season started could be as rough as the summer preseason workouts just because of the post-summer heat wave.

Mr. B picked me up at our house, which was probably the only reason Mom let me go. He had as good a reputation as Dad, at least before we found out about Laura, so she was willing to risk my going even though she wasn't particularly lenient in the best of times. Mr. B pulled up in an old woodie that he kept in primo condition. I was let in the backseat next to his daughter, Cindy, who rivaled Sandy, Leslie, Tamara, and Gloria, without being as pretty. She had her own special appeal because she was tan and athletic. At the time the only women who used weights were the freakish-looking female bodybuilders or people would have assumed she worked out. She had the broad shoulders of an Olympic swimmer that she got from her father and flawless olive skin that she inherited from her Italian mother.

She reached an arm around me for a hug when I got in. "Sorry about your Dad." She didn't smile. I liked that. She smelled of coconut oil. I liked that, too, because it reminded me of a Hostess Sno Ball. Mr. B said the rest of the guys would be coming on their own.

Mrs. B sat in the middle of the front bench seat because their Irish setter had shotgun. The window was down just enough for her to put her nose into the wind. On the other side of Cindy was her younger sister, Penelope, whom they all called Loopy. In the far back, behind me and Miss Coconut, was their only boy, Kevin, who, like Loopy, was still in elementary school. All of them surfed, even Mrs. B and Loopy, and all of them were attractive in that fresh, confident-looking way.

When we got to the parking lot, Mr. B let Kevin out to go grab a spot on the sand. He took with him an enormous beach towel with large circles of color, an oversized replica of a watercolor tin. The other Ambassadors never came. We didn't know if they changed their minds or just didn't find the right beach. I thought they didn't want to be around someone whose father had died. It turned out fine because

I was made to feel a part of the family without them acting like they had to treat me special for being half an orphan.

Loopy told me to help her father bring the large cooler and ran to find her brother. "I'll guard our place." She was so small, way below the line for Autopia, that the idea of her reinforcing Kevin was funny. She had curls like the girl in the Coppertone and legs the size of her arms.

Mr. B and Cindy carried the two surfboards that had been strapped to the top of the car while Mrs. B. brought a basket of what turned out to be some of the best sandwiches I had ever eaten. The meat was chicken, but she added herbs and condiments that I didn't recognize. She had gotten the idea from some restaurant they frequented downtown. On the way over, Cindy had asked if I knew how to surf.

"A little."

"So what can you do?"

I had no idea what she meant, so I clarified, "Very little." Actually I had been paddling once in the late afternoon on my stomach but never could stand up.

"I did it once when it was almost dark."

Of course, it being difficult for people to see me had *everything* to do with how I did, but I had not learned that as a general principle yet. Yes, I was good at school, but that just seemed to be a gift I inherited from smart parents, not the result of lots of reading and always doing my homework. Yes, my pitching had improved, and Dad and I had spent hours in the backyard working on it, but that was only one skill, and I had not worked on it all that long. And most important, I had not reached anything close to the level of achievement I wanted, which meant as good as the twins. I still had that ridiculously magical understanding that I couldn't do things because of the lack of some gift, not the lack of countless hours of making mistakes and trying again.

That day still stands out, not because Cindy and Penelope taught me to surf, which they did, and not because it was my first outing with this family, which it was. I still remember it because the whole family accepted me without any strangeness. They treated me like some long-lost cousin they had been talking about and missing for years and who had finally come to see them. I felt more comfortable with them that first time with them than I did with my family at any time, except maybe summer vacations in Texas.

I wasn't kidding about Penelope teaching me to surf. She was the one who insisted that Cindy start me on the sand so the board would be completely stable. "'Okay, good idea," Cindy said. I couldn't believe that she made a suggestion, and it was actually followed.

The last time my family went to the beach, we never saw the ocean. Dad didn't want to worry Mom about the waves, so we went to Mission Bay, where what waves occurred were caused by speedboats pulling water skiers. Mom insisted on making sure Maw-Maw did not burn by putting zinc oxide on her nose and cheeks. We used to laugh at the photo. All she needed was a Bozo nose to look like a clown.

Debbie got invited to a party of San Diego State students nearby, and the rest of the time was spent with Mom arguing against it.

"Those are men, not boys."

"They're college students." Debbie had on her two-piece that made it abundantly clear why she had been invited.

Mom looked pretty good, too, and I wondered if she would be invited next. She squinted in their direction. "Besides, I don't see any adults."

"But you just said they're men," Debbie Darrow retorted.

Dad was doing his best to distract Mom and Debbie by asking them to join him for a whiffle ball game, but they were too far gone. Mom decided that we would leave if Debbie couldn't behave, which meant if she didn't stop arguing. Of course, she didn't, so we packed up to go, even as Dad was telling Mom they shouldn't be punishing the rest of us for Debbie's sins.

"Not that you're sinful," he added to Debbie.

Maw-Maw was ignoring it all and just enjoying the sun as she leaned back in her portable chaise lounge Mom had brought for her. She made a good case for the advantages of being hard of hearing.

I cringe when I think about it now. I cringed then, too. Already a little girl was pointing us out to a man who was holding her hand. When Mom started to pack up, Debbie accused Mom of being jealous, a killjoy, a despot, and a few other epithets I hadn't heard. She was loud enough that some of the partying guys started to notice, too. They thought it was funny, which just egged Debbie on and made Mom all the more adamant.

I was glad we were leaving because I didn't want strangers to see any more of what we could be like at home. Mom usually avoided a public scene at all costs, and the penalty for starting one could be very severe.

Once Debbie called Mom a bitch at a church picnic in Balboa Park, and Mom said nothing, even smiled the rest of the time. When we got home, Mom said Debbie would be grounded for a month, which meant she would not be driven anywhere by Mom or Dad in that time. Debbie managed to sneak out now and then anyway. It seemed pretty severe to me, but she never called Mom a four-letter word away from home again.

This time with the Bodenhamers was very different. I was having so much fun with Cindy and Penelope that I fell off the board a few times on purpose just to get them laughing. But practicing in the sand did make a difference. By the time I got in the water I could do okay, managing to stand up twice and actually stay up long enough once to call it a ride.

Mrs. B. was using the other board. She'd been out while I was dry surfing. When I went into the water, she was coming out to let Mr. B have a chance. When I came in, I gave my board to Loopy. She was quite good, even though the board was too long for her. She could paddle on her knees and managed to catch the first wave she tried for even though she couldn't get the board moving very fast. Kevin was using his time on shore to construct some sand ramps for his toy truck, and a few other kids had joined him in the project.

Still breathing heavily, I sat on the beach looking toward the horizon. Except for Kevin, all of the B's were in the water. The ones without boards were body surfing. They would look for each other and wave after each failed or successful attempt at catching a wave. I don't know if they were the happiest family at the beach that Sunday afternoon, but there was little doubt they were happy. I longed to be a part of such a family. I wanted my father back. I wanted a mother who didn't bug us so much. I wanted a sister who didn't always have to be right. I wanted a grandmother that didn't have to make everything about God. I wanted a family that I enjoyed being with, that made me feel I was important but not so important that any mistake I made would destroy the happiness of everyone else.

When the Bodenhamers dropped me off at home, I had actually not been thinking about Dad and was surprised to remember he would not be at home. Ever. It made me want to avoid Billy when he looked up from his jeep.

It would be impossible for someone to work on a car more than Billy did unless he was doing it as a full-time job. But he also kept an eye peeled for anything going on in the cul-de-sac and was the first to call the fire department when smoke started coming from the Carroll's garage a year ago. So he saw me get out of the woodie and waved me over, which was not enough to get me to come to him but enough to make me pause on the sidewalk.

As usual he had on a white T-shirt that was a bit too small, and as usual he wiped his hand on the part that covered his belly.

"What a cool car." He was watching the Bodenhamers drive away. "How's it going?" Then he looked over my shoulder at the Twambleys as their car was pulling into the driveway.

I looked at their car, too, because Mrs. Twambley and Leslie were arguing loudly in the car without us being able to make out what they were saying.

Billy was looking over there while talking to me. "My grandfather died summer before last. He had emphysema for a long time so he couldn't walk far without resting and couldn't talk for long either." He looked at me and then back at the Twambleys. Leslie and her mother were silent when they got out of the car and looked over at us. Billy waved, but they just walked inside without responding.

"I know grandfathers aren't the same as fathers, but he was the first person to let me drive. It was a lawn mower you could sit on. I wasn't even in school yet."

I said, "Sorry about your grandfather," and continued walking toward the front door. If I had been older, I would have understood why people kept bringing up relatives or pets who had died when they talked to me about Dad. But then I either wanted them to limit their condolences to the subject of my father or just leave me alone. More and more I just wanted to be left alone.

Billy caught up to me, put his hand on my shoulder, and wheeled me around. There were tears in his eyes. "I'm sorry about your father passing on."

"He died," I shouted. "He didn't pass on. He's gone. Get it?" Then I leaned forward in a loud whisper like Debbie had done at church, "Just like your fucking grandfather."

Billy just stared at me. It might have been the first time I had ever said the "F" word outside my room. So that alone had to shock him, but he was also shocked that I couldn't understand that he missed his grandfather like I missed Dad. I couldn't. I was barely able to tolerate all the commiseration for Dad and me, much less absorb the pain of everyone who had "lost" someone they loved.

Mom was on the front porch, and I ignored her. I thought if she said anything to me, I might pull a Debbie and just flip her off. Maw-Maw nodded from her room as I turned into mine from the hallway.

I knew I was angry, but I was too confused to know exactly why, besides the general circumstance of being fatherless. Gloria was coming in a few weeks, but that felt like years away. Mr. B had asked if I wanted to spend the night at his house sometime, but that wasn't a possibility tonight.

I had to get away. I had to avoid Mom coming to me tonight. Besides, I just didn't want to talk or think or feel. I listened to the radio for a while, but it never helps when I'm really angry. I know I was sad, too, but all I felt was the energy of fury. I couldn't calm down even after throwing a ball into my glove about ten thousand times. I walked a lot, back and forth from sofa to window, until I actually was real tired, and it had gotten dark, muttering to myself that God ain't so powerful and loving if he could let this happen. I didn't understand the point of dying, in general or in the specific. What a ridiculous way to run a universe. Maybe God was just stupid.

Mom had looked pretty tired when I passed her at the front door earlier, so I hoped she would be going to bed early. I knew I couldn't get out of the house until she was asleep. Debbie was still at rehearsal. I hoped she wouldn't try to check on me when she came in even though she was being nicer to me since Dad died than I could ever remember.

I went to the kitchen. Mom was already fixing dinner, frying pork chops in a skillet on the stove. "I had a lot to eat at the beach," which was true, "so I don't want any dinner." I had to admit the chops smelled good, but I couldn't face a meal with just Mom and Maw-Maw. "We were swimming and surfing almost the whole time, so I'm ready for bed now."

Her eyebrows rose, and I kicked myself for mentioning surfing. She hadn't said I couldn't do it, but I hadn't said it would be a possibility either. Before she could say anything, I gave her a quick peck on the cheek. "I'll be okay tonight." I hoped that communicated that I did not want her to tuck me in, but I couldn't be sure until later, and I didn't want to stay around to find out.

On my way back to my room, I complimented myself for the preemptive kiss that would both please Mom but not give her a chance to do more than I wanted. I wanted to tell Tamara to meet me at the fort, but calling would be difficult. So I just decided to go straight to her house. Well, not exactly straight. I would take the canyon route and go up to her window. At least, I wouldn't be trying to see her undress or something. I just wanted to contact her without anyone else finding out. Of course, I couldn't be certain she was still interested in me, but I was desperate.

I folded up a blanket and a pillow and tied them with one of my belts. It wasn't long enough, so I took one from Dad's chest of drawers. I wondered if he would think it was funny, me using his belt to stage a short runaway. I didn't intend to be gone more than the evening, maybe not even all of it, but I did have to get away, and I liked that Dad was helping me.

I turned on my radio, loud enough not to bother anyone but still be heard if you stood near my door in the hall. Then I proceeded to carefully take out the panes from the louvers at the top of my bedroom window. I had moved my desk over so I was stable but it still took a lot of slow shimmying of the pane back and forth. There were six altogether, three on each side. I tried removing only the top four. I could fit, but my bedroll couldn't. When I had all the panes out, I had to climb on a chair on top of my desk so I could go out feet first. It was too big a drop to go out headfirst.

I had pushed the blanket and pillow out, when I heard a knock on my door. I jumped off the desk, put the chair down, pulled the desk away from the window, and closed my curtains.

Mom actually waited for me to open the door. "I brought you a plate just in case you get hungry before you go to sleep." She hated us eating in our rooms, so this was special. She looked around and saw the desk in the middle of the room.

"I'm thinking of putting it in a different place." I shrugged my shoulders and began to open up the sofa to pull out my bed.

She set the plate on the desk and left just after giving me a quick peck on the cheek. I guess I started it, so I couldn't complain.

I wasn't able to be grateful to her for the food, but I certainly was hungry and I ate it all. I waited until I heard her close the door to the bathroom to leave.

I was able to get both legs out and lower myself until my feet touched the outside sill, while I still held on to the bottom of the louver frame just above the large picture window. I had forgotten to turn out my light, but it was only the lamp near my bed. I read late into the night often so that would not he so unusual.

I walked over the pitcher's mound and then to the plate behind which Dad crouched to be my catcher. I picked up the plastic plate and threw it into the ice plant. I went back for my bedroll and walked through the back gate, thinking I might have some oleander leaves for dessert just to see what might happen.

CHAPTER TWENTY-ONE

I PUSHED OPEN THE trap door to the fort and threw in my bedroll. It was a good thing Mom had brought me dinner, or I'd be asking Tamara for food, too. I guessed someone could see Mom as evidence of God taking care of me. Certainly the afternoon with the Bodenhamers could be part of the case for providential care, but I was having none of it.

I wasn't afraid as I walked through the canyon. I had remembered to bring a flashlight, but it didn't illumine much, just enough to keep me from tripping on a large rock or running into some bush. Maybe it was because I was so intent on seeing Tamara again that I didn't imagine coyotes, rabid dogs, or escaped convicts. Even in the dark, I could find the trail down the canyon slope.

It was weird to be behind all the houses with their lights on. It was as if I could see the secrets that were hidden from the street side.

Tamara had a dog, but he was usually in the house at night. I could see the blue glow of the TV in their living room window from behind the fence. I didn't know where Tamara's room was, but I had a pretty good idea it was on the opposite end of the house from the garage based on what Debbie used to say about watching the boy next door. Out of the corner of my eye, I thought I saw something move, so I stayed still for a while, just like I'd seen Indians do in the movies. I couldn't see or hear anything, so I went through the gate and stopped again to listen. Still nothing.

I stood for a few minutes outside their living room to see if I could tell what they were watching. I think it was *Bonanza*, because I thought I heard Hoss's voice. I am surprised at how sneaky I was and also how bold. This could have been the beginning of a life of crime and might have if I hadn't gotten help from Mr. Bodenhamer. But then all I knew was that Tamara had been real nice to me, and I was desperate to see what she would do with me the next time. I still imagined I was staying loyal to Gloria, but that wouldn't matter in a few days, anyway.

I heard a noise and then a "Damn it." I thought I recognized the voice but was too scared that anyone else was there that I didn't put any effort into figuring out who it might be. Then I saw this figure turn the corner and walk into the TV's blue light.

"Billy?!" I almost shouted. Then, in what was becoming a Norton tradition, I whispered as loudly as I could. "What are you doing here?"

"Joey?" He laughed. "We have to stop meeting like this." He rubbed his stomach. "What are you doing here?"

"What are YOU doing here?"

"Asked you first."

"I came to see Tamara."

"Yeah, I know."

"No, not like that."

"What, she's different from my sister? And the Twambleys?"

256

Part of me wanted to tell him about Tamara in the fort, and part of me did not want to betray her. Still I had to make it clear that I wasn't here to look in her window. I wanted to *see* her as in talking to her and getting her back to the fort.

Billy turned toward the house. "They must be all watching TV because she hasn't been in her bedroom for a long time."

Billy did not have on a white T-shirt, or at least he had covered it with something darker. I wanted to ask him if he had been here before and if he had tried windows in any other houses besides the Twambleys. I wondered if he had tried to look in on Debbie. I was hoping he had because then not only would I not have to feel bad about spying on Sandy, but also I would have a partner.

"What do you want to do?" Billy made it sound like we had been on an adventure together and now that Tamara was unavailable, we would be doing something else. I knew I didn't want to go home. I had already considered staying on Billy's patio but not tonight. I wanted to mess around with Tamara first and then decide where I would be sleeping. What if Tamara would sneak me into her room?

"I'm going to stick around for a while, then go back home."

Billy didn't have a jacket so he was getting cold and that was the only thing he hated more than being hungry. "See you tomorrow."

I was relieved that he was leaving, but it didn't really solve anything. I didn't look forward to staying in the fort all night by myself, but I didn't have any ideas of how to get Tamara's attention without alerting her parents. If they saw me in their backyard, they were sure to call Mom, or maybe the police.

I walked to where Billy had come from around the house and tripped on a branch. I fell on my stomach with enough of a blow to knock the wind out of me. Slowly I raised myself to my knees and began to pray. I prayed that God would make Tamara come outside so I could see her. I also prayed that I could go live with the Bodenhamers. While I was at it, I asked that Billy and I be allowed to beat the twins the next time we played football in the street. Finally I prayed that I could get back to Dayton by Christmas.

I was moving on to other prayer topics, when the back door opened and their dog came out barking. I didn't think he had sensed me, but I couldn't be sure. I looked around the corner and could see he was barking at something on the other side of the fence. Maybe Billy. Standing in the rectangle of light made by the doorway was Tamara. She had on shorts and some loose top, probably a sweatshirt. Her hair was tied back in an unkempt ponytail so it puffed out on each side.

I didn't say anything because I was afraid she would scream. I wished I had written a note that I had left on the back porch so she would pick it up, look all dreamy and in love and then, in the Norton tradition, whisper my name loudly.

"Tamara?" I whispered too softly for her to hear.

"Scrabble, what are you barking at?" She took a few steps toward the dog, and he ran past her into the house. She stood for a moment looking in the direction of the canyon, tuned my way, and went back in. I could hear her turn the lock on the door.

Even with a jacket on I was starting to get a little cold. The hulking plant behind me must have been an orange tree because I could smell sweet blossoms. I was pretty sure I was outside Tamara's window because I could see a window in the house next door even with the tree there. I couldn't think of any movie or TV show that could offer an idea of how to contact her except for Cyrano de Bergerac and in that case the woman was on a balcony above him. Guys in the past had it so much easier. I wasn't even sure what I would say to her. "Want to go back to the fort to screw around?" "I love you. Will you let me prove it to you in the fort?" "The fort is real nice this time of night." I wished I were older or smarter. Or had an older brother to ask. Somehow being with Tamara had seemed like a perfect solution to Mom and Dad and everything. I had no plan B.

I walked slowly by the glow of the TV and back into the canyon. A half-moon was out, so even though this part of the canyon wasn't that familiar, I didn't use my flashlight to get back to the fort. I thought I saw a light flickering inside and imagined Tamara had somehow gotten ahead of me and was making things romantic.

When I pushed open the door, I heard, "Ow," and watched it slam back closed.

"Billy?"

"Joey?"

"Yeah. What are you doing in there?"

He opened the door. "Can't you think of another question to ask me tonight?"

I shined my flashlight on him. "Yeah. Why do have my blanket on?"

He offered his hand to boost me up as a way of reply. "I didn't know it was yours." He handed it to me and pretended to shiver violently as a result.

"Why don't you have a jacket?" I said in a parent tone.

"Gee, Mommy, I must have forgot it. Will you fix me a hamburger or are you too busy cleaning the house?"

I threw the blanket at him and sat down leaning against the wall.

"What now, Sherlock?" He laughed, and I couldn't help smiling a little. "When were we last in here?"

"I don't know about you, but I was here a few days ago."

He could tell from the look on my face that I wished I hadn't said anything and that there was something juicy to learn.

"Oh, really. By yourself?" I could tell he was putting together the blanket and pillow with my visit to Tamara's.

"You and Tamara?"

"What's so amazing about that?" Now I was in a bind. If I didn't offer convincing details, he would never believe a girl that much older and taller and beautiful would have spent any time with me. If I did offer details, he might tell someone that would take it back to Debbie and Tamara.

"You're not going to tell me you did it?" Every boy in the world knew the pronoun referent for "it" in that sentence. And every boy knew that the way Billy asked the question meant he *hadn't* done "it," so I might be able to make him believe I had. Then again, he had all those *Playboy* magazines, and if he had actually read some, he might know a lot more about "it" even if he had no personal experience.

"Tamara and I were here and talked about some stuff."

"Some stuff? Talked? Only?" He rubbed his stomach and patted his head. "I am such an athlete." Then, to add proof to his declaration, he patted his stomach and rubbed his head.

"Look, I can't go into it." I just wanted him gone now.

"Remember when we were all here."

"All who?"

"You know, the twins and us. I was surprised they didn't bring their trophies with them, like 'show and tell' in third grade."

I put the pillow behind me and straightened up against the wall. I did remember. I couldn't go to sleep because I was so jealous of their success. "So?"

"I mean, they could talk about nothing else. Unfortunately, they have a lot to talk about when it comes to sports."

The last thing I wanted to do tonight was to talk about the twins, my earlier prayer notwithstanding. I decided to keep quiet and hoped Billy would get the hint to leave.

"She is really righteous looking. Even if she wasn't stacked, which of course she is." He winked at me like this would get me to talk about her.

"Shut up. Don't talk that way about her." I was spoiling for a fight and, though it would be foolish to start one with Billy, I just didn't care.

"I got here first." Billy looked hurt. He probably wouldn't have stayed the night anyway: no food and not enough cover. But I just needed him to leave now before I wailed on him.

"Okay. Geez, Joey. I'm sorry about your father, but you don't have to—" He didn't finish because we heard a knock.

"Oh, I see how it is." He was smiling so broadly I thought his cheeks might cover his ears. He assumed it was Tamara, and I was sure.

"Joey?" It was a girl's voice, but it didn't sound like Tam.

"Joey? Are you in there?" I could tell the voice was angry, so I knew who it was.

"Go away. I'm all right."

Debbie said, "Look, let me in. Let me tell you about Maw-Maw."

I immediately thought Mom had sent Debbie to get me back home, and I certainly wasn't going back just because Mom wanted me to.

Billy decided it was time for him to go and raised the door. "Look out," he said to Debbie and dropped down.

He didn't even say good-bye. I thought he might stay nearby to listen in on what Debbie had to say, but I didn't care now. I was almost glad to see Debbie and, if I hadn't been so proud, I would have asked her how she was dealing with everything.

"Look, buster, I'm not trying to get you to come back home. I even thought of coming down here myself. I just think you should know that Maw-Maw decided to go back to the desert."

"What?"

Debbie climbed into the fort and closed the door. "Boy, all the conveniences of home." She wiped her hands on her pants and pulled the zipper of her jacket up to her neck. "Maw-Maw and Mom had it out. Maw-Maw said that Mom had no right to go on and on about Laura when she was anything but nice to Dad. Mom reminded Maw-Maw of all the times Dad had kept her out of the kitchen and how he resented her taking Mom's place." She scooted against the opposite wall. "This is nothing new, but Mom asked Maw-Maw why she stayed around here if things were not the way she liked, so Maw-Maw said she wasn't planning to stay."

I didn't know what to say. Maw-Maw was a bit strict about God and church, but she was also someone I could talk to. "Maybe I could go with her."

"Right. And leave me alone with the Witch of the East. No way, Toto." She crawled to the trap door and pulled it up. "I just thought you might want to say good-bye before she leaves again."

"Thanks." I meant it and watched her lower herself down like a gymnast.

She took off her jacket and handed it to me. "It might get chilly tonight."

I think that was about the nicest thing she had done for me up to that time. I wanted to tell her how much that meant to me, but I couldn't. "Thanks. I'll be okay." I had to start doing stuff for myself, especially if I decided not to go back home.

"By the way, you know how the Carrolls always act like they are God's answer to the perfect family? I saw their Mom with this other guy at the drive-in. They were making out."

"How do you know it was her?"

"Because she walked by our car on the way to the bathroom. And she looked great. Real sexy top and skin-tight pants. See you sometime."

I slammed the door and sat on it, as if someone was going to try to break in. Geez, what's going on? All we ever heard about the Carrolls was how devoted they were to Jesus and how all their strictness with the twins was just a reflection of the parents' strictness with themselves. What if Captain Carroll knows? He might make her walk the plank.

I was now hungry and cold and lonely. It didn't look like Tamara was going to show up. And I didn't want to sleep on the wood floor. I thought of leaving the blanket and pillow in case I wanted to come again and I more easily could carry a pad or something soft to sleep on without having to bring the other stuff. I folded up the blanket and set the pillow on top of it. I opened the "treasure chest" and found only a bag with a half dozen or so Cheetos. I would have gotten pretty cold by morning anyway.

I pulled up the door and jumped down.

"Ow. God, Joey, what are you trying to do?"

Tamara was on the ground, and I was on top of her.

"Are you okay? I didn't see you."

She stood up brushing off her white pants. She had on a letterman's jacket with white sleeves. I couldn't make out the color of the body, but if it was from the high school where she and Debbie went, then it was maroon. I supposed that meant she had a boyfriend, so I immediately hated the jacket that I would do anything to earn.

"You really know how to welcome a gal. Thank God, you don't weigh much."

I suppose she could have said something crueler, but I doubt it. I wanted to punch her in the face and ask her how skinny my fist felt.

"Joey, was that you in our backyard?"

Should I tell her it was Billy? If I admitted it was me, would she think it was weird? If she didn't know who it was, why did she come down here? "What do you mean?"

"Scamper heard something and I came out to check, but I didn't see anybody? I thought maybe you had come to see me."

She was taller than Mom, probably Dad, too. Her nose seemed thinner and longer at night. With the right lighting, she might look like a witch, albeit beautiful. She smelled of citrus, orange or lemon, and sounded way too sexy for her age at night when I couldn't see her lips all that clearly.

"Why don't you come home with me?"

By now I had completely forgotten about being cold or hungry. I had forgotten that Maw-Maw was probably leaving early tomorrow. Most important I had forgotten about Dad, which probably was the main reason I had been in her backyard anyway.

"Okay."

She took my hand and led me up the trail to her house. Scamper was already in the backyard, barking and jumping all over her. She opened the back door for me and led me past her parents, who were watching *Bonanza*, into the kitchen. Her mother followed us and asked if I was hungry.

"A little." I was starving.

"Would a hot dog be okay?"

I nodded and watched her go to the refrigerator. She put a single wiener in a skillet and fired up the burner below it. Tamara was sitting next to me stroking my head, like I was a puppy that had been snatched from its mother.

Mrs. Cohen asked if my mother knew where I was.

"I think so. I mean, my sister knows I was in the canyon, but she doesn't know I'm here."

I was hoping they would ask me to stay and had no extra bedrooms. "I was on my way home when Tamara came by the fort."

Tamara reddened and nodded. She didn't say she had heard something in the backyard. "Debbie said Joey often went to the fort when he wanted to get away and asked me to look out for him."

I looked at her to see if she was lying, but she looked straight at her mother.

Apparently there was a commercial playing now because Mr. Nathan came into the kitchen, too. "Smells

265

good in here." He just barely made it through the doorway without having to duck.

He reminded me of the guys who came for Maw-Maw, and I remembered she was going back to the desert.

Mr. Cohen had on a robe over pajamas and fuzzy house slippers. He had a goatee with eyebrows almost as thick as his beard. If he weren't smiling, he could look pretty menacing. "How are you doing, young man?"

"Okay."

He nodded, looking at me like he knew I was lying and sat down across from me.

"I hear you're a pretty good pitcher." I looked at Tamara who smiled and shrugged. She could only have heard from Debbie, which meant Debbie thought it was important enough to tell her.

"I only made alternate."

He looked puzzled.

"The all-star team. I was kind of next in line."

"Congratulations. I never learned to play baseball when I was young, but my father loved the Dodgers. When they were in Brooklyn. We went every week."

"My Dad likes the Yankees. We watch a game almost every weekend." I realized what I was saying and got up. "Sorry, I have to go. My mother will be worried."

I heard Mrs. Cohen say that the hot dog was ready as I went out the front door. Tamara came out the door after me, but I realized she wasn't interested in me for the reasons I wanted. She was just like everyone else. She wanted to make me feel better by being nice to me. I wanted her to be nice to me by having sex with me, but that wasn't going to be happening tonight.

CHAPTER TWENTY-TWO

I ENTERED MY ROOM the way I'd gotten out. It took a while to get all the panes back in place. I almost broke one that got stuck halfway into the metal slot, but I was able to finish about midnight without anyone but Debbie knowing I had been out.

I was real tired in the morning and, by faking a lot of sneezing and making my voice sound nasally, I hoped to get Mom to let me stay home. Debbie knew I was faking but gave me a look like she admired my acting. Some woman came to pick up Maw-Maw. I said good-bye after asking if I could come visit her in the desert.

Maw-Maw looked at Mom, who said, "As long as he doesn't miss any school."

"But they have a school there," I said.

"You can visit on a weekend," she said in a harsh voice. "Now, finish getting dressed."

At school, I found solace in my classes. I had always done well in math, but had to work extra hard to concentrate since my photo and the bio of Dad were still outside the door in the hall. We were reviewing common dominators and somehow being able to find them quickly was comforting. I had the next-to-youngest Twambley girl, Carrie, in my class, who kept looking at me. She had these eerie blue eyes because one was slightly darker than the other. Her eyebrows were light, but her eyelashes were dark and so long they looked fake. If she hadn't known about Dad, I might have thought she was interested in me.

During PE, I held my own during dodge ball. A little anger can make that ball really go. I eliminated Greg the Bully in the first round. He was so surprised that I could throw the ball that hard that he bowed to me on his way out of the circle, a fitting ending to the school day.

I had been so focused on my classes that I forgot Maw-Maw was gone until I got home. Mom had apparently decided I was old enough to be by myself or was so flummoxed by losing both Dad permanently and her mother temporarily that she forgot. I put some Velveeta cheese on saltines, one of Dad's favorite snacks, and made myself a root beer float. I watched Popeye cartoons while I ate. I hated the way his forearms were bigger than the rest of him, but loved the way he beat up on Brutus to protect Olive Oyl. During one commercial I looked for a can of spinach in the cupboard and made a promise to myself to ask Mom for some the next time she went to the store. I wished I hadn't thought of that because Dad did all the grocery shopping.

I went back to watching TV and ate some protein pills with milk while Gene Autry sang to his horse. Even though they usually lost, my favorite characters were always the Indians, especially the Apaches, so fierce and stoic. I had homework, and I wanted to start my pitching program—until I found someone to catch me, I could at least throw through the tire—but I didn't want to do anything now. If I was lucky Debbie would have another rehearsal or would go over to someone's house after school, and I would be by myself until Mom came home.

As soon as I had that thought, the telephone rang. Gloria, I hoped. If it wasn't her, I'd go ahead and call now even though it was the expensive time. I wanted to find out the exact day she and her dad were coming out to LA. I was feeling better already.

"Hello?"

"Honey, are you okay? Mrs. Carroll said she would look out for you as soon as she got home. Is she there yet?" I couldn't have been more disappointed.

"Mom, I'm fine." Partially true, since I was much better on my own than with someone else around. "I'm just getting ready to start my homework." Partially true, too, unless the twins and Billy wanted to play football or I could find another program on TV to watch. The doorbell rang, followed by pounding. "Just a minute, Mom." I went to the door. Billy had a football and was motioning for me to come out. "I'm on the phone," I whispered.

Back to Mom. "I'll be okay. I fixed myself a snack and everything."

"Okay. Be nice to Mrs. Carroll."

"Sure." Debbie said she was real nice to some guy who was not the captain, so maybe she'd be nice that way to me. She just happened to be the youngest-looking mother on the block. I told Mom someone was at the door and hung up before she had a chance to say good-bye.

"Come on. The twins don't have any chores to do. Can you believe it?"

"I'll be right out."

I went to my room and took off my school clothes and put on some shorts and a white T-shirt, just like Billy. The twins were pushing weights in their garage while Billy and I tossed the football back and forth.

"Last night. Something, huh?"

"Yeah, something." I guess he was referring to both of us being in Tamara's yard at the same time. Maybe we could make it a regular thing, meeting in the backyards of bitching girls. We could form a club of two, the scopophiliacs, Scopes for short. Even Debbie might not know what it meant. Billy *certainly* wouldn't, but he would like the nickname.

The twins walked over, their arms and chests pumped up. They seemed extra serious. Billy shocked us all by suggesting he and I be on the same team. I looked at him to see if he was kidding. Or had a can of spinach handy. He wasn't smiling, but just kept staring back at the twins.

Terry started to shake his head, but Jerry stopped him. "You're on. We'll kick off first." He stood by the manhole at the bottom of the cul-de-sac, expecting us to walk uphill, thereby giving us the advantage of both receiving and going downhill.

"Nah, you guys go downhill." Billy looked grim, like he'd just been forced to clean the bathroom toilet and wanted to get it over with.

Jerry shrugged as if to say he'd tried to be nice, but we wouldn't let him. They walked slowly uphill, talking to each other as they went. They like winning so much that they didn't want to take a chance at leaving out discussing strategy in case being faster and generally more talented wasn't enough as usual.

Jerry threw the ball way up in the air. For a moment I thought it might hit the telephone lines. Billy grabbed it and ran right at them. We always played two-handed touch because, one, our parents wouldn't have sanctioned tackle, and two, even the toughest guys didn't play tackle on asphalt. He barreled right into Terry, who was so stunned he only got one hand on him. Jerry was next but didn't want to be knocked down and didn't get close enough to tag Billy until he was already by him. Billy wasn't fast enough to make it to the goal line, which was the street corner, but he was only a few yards short when Jerry caught up to him.

I was dumfounded. Billy had almost scored, but more important he had intimidated them. With all their weight lifting, they were pretty muscular, but Billy, because of his size and all the work he did on his car and the family car, was quite strong himself. He still wasn't smiling when we huddled to call the first play. He suggested I pass to him after he had run straight into Jerry, who was playing back to cover the pass. He said just throw it at his back and he would turn around in time to catch it. It didn't work the first time, I just hit him in the back, but he said he wanted us to look inept. Ironically, Jerry had given him enough space that if our timing had been better, he could have scored since he was already over the goal line when I threw the pass. The next time, he said he would do the same thing but that I should lob it over his head because he knew Terry wouldn't expect us to try anything different and, further, he wouldn't expect that Billy, who was way slower than Terry, would try to run past him. He said give a quick arm fake as he turned toward me. Billy hiked the ball, almost ran over Jerry, who was rushing, and ran right up to Terry before he stopped and turned to face me. I did a wimpy pump fake, but it worked, and he took off past Terry. I overthrew him, but he still caught the ball. Touchdown.

We looked at each other and then at the twins, who were walking disconsolately down the street to get ready for the kick-off. They ended up beating us again, but we learned something. They could be unsettled by aggressiveness, by guys who weren't intimidated by their prowess. We had a new respect for ourselves. I think they did, too. When all the stuff came out about their mother, and their parents had separated, they lost to us in a Wiffle ball game, too. It was a good lesson to me. Attitude can conquer anything. I felt sorry for them because it became obvious that they were devastated by any lack of success in sports. They were college scholarship material, but they never again had the same swagger around us that I used to envy in them.

We had a quiet dinner that night, just the three of us. Debbie and I retired to our rooms to do homework, an activity that would guarantee Mom leaving us alone. She had a meeting at church anyway.

Later that night, there was a knock at our front door. It was before bedtime but still pretty late. Leslie Twambley was at the door, still in her school uniform, plaid pleated skirt and plain white blouse. She had obviously been crying. "I know it's late, but could I talk to Debbie?" When I told Debbie, she looked as surprised as I was and came to the door.

"Hi." That's all she could say before she began crying again. They walked to Debbie's room and closed the door. I'm not proud of it, but I did my best to listen in. Just like I'd seen in the movies or a cartoon, I put a glass on the bathroom wall with my ear on the glass while standing in the tub, but either the walls were better built than Dad claimed or Debbie and Leslie were mostly whispering.

Leslie stayed for about an hour and left before Mom got back. After Debbie escorted her out the door, she joined me in the kitchen. I was having some Oreos and milk and offered her some.

She took a cookie but waved off the milk. She was shaking her head. "Boy, you never know." And she shook her head some more while she had another cookie. This time she separated one side from the other and licked off the filling first.

"What?" I said, trying to sound like it didn't matter if she told me or not.

She looked at me like she was sizing up my reliability. I think she also calculated that with Dad dying I deserved trust that she normally wouldn't grant me. "If I tell you, you must promise to tell no one, not Mom, your buddies or anybody. Not even Gloria."

I felt proud that she mentioned Gloria and that she mentioned her last. It was an acknowledgement that Gloria and I had a real relationship.

"Leslie is having a baby. Or she could have but doesn't want to."

At some point in everyone's life, you learn that things are not what they seem to be, and I'm not just talking about Santa Claus and Disneyland. Something happens that removes the sweetness and light that seem to cover everything and have obscured the darkness. I remember the first time I saw the street being torn up to put in sewer pipes. I was eight or nine, and I was shocked. I knew streets were paved by humans and that the asphalt or concrete had dirt and rock underneath. I knew that the street was not some permanent fixture like a mountain or the earth, but I didn't realize how easily that pavement could be ripped up and replaced. I guess it should

273

have been encouraging to me. I could have seen it as hopeful that a problem could be fixed so easily. But it had the opposite effect. It made me realize how transient everything was, that you could depend on nothing always being there. I began to understand why words like "everlasting" and "eternal" came up so often in church. At the time the effect was to make me believe that all these things I had assumed about life and people were just not true. Some of the strictest religious people had affairs, and others just as devout couldn't keep their teenagers from getting pregnant. And your Dad could die before you grew up and left home.

I was musing on something close to this but not quite as articulately when Mom came home. She knocked on my door and again waited until I answered before she opened it. "Would you come into the kitchen? I want to show you something."

Reluctantly I followed her. On the table was a box that seemed to be moving. I could hear a soft whimpering, like a child who has been crying for a long time and has run out of steam for the full-blown sobbing. I looked at Mom who was beaming. "I know it will take a lot of care and we'll all have to pitch in, but, well, see what you think."

She stepped back and let me struggle to undo the crisscrossed flaps. Inside was a fluffy round blond puppy with a dark black nose and matching eyes. He, not that I had checked for sex yet, looked happy to see me. I looked at Mom who nodded approval to pick him up.

"The Kramers' golden retriever had puppies and they brought two of them to church tonight. It still needs its shots and we can take, ah, *him* (she was looking at him as I held him just under his front legs) back if we can't take care of him."

I pulled him close to me as if someone was threatening to kill him.

"It seems that Puppy ought to have a puppy." Mom was referring to a nickname that I was called in the first few years after a dog, which Debbie had found in the street and we had tried to nurse back to health for a week, died. It was my first encounter with the death of someone I loved.

I have to admit that Mom was right, if her idea was to give me something that would get my mind off Dad for a while. We called him Earl at first and then Duke once he was housebroken because both Debbie and I loved the Gene Chandler song. Also, the puppy was so small and roly-poly and furry that calling him an adult-sounding name was funny.

I was devoted to the dog and got irritated if anyone else even attempted to feed him. Mom let me keep him in my room, which meant I got to clean up the newspapers he peed and pooped on until we got him house-trained. It also meant that he slept with me, at the foot of my bed, inside the space formed by my curled up legs. During the day he stayed in the garage in an area Debbie and I fenced off with some leftover chain link.

Had I been older, I might have been more reluctant to let in what would hurt so much when it inevitably was taken away, but at the time, I was completely smitten.

I was the toast of the neighborhood when we went out front. Leslie was one of the first to pick him up, and I wondered if she was thinking of her baby when she cooed to him. Billy wanted to call him Furball and laughed at everything he did. The twins came over and petted him with the caution of people who have had to live through the death of a pet. Their cat was run over by a delivery truck.

Earl was not a full-bred golden retriever but mixed with a cocker spaniel, which made him even cuter, if that was possible for a puppy. Everyone was on our front lawn wrestling and petting him. I told them he knew Spanish so everyone started using their limited vocabulary (mostly food words like taco and burrito) on him. It was the second time in a week that a lot of the neighbors gathered at our house.

CHAPTER TWENTY-THREE

MOM LEFT ME ALONE the rest of the week, mostly. We were all preoccupied with Earl and didn't even watch much TV in the evening. I was sorry Maw-Maw wasn't here to see him. She used to talk about her family's coonhound bitch (it was the first time I learned you could use the word without cussing). The dog chased down raccoons Maw-Maw's family killed for food. Also, she gave them pups that they sold to their neighbors.

Debbie had read that to housebreak Earl someone had to take him out whenever it looked like he was ready to pee. She agreed to do it in the afternoon, but it was up to me at night since he was sleeping on my bed. A few of the times that I tried to get him outside in time, he peed on me and the carpet. Mom, always super neat and super clean, did not complain though she spent hours de-staining a bunch of places in the hall and living room. At first I hated the urine smell on the emergency newspapers in my room, but since it was associated with Earl, I came to kind of like it the way people who own horses feel about horse poop and hay.

On Sunday afternoon, Mom asked if I would help her prepare food for the returning missionaries' dinner, and I said yes. I felt sorry for her and grateful for Earl, so it didn't seem like too great of a sacrifice.

But after a few choice comments by Debbie, I felt like a hopeless wuss, destined to be a momma's boy for the rest of my life. I imagined myself in the future coming home with gray hair, about Maw-Maw's age now, and Mom giving me a snack of milk and homemade cookies. Then I would watch cartoons until dinner that she had fixed after finding out what I wanted. She and I would go to movies together and share a tub of buttered popcorn. I would never marry because none of the prospective brides could ever measure up to Mom's incessant coddling.

Not that Mom was anything but businesslike and in charge when she was doing chores or fixing meals, like this one for the missionaries. For instance, the iceberg lettuce chunks had to be a perfectly symmetrical eighth of a head. I only got four sections out of the first because I had to keep adjusting the edges to look like the other ones until there was nothing left of four pieces. I was in charge of cutting the green beans, too. They were a little easier to make a uniform length.

Today Mom talked a lot while we were working and, for part of it, Debbie listened in. Mom was always more relaxed when she was busy. She was reminiscing about her dating life and told us that she was so popular in Beaumont when she was a young working girl that some of the guys would play poker games for the right to call her. They had a gentleman's agreement that no one else would call except the guy who won. She said that Dad had lost once but didn't keep his promise to the other guys and called her anyway.

"I first saw him in his army uniform. He was one of the few to graduate from college and therefore one of the few to be an officer. Major Sam Norton. In those days, being an army officer was like being a doctor or a lawyer." Mom was opening a can of cream of mushroom soup to pour over the green beans with this dreamy look in her eye. I tried to remember the last time Mom looked like that around Dad. "After the war, World War II, your father would come by when I wasn't there and so charm your grandmother that she would bake cookies and pies and whole dinners for him to take with him to the night shift at the oil refinery. I'd walk in on them, and she'd be giggling like a school girl."

Debbie had had enough. "So what happened?"

Mom was startled back to the present, having forgotten Debbie was there, and dropped the can opener. "What?"

"What happened," Debbie said a little too loudly, "because Dad wasn't getting anything special from you or Maw-Maw here?"

I don't think Debbie intended what she said to have sexual overtones, but, in the light of Laura, it had to for Mom. It may not have mattered at this point because Mom had had enough other problems with Dad that whatever did or did not happen in bed was just another nail in the coffin of their relationship.

"Now, Debbie, we don't need to upset Joey."

I was both surprised and honored. Did I now merit the special treatment previously reserved for Mom? Of course, I know now that what she really meant was don't upset her.

"Oh, get off it. You make it sound like you had no part in what happened."

Mom wheeled around to face Debbie, her mouth wide open.

Debbie was pouring it on now. "When did Dad ever get a modicum of respect from you or Maw-Maw?"

I would look up "modicum" later.

"And when did Maw-Maw ever get any appreciation from you or Dad?"

I couldn't tell if Mom agreed or if she was just intimidated like most of us were when in verbal combat with Debbie. All I know is that she didn't interrupt.

"Geez Louise. Maw-Maw's your mother, and she had to be quarantined in her room with that tiny TV you guys bought for her." Debbie pulled her hair back from her face and thrust her hands in the back pockets of her jeans. I thought she was about to start a fist fight with Mom and was giving Mom the courtesy of throwing the first punch.

Mom finally managed some defense. "I didn't send her off to some hippie commune. She's been talking about it for years. She only stayed because you and Joey needed taking care of."

"Bullshit."

Debbie had crossed the line now. Mom took a lot of guff from Debbie, and it was around Maw-Maw we were most careful about our language, but Mom never used cuss words, and she expected the same from her children.

"Go to your room." Mom had thrust her arm and first finger at shoulder height toward the hallway like a queen in a Shakespearean play pointing off stage.

I thought Debbie might make things worse by laughing, knowing Mom couldn't really make her do anything she didn't want to do. Instead, Debbie stood still for a moment before she put her head close to Mom's arm and looked down it like she was trying to get a sight on where Mom was pointing. She walked to the hall doorway and turned around.

"You can only blame other people for so long. Pretty soon even Joey won't be left to defend you."

Once Debbie left the room, I knew I should put my arm around Mom and tell her that I would always stand by her. But I couldn't make myself do it.

Mom said nothing the whole time she put together the salad and covered the beans for baking. She then began heating the Crisco for the chicken. She asked me to put the chicken pieces in the paper bag to which she had already added flour, pepper, and salt. She knew I liked that part of the preparation best. I put a few pieces in the bag and shook them until I had gone through the four chickens she had cut up. She said nothing that didn't relate to what we were doing.

"Thanks. I can take care of the rest." She looked sad. Was she finally feeling the loss of Dad? Or was she now mourning the fierceness of her daughter's disloyalty? I assume it was a little of both. Mom's appearance could change radically according to her feelings. Now she looked like the average dumpy housewife rather than the gorgeous date men use to compete over just to call her up.

Boys need their mothers to make them feel safe, safe enough to be willing to not only try risky ventures away from home but to leave altogether. I didn't feel safe with Mom, and all my adventures came out of desperation to save myself from a home that seemed only to offer accusations and neediness.

Mom didn't ask me to go with her to church, and I didn't offer beyond helping her to load the trunk with all the food. Had she asked, I would have used the trump card of homework to get a reprieve. As soon as she was gone and the music in Debbie's room was cranked up, I went into Mom's bedroom to call Tamara.

I have heard stand-up routines on what guys go through before a phone call to a girl, whether for a date or just a feel-her-out chat. The phone call itself is almost anticlimactic. So I screwed up my courage and picked up the receiver.

One small problem: I didn't have her number. Now I would for the first time do what boys (and men) all over the United States did: search the phone book for possible numbers. I used her last name, Cohen, and the name of the street, Cabrillo Mesa Dr. There weren't that many Cohens and only one on that street.

I practiced dialing with the hang-up button depressed. I also practiced what I would say. I was sitting on the bed, on Dad's side, and facing the door in case Debbie needed a break from James Brown and Sam Cooke and decided to come looking for me.

"Hello, may I please speak to Tamara?" Too polite. "Hi, is Tamara in?" Sounds like a business call. "Hi, could Tamara come to the phone. I won't keep her long." Too apologetic.

When the music got louder, I figured Debbie must have opened her door. I could hear the refrigerator open, so I hightailed it to my room before Debbie asked me what I was doing in our parents' room. I sat on the sofa and looked at the dark window, wondering if someone was looking in.

"What're ya doing?" I let out a shriek, and then waited for her to make fun of me. Miracle of miracles, she actually apologized for scaring me and said if I needed anything just knock on her door. She was closing her door behind her before I could double-check to see if that was really my sister.

I felt more courageous now until I realized that there could be more than one Cohen on Cabrillo Mesa because Tamara's family might have an unlisted number. Then I had a comforting thought: if it were the wrong number, I wouldn't have lost anything.

I pulled up a chair to avoid sitting on the bed. I had closed the phone book when I heard Debbie and had to find the number all over again. That made me nervous once more, so I had to hurry up before I completely lost my nerve. I dialed slowly, asking God to at least do this one small thing for me while I waited to circle the last number on the dial.

"Hello."

It was Tamara. It never occurred to me she might answer. Now, I had nothing to say.

"Hello? Who is this?"

"It's me. I mean, Joey."

"Oh, how are you?"

She sounded truly concerned, like Gloria or Mr. Bodenhamer might rather than like Debbie's friend who had done stuff with me in the fort.

"Okay."

She whispered now. "Do you want to meet at the fort?"

That should have been enough to make me a believer in prayer, but I wasn't thinking theologically then. "What? I mean, yes," I said and then crunched my face in anger at what I said next. "Unless it's too much trouble."

"Now?"

I heard a Debbie response in my head: "No, next Christmas." Out loud I said, "That would be great."

"Okay," she said, "see you soon," and hung up.

This was too much. I kept saying thank you, Jesus, as I started planning how to get out of the house undetected. I told Debbie that I had just been on the phone (at least I started with the truth) to Billy and he invited me over. He and I had never talked on the phone, but Debbie didn't know that. She did a parent thing and said I shouldn't stay too late.

My heart was beating so loud, I was sure she could hear it even with her music on. My hands were sweating while I tried to figure out what to take. The same pillow and blanket seemed too boring. I remembered Debbie's new sleeping bag she used when she stayed up all night in line to get tickets for Ray Charles.

I grabbed a box of vanilla wafers, stuffed it inside Debbie's sleeping bag, and rushed out the back door. Halfway down the canyon I realized I had forgotten the pillow but didn't want to risk going back. Besides, I wanted to get their first. Tamara must have already been planning to come before I called because she had candles (some already lit) and her own sleeping bag. She had a pillow, too.

"I'm glad you called." She looked a little more serious than I would have preferred, but still looked beautiful, even with only candles for light.

She used the melting wax from the ones already lit to make a base for the others. She had created a half circle with her sleeping bag in the middle. I figured we could put out any candle that tipped over before it ignited the wood floor but was a little nervous anyway. She had trouble striking one of the matches, so I offered to help. Mine struck fire immediately, and I lit the candle she held out for me.

I moved close enough to be able to kiss her, but I wasn't tall enough to reach her lips. I jumped and pecked at her, but pushed a little too hard and we hit teeth instead of lips.

"Ow. What are you trying to do?"

She stepped back and looked at me in the dim light. I tried to look bigger by tightening my chest and biceps.

"Joey, why did you think I came down here?"

I was plenty confused now. A gorgeous older girl lets me touch her the last time and eagerly agrees to see me again and now she wants to know what I want?

"I thought we could talk about why you don't think Jesus is the Messiah." Sometimes I hate Debbie's influence over me.

She slapped me, looked at the shocked expression on my face, and immediately apologized.

I put my hand to my cheek where she had touched me. I tried my best to keep from crying, but I couldn't. I wanted to tell her that I wasn't crying out of pain because I wasn't. It wasn't out of shame either. I was crying because I didn't know what I could expect or how to ask for it. I believe now that if I said I wanted to sleep with her, she would have obliged, out of pity. I think she might have said I could have whatever I wanted. Then all I knew was that I was lonely and turned on by a girl who could easily match the beauty of any actress I'd seen on TV or in the movies.

She pulled me to her, making sure my face rested against her breasts. I thought she was going to offer to nurse me for a moment.

"Look, let's spread out the blankets and lie down. I'll give you a massage to make you feel better."

I was bursting out of my pants and had to sneak a quick adjustment to avoid pain as I lay down. She spread her sleeping bag out and crouched down, patting next to her on the bag. I went to my knees like I was kneeling before an altar. I felt a lot more like worshipping her than worshipping God, the one who killed my father.

"Relax." She pulled me down on my back and began to stroke my forehead and cheeks. I wanted to pull her down and kiss her like I'd seen some actor do, maybe Steve McQueen. I would have given anything to be older or bigger or taller or heavier, something, anything but my puny self.

She began to move down my chest and into the space between the buttons on my shirt. I quivered in excitement, and she took if for a chill. "Here, I'll get the other bag." She stood above me and unzipped it. I imagined she was unzipping her pants. She came down to me with it over her head like it was the cape of a vampire. I turned on my stomach to try to avoid going off in my pants, but I couldn't stop. She stroked my back in slow circular motions and hummed a familiar song that I couldn't quite place.

"Joey, do you want to touch me again?" I was definitely in full shiver now. I felt like I had a fever and couldn't answer because my teeth were chattering so much. She lay on top of me, and the heft of her body made me feel secure. She kissed the back of my neck, and her warm lips gave me goose bumps.

When I woke up, she was gone. I must have been sleeping for a while because I had a crick in my neck. The lemony scent of her hair lingered on the sleeping bag, and I ached to have her beside me, or on top. I was overcome with desire and would have given anything for her to be my first experience. I felt incredibly alone and heard a dismal voice say that this is just the beginning. First Dad, then Tamara. Gloria would be next.

I started to get up and then felt this overwhelming fury. I wanted to tear the fort down. I beat on the sideboards and stomped on the floor. I wished I had one of those spiked steel balls from medieval times and could swing it around until the walls started to collapse, like I was my own wrecking crew. I had never been that angry. Over and over in my head and sometimes out loud I shouted how unfair everything was. I got all kinds of crazy thoughts about sneaking into Tamara's bedroom or burning down the fort or getting Dad's derringer and putting it to my head.

I didn't seriously entertain any of those ideas very long, but I had to do something or go somewhere. Anywhere. Just not back home.

I opened the trap door and jumped down. I started walking down the canyon. I looked back at the fort. I could see a dim light through the cracks. It occurred to me that I should go back and put out all the candles, but I kept walking, wondering if I could make it to the beach before dawn.

CHAPTER TWENTY-FOUR

BY THE TIME I got to Friar's road, I was cold. It was then that I thought about Earl. He was still in the garage when I left and would be sleeping with me in my bed by now. I knew Debbie would look after him, but I was more concerned with whether he would remember me when I got back than if he would be taken care of. But I just couldn't go back to living with Mom.

After a city bus whizzed by, I ran across the road and found my way into the streambed that ran through Mission Valley. It was mostly dry, and the moonlight helped me avoid the few pools of water. I had never been down here at night, but I wasn't scared. So far, anyway. I was still angry at the unfairness of it all, feeling that I wanted to hurt someone or be hurt myself. Someone ought to be punished.

I saw a shadowy figure above my left shoulder. It swooped just a few yards above my head, an enormous flying body. Silhouetted against the moon I could see it was an owl, with the eerie silence of his flapping wings. Coming from its apparent destination, I could hear the hoo-hooing of what was probably its mate. How long would it take him to get to the ocean?

If I decided against the beach, I had two other destinations in mind: Tijuana and Mr. Bodenhamer's. Even though I was walking pretty fast, I wasn't building up enough heat to combat the cold. I knew I was headed in the right direction, but that meant a lot more walking. Tijuana was even further than the beach, and neither of them offered immediate warmth. I became less focused on what angered me and more on how to get out of the cold, and maybe to get something to eat, too.

I decided on Mr. B's and immediately felt better. I had been there enough times with the Royal Ambassadors to know where he lived, just off Linda Vista Road, a few miles beyond our church. This time I would be approaching it from the other direction, but I remembered that the corner had some palm trees.

I walked up the embankment onto Friar's Road and turned left to cross under the freeway. Ulric was the first street heading north from Friar's. I didn't know what time it was, but it had to be past midnight since there was little traffic and most of the houses I passed were dark, except for a couple of porches. A dog barked, and I thought about Earl again. If Debbie didn't take good care of him, I'd just kill her the next time I saw her. When I got to the corner of Ulric and Linda Vista Road, I was still a ways from our church, which meant it was even further to his house. Fortunately I saw no patrol cars.

I sank down on a bus bench and hugged myself for warmth. I had put on a baseball windbreaker to go down to the fort, but it was too skimpy to keep me warm now. I was now about as far from Mr. B's as I was from home. I didn't know which would be worse, being discovered sneaking back into my room or to have to wake up the Bodenhamers.

I remembered Mr. B making a big deal of the passage in the Bible about taking in the stranger. He used to tell this World War II story about a French couple sheltering him from the Nazis when he was separated from his platoon. I hoped the principle also applied to people you already knew during peacetime.

I had decided that if Mr. B didn't want me I would go to Mexico or maybe Arizona. I had Gloria's number memorized, so I could still make contact with her. Maybe I could meet her in LA where her dad was going for the job interview. They could take me back to Texas with them.

A bus stopped in front of me and the door opened. I shook my head to indicate I didn't need a ride, but the driver motioned for me to come closer. "On your way home?"

I nodded slowly, a bit suspicious.

"No money?"

I nodded again.

"How far?"

I shrugged. "Just down the street."

"Come on."

I hesitated, but he waved me in impatiently. I watched him put some coins in the cash box. I sat on the seat behind him. In the middle of the last seat, the only other passenger was bouncing to some beat I couldn't hear.

The bus driver called me closer to him. "What's your name?"

"Joey."

"Okay, Joey. Your parents know you're out?"

I started to say I had only one parent now. "Not exactly."

"If I take you close to your house, you'll go straight there? I mean, you don't want me calling the police, do you?"

"No, sir," I said a little too loudly.

He had short hair with a handlebar mustache, like Buffalo Bill's, only his was black. An upper front tooth was silver. On his right forearm, he had a tattoo that rivaled Popeye's. "We'll get you home, son. And you stay close to me, away from Mr. Rhythm in the back." The guy was now tapping his feet like he was crushing invisible bugs.

I looked at the snapshot of the driver above the windshield. The man in the photo looked young enough he could have been his own son.

"You tell me when to stop."

I went to the seat opposite the driver so I could see out the front more easily. We were just passing our church, and I wanted to tell him it was my church, perhaps as a way to get him to believe me. I wasn't sure how much further Mr. B's house was, but I knew I could find it on foot. His street connected to the one we were on and started with "San." Just ahead I saw a trio of palms, like the three bears, one short, one tall, and one medium on the corner. "Here."

The guy in the back said, "What?" but didn't stop nodding his head and tapping the floor. He had now added some weird movement with his shoulders, but it was all in the same rhythm and looked cool, like some jazz player enjoying another band member's solo.

The bus stop was a few blocks from the corner of what turned out to be Santa Theresa Way. At least I remembered the saint part. The driver drove past the bus stop to the corner. I thanked him and made a mental note to be extra nice the next time I took the bus. The thought made me feel like I wasn't a moocher. I wondered if he knew Dad.

I remembered Mr. B's house having a hedge about my height. I was looking for the woodie in the driveway, but realized it might be in the garage. No houses on either side looked like his until I came to a house without a hedge but definitely Mr. B's car in the driveway just before the next cross street. I walked up to the car and could make out the pair of extra swim fins he always kept in the back.

I was cold and didn't want to walk all the way back home, but I didn't want to wake them up either. I also didn't want to sneak around looking in windows like some peeping Tom, which I had not yet admitted to being. I wished Billy were here to come up with ideas.

I sat on the porch and figured I might just stay here until they got up in the morning. Since Mr. B was one of the older lifeguards, he usually had an early shift, sometimes even leaving before dawn. I hoped Monday was one of those days.

As it turned out, I didn't have to worry about waking them up because their German shepherd started barking. I hadn't even made any noise, so he could have been barking at something else. Or maybe he could smell a stranger on the other side of the front door, but whatever the cause he was going crazy now. He was always friendly, even with lots of people he hadn't met, like a house full of us RAs. He was easy to like since he was a ringer for Rin Tin Tin. The Bodenhamers called him Rinty. This reminded me of Earl again, and I reassured myself that Debbie wouldn't take out on little E her anger at me.

"Heh, buddy, what's going on?" I could hear Mr. B 's voice. Rinty calmed down, so before they both went back to bed, I knocked on the door. That put the dog in a real frenzy. He was growling and sounding like those junkyard guard dogs. I was about to run when Mr. B opened the door. He was bent over because he was holding his dog by the collar. Rinty was baring his teeth, and I hoped Mr. B was as strong as he looked.

"Joey?"

My God, he wasn't sure who it was. Now I really was sorry I came.

"Heh, come in. Are you shivering?"

Until he said it, I didn't realize it that my arms were trembling and my jaw chattering. I bet the guy at the back of the bus would have been jealous. I wanted to say I was okay, but I couldn't get my mouth to cooperate.

Mr. B pulled me in and told me to stand there. Rinty had calmed down as soon as he realized Mr. B considered me a friend. "Just a minute."

He came back with a blanket that he wrapped around me. He turned on the light in the kitchen and looked at the clock. "Doing some street preaching tonight?" He had on a tan T-shirt and boxers with tiny pine trees. "Or are you delivering milk now for a few extra bucks?" He crossed his arms over his chest. "We like having visitors but normally when we're awake. Of course, I am awake now and have *you* to blame for it." He turned to Rinty, grabbed his head, and swung it back and forth, about which the dog grumbled goodheartedly.

"What brings you to our humble domain?"

"I'm running away."

"Hmmm." He looked at my shoes like he was Sherlock Holmes gathering evidence. "From whom?"

What did he mean, from whom? From my house. From my mother. From my sister. But not, of course, from Earl.

"We have a puppy. Duke of Earl. We decided to call him Earl until he's older and then call him Duke." Running away didn't sound so great when I was doing it without

Earl. "I'm not sure how I'll take care of him, but I'll figure it out later."

"I take it your mother doesn't know you are here?"

"I don't think she even knows I left the house."

He paced back and forth like I had asked him to invest in my company and he couldn't decide if I was a good risk. "Let's do this. I'm getting up in a few hours anyway. I'll let your mom know where you are as soon as I wake up. Again." He squinted at me. "I'll get you a pillow and another blanket for the couch. Can you sleep in your clothes?"

"Sure."

Rinty followed him down the hall. When he came back, he tossed the pillow and blanket at me.

"Nice catch," he said when I kept both from hitting the floor.

"How about I ask your mother if you can come to work with me? You'll have to get up in another three hours, but that way you can tell me then why you decided to visit us so early in the morning."

Now that I was warmer, I was yawning nonstop and would have agreed to anything. I nodded and he did, too. "Come on, Rin."

Had I been older, I would have seen the irony of sleeping on a sofa just like I did at home. If Earl could get along with Rinty and vice versa, I wondered if Mr. B would let the two of us stay here for a while. Though I was yawning continually, I couldn't go to sleep. I kept thinking about Earl and Tamara and Gloria. I imagined seeing Sandy in her room and the rest of the neighborhood boys, even Billy, watching at her window.

I must have slept some because I had a dream. In it Gloria and Tamara came to my room and, while Tamara made out with me, Gloria took Earl. She claimed Grandma said he needed to be in Dayton to be appreciated. Then Tamara and Gloria drove away with Earl, in the same convertible that Darin used to take Debbie to Galveston. Mom and Dad were on Grandma's porch waving to them like they were relatives leaving after a long visit.

When I woke up, I could see a light in the kitchen. It was Cindy. She had on panties and a short-sleeve shirt that did not cover her behind. The light came from the open refrigerator door. She was shuffling stuff around to get something in the back. I had a direct line to her butt.

Now there was no way I would be able to get to sleep until I did something, and I wasn't sure I could in their house. I hoped she would notice I was here and want to lie down with me. She drank what looked like some milk and went back down the hall.

I got up to see where her room was. I could hear running water and saw a light from under a door. I felt like my head was expanding and contracting with each heartbeat, like in a cartoon. The water stopped, and I heard the toilet seat cover hit the toilet. I stood there, feeling like a trespassing thief in a stranger's home. Rinty came bounding from the other end of the hall (maybe he slept with her) and started barking. Facing him, I backed slowly into the living room and ducked under the covers. If Cindy had not followed him into the living room telling him to shut up, he might have attacked me in bed.

"What's with Rinty now," I heard Mr. B say. Mrs. B. was either a naturally sound sleeper or took pills like Mom did. "It's Cindy, you crazy mutt."

"What are you doing up?" I heard Mr. B say to Cindy. "I just got something to drink and went to the bathroom, then Rinty started barking and ran in here."

"Oh, I see."

I hadn't done anything, but I felt guilty for what I wanted to do: ease the bathroom door open to see how much of Cindy I could see. I thought Mr. B might say something to me, but he just called Rinty to follow him and everything went quiet again.

I was still awake when I heard an alarm clock and Mr. B opening a door off the kitchen to let out Rinty. Mr. B jostled my covers and asked if Grape-Nuts was okay for breakfast. I said yes from under the covers. I still had my clothes on and went to the bathroom to pee. Apparently no one else was up, which was not surprising since it was 4:30 a.m., according to the Mickey Mouse clock above the toilet.

Mr. B was standing in the hallway when I opened the door. "Can you get the cereal for yourself? I need to shower now."

I nodded, hoping Cindy got up early, too. After trying a few cupboards, I found the Grape Nuts and poured some into two bowls. I didn't think he would want it softened by soaking, so I didn't ask. I found some sugar on the dining room table and added enough to mine to make it as sweet as Trix. I enjoyed the crunch, and wished I could ask Dad why he didn't.

When Mr. B sat down to eat, he was dressed in a sweat-shirt that said "San Diego Lifeguard," some white shorts, and a pair of flip-flops. His hair was still wet.

"Find the sugar?"

I nodded while I chewed.

"That Rinty is something else, huh?" Just then I heard a scratch at the door, and Mr. B got up to let him in. "Yeah, even in the dark he never barks at one of us, so when he was barking last night I knew he smelled or heard something. I thought it was a loose dog."

He looked at me like he was sizing me up for a "tell" in a poker game. "Yeah, he's something all right. That's why him barking at Cindy was especially strange." He looked at me silently for a little too long.

Mr. B called Mom and asked if it was all right for me to miss school today. If it was, he said he would bring me by the house on his way home from work. To me he said later, "Unless you want to run away still. I bet Earl misses you already." I wanted to believe that, and it was enough to make me willing to consider going back home.

We stopped at a coffee shop to have something else to eat and talk a little bit.

"Joey." It was Laura in a white uniform with a pink apron. I cringed, partly because she made me think of Dad and partly because of her relationship with Dad. Mr. B seemed to know her and asked how she knew me.

"Sam used to eat here sometimes."

Her hair was tied back with lots of red strands hanging over her ears and cheeks. She was looking sad behind her smile. "How do you know each other?" She said looking back and forth at me.

"We go to the same church," Mr. B said.

"He's my Royal Ambassador leader."

Mr. B explained what RAs were briefly while she took our order of coffee, hot chocolate, and cinnamon rolls. "A friend of the family, huh?" I glanced at him thinking he was being sarcastic like Debbie would have been in the situation. He wasn't smirking so I just agreed and looked at the surfer photos on the wall behind the counter.

He said he took the woodie to work today because he knew I liked it. Usually he takes their old VW bug and saves the woodie from the salty air. We stopped at a building a few blocks from the beach where he said he needed to check in before making a tour of the lifeguard stations from La Jolla to Ocean Beach. "I may need to fill in for someone who called in sick."

He left the radio on and one song after another reminded me of Gloria. We hadn't talked in a while because I knew she was coming out for a visit, but I was beginning to doubt she still felt the same way about me. Would she be upset to find out I ran away? Would she be even more excited to see me the next time like she had the last time? Would I get to go to Dayton anymore now that Dad was not around? By the time Mr. B returned, I had heard "Big Girls Don't Cry" and "Breaking Up is Hard to Do."

"I've got to drive out to Pacific Beach to see if Jeff showed before I check messages at the office. He's been late a lot." He started up the motor, and it coughed a few times before catching. "My daughter says it's the cheap gas."

He drove the few blocks to the beach, and we parked facing the ocean. Some surfers were already out, the waves neither large nor shaped well. These guys were pretty experienced because they never got separated from their boards. Over each wave that collapsed, they would do a 180 degree reversal and, still on their boards, paddle out for the next set of waves.

"I was just looking for the bathroom last night. That's why I was in the hall."

He looked as if I had said I had been born on Mars and was trying to figure out how humans organized their houses.

"But you didn't use the bathroom."

"I, uh, forgot. I mean, Rinty surprised me, and I felt bad about waking everyone up again."

He pointed to a surfer who had thrown his board back over a wave and the board flew up high and just missed a guy that was sitting on his board. "Close call. That sometimes calls for us. A whack on the head and he's out cold. We usually can't get to him before he drowns so we count on his buddies to keep him above water until we can pull him into shore."

I wondered if I could ever get confident enough or strong enough to catch waves at wimpy La Jolla Shores, much less here at Windansea. I knew there were reefs that caused the deep troughs and, while the ride was good, the coral was also very hard.

"Look, Joey, I used to sneak looks at my cousins when they came out here to go to Disneyland. And my daughter is definitely something to look at."

"Oh, Mr. B, I wouldn't do anything like that. To Cindy." I started to say to someone I knew, which was partly true. I really didn't know Sandy much, and I knew the Twambley girl even less.

"I'm not saying you were, but we guys have to deal with our urges and sometimes we do stupid things."

I wanted to ask if he had been talking to Tamara. "Mr. B, I don't know if I believe in God. Even Jesus."

He nodded, still looking ahead. "Whoa, now that's an experienced surfer. He was able to kick out of the wave and avoid hitting those guys on each side of him. I wonder if they're thanking the guy or God for taking care of them."

I was missing Earl. I was also missing school. I wanted to tell Mr. B to take me to school since I could still get there in time for my second class. I wanted to ask him to use his office phone to call Gloria and find out when she and her dad were coming out. I wanted him to get Maw-Maw to come back. "Is God in control?"

"Yes."

"Can anything happen without his permission?"

"No."

I watched a guy paddle furiously and not catch the wave. "Does he love us?"

"More than a father loves his own children."

"Then, why?"

"Joey, can I tell you a story?"

I nodded.

"I was eighteen when I enlisted in the army. I had not seen photos of what was happening in the concentration camps until after I was discharged. The more I see, the more I can't believe it. Have you seen any of the documentaries?"

"We saw the movie of Anne Frank in sixth grade. My teacher was Jewish."

"I liked that one because it created the feeling without showing all the emaciated bodies and the violent cruelties."

"So God allowed that?"

He shifted in his seat and nodded. "He allowed it in the sense that once he has set certain things in motion, the inevitable will happen. I heard a pastor on the radio talk about God suffering with us in our pain. I don't quite understand it all but it seems to be the best answer to why God doesn't do away with pain."

"So God suffers?"

He looked at me like he was trying to find the answer in my face. A kid on a small board was getting buffeted by the breakers but kept going back each time he was pushed toward the shore.

"It's like that kid. God doesn't all of a sudden suspend the laws of motion to give the kid some help. But he will help him have the courage and hope to keep practicing until he can get outside without as much effort."

He started up the car and backed out of the space just as two guys in a VW bug with boards longer than their car attached to bars on the roof pulled into a spot next to us.

"I've got a few more places to visit before I see if they need me to sub for someone who called in."

CHAPTER TWENTY-FIVE

NOT ONCE ALL DAY did Mr. B ask me why I came to his house last night. He showed me how to find a riptide and where he had made rescues. He told me about a boy much younger than me whose father was killed in a swimming accident a few months ago. He and his family went to our church, but they had only joined last year. When we came back to his office—the lifeguard he was going to sub for showed up—he asked if I would talk to the boy sometime.

"I don't know what to say."

"You could just tell him about how you feel about your father." He was turning back and forth in his swivel desk chair slowly, alternately looking out the window and at me.

"Okay," I said and wanted to add, "if you will let me come live with you," but I didn't dare after he found me in the hallway outside the bathroom where his daughter was.

The phone rang and startled us both.

"Bodie." He turned to look at me while he continued to talk. "Oh boy. When?" He swiveled back to face his desk and wrote something down. "All right. I'll get him over there as soon as I can."

He looked at me for a few seconds and then shook his head. "That was Sharon." I thought that was his wife's

303

name, but I knew her as Mrs. Bodenhamer. I was too scared about the phone call to ask him. "Your sister called to say that your mother was just taken to the hospital."

I stood up.

He put up his hands. "She's okay. Well, at least she's not in danger. Apparently she fainted after saying the same thing over and over."

"What?"

"Sammy and something else."

My head was swirling. I had spent part of last night walking in the canyon after being with Tamara in the fort, I had been about to ask Mr. B if I could live with him, and now my only surviving parent was in the hospital.

"Which hospital?"

He hesitated and looked away. "Mercy."

Did he say she was fine because the last time I went there someone died and he thought I expected Mom to die, too? "When did she go?"

"This morning."

I figured it was after he called, but he didn't specify and I didn't want to call attention to the possibility it was my fault. I don't know how I had enough awareness to avoid asking about something that could bring on guilt. I guess that's the kind of thing that would signal hope to a therapist. It certainly makes it clear that I was more aware than might be expected.

"I'm going to take you home. Apparently your grandmother is coming back. Was she travelling?"

"Yeah, kind of." I didn't want to talk about the commune. "Can't you just take me to the hospital now?" I didn't want Debbie or Maw-Maw to find some reason to make me stay home while they went.

I could tell Mr. B was having trouble deciding what to do. He tugged on his shorts and adjusted the straps on his sandals. Though I hadn't told him why I ran away, he might think he was being cruel by putting me back in the middle of it. He had to know that the main reason for leaving had something to do with my mother. Maybe he wanted to make sure I was not going to be alone with her.

"I tell you what. I'll take you home, and we'll find out when they plan to go to the hospital. If it's going to be quite a while, I'll see if they will agree to me taking you right now."

He clicked on his intercom and told Annie, his secretary, that he had to go out for a while but would be back before two o'clock. It was almost noon now. "Have a nice lunch," was her response.

When we drove up our driveway, Debbie came out to meet us. I wondered how she had gotten home. I knew Mom's condition had to be serious because Debbie had not changed out of her school outfit, navy blue pleated skirt and frilly white blouse. She had a white ribbon around her ponytail. Men noticed her everywhere she went, but I didn't catch any of that in Mr. B.

"How is Earl? Did he sleep with you? Have you fed him already?"

"Nice to see you, too." She stood in the doorway. "Maw-Maw is supposed to be here in a few minutes. The people bringing her are going to take us all to the hospital."

I looked at Mr. B, who nodded and said to call him when we found out more. I looked at Debbie to see if she looked worried, but I didn't notice anything.

"So you had a little adventure last night." I knew instinctively then what I had to relearn as an adult: better to keep your mouth shut until you know for sure how bad things are before saying something that will definitely make it worse. She could have been talking about Tamara, she could have been talking about me out late, or she could have just been referring to last night at the Bodenhamer's.

"Better than staying in the fort all night, eh?"

I responded with a thin smile, still hoping she didn't know much.

She walked onto the front porch and waited for me to follow. "I need to tell you something. You're going to find out soon enough."

I hated introductions like that.

"Mom found out you were not in your room when Mr. Bodenhamer called to tell her you were with him. When she hung up, she started going crazy, imagining the worst possible scenarios." Debbie looked at me. "You know, situations."

"I know what sen-ar-reo means." Debbie was always acting superior, even when she thought she was being considerate.

"Anyway, she just kept talking like some tape recorder gone bad, repeating your name and Dad's, like she was calling you both in for dinner." She smiled. "I yelled at her, shook her, and finally had to slap her."

When she saw my eyes widen, she said, "Not hard, but maybe I should have because she didn't break out of it until the ambulance men strapped her to the gurney."

Debbie went into the kitchen and sat down in front of a bag of potato chips and a coke. She put a couple of chips in her mouth and had a swallow of the soda. "So I called Dr. Carver. When I described what she was doing, he said he would send an ambulance immediately."

I sat down. She went to the refrigerator and got another coke. She extended it in my direction, and I nodded. She put a few ice cubes in a glass and poured half of the bottle into it.

Usually the frizzing sound the coke made as it hit the ice cheered me, but it just irritated me now. "When is Maw-Maw coming?"

"Looks like right now."

I followed her to the window, and we watched this tall skinny kid, who looked like one of the guys who had picked her up, open the door for her and then get a couple of suitcases out of the trunk. It wasn't everything she had taken with her, but it was more than enough for just a few days. She said something to him as he followed her to the door, and he set the suitcases down.

"Debbie? Joey?" she called as she came in the front door. When we approached, she pulled us into her for a group hug.

She turned to the tall skinny boy, "Do you remember where you got them?" The boy nodded and went past us down the hall.

"This is Jeremiah," she said as he walked away.

He turned back to us and said, "Hi." He was definitely checking out Debbie, whose blouse seemed ready to burst if she expanded her lungs just slightly. Her skirt was right at the edge of what was allowed at the high school, but, as usual, everything she wore left no doubt what her shape was underneath. He glanced at her again as he went back to the car.

"Are you two ready? Not that it's possible to be ready for all this." She turned to Debbie. "You can tell me more on the way there. I just need a quick trip to the bathroom."

"Maw-Maw, we have a dog." I led her out into the garage. Earl started going nuts. He kept jumping at the wire fence and falling back over himself like he was doing somersaults. "Wait a minute." I could see he was starting to get in peeing position. I grabbed him quickly and held him as far as away from myself as I could. He managed to hold it until we were just past the concrete patio but started letting go before I had set him down.

"Good boy, Earl, good boy." Maw-Maw and I petted him a little and then put him back in his garage pen.

Since Maw-Maw didn't mention it, I supposed Debbie hadn't told her about me running away. I wanted to take a shower and put on some fresh clothes, but it looked like I might be left behind if I did. I went to my room and took off my jacket and shirt and put on a polo shirt that I didn't tuck in.

In the car Maw-Maw explained that Jeremiah had to get back to do his chores and that when we wanted to return home Mrs. Bodenhamer had offered to come by. Debbie looked at me like this had something to do with me staying the night at the Bodenhamers. At least that is what I imagined because I could only see her out of the corner of my eye. I stared out the window on the way there, counting all the fast food places, and wondering if it's okay to feed puppies hamburgers and fries.

Before I saw the sign, I recognized the palms along the semicircular drive to the entrance. I wondered if palms had been present at all major events in my life. Jeremiah let us out and said if we couldn't get a ride to call him. Before we went in, Maw-Maw bent down to the front passenger window and said something to him we couldn't hear.

When Maw-Maw and I walked through the front doors, Debbie had already located the ER. We followed her to the same kind of curtained room Dad had been in. A nurse said that Mom had been given something to make her drowsy, but not enough to knock her out completely. She was mumbling something we couldn't understand. "We've ordered a psych eval," the nurse told Debbie. When Maw-Maw and I looked confused, Debbie said, "They're going to give Mom a psychological evaluation." I think Maw-Maw just didn't hear, but Debbie said it like she was talking to two more people with the vocabularies of illiterates. Maw-Maw shuffled up to the bed and held Mom's hand. Mom looked up but didn't seem to recognize her.

The nurse said Mom would be out of it for a while and we might want to go to the waiting room. Debbie said we'd wait here until the doctor came. The nurse looked displeased and said Debbie and I would have to stand because each room had only one chair, which she pulled up for Maw-Maw. Maw-Maw, still holding Mom's hand, asked Debbie what happened this morning.

"Joey ran away last night." Debbie gave me the okay sign and winked. "Mom was hysterical for a while and then just kept repeating Dad's and Joey's names, like she believed it would bring them back. When Mr. Bodenhamer called to tell us where Joey was, Mom stopped saying Dad's name and began saying Joey's full name like she would when she was disappointed with him."

Maw-Maw pushed on the arms of the chair to get up. Debbie came over to help, but she waved her off. "But what made you call an ambulance?"

"Dr. Carver. I called him, told him how she was acting, and he said she needed to get to the hospital immediately." Debbie went to Mom and stroked her arm once before she backed off. "Then she started to talk to Joey and Dad again, telling them that dinner was getting cold."

"Yeah and then Debbie slapped Mom." I wanted Maw-Maw to know that Debbie shouldn't get too much praise for helping Mom.

"Mrs. Cagney, huh?"

Debbie smiled until she saw that Maw-Maw was not.

"Excuse me," came from the other side of the curtain, and a man just a little taller than me, but not quite as tall as Debbie, came in. "Dorothy Norton, I presume," he said smiling and nodding in Mom's direction.

None of us returned his smile.

"Mrs. Norton will probably not be able to talk much for a while. Why don't you come back tomorrow? I can tell you more then." He smiled like he had just done something so wonderful his parents would be forever proud of him.

Maw-Maw looked at us and shrugged. "You two want to go home now, and I'll stay until they know something? Mrs. Bodenhamer can take you home without me."

Would this be the new regime that allowed us to stay home by ourselves?

"Are you coming back?" I said, not ready to be under Debbie's authority.

Maw-Maw looked at her blouse while she fumbled with a button that was half in and half out until she had pushed the button completely behind the slit. "In case she comes back to consciousness soon, I want to be here. I think it would be good for her to see a familiar face. If she doesn't come out of it soon, I've got plenty of praying to do." She sat down and picked up Mom's hand again. "Debbie, will you call Ethyl to have her let the church know your mother's in the hospital?" She looked at me. "Yes, I'm back."

Debbie nodded. I knew she would agree to leaving, but I also knew she didn't like Ethyl and might try to get me to call for her. I wondered what she would be willing to trade in exchange for the favor. Debbie grabbed my hand to lead me out.

I pulled my hand back. "I'm staying with Maw-Maw."

Debbie rolled her eyes and shook her head like she couldn't believe she was related to such an idiot. If Maw-Maw hadn't been there, I wouldn't have wanted to stay, but I wanted even less to be with Debbie at home. Besides, maybe Mrs. Bodenhamer would take me to her home.

A nurse about Maw-Maw's age came in to say that they had found a room for Mom and would be moving her in an hour. No sooner did the nurse leave than a man in a white uniform came in and began releasing the brakes on the bed wheels. He said we could go with him. Debbie looked defeated as she followed Mom and us to an elevator that had doors on both sides. I wanted to tell Mom that Earl is doing fine and almost house—well, garage—broken, but I never got the chance.

CHAPTER TWENTY-SIX

THEY PUT MOM IN a double where the other bed was empty. The room was filled with red carnations in vases on a table, small ficuses in pots on the floor, and across the window a large banner with ski stickers that said, "Go Get 'Em, Mabel." Either Mom's roommate had been in an accident or her getting back on the mountain would be evidence of her healing. As two orderlies transferred Mom from the gurney, Debbie started reading some of Mabel's cards. Mom moaned as they dropped her onto the bed, but she wasn't conscious.

Maw-Maw sat down next to Mom and picked up her hand again. I remember Mom doing the same to me when I was sick. "I reckon she'll be here for a while. Y'all want to get something from the cafeteria?"

"Sure." I held out my hand for some money.

Maw-Maw gave it to Debbie and said to bring her a sandwich. "You can eat down there or up here."

I figured Debbie would want to stay in the cafeteria. She wasn't wearing anything special, at least for her, but everything she wore seemed to shout out, *look at me*. I offered to bring back Maw-Maw's sandwich. I was afraid I might miss Mom's last few moments if she was dying. Besides, I felt it was my fault Mom was here. In the cafeteria Debbie ran into a friend whose brother was in the hospital for a broken leg. They sat together and began rating all the guys that looked like doctors.

When I got back to Mom and Maw-Maw, Pastor Bob was standing at the foot of Mom's bed looking like he was trying to appear sad without revealing his pleasure to be near Mom. The further I get from my childhood years, the weirder he appears. He had on tan slacks and a white short-sleeved Mexican wedding shirt that contrasted nicely with his bronze arms. We had a sister church in Tijuana, and they gave him presents to thank him for the men he had brought down there to work on their new sanctuary.

"Joey. How are ya, buddy?" He smiled broadly and then, like he had forgotten what we were here for, pursed his lips.

I nodded, trying to hide my irritation. He was like a lot of people who had a great personality for being in front of an audience but were too much up close.

"I hear you had a sleepover at the Bodenhamers."

"Kind of." So that was how he found out about Mom. Fortunately he didn't say anything about how I got there. If he knew.

He opened his mouth wide and raised his eyebrows slightly, laughing a little too loud. I wasn't sure what he thought was so funny. Mom seemed to notice someone new was in the room, but she didn't recognize him because she would have gushed over how nice it was for him to take time from his busy schedule to visit her.

He seemed confused about what to do or say next. It makes me wonder what he expected. He surveyed the whole room and then focused on Mom. "Your mother probably just needs some rest after all that's happened."

Was he referring to what happened to Dad or to me?

"She'll be on our prayer list for Wednesday night." He looked at Maw-Maw when he said this.

She said, "Thank you," without looking up.

I learned later that he didn't approve of the desert group Maw-Maw had joined and also didn't like it that Maw-Maw had given up her position as Sunday School Superintendent on such short notice. No stranger would have noticed anything awkward in their conversation. He was as solicitous and Maw-Maw was as polite as anyone who had been brought up in the South.

When Debbie returned, she didn't hide her sneer upon seeing Pastor Bob. He had a wider grin for her, but managed to stare at her breasts only briefly. She returned his hello and asked Maw-Maw if there had been any change.

"Not yet."

I suppose because he sensed the cool reception, after he said again that Mom needed rest, he left.

Debbie pulled up a chair from the other bed and handed Maw-Maw a tuna sandwich, abruptly asking her about going to the desert. "You wouldn't have gone if you were treated better, would you have?"

Maw-Maw looked surprised and dropped Mom's hand. "What do you mean?"

"Come on, Emmie, you know what I mean." Debbie hadn't called Maw-Maw that in years. "Mom and Dad treated you like a glorified maid."

Even I could tell that this wasn't the time to bring this up and said so.

Slowly Debbie turned her eyes to me. "To the oppressors, there never is a good time." We were about to get a lecture laced with quotes from Martin Luther King and Gandhi, but Maw-Maw spoke next.

"Look, sweetie, people under pressure do a lot of unkind things. Your mother was battling for her family." She looked at Mom and patted her hand. "She needs us now to battle for her."

"Mom gets away with murder, and you know it." I didn't think Debbie was referring to Dad as a victim of homicide, but it was possible. For all her intelligence and mature insights, Debbie said a lot of dumb things without thinking. Her friends once gave her an award: a cardboard replica of a Civil War cannon. When you pulled the trigger, it shot out a flag that said "The Loosest." It was pretty realistic because a friend of hers had a father who worked as a set designer.

Debbie stood up, putting her hands on her hips in prime disgust posture. "My God, she blamed Dad for everything that went wrong."

I wanted to defend Mom and talk about how hard she worked. I wanted to remind Debbie of Mom taking a second job as a cashier when Dad was laid off from Ryan. I wanted to ask Debbie how many times Mom had driven her to rehearsals.

But that didn't mean I wanted to live with Mom. With her in the hospital, maybe the Bodenhamers would feel obligated to take me in. Then Maw-Maw could go back to the desert, and Debbie would be free to go to Los Angeles to pursue her acting career. Mom moaned again, and we all looked at her.

"It's okay, Dodo, we're right here." She stroked Mom's hand while she spoke.

"Sammy? Sammy? Dinner's almost ready."

"Dad's dead, so you don't have to worry about dinner." Debbie often deserved to be slapped, and Maw-Maw might have if a man had not appeared at the door.

"That's right, no need to worry about dinner. The food here is actually pretty good." The man stayed in the doorway. He had on a dark suit and a skinny, knitted, black tie with a straight bottom. His mouth slanted slightly, like he wanted to be happy but just couldn't quite believe it was possible. Even so he seemed more sincere than the pastor. "Good afternoon. I'm Dr. Calmwell." He was slim, but not skinny, with a sharply angular face and obviously too young to be bald. "I want to talk to your mother for a few minutes, then I can answer any questions you might have."

We walked out into the hall as he pulled the curtain around the bed. Debbie said, not caring if he heard, "With a name like that, he must be the shrink."

That struck me as funny, and I started giggling. Debbie liked anyone who thought she was clever enough to be funny, but looked at me skeptically at first. Then she started laughing herself. Before long Maw-Maw joined in. Anyone walking by would have thought we just got some great news about the person we had come to visit.

I had some idea of what went on in hospitals from shows like *Ben Casey* and *Dr. Kildare*, but I didn't think they affected me that much until a few years ago, when I was asked what I wanted to be and I said a doctor.

As a family though, we were much more dedicated to the domestic comedies: *The Adventures of Ozzie and Harriet*, *Father Knows Best*, and *Leave It to Beaver*. But I don't think I learned anything more helpful on TV about families than I did about the medical field from the medical dramas. What I did learn was that my family was not like them. I envied their never encountering a problem that didn't bring the family close together by the end of the show. And they seemed to like each other, even when they were angry or disappointed. I so believed they had the secret to happy family life that I was sure all we needed was to move into a two-story house like theirs. I couldn't have been the only kid who measured his family up against the TV versions and found his wanting. Of course, Ozzie Nelson never went to work, but all I saw was how much he enjoyed his boys and his wife, even when they were complaining about him.

Maw-Maw sat on a bench while Debbie was pacing back and forth. A woman in white was pushing a cart with bottles of medicine and almost collided with Debbie. Maw-Maw patted the space on the bench next to her and Debbie sat.

"Look, honey, your mother has never had it easy, especially with her father dying when she was so young." She then looked at me. I guessed to see if I was as young as Mom had been then.

"My God, Emmie." Debbie almost shouted out and toned down her next comments to a fierce whisper as a gurney with an emaciated old man came by. "She's always nagging Dad even when he's doing what she asked. Once she had been going on and on about how junky our yard looked because the bougainvillea had not been pruned lately and the edge of the lawn wasn't trimmed correctly. He had just finished one section with the edger and she was on her knees right behind him, with clippers, supposedly making it straight. When he noticed what she was doing, she told him to go do something else since this was one more thing she had to do herself if she wanted it done right."

The doctor came into the hall and motioned for us to come back in. "Your mother is still a little groggy and keeps calling for Sam. Is that your father?" He was looking at Debbie and me.

Debbie nodded. "He's dead."

Dr. Calmwell's eyes widened slightly, not more than you would expect from someone who had just heard that it would be warmer than expected tomorrow.

"We won't know exactly what happened to Mrs. Norton until she can talk and we run a few tests. Has she been upset lately?"

"Her husband just died." I guess Debbie was planning to keep repeating this information until she got a rise out of the doctor, but apparently he was well trained in dealing with troublemakers like my sister.

Maw-Maw said, "We've all been a little out of sorts." She looked at me. "Because it happened so suddenly." She tapped the left side of her chest.

Debbie interpreted. "The 'it' is Dad dying." I wondered which she enjoyed more: acting or irritating people. She had said that she would be perfect as Kate in *The Taming of the Shrew*. Typecasting, I had thought.

But this time, with little sleep, I had had enough. "Shut up, Queenie, just shut up."

I thought she was going to punch me. She hated to have anyone use Mom's nickname for her, especially in public.

Maw-Maw stood up and put her arm around Debbie.

Dr. Calmwell offered Maw-Maw and Debbie seats next to Mom and looked at me. I shook my head to let him know I did not need to sit. "This is a lot to go through, with your mother in the hospital after your Dad was here a few weeks ago."

"You mean, when he died?" Debbie the irrepressible.

The doctor's smile tightened into a thin grim line. He did not look at Debbie as he continued. "I would suggest you go home and let me call you when we know more." When Maw-Maw frowned, he responded. "She needs rest now. You could come back around dinner time."

When Maw-Maw said we didn't have a ride, Debbie reminded her of Mrs. Bodenhamer's offer. "I'll go call her." Debbie was out of the room before anyone could reply.

The doctor said the nurse would send for him the minute Mom woke up and that he would be in the hospital on rounds for the rest of the day. "Her vitals are fine and it may be that with just a little rest she'll be as good as new."

Maw-Maw picked up Mom's hand as if by feeling it she could determine whether the doctor's prognosis was reasonable. I don't remember seeing Mom and Maw-Maw touch each other this much, so every time Maw-Maw held Mom's hands now it seemed spooky, like she was only doing it because it might be the last time they would be together.

The doctor said to make sure we had given them our phone number and left.

I didn't know what that meant for me. Would it be okay to go back home since Mom wasn't there and Maw-Maw had come back to live with us? Would I have a chance to call Gloria or was she already in California? I had been worried about her feelings for me since I had become less sure of my own, especially after Tamara. It horrified me to think Gloria might find out. Every time I was around anyone attractive, like Mr. B's daughter, I wondered if I had fallen out of love. Songs on the radio were no help since for every one that talked about love being forever there were two talking about heartbreak. I think the subconscious influence of the songs partly explains my disbelief in Gloria's loyalty despite all her frequent assurances of her love.

"Mrs. B will be here in about half an hour." Debbie walked in the door and sat down, staring at Mom, either willing her to get better or willing her to stay sick so we wouldn't have to deal with her for a while.

We met Mrs. B in front of the hospital so she wouldn't have to park. She said how much they enjoyed having me stay with them, as if it had been a planned sleepover with one of my pals. I wondered if she knew about Mr. B finding me in the hallway outside the bathroom.

I felt that by going back home I was admitting to being a failure, that I wasn't tough enough or smart enough to make it on my own. Somehow it seemed to be another test of manhood.

Maw-Maw said she would fix us something to eat along with a lemon meringue pie for dessert. Debbie was uncharacteristically enthusiastic and offered to help. I offered, too, and Maw-Maw said I could do the dishes after we ate. I was relieved to be off the hook for a while and went into the garage. I didn't have anything in mind. I just wanted to avoid my room at present. I picked up Earl, petted him, and watched him run around both to make sure I got him outside to pee and just to enjoy his puppy antics. A fly began to bug him and after swatting at it a few times, he chased it until he ran into the garage door. Not fazed he jumped up and ran in the opposite direction, as if to say that no wooden barrier will keep him from his prey. Then he flopped down and went to sleep.

A few years ago, when I had asked Dad about what he did during the Korean War, he showed me a small Derringer, which he said he had carried with him in case he got captured. He shocked me by saying that it was not for the enemy but for him. He said he didn't want to be brain-washed and since he was already willing to die for his country and so Debbie and I could remain free, he was willing to die to keep the enemy from turning him against his fellow soldiers.

I remember he had taken the gun out of an old toolbox that had a board front that slipped down a slot on each side. Once you pulled that up and out you could access the series of small drawers with nails, screws, and other small items. I found it under his workbench, but it was locked. I thought I would try a few old-looking keys hanging on the wall, and one of them opened it. I found the small gun in the third drawer. It was wrapped in an old oily cloth. There were bullets in a small box next to it that was oily like the cloth.

I unwrapped the cloth and looked at the gun's rounded handle and tiny hammer. I would take it with me to protect myself if I ran away again. Of course with Mom gone, I wasn't sure what I would be running away from. I pulled the flap up from the box of bullets, and it fell back on a small notebook that had been under the box. The cover was a made of soft leather and the edges were soiled. I wondered if Dad had carried this next to the gun. I tried to open it in the middle but the pages stuck. I carefully wedged a finger-nail between two pages and ran it around the edges.

December 24, 1952. [I recognized Dad's cramped long handwriting.] *Nothing much today. Dreamed of Mee last night. Ready to go home.*

I went back to the first page and thumbed through ten or twenty pages. It looked like he wrote something in it every day. I heard some noise in the kitchen, held the book behind my back, and waited to see if anyone was coming out the door to the garage. Then I went back to reading. I wasn't sure if I would show anyone. Certainly not Debbie, at least not until I had shown someone like Mr. B or maybe Billy.

January 6, 1953. *Rumors of the war ending soon. Coldest I've ever been. Must be really bad for the dogfaces. Hope I can get her out of my mind. Maybe better if I died.*

Dad never talked about what happened in the two wars he fought. In college, I read Steinbeck's essay on why soldiers don't talk and wondered what Dad's trauma had been that kept him quiet. At the time I looked at war as a little more serious game than cowboys and Indians. My hands were shaking while I held the little book. I knew I would read the whole thing, but I didn't know where. I could figure out when, as soon as I could decide where.

Running away was now officially on hold, and not just because of finding the diary. I felt Maw-Maw, maybe even Debbie, needed me. I had some of that feeling I'd seen in so many movies, where the dying father tells the son that he is now the man of the family. I also didn't want to hurt Maw-Maw any more. She was usually even-keeled, but I could tell she was pretty worried about Mom. She kept asking Mrs. B how she knew to come pick us up. Debbie looked worried, but Mrs. B took us both aside and said it was probably just all the strain over Dad, moving back, and Mom sick. She had talked to us after she helped Maw-Maw into the house. She gave us both a hug and said to call if we needed anything. I had forgotten that Debbie used to have Mrs. B. in Girl's Auxiliary and that she was one of the few church people Debbie talked about without sarcasm.

I put the book inside my pants in the back and let my shirt cover it and picked up Earl. I opened the door to the kitchen slowly. There was a drawer by the door that had recipe books in it, and we were supposed to keep the door locked when the drawer was open, but almost everybody forgot. It was closed this time. Maw-Maw was just separating the yolks from the egg whites and putting them into a mixing bowl for the meringue. She loved cooking in general and adored making desserts. They were her specialty and could have easily won prizes at a county fair. Dessert was the primary dish her restaurant was known for when Mom and she ran one after the grandfather I never met died. She said to wash my hands thoroughly after messing with the dog and that dinner would be ready soon. I nodded and went to my room. I put Earl down, watching to see if he had to pee.

I wanted to tell someone about the diary, but I figured I'd better read it first. If I were still in Dayton, I would have waited to read it with Gloria. I thought of reading it to her over the phone and promised myself that in the future I would make enough money so that we would never have to worry about what time of day we could call and how long we talked.

I decided to read it with my back to the door and my shirt partially unbuttoned. If someone came in uninvited, I would stuff it in my shirt before even turning to see who came in. Or if anyone knocked first, I could just stay with my back to the door and say I would be out in a while and then hide it somewhere in the closet. There really wasn't much danger of it being found because the only person who searched my stuff was Mom. Debbie would quiz me about something that seemed suspicious but was too guarded about her own stuff to look through mine. I could imagine her searching my things if I ran away again, so I decided that it would come with me.

Maw-Maw called us for dinner and even though I was hungry and dinner was pretty good, I couldn't wait to get back to reading the diary. Debbie kept looking at me like she could tell I had something going on but never said anything. Despite all that had happened, she seemed calmer in general. I think she was relieved to have Maw-Maw back and to have Mom out of her hair for a while.

I asked if I could eat my pie in my room.

"As long as your puppy doesn't get any. It's not good for dogs to get used to people food."

"Okay."

Sometimes Mom would allow us to eat in the living room while we watched TV, but this was a special exemption for Maw-Maw, since she thought you shouldn't eat anywhere but the kitchen with family or in the dining room when we had guests. She agreed if I would set up a TV tray in my room. I did, placed the piece of pie on it, and got out the diary. The oil from it had already stained my shirt so I found some Kleenex to hold it with. I hated having sticky hands from sugary things and greasy hands from oil or fried food.

I sat down leaning against the sofa arm that was closest to the door. That way no one could see the diary when they first came in. I held it in both my hands, fingers behind and thumbs on top, like it was a picture. I brought it to my nose to smell the leather but it reeked of oil only. I took a bite of the pie and wished I could share this with Gloria, both the dessert and what my father wrote. Everything seemed a little less without her. Or I just anticipated it would feel more with her.

I opened to the first page. *This is for me. I don't intend anyone else to read this. If you are reading this and I am gone, please destroy it.*

I put it down and looked at the pie. It looked sickeningly sweet. I didn't feel hungry because I knew I had to read it even though it meant betraying Dad. Maybe I would show it to Debbie after all because she would never let this stop her. She was a master at making anything she wanted to do seem her right, no matter what anyone else said, or, in this case, what anyone wrote.

I pulled it to my chest and lay down. I closed my eyes and imagined asking Dad if it was okay. "Why would I want it destroyed if it was okay?" I heard him say.

"But you're gone," I said out loud, "and I'm already forgetting things about you."

I heard a knock on my door. "What's going in there? You got someone other than Earl with you?"

Debbie knocked again, and I put the book underneath a sofa cushion. She waited until I opened the door and came in looking around, like she thought that someone was hiding in here. "You gonna finish your pie?"

It was amazing she wasn't 200 pounds the way she put away sweets. I guess she compensated by skipping meals and dancing, in classes or with friends, every chance she got.

"Nah, you can have it."

She went at it immediately using my fork. In between swallows she yelled, "Maw-Maw is back!" She was sitting on the cushion that was on top of the diary. Earl was nuzzling her leg for attention, but she was only eating pie now. She had amazing powers of concentration. I suppose honed by her acting.

I decided to wait until she finished eating, which wouldn't take too long anyway. As much as she hated Mom, she was just like her: both of them got noticed by men everywhere we went and both wolfed down their food. You didn't notice it as much with Mom because she talked a lot and was always getting up to serve people in between bites.

Debbie wiped her mouth with the back of her hand, like a cowboy at a campfire. "So what' going on?"

"What do you mean?"

She stared at me.

"Get up," I said with as much authority as I could muster.

"I'm not leaving until you—"

"It's under you."

She jumped like there was a rat or a spider there, two of the myriad of animals and insects she was deathly afraid of. She still hasn't forgiven me for putting a pretty realistic rubber spider on her stereo. I can still remember the delicious chill of her scream.

I pulled back the cushion and retrieved the little book.

"Sit down. I'm going to read something to you."

She was uncharacteristically obedient. I then read her dad's admonition and closed the book, holding it behind me.

She said he had told her he used to write some, but she thought he meant poetry or short stories in college.

"He could have written those, too," I said rather astutely.

She nodded and held out her hand.

"He said to destroy it."

"So. He's dead. He's got no say anymore." She extended her hand a little further.

I was now fed up with her having to use the word "dead" all the time. As an adult I now hate all the euphemisms, but then it seemed unnecessarily harsh to not use them.

327

"Look, you found it. You get to keep it. But I've got a right to read it, too."

I was just as worried about not understanding it by myself as I was about defying Dad's request.

"How about this?" I sat on the sofa. "We'll take turns reading."

She agreed, and I began with the second entry.

September 3, 1951. Not much today. Main goal still just to keep warm.

September 4, 1951. Feel guilty that we're protected here so far from the front.

"My turn."

I handed it to Debbie, and she leafed through a few pages. I wanted her to read it in order, but it wouldn't do any good to tell her that.

November 13, 1951. Met Mee Kyoung yesterday. She was carrying her daughter and weeping. We gave her a lift. She knows English quite well.

November 14, 1951. No good news from first attack by Chinese. Mee invites me for tea.

"Well, this looks interesting."

I grabbed the book from her. "My turn again."

"Okay," she said, pulling her face back into her neck to suggest I'd completely overreacted.

I jumped to December 25.

Miss Dorothy and the kids. Can't ever let them find out what happened, but got to write about it or I'll go crazy.

Maw-Maw knocked on the door and asked if we wanted any more pie. I said, "No, thanks."

Debbie opened the door, and I put the diary behind me. "But it was good."

Maw-Maw looked at the half eaten pie slice.

"I'm savoring it." Debbie took another bite and chewed it slowly.

"I'm gonna take a nap. Without my hearing aids. So let me know if the doctor calls."

We both said, "Okay."

I pulled the notebook out again.

"Let me read it fast, and I'll let you know where the good parts are." She adjusted her bra strap over her shoulder and pulled the legs of her shorts down. I let go of it and she began reading.

January 1, 1952. Mee's husband had been killed last year by friendly fire from the UN forces, but she hated the North and the Chinese so much she accepted it was the price her country had to pay. I visit her every day after work. Mostly just issuing supplies at base so free almost every evening. She is gorgeous. I've never seen a woman that could make it hard for me to breathe, just to look at her. We first met last July.

January 15, 1952. Mee paints and sings. Sometimes at the same time. She's like a Korean cultural experience all on her own. She's beginning to show. I have a hard time writing Dorothy without spilling the beans.

"Oh, my God. We have a brother. Or a sister." Debbie is walking around my room waving the diary in the air.

"What? This woman had Dad's baby?"

"Sure looks like it. Wait." She shuffles through a bunch of pages. "Here."

April 10, 1952. Fortunately he looks like her. Sun Ki is his name. She said it was as close as she could get to Sam.

"We have a Korean baby brother who is about eight years old."

"Let me see." I read over the passage again and sat on the floor with my back resting against the sofa. I wondered if he's skinny like me. Did he play sports? Did he know about us?

But Debbie asked the important question out loud. "I wonder if Mom knows."

CHAPTER TWENTY-SEVEN

IT HAD BEEN A few weeks since Mom was in the hospital for what Dr. Calmwell decided was a nervous breakdown. Even though Mom was able to come home, Maw-Maw stayed with us. Debbie put off going to LA for an acting internship, and I was glad.

Since Mom was on pills to keep her from getting upset, she'd been easier to live with but weird, because it was more like a personality change. She took a pill to wake up and another to go to sleep. She took a third when Maw-Maw sensed she was getting agitated during the day. She finally went back to work, but didn't drive herself. She didn't put in extra hours like she used to either.

Nobody referred to Dad much, and I didn't mind. Debbie and I read the rest of his diary, but found nothing as sensational as our Korean half-brother. He got a little of what Debbie called graphic about his relationship to Mee Young, but I didn't quite understand. He used words that had more to do with eating, but I could tell they were referring to something else by the look on Debbie's face.

The one part of the diary that surprised me was how guilty he felt for having to see all the guys who had been wounded coming back to the base where he was safe. Debbie talked about writing the Defense Department to see if they knew how to get in touch with Sun Li or his mother, but once she got back to rehearsing for her next play, she lost interest.

I hadn't talked to Gloria in about A MONTH. When she came out to the West Coast with her dad, they didn't have time to come to San Diego. They invited me to meet them at Disneyland, but I had no way to get there. I tried to stay true to her by ignoring other girls most of the time. I cried almost every night and began to formulate the principle that everything good is always taken away from you and that anything joyful is just a way to get you even sadder than you were before the happy times started. I spent a lot of time watching baseball and used one of Dad's old notebooks to keep score. It seemed one of the few things I could watch on TV and not feel worse. I couldn't stand any of the family sitcoms we used to watch. I kept Earl close to me whenever I was home.

Every ordinary daily activity seemed to take forever. When brushing my teeth, I had to concentrate on stroking each tooth and then couldn't remember which ones I had missed. One time while I was peeing, I looked down to see that nothing was still coming out and then wet my pants after I had tucked myself away. I stayed on the toilet forever trying to figure out how to get out of the bathroom and into my room without anyone seeing the large dark spot.

In the neighborhood, I took no joy from playing with Billy and the twins and made lots of excuses for not joining them. Then they found some guy up the street to make four and stopped asking.

I was as depressed as I had ever been when Mr. Bodenhamer invited me to join his family on vacation. I knew they took a rafting trip every summer. This time they were taking a week to do the Grand Canyon. They were paying for everything and were trusted by Maw-Maw, them being from the church and all, so I was allowed to go. Mom still got asked for permission, but she deferred to Maw-Maw most of the time anyway. I don't remember Mom ever giving in to Dad, much less Maw-Maw, but she had simply lost all confidence in her own opinion. She still came into my room at night but didn't do or say much. It was like she forgot what she came in there for or thought she had mistaken my room for hers.

I wanted to reread Dad's diary on the rafting trip, but Debbie convinced me that I would never forgive myself if I lost it or got it wet. I memorized a few passages from it instead.

Since the hall episode at the Bodenhamers on the night I tried to run away, I thought Mr. B would never want me near his daughter. I felt guilty about trying to see her and simultaneously began scheming how I could try again on the trip. I'm sure part of the reason I was obsessing over her was because I felt I was losing Gloria. Before Dad died there was a possibility that Debbie and I would fly back to Dayton over Christmas vacation. He had promised us that he would get Mom to give the okay. Now I wasn't sure I would ever get back there before I was old enough to pay for it on my own.

Mr. Bodenhamer gave me a list of stuff to bring or I never would have been able to decide what to pack: underwear for six nights, two pairs of shorts that dry fast, sandals that can get wet, a pair of tennis shoes, a few pairs of socks, long-sleeved and short-sleeved T-shirts, a hat, and sunglasses with a strap that floated. He knew I might not have a lot of that stuff and said that his older son, who had left for college recently, probably had a few things that would fit me. I was to come over and try some of the clothes on. He said Mrs. B was going to Marston's and would pick up for me what I couldn't find among Jeff's. Debbie said I should make sure to find only a few things so I could get a lot of new stuff.

In the toolbox, near the gun and the diary, I remembered Dad had kept a pair of binoculars. I packed them, along with an old penknife I found in the canyon and my baseball glove. As far as I knew, Mr. B didn't even like baseball, but I wanted it to make me feel comfortable away from home, I guess the way salesmen bring photos of their family on business trips to put on the night table in their motel rooms.

Debbie kept trying to scare me while she stood at the door watching me pack. "Got something for the alligators? On land you got to watch out for scorpions and rattlesnakes."

I didn't bite but wasn't sure if she was only kidding.

"This is summer, buddy. You'll be lucky if you even need clothes." She rested her hip against the doorjamb, making it look like she wanted to collect in her jeans pocket anything that might be traveling down the wall.

"Can't you be nice for a few moments before I leave?" I threw in my glove out of anger and hesitated before throwing in the binoculars until I realized there was nothing in the duffel bag that could have broken them.

She said nothing for a few minutes. When I looked at her again, she was staring out the window and twirling a strand of hair above her ear. She looked sad. "You're right." She turned to me. "I hope you have fun." She turned back to the window and wiped something off of it. "And I hope you come back without any broken bones." Before I could sock her, she went on. "I do hope you have a good time, and I will miss you." She walked up to me and put her arms around me from behind. She held me a long time, even after I began squirming to get loose. She might have hugged me before, but I couldn't recall it. When she let me go, she told me again to have a good time like I was going on some dangerous mission that I might not return from.

Mom walked by and looked in but didn't ask what I was doing. Even though she had given permission for me to go, if you can count her being told and not saying anything in response, she didn't seem to know what I was doing. She had on a terry cloth robe that she had not tied so I could see her bra and panties. When she noticed that I noticed, she said, "What are you looking at?" and pulled the sides of the robe together. I was glad to be going away.

When the Bodenhamers arrived, it wasn't even light. We could barely see the cookies Maw-Maw had baked but the smell made it unnecessary. "This is a new recipe I tried, so I hope they're okay." I had two immediately. They were sweet and chewy, with a lemony tartness. I told her they were great as I dragged my duffel bag out the door to the Bodenhamer's station wagon. Mr. B hoisted my bag over the back door and on top of their stuff. Their youngest two weren't coming and their oldest wasn't living at home, so it was just Cindy and me in the backseat. I thought of Gloria to keep from staring at Cindy.

"Okay, my building and loan pals, we are on our way." He had parked parallel to the curb with the back end of the car extending over the driveway. All he had to do was keep circling around our cul-de-sac to leave. The RAs had seen *It's a Wonderful Life* at his house every Christmas for the last few years, so I recognized his "building and loan pals" comment. He had said if we hadn't been given the gospels, this movie would have been the next best thing.

Debbie and Maw-Maw stayed on the porch until we disappeared around the corner. They kept waving like they were going to miss me.

Before we got on the freeway, Mrs. B. was already passing out Maw-Maw's cookies after putting one in her own mouth and one in her husband's. "Scrumptious," she said as both Cindy and I took one. I looked out the window at some kid playing in the sprinkler on his front lawn. Next door a tiny Chihuahua was barking frantically at a girl walking down the sidewalk. I watched everything closely like it would be the last time I would see any of it. It was then that I realized I hadn't said a special good-bye to Earl. I wanted to ask them to go back but felt they would think I was stupid. According to Maw-Maw, Debbie had taken good care of him when I was with the Bodenhamers the last time. If something happened to Earl, I would probably kill myself.

Already I was comparing how the Bodenhamer's acted on vacation to how my family acted. The biggest difference was the way Mr. and Mrs. B talked to each other. They didn't seem any different than they did when I saw them at church or in their home. They would point out something that they saw or remind the other about something involving the three kids who weren't there. That was the only time they seemed even slightly sad and would cheer each other up by remembering something funny that they would get Cindy to confirm the details of.

Even though Cindy wasn't as pretty as Gloria and Sandy and the Twambley girls, she had a self-assurance about her that made her seem all the more alluring. She styled her hair much like Annette Funicello, to her shoulders and puffy.

Mrs. B. controlled the radio and surprised me with how many popular songs she knew. She loved Jerry Lee Lewis and made a point of turning up the volume when one of his songs came on. Cindy would sing along, too, but not with quite as much fervor. Our pastor use to rail against rock and roll and had lots of support from many of the parents. The Bodenhamers were always a little bit suspect for his surfing and her trying to get the church to have dances. If it had ever been allowed at a church event, she would probably have been the first one on the floor.

We made it to Las Vegas just before noon. "Same park as last year?" Mr. B was talking to his wife and daughter.

"Sure," Cindy said and Mrs. B. nodded. We had tuna sandwiches, Fritos, and German potato salad that was good after I got over the sourness.

Mr. B was looking at a billboard that advertised Sammy Davis Jr. and asked if I knew where he had to stay when he performed.

"He didn't stay in a hotel?"

"They wouldn't let him. People paid big bucks to see him but no hotel on the strip allowed Negroes to have a room. It only changed recently."

I wasn't sure why he was bringing it up. I had heard a little bit about the husband of one of Maw-Maw's sisters who was in the Ku Klux Klan, but I didn't remember ever telling Mr. B. At our RA meetings, we talked a lot about guilt and forgiveness, especially in the light of the Sermon on the Mount. He said we could carry guilt from past generations and not even be aware of it, except we might be irritable, or if it was a lot of guilt, it might make us depressed even when things were going well.

We stopped at a park on the north side of town where there were mothers with their children and a few dogs. I watched how the Bodenhamers did everything: the way they offered food without any demand, stated or unstated, to be eaten; the way some story of other rafting trips would be brought up to protests from Mrs. B or Cindy, but you could tell they really wanted to hear it again.

Mr. B was using his sandwich to mimic his son. He stretched his arm way above his head. "Remember the Red River trip when Jeff was screaming for all of us to look at what he thought was a bear."

"That turned out to be a bush shivering in the wind?" Cindy said laughing.

"But I forget how he fell out," Mrs. B. said.

"Are you kidding? He stood up to get a better view and knocked that girl over the side." Cindy was shaking her head. "Then he jumps in to rescue her and she ends up pulling him to the shore. I never knew skin could get that red without makeup."

Mrs. B offered me some of Maw-Maw's cookies. "They still write, and I suspect she's been visiting him at college since they have breaks at different times." She looked at me to explain. "Her school's on semesters and his is on quarters."

They reminisced about a few other trips, which just made me all the more lonely for my family. Or, more precisely, made me wish my family was as comfortable together as this one was. Fortunately, Mr. B coaxed us all into a little Frisbee throwing before I thought about how there wasn't much of my family left.

On the way out of town, Mr. B told us more about black performers, in addition to Sammy Davis, Jr., who couldn't stay in the hotels where they were performing. He mentioned Louie Armstrong. He also said the Mafia had a lot of money in the strip and that Frank Sinatra was implicated at various times. I wasn't sure why he was telling us. Both his wife and daughter didn't seem to be paying much attention, so I figured they had heard it before. So why was he telling me? Did he think I was ignorant of stuff like this? If only Debbie were here. But the fact was I didn't know much about the civil rights movement or about what Debbie referred to as La Cosa Nostra, even though I knew a little about Martin Luther King, and I had stayed up late to see *Little Caesar* with Maw-Maw one night Mom and Dad were gone. Sometimes I felt Mr. B was treating me like an orphan, which, given Mom was so out of it, I technically was.

We spent the night in a small motel a few miles from all the casinos with shows. I would gladly have gone to see any of the Rat Pack guys performing, but I wasn't sure anybody from our church would approve, even cool people like the Bodenhamers.

Mr. B and I had one room with two double beds while the girls had another. I almost suggested the kids have one room and the adults the other, but that might not be taken as a joke. We had to get up early to catch the bus to our drop-off place on the Colorado River, and if we missed the bus, we missed the whole trip, so Mr. B had us up at dawn.

On the bus, I sat next to a guy who'd been on countless trips down the Grand Canyon and might have told me about each one if we had had more than the five-hour bus ride together. I had never met someone who could talk as

339

much, especially when he seemed to have trouble breathing. He would stop to hack a half dozen coughs and then go on.

At the drop off point, the bus pulled into a parking lot, where there were regular flush toilets—the last we would see for a while. Nearby the boat was already being loaded. We would form a bucket brigade to load the water and to pass along our belongings, which were in waterproof bags they had given us at the hotel before we got on the bus.

Skip was our captain, and he looked no more than a year older than Debbie. He was tall and wiry strong, so I guess that's how he got the adults to respect him. He was actually thirty and had been on so many rafting trips, though our boat was much stronger and nicer than a raft, especially if you're thinking of Huckleberry Finn, that it was hard to believe that anybody older than him could have had much more experience. He paid a lot of attention to Cindy since she was the only girl in our group.

The river was calm at the drop-off point, but I knew there were rapids ahead. We were taking the seven-day trip—there were two- and three-week possibilities—but I was already homesick. Everybody was nice to me, and Cindy seemed to be going out of her way to make me feel that had I been older we might even be dating. Skip assumed I was her brother, which was the last thing I wanted anyone to assume.

"Just a few rules to make our time together more enjoyable." Skip looked at Cindy so much while he was talking that you would have thought she was the only one going and we were just there to see her off. "Life jackets must be on whenever you are on the boat, even if we are docked. When we approach a rapids, everyone must be seated and holding on to something, not someone." He winked at Cindy.

I looked at Mr. B to see if he was noticing all this attention being given to his daughter, but he was looking at the canyon walls opposite us, grinning like he'd just been told someone was giving us two weeks for the price of one.

Cindy was something else today. Long dark brown hair and eyebrows that were so dark they seemed to have been loaded with mascara. Her skin was tanned but only lightly, like she limited her daily sun time, which had to be impossible in her family. Like her mother, she was slender with a pronounced waist, an hourglass shape that wouldn't seem to be possible on such a thin body. You wouldn't call her skinny like me. She did have a sharp nose, like she could have played the Witch of the West in *The Wizard of Oz* if it had been longer, but she was way too pretty. Her cheekbones reminded you of Katherine Hepburn, and her irises were so dark brown that you couldn't see the pupils so her eyes seemed twice as large and gave you the feeling she was luring you into some deep, mysterious place within her. Some guys thought she was part Mexican. All she would need was a few words and a believable accent to convince anyone she was an exchange student the Bodenhamers had taken in.

We finally took off and mostly floated the first afternoon, though the motor was on all the time. Apparently it was mostly needed for navigating the rapids and, as I learned later, to get to Lake Mead sooner than planned in the case of an emergency.

Skip kept asking where we wanted to stop during the day to explore one of the many canyons. Some were dangerous during the rainy season. Because the walls were so steep and so close together, there was no escaping a flash flood. Some photographers had drowned just last year according to Mrs. B, so she made Skip swear that there was absolutely no chance of rain anywhere near here.

"Ma'am, you would have to bring in about a thousand water trucks and have them dump all the water in the one slot canyon we were in and even then I doubt it would be enough water to bother us." He smiled broadly at Cindy, who did her best to look shy, demure, and flattered all at once. If it were a performance, Debbie would have been jealous.

Skip seemed to grow taller and more muscular during the trip. He wore only T-shirts and shorts, with tennis shoes on the boat and flip-flops on shore. His feet were huge, fourteens or more, so he looked a little like he was related to Gloria. When he stood next to Cindy, she barely reached his shoulders, and she was tall for a girl. When I stood next to her, I barely reached *her* shoulders. It was unfair, but I was supposed to have a few growing years left.

The first night camp was set up after Skip and his assistant, Bart, who looked like he could be cast as a pirate or an ex-con in a movie, found a suitable spot for the toilet. They had two criteria and both had to be met. It needed to be hidden from view of the campsite and yet have a nice view of the canyon for the user. That meant they would find a spot on a bluff that had a tree or large bush on it.

Then they set up the dinner table, usually as close to the boat as possible. There was no fire unless it really cooled off dramatically, which apparently never happened in the summer. Bart complained enough about how it was cozy and nice for community spirit that on the final night, Skip allowed him to fix one. That night we sang well past midnight, our faces flickering in the flames.

We had gotten up so early the first day for the ride from Las Vegas that everyone was in their sleeping bags by nine o'clock. I had no trouble going to sleep immediately.

For the next few days, we hit a major rapid at least once a day. In the smooth in-between sections, Skip let those of us who wanted to steer. I was too nervous and no one else was game except for Cindy. Skip declared her a natural and even suggested she consider signing up to be an assistant. I think Bart smirked, but it was hard to tell since he had so much facial hair. He had not shaved in a few years, I guessed, and his eyebrows were dark and thick enough I figured he could comb them back over his head when he started going bald. You could only tell what he was feeling by looking closely at the corners of his eyes.

By the third day, I was going nuts. I missed Gloria. I couldn't look at Mr. B without wishing I had treated Dad better. Mrs. B. was making me crazy with all her concern for my safety on the boat. I hadn't felt comfortable enough to masturbate at night since I was sleeping next to Mr. B, even though we were in separate sleeping bags.

Cindy and Mrs. B. each had a tent while Skip and Swarthy Bart had a tent up for their stuff, but slept outside like Mr. B and me. They kept close to the boat, and I hoped that wasn't because of possible pirate attacks.

The moon was almost full so when I got up to pee, I didn't need a flashlight. I had positioned my pillow and my jacket, which I didn't even need in the middle of the night, so it would look like I was still in my sleeping bag. I peed as far away from the river as I could without going back into the brush at the bottom of the canyon wall. I thought I smelled mint, something sweet at least, and had this desire to chew spearmint gum. I probably just wanted something

I couldn't have, like a living father and a trip to Dayton and our family all together and "normal" again.

I could see a light on in Cindy's tent and, just like in the movies, could see her outline on the wall of it. She was either putting clothes on or taking them off, I couldn't quite tell. I sat on a rock, alternating between looking at her outline and checking to see that Mr. B was still in his sleeping bag and not getting up to pee like I just did.

I stood up and moved closer to her tent, my heart pounding just like it always did in these situations. Something crawled over my foot and I sucked in air, but let out no sound. I could hear some music faintly. I knew she had brought a transistor radio but Mr. B had said she wouldn't be getting any reception down here. She said she just wanted it for the ride to and from the drop off. Then I realized she was singing. I got close enough to hear some of the words, part of the chorus. It was the Sam Cooke song, "Twisting the Night Away." Her outline was twisting and I wanted to see her, not just her shadow.

I snuck around back so no one else in the camp could see me. I thought of crawling under the edge, but there didn't look like enough space, even for my skeletal head. The more I heard her sing, the more excited I got. For a while I just listened.

Here they have a lot of fun/Puttin' trouble on the run/ Man, you find the old and young/ Twistin' the night away/They're twistin', twistin', every-body's feelin' great/ They're twistin', twistin', they're twistin' the night away.

From this angle I couldn't see her shadow so I just imagined her hips and arms moving. She had a high, clear voice, the kind I assumed Gloria had, too, but I had never heard her sing.

"What the hell are you doing?" I couldn't see Mr. B that well because the moon was behind him. His breath smelled garlicky from the steaks at dinner.

"Who's out there?" Cindy called from inside the tent.

Skip called out from his sleeping bag to ask if everything was all right, and Mr. B said he was taking care of it. He grabbed me by the neck and marched me back to where our sleeping bags were. He made sure Cindy saw me as she stood just outside the entrance to her tent.

"What the hell were you doing?"

"Listening to her sing." I was almost in tears but did everything I could to keep them in.

"Do you have a problem?"

He had let me go, and I was standing facing him, hoping he could send me home, even though it wouldn't have been possible now. I heard a howling that I assumed was a coyote and thought that one way out would be to be eaten by animals.

"Look, Joey, you've had a rough time these past few weeks. Your Dad passing, your mother in the hospital, you running away. I'm trying to understand, but some things just ain't going to happen."

"I'm sorry, Mr. B. I never should have come. You were just feeling sorry for me anyway."

I sat down on my bag and took off my shoes. I put my legs in the opening at the top of the bag and scooched my butt down until I was completely inside. I hoped Gloria would never find out, but right now I didn't care. I just hated my life and everybody in it and would have run away again if we weren't stuck in this stupid canyon.

Years later I would not be able to recall any of the majesty and enormity of being at the bottom of the Grand Canyon. I had forgotten what the colors were and how strangely wonderful the dozens of slot canyons were until I saw a documentary on a rafting trip. I had forgotten everything except that Skip liked Cindy and Mr. B caught me outside his daughter's tent while she was singing "Twistin' the Night Away."

CHAPTER TWENTY-EIGHT

THERE WAS ONE OTHER event, or series of events, that I remember from that trip down the Colorado. We had just made it through a particularly tough set of rapids. I believe they were called Lava Falls, one of the most treacherous in the Grand Canyon even when the water is low. Skip had warned us to have something to hold onto and reminded us more than once to make sure our life vests were on tight. Swarthy Bart came around and double-checked everyone's buckles, giving mine an extra tug.

I was in the front on the port side, Mr. B was in the middle next to me, and Cindy was on the starboard. I had zinc oxide on my nose and a sleeveless T-shirt, exposing my already sunburned shoulders. It had been a few days since Mr. B found me outside Cindy's tent. He had been polite, but I could tell that he was disappointed or irritated or both. It reminded me of the way Dad would act after I had taken Mom's side in one of their arguments.

Skip had explained how the boat might spin around and how that didn't mean he had lost control. He said he had never flipped a boat but that he knew many experienced raft guides who had at least once in their career. I thought this was just his way of trying to make it more exciting. It worked for me.

When Skip warned us that the rapids were coming, in the distance we could see the river drop away beyond some swirling dirty water. I gripped the bar in front of me. When we got closer, the noise of the rapids make it difficult to hear what Skip said, but I assumed he was just repeating what he had said earlier.

He swung the boat to the left and bumped through one eddy. Then we went almost perpendicular to the shore to avoid a large boulder. On Cindy's side of the boat, there were waves going in three or four directions with water spinning around us like we were in a gigantic bathtub and someone had just pulled the plug. We bounced left and right and then dropped a few feet crashing into the water nose first. I didn't notice I had been screaming until both my mouth and nose filled with water so I couldn't breathe. I was so desperate for air that I let go of the bar while I coughed up the water. Then my head hit something as my feet flew upside down. There had been such an enormous amount of water pouring into the boat from so many directions that at first I didn't notice I was actually in the river. When I dropped into a water hole and popped back up, grazing my shoulder on a rock, I realized I was a boy overboard.

Like everyone who prepares people for some dangerous situation, Skip had said to remain calm if we fell overboard. He assured us that the vest would keep us above water until the boat came back to pick us up. I was anything but calm. I tried to see where the boat was but couldn't. I thought I better try to avoid slamming into the rocks at least. I was surprised that the water was neither salty nor chloriney, not thinking that the only swimming I had ever done was in backyard pools and the ocean. Why I thought of it then I don't know. The thought left me when I felt this enormous pain in my head like someone had whacked me with a baseball bat. That's all I remember until I was lying on the ground and Mrs. B was asking if I could hear her. I tried to answer, smiled, and then went unconscious again, according to what Mr. B said later.

With lots of embarrassment and a small amount of pride, I learned that Cindy had saved me. I had made it past the rapids but was floating without any movement. She had turned me over in some calm water behind a large boulder and gave me mouth-to-mouth. She said I responded pretty quickly, but when I was pulled back on the boat I kept talking crazy so they figured I must have had a concussion. They said I was talking to somebody named Billy. I learned later to my delight that Cindy had eaten a peanut butter and jelly sandwich before we entered the rapids.

"Can you stand up?" Skip was kneeling next to me. "Try it slowly. I've got you in case you're dizzy." He had his hands in my armpits and made me feel a little violated.

I stood up and felt okay except for being sick to my stomach. I managed a few steps before I began throwing up. I didn't remember having eaten that much. Then, they told me later, I fainted right into my own vomit. After I was cleaned up, they put me in my sleeping bag in Cindy's tent. She slept next to Mr. B where I had been. I don't remember anything else until the next morning when Skip was standing over me again.

"Think you can get on the boat?"

"Yeah." I really did feel better but, of course, I was still lying down.

He squinted, not believing me. "How's your head?"

I touched it and felt a bandage. "It hurts a little. Who put on the bandage?" I hoped it was Cindy.

"Captain Skip, MD, at your service," he said saluting.

Cindy had come over, and I wanted to thank her for saving me, but she was obviously more interested in Skip than me. She had on a white T-shirt, maroon shorts with cuffs, and no shoes. She looked like a girl in one of those beach party movies that would become so popular in the next few years.

"How are you?"

"Fine." I smiled weakly. "I think."

She took my hand and patted it. "Boy, you had quite an ordeal." She was talking to me but looking at Skip, who nodded in confirmation. I nodded, too, since I didn't remember much about it except that she was involved.

Mr. B walked up and said they didn't have to go on today if I didn't feel like it.

"I'll be fine. I mean, I can do it."

Skip heard and immediately started to load up the food. He asked Mr. B to help Bart load the toilet. I was able to pack up my sleeping bag and help Mr. B take down one of the tents. He smiled at me, probably enjoying the irony that it was Cindy who rescued me.

I didn't say much on the boat and was dazed enough that I just watched the scenery. Skip pointed out some bighorn rams that were sparring. Watching the fight from a distance were other sheep. There was so little footing for the spectators it looked as if they were standing on the vertical wall. He told us to be on the watch for deer in the offshoot canyons and to check the sky now and then for condors. Bart pointed out striations in the rock walls and the millions of years ago they represented. It turns out our pirate had a degree in geology.

I was so tired that it was soothing to just let my head lie back, like I would sometimes do on a long trip in our car, and watch the canyon walls go by. I thought of Gloria and the pitching mound and felt sad. I saw Billy in the backyard of the Twambleys scraping dog poop off his shoes and smiled. I had a vague pain in my right foot, but was banged up in so many places it didn't seem unusual.

We didn't encounter any rapids to speak of that day and made camp on a beach one last night. By this time my foot was hurting way more than my head. When we got off the boat, I couldn't stand on it. I looked at it and it seemed a little bigger than usual. I had this crazy idea that somehow I was getting bigger, at least less skinny, and that my body was expanding starting with my feet. It reminded me of the giant Rumblebuffin statue in *The Lion, the Witch, and the Wardrobe* when Aslan breathed on it and he came to life slowly from the bottom to the top. I knew I couldn't be growing that fast and that, while the food had been good and I had absorbed a lot, I had thrown up too much in the past few hours not to have lost some weight. Mrs. B. saw me limping and asked if I had stepped on something.

"I guess so."

She looked at it and said, "Oh, my. Your foot is really swollen. Bodey, come over here."

Mr. B took a look and called over Skip. Cindy came with them.

"Yep. Looks infected to me. See this cut here." He pointed to the bottom of my foot. "I'm sorry to say that not everybody is as careful as we are about sanitation. Though it's required, some don't even carry a toilet." He gestured toward the water. "It's a lot dirtier than it used to be."

Mrs. B stood up. "What do we do? His foot looks like it was stung by a sting ray, doesn't it Bodey."

"Well, it sure looks more swollen than a few minutes ago."

Skip took off his straw hat and was nodding. "I've seen it before. Swelling from infections seem to take off fast down here. We had to helicopter one guy out it got so bad. Either that or amputate."

Skip noticed my eyes getting real big. "But that was because it happened at the beginning of the trip. We're out tomorrow afternoon. I think if we can heat some water with salt and have him soak the foot tonight and tomorrow, he'll be fine until he can see a doctor in Las Vegas."

My foot hurt a lot. Cindy redressed the wound a few times more than seemed necessary, but I enjoyed all the attention. I think she sensed that Mr. B had been upset with me and, since she didn't know why, she took my side like any good teenager would against her parents. Also, it often required some medical advice from Skip.

That night I was pretty tired and went to sleep right after a dinner of barbequed chicken, country fries, green beans, and apple cobbler with whipped cream.

By morning I could not put on my shoe, and I had this fever that made me shiver like I was freezing. It was already in the eighties and would reach one hundred by noon, but I couldn't get warm enough. I had on a short-sleeved T-shirt with a long-sleeved one on top. I put on a jacket, too, but still I shivered. Mr. B gave me his windbreaker and they undid one of the sleeping bags so I could wrap it around me. I thought of the term used for dogs that are sexually active—being in heat—and felt it applied more to me. I was burning up and my teeth were chattering. It was like I was having a seizure, but my movements were trembly rather than rigid.

Once they got me to an emergency room in Las Vegas, I got an antibiotic drip. In a few hours, I stopped shaking.

I noticed there weren't any blacks as patients but just a janitor picking up trash. I wanted to ask Mr. B if there was a special hospital for them but forgot about it once I was feeling a little better. I had many times wished I was sick enough that everyone would fuss over me, but when it actually happened, I was a lot more interested in getting better than being made the center of attention. One nurse kept leaning over me so I was only a few inches from her breasts and every time she did something to me—put a thermometer in or checked my blood pressure—her thigh would rest against my arm. Thank God I had a sheet and a few blankets on me or she might have noticed the effect on me.

On the way home in the car, they sang while I slept. I thought they were the least religious serious Southern Baptists I knew, and I had no doubt now that being adopted by them would be a close second best to getting to move back to Dayton.

CHAPTER TWENTY-NINE

WE STOPPED IN STATELINE to get gas and use the restroom. Mr. B took me aside while we were waiting for Mrs. B and Cindy to come out of the women's. Slots rang in the background, and all the flashing lights and the red carpet with gold streaks made me a little dizzy. He ushered me outside to a tall palm tree.

"Joey, can I talk to you about something serious?"

I nodded, but wanted to say no.

He looked up at a black bird squawking. "Every boy is curious about the female body. Sometimes I think we are messed up some by our church."

I didn't look at him. He was talking softly enough that he didn't seem angry and, more importantly, so that people walking by couldn't hear. "But a little bit older and you can get arrested for that stuff."

"But, I was only..." When I glanced at him, he held up his hand.

"Look. Every kid, well, every normal kid, does his share of looking. In person or in magazines."

I wanted to ask him what his share was, when a couple with a stroller stopped near us. The woman gave her baby a bottle and then signaled for the man to resume pushing.

Smiling, Mr. B watched them for a while. "What I'm trying to say is that now is when you're making decisions that can have consequences for years to come."

At that moment Mrs. B. called out behind us, "So there you two are. Let's get out of here before I get the idea that dropping hundreds of quarters in a machine and pulling a lever are fun."

Mr. B winked at me like we had just discussed playing the slots ourselves.

On the road Mrs. B switched back and forth between a rock and roll station and one playing country-western music. At least one of them—Mr. B, Mrs. B., or Cindy—knew every song on each station. When "Tumbling Tumbleweed" played, I felt an ache. Dad loved the Sons of the Pioneers and would sing parts of "Tumbleweed" when he worked in the yard. He hardly ever got the tune right but either didn't know or didn't care. Mom would smirk and shake her head, probably because he was having so much fun with a song that she could tell didn't sound right.

I didn't notice any off-key singing among the Bodenhamers. Both Cindy and Mrs. B would alternate with the harmony, sometimes above his melody line and sometimes below. I thought that their love made the harmony possible.

I hadn't had any feverish chills since the time in the emergency room. The doctor had given me antibiotic pills and said I should be fine, but if there was any more swelling to go to the hospital at once in San Diego. By the time Mr. B dropped me off at home, I wasn't even limping any more.

When I grabbed my duffel, Cindy picked up my sleeping bag and escorted me to the front porch. Out of the corner of my eye, I could see Billy watching from his jeep. Cindy had on shorts that seemed shorter because her legs were so long, like those pinup girls that soldiers had everywhere during World War II. During the rafting trip, she had added to her already coffee tan. Her hair was pulled back with a barrette on one side, and it flowed over her bare shoulders that were as creamy brown as her legs.

I hoped she would hug me good-bye and add a little peck on the cheek to give Billy, and anyone else watching, something to talk about. But she just waved over her shoulder as she returned to the car. Mr. and Mrs. B were waving a little too enthusiastically for a good-bye.

I pulled my stuff into the house, wondering why no one noticed I had arrived. Debbie was in the kitchen on the phone and waved like she was happy to see me but not enough to stop talking. She made a signal to be quiet and mimed someone sleeping. Mom was usually doing chores all day Saturday, so—since I didn't hear the vacuum or her huffing and puffing—I assumed she was the one sleeping.

"Where's Earl?"

She pointed to the garage, and I dropped my stuff on the floor. He saw me coming and his tail started wagging furiously like he was about to shake it off. I picked him up and immediately he began to pee. I was so happy to see him and had been cold so often the past few days that the warmth of the liquid felt good. I took him to his outside spot, but he didn't have anything left. I got a rag from the garage and wiped off my shorts as best I could.

He ran to me and then away. The drop-off from the concrete patio to the dirt was just enough to make him tumble as he ran off it. I laughed like someone who had not seen anything worth laughing at for months and. I don't remember laughing that much since Dad pretended he was a ghost at Halloween and Debbie screamed when he surprised her in her room.

I waited for Earl to pee one more time and then let him follow me to my room. In the hall I heard snoring but couldn't tell if it was Mom or Maw-Maw. Since both their doors were closed, I went back to the kitchen for a Coke. As I was dropping cubes into a glass, Debbie hung up and told me that Mom was back in the hospital. She reached down to pet Earl, who immediately rolled onto his back for a tummy rub. I was surprised that Mom was gone again but shouldn't have been since she was hardly normal while she had been home.

"What happened?" I said, trying not to sound upset.

"She kept crying all the time and you and I both know it was more than just Dad." Debbie took off the Yankee baseball hat Dad had given her, smoothed her hair, and put it back on.

I took a large swallow from my glass, and the carbonation tickled my nose. "So, what's going to happen?"

"Well, she's not in a regular hospital. She's basically in a loony bin."

It never took long for Debbie to say something to irritate me. But with all I had been through on the trip, I found myself a lot calmer, like I had matured in just a week. Besides, it was hard to get upset with our blond furball getting our attention.

"Where is it?" I got some Fritos out of the cabinet near the phone. "Have you been there?"

"Somewhere near Point Loma. She only left yesterday. She started crying over some spilt milk."

Debbie made everything into a joke, if she could. I did my best to look unpleased without saying anything.

"I mean, she actually spilled some milk on the table while she was pouring some for me and started crying. She couldn't stop until Dr. Thayer came over and gave her a shot."

I joined in petting Earl and then got ready to take a shower. I thought of bringing Earl with me but decided I would see how he responded to water when we were alone first.

After a mostly quiet dinner during which I told them a little about the trip, the three of us watched *The Lawrence Welk Show* together. Debbie joined us even though she hated the music, especially the polkas. I thought the Lennon Sisters were great, but not just for their singing and their good looks. It was the idea of four siblings doing something important together. When I found out they came from a family of twelve, I immediately thought of *Cheaper by the Dozen* that Mrs. McDooddle read us in sixth grade. Maybe, if Mom and Dad had had a few more children, our family might have been happier.

We sat on the sofa, right on the actual cloth. Debbie told me how she had removed the plastic one night when Mom went to bed early. Maw-Maw didn't approve at first but had to agree with Debbie's argument that it was ridiculous to save the sofa for some time when we will all be gone and never get to enjoy it as it is. Maybe the plastic covers would come off the car seats next. In the summer sometimes my legs would sweat and stick to them so strongly I was afraid I would rip off some skin when I got up. I had a curious thought: if the plastic could be removed, then anything could change.

While I missed the constant attention I got from Mom, I had begun to see that it exacted a price. Even with Dad gone, I was beginning to feel better without Mom than with her. It scared me. It was ironic that we were watching Lawrence Welk since it was the one Mom chose on Saturday nights, but a lot of irony accompanies all tragedies. "Anna one, anna two, anna…" I laughed at Mr. Welk's accent and didn't mind that we were missing Dad's favorite show, *Have Gun, Will Travel*. I think I liked the theme music more than Paladin, but any time Dad wanted to watch it, I would join him. Mom watched, too, but not because she enjoyed it. She just didn't want to be left out of our fun.

At church the next day, we got to hear a lot of people sympathize with us over Mom having problems so soon after we lost Dad. Some said it wasn't fair, but most made a point of saying that it was all in God's hands and would work out for the best. Mr. B didn't say either, but just shook his head, asked me how my foot was doing, and gave me a hug.

When we got back to the house, the twins asked me to go to the beach with them, something they had never done before. Was it Dad's dying? Did they hear Mom had gone to a mental hospital? Was it something they thought they were supposed to do as Christians? Was it that I had struck them out?

I loved the beach and wanted to get out of the house, but I didn't really want to be compared to such beautiful physical specimens all the time. Once some muscular kid had said that not even Charles Atlas could help me. Everyone told me I would get taller and bigger in a few years, but it was looking more and more like I would never be tall or big enough.

I figured Maw-Maw would nix me going the way Mom always did since Mr. Carroll was just going to drop us off and pick us up around dusk, but she looked at me like she was thinking it might be good for me.

"I know how to swim real well," but I don't think she was worried about an accident in the water because she already knew about the lessons I had taken up the street when the Y was using backyard pools in the area.

"You can go if you promise not to get burned."

The last time I went, not with the Carrolls but with the RAs from church, I was so badly burned that Mom said she could feel heat emanating from my skin. Within a few hours of getting home, my whole back was a series of blisters like I had been roasting on a spit.

Maw-Maw said, "Well, do you know where the suntan lotion is?" I ran to the bathroom and let her put some on my back, wondering if it would bleed through my T-shirt.

In the car Jerry made some crack about how I smelled, and I explained my serious sunburn. But he was only joking. I had gained a modicum of respect athletically ever since our Little League game. Mr. Carroll asked to see the lotion the twins were bringing and reminded them to use it.

There was no music on the Captain's car radio, just news, about which he would shake his head like a parent greeting an obstinate child. The twins didn't even ask for another station. It was completely different with their mother. She always had on a rock and roll station and knew more songs than any of the kids in the neighborhood. She could sing pretty well, too. With her knockout body, kind of an American version of Brigitte Bardot, and her being fifteen years younger than her husband, you would have thought she was an older sister and not their mom.

The Captain let us out in a parking lot near one of the lifeguard stands in Pacific Beach. I wondered if Mr. B had been covering for one of his guys. I had a towel and zorres with just a T-shirt over my trunks. Surfer jams were in fashion and nobody wore the show-all tight ones except indoor swimmers. Mine made my legs look even skinnier, but no one would be noticing me as long as I was with the twins.

They brought fins for body surfing, and I joined them for a few sets of waves. I didn't catch anything but was driven into shore a few times by waves after they broke. I had never heard about body surfing contests, but there was no doubt the twins would have been competitive if they had entered any.

I went in to rest on the beach while they caught a few more waves. Already they were getting attention from a group of three girls. They had been watching the twins catch one wave after another and, when Jerry and Terry finally came in, I thought they might go off with the girls and leave me behind. Little did I know the twins had something else on their minds.

Jerry never seemed to enjoy the attention, but Larry more than made up for it. If you hadn't known he had spent almost an hour frantically stroking to catch waves, you might have thought he had been flexing his muscles like some body builder getting ready to go on stage. God, I wanted to be both like Larry, who basked in the attention and like Jerry, who could be aloof. Mostly I just wanted a body that looked like something a girl would want.

One girl wrote her phone number on Larry's leg. Where she was carrying a pen I don't know because she barely had enough on to cover her female places. None of them were quite up to the standard of Ursula Andress in *Dr. No*, which I would see next year, but they were pretty good teenage versions. Finally the girls said good-bye but kept looking over their shoulders at the twins, who seemed to have forgotten altogether about the encounter.

"Want to go beat up some queers?" said Jerry. Now he was as excited as his brother had been a few moments ago when they were surrounded by the bikini brigade.

This was almost as repulsive as someone asking me if I wanted to throw a puppy off the pier. Even before Earl, I would sooner have wounded a person than a dog, but violence of any sort made me sick to my stomach. I had heard Debbie talk about high school guys that made a habit of finding gays to hurt on the weekend, but I just couldn't believe that the super religious Carroll twins were suggesting we do this. I also wondered what made them know where to find them and whether they would be able to keep us, I mean me, from being beaten up in return.

"Well?" they said in unison.

I didn't really want to, but I wanted less to be left alone, so I went. Oh, the things I did just to avoid feeling alone. They said they knew of this bathroom where these men hung out to meet each other.

The only thing worse than being called a queer was being called a girl and probably for the same reason. Anyway, I remember doing my best to walk like a cowboy when someone in fifth grade said I swished. I wasn't exactly certain what was wrong with the way I had been walking, but I watched some Westerns every day for a week until I could imitate them so well that Debbie asked if I was angling for cowboy boots for Christmas.

Larry said that the homos wouldn't be around for a few more hours, so why didn't we get something to eat. We each had a corn dog and a Coke, which they paid for. I loved the crushed ice they used at the stand and almost forgot about what we were going to do while I ate and drank. Jerry put mustard on his corn dog while Larry put ketchup on his. I sometimes wondered if the little differences between them were conscious.

We strolled down the boardwalk, checking out the girls. Well, I checked out the girls. With the twins it was mostly them being checked out. Even at twelve, I was aware it could get tedious to always being noticed, but just for a few days (months?), it might be nice. We walked by a surf-board shop, and both of them looked at the prices and touched the boards like they could sense how many waves they each had in them. I stayed outside watching the crowd: a woman in a bikini with a man's shirt over it was carrying what I assumed was a full-grown dog but was so small it fit in her purse. A guy with long stringy hair but a big bald spot, wearing Levis with cuffs dragging the ground and no shirt, bounced by to the same beat as the guy on the bus.

When the twins came out, they stood for a while looking toward the ocean at a salmon concrete structure that had outside showers. They looked at me and nodded knowingly. There was a women's and a men's entrance, but only men were milling around outside it. Most of them had bodies that you see in *Muscle and Fitness*.

"Later," Jerry said to Larry, who nodded.

Apparently they were going to wait until it was darker to do the deed. I was now trying to figure out a way to get out of this. We walked all the way to Belmont Park, but none of us wanted to ride the roller coaster. Instead we each bought some cotton candy and headed back to the restrooms. It was only a half hour until Captain Carroll was supposed to pick us up. Being late was not an option, so the twins were desperate for a queer.

I trailed behind as they walked through the outdoor showers. Some kid who looked like he was in college had his head under the water. He was rubbing his hair like women did in those shampoo commercials. He was taller than any of us but as skinny as me. He smiled when Jerry approached him.

"We're looking for someone to show us around San Diego."

I didn't know if this was some kind of special code, but the guy reached for his towel and walked toward the men's door opening. He glanced over his shoulder to see if Jerry was following and smiled when he saw both Jerry and Terry coming toward him. Jerry waved frantically at me to join them. I took a few steps in their direction while they disappeared around the corner and into the toilet area.

I heard a loud "Heh" and then the awful sound of fist pounding flesh. A muffled "Help" was followed by "Oh, my God." The twins came running out and past me. I wanted to go inside and see if the guy was all right, but I was afraid I could be blamed for whatever happened. I imagined a headline in the *San Diego Union* the next day detailing the killing of a young man by a gang of three delinquents. The twins and I ran all the way to the pick-up place. We got there well before their father arrived. "Geez, he looked scared." Jerry was laughing.

Larry wasn't laughing. "I wouldn't have hit him in the face if he hadn't touched me. Damn, how can they act like that? With someone they don't even know?"

I started to give them a theory I had heard from Debbie before I realized it was a rhetorical question. I shook my head in agreement with their view of this disgusting homo behavior.

Captain Carroll thanked us for being ready when he came but didn't apologize for being a half hour late. If the twins had known he would be late, would they have tried to find another victim? Every time they referred to the incident by looks and gestures, I acted supportive. When their father could tell something was up, he stopped the car and told them to tell him what happened. He had Jerry and me get out of the car while he talked to Larry. Jerry kept making eyes at me as if to say I better keep my mouth shut. Fortunately, I didn't actually see anything, so I could say that without lying. It wasn't so much that I was so truthful, but that I was such a lousy liar that the Captain would have been able to tell immediately.

I thought he would want to talk to Jerry separately, too, but he seemed to believe Larry's version. I could see why. Larry had told part of the truth. It was true that the guy had touched him first, but he left out the whole part about them approaching the boy and having planned it all way before we were at the beach. Thus, it made Larry appear to be defending himself from a Godless pervert.

"I never approve of unprovoked fighting, but sometimes you have to protect yourself. What were you doing, Jerry?"

"I, uh, was right there, but, I mean, there was nothing for me to do. Larry had already creamed the guy. He'll think twice before doing something like that again."

The Captain took in a deep breath and started the car. "Oh, I wish that were true." Then he began to outline what I had sensed from my church but had never heard, a reasoned religious argument for the case against homosexuality.

He mentioned Genesis, about a man leaving his father and mother "to cleave unto his wife." He said that heterosexual relations are God-ordained. Then he gave a quick overview from Leviticus and the letters of Paul. He used the word abomination a few times and said that only hell would welcome such deviant behavior. "I'm proud of you boys."

As I've already said, being called a fag was worse than being called a girl, but what they did wasn't right. The Captain's argument lost a lot of its power when the twins showed us some of his bodybuilding magazines they had discovered when cleaning out their garage. And Captain Carroll was no weightlifter.

CHAPTER THIRTY

THE POLICE CAME TO the Carrolls and asked about the kid that was beaten up. Turns out he was on vacation visiting a SDPD detective. How they found out it was the twins I still don't know, but the Captain had a convertible VW bug with NAV 555 on it and was pretty easy to remember since there were many navy personnel in San Diego and the number is so close to the dreaded 666.

Anyway, they came over to talk to me but I again said, truthfully, I didn't see anything. I left out the fact I heard those horrible screams. The twins were unrepentant because they were taught at home and in church that homosexuals defy God and they would destroy our civilization if tolerated. The Captain didn't quite say he was proud of them, but he made the officer understood his boys were just defending themselves from a pervert. That they were beautiful aided that interpretation. Apparently the Captain had a lawyer brother who said that without a witness there was no case, especially since the twins had no previous record.

I didn't know what to do. I'd never seen this part of them. I would have taken another trouncing by Billy or something worse to have their looks, but I didn't want their life, even though both of their parents were alive and functioning. I admired the Bodenhamers' relationships but couldn't really see me living with them permanently, even if I hadn't been caught trying to look at Cindy a second time. Too much for a twelve-year-old to have to think about.

Mom was not getting out of the hospital any time soon, so Maw-Maw put off her plans to return to the commune, and it seemed that life at home might not be so bad even with Dad gone. Debbie had been talking about going to LA to pursue an acting career for years but said she probably wouldn't leave until next year. I wanted to think it was concern for me that made her put off her plans. My attempt at running away made me see how much I wanted to live in our neighborhood, even without parents. Besides, everybody was especially solicitous of Debbie and me. Regularly they would suggest one or both of us go places with them like the Bodenhamers had with me.

In the afternoon on Monday, Billy came over. He asked Maw-Maw before talking to me if I could join him at the fort. He was pretty good at dealing with adults. I think his chubbiness made him appear innocent.

"Sure, Billy. How about some cookies to take with you?" Maw-Maw had gotten to baking something every day since Mom was taken away.

"Yes, ma'am."

I was standing behind Maw-Maw while she wrapped the cookies in waxed paper and put them in a lunch-size sack. Billy glanced at the bag he brought and winked at me. I assumed he was acting that way because he had some of his dad's magazines. I winked back.

"Now, you two be careful down there and get home plenty before dark."

We nodded vigorously and left through the kitchen. In the backyard Billy tripped on a rock near the gate and fell into the chain link.

"I'm okay," he said shaking his head like he was feeling dizzy. He was bleeding from a scratch on his cheek but otherwise seemed fine. "You won't believe which one I got this time." He gave the bag a few quick shakes like I could tell from the sound how choice it was.

I knew that "one" meant one of his dad's *Playboy* magazines, and my heart started racing. Sometimes I would get this slight buzzing in my face like I was leaning back on a vibrating chair when I was about to see some nudity. It got me through many evenings of despairing over ever having a happy family or a girlfriend. I was actually afraid I might lose the capacity to get excited now that I had Gloria.

I was dreading having to help Billy into the fort since it was a two-person job and usually the two were the twins, each of whom was like two of me, as far as strength goes. When we got to the fort, I was surprised to see a stepstool Billy had brought down earlier. He could get high enough by jumping from it to get his belly onto the floor. Once he was almost into the fort, he just used my interlocked hands below to make the final push in, which knocked me over.

Thank God for Maw-Maw's cookies to keep Billy satisfied while I could focus on the magazine. I would eat a cookie or two, if there were any left, but he had already eaten three on the way down here. He looked into the bag of cookies now and offered me two. "That's more than half," he said as he began to eat two together, sandwich style. "Man, these are good," he said wiping some of a melted chocolate chip from his cheek with the back of his hand.

"And what about that?" I pointed to the paper bag he had tossed onto the floor just after he had boosted himself up.

He smiled and picked it up slowly. "Gee, I wonder what's in here?"

For a moment I despaired that it was more food and a *Playboy*. I reached for the bag, and he pulled it back. "Now, are you sure you know what's in here because …"

I snapped. I wanted to get on with the business of looking or just forget it. "Let me have it," I said and reached for the bag again.

"Hey. Take it easy, buster."

I was so angry I considered punching him until he started crying, as if I was actually capable of hurting him that much.

He held the bag behind him and laughed. "Somebody's awful horny."

At this point I think I could have hurt him and that realization was both frightening and exhilarating. I could have taken on Neanderthal Greg I was so pulsing with rage.

With the trap door still open, I jumped down and began running up the canyon. I looked back and stopped running when I could see he wasn't following. I walked between a few palms across the small amount of water that collected near them. Not much of an oasis, but then I wasn't far from houses and garden hoses should I need water.

My heart was pounding. I felt that I was twice as strong as usual and that if anybody so much as said hello I would beat on them until they were unrecognizable.

I had nowhere to go and just paced back and forth between the poor excuse for a stream and a boulder covered with bird crap. A couple of crows brought what looked like the remains of a squirrel and dropped it in front of me. They took turns pecking at it, while keeping an eye on me. I couldn't figure out what to do with all the energy I had. "Leave me alone or I'll squeeze you to death."

From behind me I heard Billy's voice, "You don't get what you want when you want it and you run off?"

"Shut up." I said it so fiercely that he took a step back. I didn't tell him I left to keep him from getting hurt. He would have just laughed.

He looked puzzled. I didn't usually talk this way to him, or to anybody. I felt I had entered *The Twilight Zone*, and Rod Serling would come out and explain how weird things happen when kids lose their parents.

Billy sat down. He had the paper bag in his hand. "Here. It's the first issue, so I brought gloves for both of us. They're in the bag, too." When I didn't respond, he took out two pairs of women's gloves and asked which I wanted. One was made of white cloth and reached almost to my elbow. The other pair was real soft brown leather, the kind my mother called kid gloves. Until an adult I thought it meant they were for children or women with very small hands.

I took the long ones and struggled to get the second one pulled up high enough to fit my fingers on my left hand once I had a glove on my right hand. Billy's hands were almost too big, but he squeezed them in his pair. I wondered if we would have to cut them off to remove them.

Billy opened the magazine so only he could see and then slowly turned it toward me. God, she was gorgeous. Her legs were turned just enough to cover you know what, but her upper body was in full unadorned view. This wasn't the only photo of a naked woman I had seen because Billy had shown us lots of other centerfolds but this was the very first issue of *Playboy*, and he had never brought it when all four of us got together to see the others. I think this was his way of saying that the incident with me outside his sister's window was over. I knew for sure he had forgiven when he said, "Why don't we try the Twambleys' tonight?"

I had never done any of this with a partner. I hadn't done it all that often alone. But after we saw Miss Monroe together, it seemed like the next logical step would be to go to a live show.

"I'll knock on your window. What time?"

I was still trying to decide if I would go, when I said, "I guess about eleven." Maw-maw takes her hearing aids out at night, so she is not a problem. Debbie stays up late, but she always has the radio on. I looked at the centerfold again. "I don't have an alarm, so you'll have to wake me up. When I hear you, I'll go to the window to let you know I'm up." We shook hands on it like we had just made a business deal. I had forgotten about Earl, but he usually slept pretty soundly.

Dad used to wake us up for school. Mom took over for him until she had her breakdown. Then Maw-Maw did it because she got up early to pray and read the Bible anyway. Tonight it would be Billy.

More than worrying this was wrong or something we could get arrested for, I wondered if it would ruin me for Gloria. I felt some disgust with myself but much more excitement. Having Billy go was risky since he was not as agile as me, but it also meant someone else to share the blame. Maybe even take all the blame. I mean, it was his family who had the magazines. Did his mother have stuff she looked at, too?

Maw-Maw asked me if I was sick because I didn't eat much dinner. Any other time I would devour her pork chops and buttery mashed potatoes. I even ate more spinach than I did meat. But my mind was playing a film of Marilyn Monroe. It was like her centerfold was in a stack of cards and with each card she shifted her position slightly. I could hardly concentrate on anything anyone said at the table. I pretended I was sleepy and went directly to bed.

I thought about Miss M just enough to get some release so I could sleep. I considered that it might make me less interested in going next door with Billy, but I didn't care now. Besides, there would be a few hours between now and trying to see one of the Twambleys, so it should be plenty of time to recharge.

I can't believe I thought about such stuff at twelve, but I did and it makes me sad to remember I resorted to such stuff in order to feel some kind of connection. If things had worked out better with Gloria, if we had been closer, geographically, or if we could have figured out some way to get to see each other now and then, maybe I would have learned how to give and receive love from her. In our family, love was manipulating another into giving you what you thought you needed. Tonight I could see a Twambley in some stage of undress, and I wouldn't have to manipulate anyone. Improvement?

When Billy rapped on my window, I was in the middle of a wonderful dream. I was pitching to Gloria, and Mr. Bodenhamer was at bat, but he was a much smaller version of himself. Dad was the umpire. In the stands were the Twambleys and Carrolls and Marilyn Monroe. She was cheering loudly but in that breathy voice. "Hey, battah, battah. Hey, battah, battah." Behind me was Maw-Maw offering me a gigantic fried chicken leg, bigger than a whole chicken.

"Joey. You up?" Billy had used a small rock to break into my dream world.

I shook my head and threw back the covers. At the window, in my now well-practiced loud whisper, I said, "Yeah, okay. I'll be right out." I had slept in my clothes so I only needed to put on shoes and get a jacket from my closet.

Once I was out back, I could see the flashlight beam running over the pepper tree and traced it back to Billy who was on the far side of the yard, next to the Twambleys' garage.

"Psssst." Why he said anything I don't know since it was obvious where he was, like a car dealer with a searchlight. This time we knew to watch out for dog poop and had decided we would come back at the first sight of the pooper. I had a piece of meat if we needed to distract him while we escaped. I had seen it done in a movie.

We used a patio chair to get high enough so we could swing our legs over the fence while holding on with our hands. I wasn't sure I had enough strength in my arms to make it over. I wasn't sure Billy could get his legs that high. But we both did fine. Billy landed in something squishy, but it turned out to be near the end of the hose so the dirt was just extra soft in that area.

We used hand signals like we were on some secret military operation. Peeking around the back of the garage, we saw one window with a light on. We hadn't even considered that everyone could be in bed. But it was summer and most everyone, even the Carrolls, stayed up a little later. It was the last window on the other end of the house.

My heart was pounding like we really were soldiers in enemy territory and could be killed at any moment. We ran to the house and paused. More hand signals and then I went first, ducking down as I passed each unlit window, knowing that it would be easier for someone to see out when it was dark inside. When I was next to the lighted one, I stopped and waited for Billy to catch up.

"Come on," I hissed.

Even in the dark, I could see that he was putting something in his mouth. My God, I never knew anyone who had to eat all the time. Later I would learn that he did it whenever he was nervous, and he was nervous a lot of the time. Then a bright light blinded us.

"What the heck are you doing?" It seemed funny that the person with the flashlight used "heck" instead of "hell," but only for a moment.

"Well?"

"We were looking for my cat."

I didn't know Billy had a cat.

The flashlight spoke again. "What made you think it was over here?"

By this time lights started coming on in the house and I could hear voices from inside.

"Well?"

"Gee, Mr. Twambley, you just never know where he might go."

"Look, I bet your parents don't know you're out here."

Billy saw an opening here. The light had been on Billy only, so he pulled me into the beam.

"Oh. Joey." Mr. Twambley's tone completely changed.

"Jim, what's going on?" Mrs. Twambley came out in her robe. Her hair was in curlers and in the half-light, she looked kind of scary.

"Nothing. The boys are just looking for Billy's cat."

I knew he didn't believe us, but you got a lot of slack when your dad had just died and your mother was in the hospital. I don't know if they knew it was a mental hospital, but in our neighborhood, that kind of news got around pretty easily.

"Okay." She touched her hair as if to make sure her curlers were still there and went back in.

Mr. Twambley came close to us and turned off his flashlight. "Listen to me. I don't know what's going on, but we've had some prowlers around here recently, and I don't want to think it's been you two." His breath smelled of alcohol. "Now, get home."

Billy started to go behind the garage and retrace our steps but decided it would be better to go down the Twambley's driveway and out the front. We didn't talk on the way back, but I was thinking about the next time already. I would make some noise and wait to see if he came out, then go on with my viewing. I thought it might be better to do it earlier in the evening because they were more likely to be up and Mr. Twambley might be more likely to think some criminal would wait until they were asleep.

CHAPTER THIRTY-ONE

I WOKE UP WITH a headache but felt hungry. When I came into the kitchen, Debbie was arguing with Maw-Maw. "Don't you trust my teacher? She wouldn't recommend me for something that was bogus."

Debbie still had her pajamas on. Well, she still had on what she slept in. This time it was a pair of men's boxer shorts (some actress must have worn it in one of those weird films she saw at the Capri) and a men's tank top, the kind Dad used to wear under dress shirts. She was pacing between the phone on the wall and the refrigerator. like she couldn't decide whether to have food delivered or eat something we already had.

"It's only four weeks. We rehearse almost every day and then perform on the last day. Miss DeSantis thinks I could get a major role. She knows the director."

"You're leaving?" I didn't mean to say it out loud, but Debbie and I had only just begun to get along, which meant Debbie had stopped finding every possible excuse to make fun of me. I had been so close to Mom that with her and me on the outs and Dad gone, Debbie could actually sympathize with me.

"Woah, Superboy's back."

Mom had bought a Superman costume for me for Halloween years ago, when I used to wrap a towel around my neck and jump off a chair to pretend I could fly. Last year she saw some pajamas with red-and-blue pants and the red-shielded blue top on sale. I wore them for the first time last night. I had a cape, too, but it was too much trouble to sleep in.

Debbie turned to Maw-Maw and started to say something, but Maw-Maw held up her hand like she was a cop signaling traffic to stop. "I'll think about it." Debbie stared at her for a while, then walked to the refrigerator, took a dill pickle from a jar, and began to suck on it.

I was watching her like she was some foreigner with odd habits. She took it as a criticism of her wanting to leave. "It's only twenty-eight days," she said, as if she was reneging on a promise to be around all summer.

While Maw-Maw fixed me some pancakes and bacon, I sat at the table looking at the salt-and-pepper shakers. Mom had a large collection, and this one was a Mickey and Minnie Mouse combo. Debbie sat nibbling at her pickle. Maw-Maw, after serving me, went to her room to begin preparing for her Sunday school class.

Before eating, I cut each of the three pancakes in half and then half again. With each of the twelve quarters, I cut off the tip and ate those first. Then I cut each quarter into three pieces. I would stab a piece with my right hand and hold a strip of bacon with my left. Then I would put the pancake bit in the right side of my mouth while I bit a piece of bacon with the left side. It took some practice but by the time I finished one whole pancake, I had it down.

Debbie didn't say anything. She seemed to sense both that I wanted company and that I didn't want to talk. She had her own thing going with the pickle, like she was trying to make it last all day. Someone watching might have thought we were engaged in some Zen exercise.

On Thursday, after Maw-Maw agreed to talk to the drama teacher in person, Mrs. DeSantis accepted Debbie's invitation for dinner and made a strong case to Maw-Maw that this was a special opportunity offered to very few high school students. It didn't hurt that she was from the South and kept a constant chatter of amazement over Maw-Maw's collard greens, red beans with rice, and rump roast. By the time the boysenberry cobbler with vanilla ice cream was finished, I think Maw-Maw would have agreed to let the woman adopt Debbie if she had asked.

Earlier that afternoon, either to seal my loyalty to his cat story alibi about being in the Twambley's backyard, or out of guilt for us getting caught, Billy brought me a few *Playboys* to keep. I decided to hide them in the closet under my shoebox of baseball cards because I planned to take out a card and pretend the baseball player was looking at the magazine with me. We would talk about how she looked and what we would do to get to meet her.

The next day I was in my room while Tamara was in Debbie's room listening to records. All the more reason to look at the *Playboys*. I knew Tamara was going to miss Debbie, too. I had already been missing Tamara, who seemed to act like nothing had happened between us. If I had been given the choice, I'm not sure which I would have chosen: the magazines or Tamara.

I spread out the three centerfolds and was imagining that the women were ignoring the baseball players and fighting over who would go with me to the next school dance. In the real world, I hated the dances. First, I was afraid to ask anyone to dance because they might turn me down. Second, when I did get the nerve, I was embarrassed at how I danced. I went anyway because that was the main way to get close to girls. I didn't know that the ones who danced well, boys and girls, had spent hours and hours copying what they saw on *American Bandstand*. I thought I was just cursed with being terminally uncool.

From Debbie's room I heard a sudden burst of "Twist and Shout." I thought they had just turned up the volume, but the sudden loudness must have come from them opening her door because a few moments later, the two of them came dancing into my room. I tried to hide the magazines, but only managed to throw one to the floor between the sofa and the wall.

"My, my, little brother. What have we here?" They were giggling and poking at me while saying things like, "Is this someone you know?" "I wonder what her mother thinks," and, "Do you think it's their diet?"

"Stop it and get out." I said it as angrily as I could, but they were having so much fun that I couldn't quite maintain my indignation. I think I wanted them to disapprove, so I could defend myself. I wanted to say that it's not that much different from bikinis at the beach or nude paintings in museums. I don't know who I had heard that from. It's a bit amusing since it is the kind of argument that Debbie would mount, and I had spent most of my life, with Mom's help, trying to prove how different I was from my sister.

"Lordy, what is all this noise about?"

I had forgotten about Maw-Maw. Debbie and Tamara were having so much fun with the centerfolds that I had not put them away. Maw-Maw just stood there looking at the magazines and then at me, like she had just been told

I had murdered my mother and couldn't believe I still had the knife in my hands while sitting next to the bloody body.

She shook her head slowly. She seemed equally disappointed and disgusted. She kept wiping her hands on her apron as if they had been dirtied by seeing the pictures. She held out one hand, and I gave her the two magazines she could see.

"Those aren't mine…" I stopped because I didn't want to get Billy in trouble. Although, for all I knew his parents allowed him to look. I mean, they were the atheists, weren't they?

"We'll talk later." Maw-Maw looked at Tamara when she said this, probably because she did not want to discuss this in front of someone who wasn't family. She, like Mom, believed that the extent of shame was directly proportional to how many people found out.

Tamara took this as a cue to go, and Debbie objected only mildly. I closed my door and almost felt relieved that they all now knew, especially since Debbie and Tamara thought it was funny and not nasty. To ensure some privacy, I leaned the top of my desk chair against the door just under the knob like I'd seen in gangster movies. Even if it only slowed an intruder down, it would give me some time to hide the incriminating evidence before anyone got into the room. I put one *Playboy* I still had in the closet and pulled out Dad's journal.

I sat down holding it in my lap, trying to conjure up Dad. It smelled dusty, like my shoes do after walking in the canyon, but not stinky. I imagined how it could have saved Dad's life in Korea by being in his front pocket and stopping a bullet before it got to his heart. Would Dad have been upset to see the magazines? I mean, he had this other woman. Who knows what else he had done that our church preached against.

I had not closed my closet door, a sin in Mom's world, and noticed my swim trunks hanging from a hook. I stared at them until I imagined my way back to Dayton and the first time I saw Gloria at the town pool. Then I saw Gloria walking down the street, her hair flipping back and forth over her shoulder each time she looked back at me. She kept getting smaller and smaller like when you look in a mirror that has a mirror on the opposite wall so one image shrinks inside the other back and forth until it's too small to see.

I went to my desk, opened the top right-hand drawer, and pulled out a notebook with a stuffed cover and a small gold-colored clasp that made it seem importantly private. I had gotten it as a prize for not missing a day of school in sixth grade. Mr. Clapper had handed it to me with the encouragement to fill it up with my thoughts at random, suggesting I had a gift for words. He even said I might be a writer one day.

I turned to the first page and wrote, *Thursday, August 16, 1962. My name is Joey. My father died a month ago and my mother is in the hospital for crazy people. My girlfriend's name is Gloria. Billy gave me some Playboys and Maw-Maw just took them away (except for the one I hid). I struck out the twins, and they beat up this homosexual kid. Billy and I were caught in the Twambleys' backyard trying to get a look at one of the girls. I want to be bigger and taller and never want to see the Grand Canyon again. I ran away and now I'm back home. I didn't walk the aisle at church, and Debbie is going to LA to be an actress.*

Writing it made it seem like someone else's life. I also felt more mature, like the act of writing made the events more controllable. It was a little like that day at Disneyland when I was first tall enough for the Autopia cars you could actually steer. I read what I had written again and waited to close it, seeing if there was something else I needed to say. Then something came to me almost like a voice whispering in my ear. I opened it and wrote: "In excelsis Gloria."

That night I tried our old phone signaling method to get ahold of Gloria. I had been too upset to talk with her since her father didn't let her come to San Diego on his business trip to California. That was when I returned to Sandy and the Twambleys and Cindy in my fantasies.

I found Dad's alarm clock and set it for 11:55. I put it under my pillow, so only I could hear it. Debbie was staying up late packing, even though she wasn't going to leave for a few more days, so, once she was asleep, she would be good until morning. I tried going to sleep without my usual relaxer but couldn't. I used the only *Playboy* left to help me get excited enough for release. I must have gone to sleep immediately because the next thing I remember was this irritating buzzing coming from my pillow.

I opened my door slowly and listened. I could hear Maw-Maw snoring and nothing else. I walked up to Debbie's door and didn't even hear music. Then I ran to the kitchen and dialed Gloria's number as fast as I could. I let it ring once, like we always did and waited for her to call back. Since we had not been calling for a while, there was no reason to believe she would be up to hear the one ring. If she did hear it, would she even want to call back? I forced myself to wait five minutes. To pass the time, I tried Debbie's dill pickle meditation, but I couldn't make myself like it enough to suck on it more than a minute. Then I timed my walking from the door to the garage, which was next to the wall phone, and back to the doorway to the hall using the clock above the stove. It took exactly four seconds. I figured that was fifteen trips a minute, or seventy-five trips for five minutes. I walked using a finger to indicate when I had reached a multiple of ten. For some reason I thought that that was easier than just walking back and forth watching the clock until five minutes was up.

I called again, let it ring once, and did another seventy-five laps. Now I had no idea what to do. I had convinced myself I needed to see Gloria as soon as possible. The first step was to talk to her, but what to do now? Risk waking her parents? Sneak into Maw-Maw's room and take enough money from her purse for a bus ticket? Start hitchhiking?

I sat at the table and began to pray. "Please, God, tell me what to do. Don't I deserve some help? Please help me." I thought of the scene in *It's a Wonderful Life*, when Jimmy Stewart is crying and just wants his old life back.

I called again and just let it ring. A man answered and asked who it was.

"Could I speak to Gloria?"

"Who is this?"

I hung up. I went to my room and got out the *Playboy*. I looked at a cartoon of a man and a horse that was asking how his date went. I didn't understand it and got furious that I had given the other two to Maw-Maw.

I went back to the kitchen and called Gloria again.

A woman answered, "There ain't no Gloria live here," and slammed down the phone.

I sat at the table. I was trembling. I couldn't decide what to do. Did I have her number wrong? I had memorized it, so I had never written it down. Then I heard a faint knocking at the front door. I went closer and heard it again. I turned on the porch light and opened the door slowly. In my fantasy world, I thought it could be Gloria.

"Hi, Joey."

Leslie Twambley was standing there and had obviously been crying. "Could I talk to Debbie?" I started to say I would check and then just let her in. She had on a windbreaker jacket over shorts and no shoes. Her hair was pinned up but obviously in a hurry, so it was kind of going in all directions. She thanked me and asked if she could sit down. She smelled of alcohol but didn't seem drunk, just real scared.

"I'll get Debbie," I said as if it were the afternoon and she had just come over for a friendly visit.

Debbie was just opening her door as I got to her room and groggily asked what was going on. I told her Leslie was here and wanted to talk to her.

"Twambley?"

I nodded and said I had to go to the bathroom. Debbie patted her cheeks and walked down the hall to the kitchen. In the bathroom I looked at myself in the mirror and realized my hair was a mess, as much as it can be when it's only about a few inches long. I also had completely forgotten I was in my Superman pajamas. I went to my room to change. I was wide-awake and didn't want to go back to bed. I put on a white T-shirt with blue horizontal stripes, like you might see on a guy who worked on a sailboat, and some old gym shorts. I walked slowly down the hall until I could hear clearly what they were saying.

Leslie was talking. "I can't keep it from them much longer. I know they'll want me to have it."

Debbie, still sounding a little sleepy, said, "You mean to give away or to keep?"

"I don't know." She started crying and with the sound of shifting chairs, I imagined Debbie was probably getting in a position to hug her.

I heard someone, probably Leslie, blowing her nose then the refrigerator door opened.

"Want some?"

Leslie said, "Yes. We met at a church meeting. He's about to go on a mission. I think it was that old line that got me, you know, 'I'm about to go off to war and may not come back, so let's do it while we still can."

"At least he didn't say, 'If you really loved me, you'd…'"

"Oh, he said that, too." A long pause. "I haven't been able to decide what to do."

Debbie asked Leslie if she wanted more to drink and offered some chips. God, are they going to stay up all night? It was like being in the fort. I wondered if Debbie would get out the Oreos next. Everything was said in barely audible tones, but I could hear it all.

"I have a friend whose older sister didn't want her baby. She went to this place in Chula Vista. It was a little scary because she bled quite a bit. But she's fine now and has a couple of kids."

"How much was it?"

I was surprised that Leslie didn't ask more about the bleeding. I guess she was already pretty desperate.

"I don't know, but I'll call my friend and see if it's okay to give you the number of the clinic."

I heard chairs moving again.

"Could I ask you a question?" Debbie was talking in more normal tones now. "Why did you come to me in the first place?"

"You're not gonna like it, but you always dress a little weird. I mean, I like it, but my parents would never let me dress like that. Anyway, I just thought you might know someone who had had it done."

Debbie didn't respond verbally, but I had to believe she was complimented. The worse thing in life would have been for her to be seen as normal.

I went back to my bedroom before Debbie walked Leslie out the door just like Dad and Mom always did with guests. She couldn't walk her to her car, so I wondered if Debbie would walk her to her door.

I took out my journal and recorded Leslie's visit. I don't know if they had ever talked before, but we certainly had never done anything together as two families. The Twambleys had sent flowers to Dad's funeral and I heard Mrs. Twambley offer to fix dinner for Mom, but it never happened since we had so many people from church helping out. I went to sleep wondering what I would do if I got Gloria pregnant. Then I wondered if I would ever see her again to get the chance. Earl stretched and rolled over to his other side, and I joined him in a surprisingly peaceful sleep.

CHAPTER THIRTY-TWO

IT HAD BEEN A month since Leslie talked to Debbie. Debbie had gone to Los Angeles and got back last night. I had been spending a lot of time with the Bodenhamers and hadn't thought of running away for a while. I couldn't get the courage to call Gloria again because I couldn't figure out how I got the number wrong and because I was afraid, if I did remember, she would be able to tell I had been thinking about Tamara and Cindy and the Twambley girls, especially Leslie.

About a week ago, I saw Leslie's father helping her put some luggage in the trunk of their car before they drove off. The rest of the girls and Mrs. Twambley stood in the driveway waving good-bye. You would have thought she was going away to prison from the way they looked.

Mom was still in the hospital, and Maw-Maw had not even talked about returning to the desert. I was back to playing regularly with the twins and Billy in the street when I wasn't going to the beach with the Bodenhamers. If you had observed me, I'm sure you'd have had no idea of all that had happened.

During the summer the Bodeys went to the beach on Saturdays and Sundays, plus Tuesdays when

Mr. Bodenhamer got off work early. In the fall, they still went at least one day every weekend. Now I understood why they all had such dark tans by the time school started in September. I had an open invitation to go with them any time, and I took them up on it regularly.

We visited Mom every Saturday and at least one other day during the week. She was getting somewhat better, but every few days she would act real weird, talking to herself or acting like someone was trying to hurt her, according to what I heard a nurse telling Maw-Maw when she asked if Mom would be able to come home soon. The nurse said Mom had to be stable for a few weeks before they would consider releasing her.

I was getting more and more used to not having any parents around. Even with Maw-Maw, it sometimes felt like I had actually run away and was in charge of my life. With Debbie doing more and more acting—she was auditioning for a part at the Old Globe for December—I felt it was time for me to figure out what I was going to do. Adults all the time asked me what I planned to be, and I thought that since I was so good in school I might become a teacher. I didn't tell any of my friends, but the more I thought about it, the more it seemed to fit. I probably wanted something that would give me a semblance of control over others. Also, I was aware of how teachers have lots of time off—summers, Christmas and Easter vacations—because Dad used to complain that teachers never heard of a holiday that wasn't worth missing work for.

While she was in LA, Debbie called almost every night to talk to Maw-Maw *and* me. Maw-Maw said Debbie was homesick. Possibly, although it's hard to think of Debbie ever needing anybody. I wanted to think that it was because she was worried about me.

Like I said, Debbie had come in on Monday night. It was now Wednesday afternoon, and she agreed to go with us to visit Mom. Mrs. Bodenhamer usually drove Maw-Maw and me, but today it was Mr. B

"So, how's the movie star?"

Debbie blushed as she got in the backseat with me.

Maw-Maw said, "We're just waiting to see her on Jack Paar. I promised her I would stay up late that night."

Mr. B laughed and looked into the backseat through his rearview mirror. "Need to practice your interview skills?"

Debbie rolled her eyes, but I could tell she was enjoying the attention. She pretended to be preoccupied with folding her shirtsleeves until both were above her elbows. Then she concentrated on smoothing her skirt. Her outfit made her look like she was on her way to a high school chorus performance.

At the hospital Mr. B let us out without parking. He said he had to go back to work and for us to call his wife when we were ready to leave. He and Maw-Maw talked to each other a few moments in private before he drove away.

The hospital looked more like an old high school, the kind you see in small towns back east. At the front wide concrete steps led to tall double doors on the first of two floors. The entrance was flanked by bushes in concrete planters. The outside walls had been painted recently so there were no cracks visible.

The lobby ceiling was at least twenty feet above us and a large wooden counter sat in front of a set of double doors with wire in the glass that led to the patients' rooms. Fortunately we never heard screams or moans or any of the things I'd seen in movies. This was the second place Mom had stayed and one might have mistaken it for an expensive hotel if it hadn't been for the locked doors and security offi-cers. It always felt a little creepy coming here, like it must feel when you visit someone in prison.

Mom had moved here after Debbie went to LA, so this was Debbie's first time. I was interested in how Debbie would react. I had been here often enough that it didn't make me as nervous as it used to. I could even respond to the woman who always sat in a chair just outside the inner doors without feeling weird. She said hello every five sec-onds (I timed it) and never changed her pattern whether someone returned her greeting or not.

A nurse came out of the door and ignored the three or four hellos she got as she escorted us through the doors and past the guard. Mom's room was at the end of the hallway. She shared it with a woman whose whole family was killed in a bus crash in the mountains just outside Monterrey, Mexico. The woman was polite and would respond to a simple hello and good-bye but nothing else. Her hair fell in long strands down the side of her face, giving her a kind of hangdog look. It seemed all her energy was used up with greetings.

"Hi, Mrs. Connor." We had to pass her bed to get to Mom.

"Hi, Jimmy." She never got my name right but at least always picked one that began with a "j." Once in a while she used a girl's name like Joan and Jill. She had a smile on her face until the hello or good-bye was finished, then she went back to a puzzled look that she worked on when she wasn't staring out the window.

Mom was sitting on the edge of her bed and nodded when she heard me greet Mrs. Connor. "Hi, Mom." While I had not worked through anything with Mom and wouldn't for years, I had very little anger for her in this condition. She just wasn't Mom.

Debbie sat beside her and took her hand. If you walked in the room at that moment, you might have thought she was a psychiatrist, albeit an unusually young one, who was trying to make her patient comfortable while she evaluated her state of mind. Mom looked at Debbie warily, like she expected to be chastised.

Maw-Maw had settled into a chair at the foot of the bed. She seemed to have grown older in the last few months. Her hair was the same gray and her eyes no less alert, but her face sagged more and she, a stickler for good posture, slumped. Maybe she was just tired, too.

"Mom, I got a part in *Romeo and Juliet* at the Old Globe. I get to play Juliet."

Maw-Maw and I looked at each other. It was the first we had heard.

"That's nice," Mom said, like Debbie had just revealed how she had had her eggs cooked for breakfast.

"Joey went down the Grand Canyon with the Bodenhamers."

"The Bodenhamers went to your fort?"

Mom was thinking of the canyon behind our house, but did her best to be excited for me anyway since Debbie acted excited when she said it. I don't remember what else we talked about, but we weren't there long. Mom always seemed to lose energy rather than gain it when we came, the opposite of what you'd have expected since she spent so much time alone.

Once we were back in the lobby, I stared at the "hello" woman, wondering if she had children or a husband. The security guard started to walk toward me like he thought I was going to something to her, so I turned to follow Maw-Maw and Debbie out the door. We said little as we waited for Mrs. B. There was a slight breeze, just enough to make the tall evergreens whisper. Gloria said her grandmother used to say it was God reminding us that everything was going to be okay.

On the way home, Maw-Maw asked what we wanted for lunch. Debbie said macaroni and cheese. I nodded in agreement. Mrs. B asked how Mom was, and Maw-Maw said there wasn't much change. "She still recognizes us though."

I realized that meant there was a chance that someday she might not and felt a shiver of fear. Debbie gently grabbed my hand, and I let her hold it all the way home. When Mrs. B let us out, she asked if Debbie and I wanted to go to the zoo. I nodded vigorously and looked at Debbie, hoping she would want to go, too. Debbie looked at me, winked, and said, "Sure."

Acting had a wonderful effect on Debbie and from then on, I would always look on it as a profession that made people kinder. Whenever I heard of actors or actresses being mean or selfish, I would assume they were just having an uncharacteristically bad day.

"We'll be back for you at four." Mrs. B smiled that kind of smile you use on people who are having a rough time, but you're glad it's not happening to you.

As we walked to the front door, I noticed that Jerry was mowing the lawn and Terry was using hand clippers to trim the edges. Billy waved from his jeep, where he was using a canister vacuum cleaner on the inside. I think he would have been twice as big if he didn't have the jeep to take up his extra eating time. I think he could have dealt better with the death of his father than with losing his jeep.

I went into my room and just sat, not even wanting to look at the *Playboy* I saved from Maw-Maw's confiscation. After a few minutes, Debbie knocked lightly on my door even though it was already open. I looked at her to give her permission to come in. She pulled up my desk chair and straddled it so she was leaning toward me, her chin on the backrest. She had hiked up her skirt so she looked like some taxi dancer taking a rest.

"You know, lots of kids have to deal with a mother like ours."

I looked at her like she had just said that I should be careful flying when I put on my Superman cape.

"Mom is what they call a narcissistic mother. She really can't think about what other people need."

Debbie paused like she could tell I had a question and didn't want to confuse me anymore. The only question I had was why she was talking about this at all.

"Is this about the magazines?"

She laughed and then said rather seriously, "Well it could be." She stood up, walked around, and sat down in the chair again, this time in the normal position.

"What happens at night when Mom tucks you in?"

"She doesn't do it anymore."

"Okay. But when she did."

I sat up, as if a better posture would make this easier. She leaned forward, resting her elbows on her knees. "Mom should never be allowing you to attach her bra or to zip her up. And she certainly shouldn't be lying in bed with you at night."

"I would appreciate it if you would leave." I stood by the door like that security guard at Mom's hospital.

Debbie stood up and shook her head. "Do you know what incest is?"

397

Now I have never asked Debbie where she got all the information she was laying on me that afternoon. She was smart, read a lot, and acted like she was savvier about psychological stuff than any of the grownups in our family, which she probably was. Certainly she knew a lot more than me. At this point, I knew I was ashamed about what Mom did and would have been mortified if anyone found out. It was embarrassing enough that Debbie might know about it, though I didn't know how since I couldn't imagine Mom telling her.

She sat again and smoothed her dress the way Mom used to. "If Dad did to me what Mom has done to you, he would be arrested."

Maw-Maw appeared at the door and said that we only had a few minutes before the Bodenhamers were supposed to come by.

"Yeah, I have to get ready," I said, gesturing with my head for Debbie to leave my room.

She paused and nodded slowly, as if to say, "I'll leave now, but we're not done."

I closed my door after her and got out a polo shirt that Gloria had said made me look muscular because it emphasized my biceps. Well, she didn't exactly use the word "muscular," but she definitely said that I didn't look skinny in it.

The Bodenhamers arrived without their kids. I was both relieved and disappointed. On the way to the zoo, they talked about the next time I was going with them to the beach, on Saturday, and asked Debbie if she wanted to join us.

"I'll have to check with my grandmother." That was only partially true, since Maw-Maw had been much less strict with Debbie once she got the report on how well she acted (on and off stage) while in Los Angeles and when she saw how much she had changed toward me. So what she really meant is that she didn't want to say now that she didn't want to go.

"Cindy will be disappointed if you can't come." Mrs. Bodenhamer didn't know how much of our church's teaching Debbie questioned, if not outright opposed, but it was true that Debbie was popular with most of the kids her age at church and Cindy was one of them.

I still got in free, but Debbie had to pay for the first time, a point of honor for her. We took the tour bus like we were from out of town and didn't know much about our world-famous zoo. Of course, most of the times we went because of people visiting, who always wanted to take the tour, so we almost had the script memorized. I loved the part where the driver drove by the area next to the zoo grounds. "Notice on your right the fences are three times higher than anything in the zoo. They house the most dangerous and unpredictable animals in the US, the modern teenager." Since most of the large mammals at the zoo were separated from us by moats and not by wire, it was a great contrast. On the other side of the fence, the "animals" he was referring to were high school students on racquetball courts. Though I knew not only what he was going to say but also when he was going to say it, I laughed every time.

When my wife, our girls, and I visited San Diego recently, I found out the bus drivers were no longer allowed to mention the teenagers because the students had begun to make comments back to the tour buses (not because the zoo felt they were less dangerous).

After the tour, Debbie and I decided to wander down to the large cat enclosures while Mr. and Mrs. B ate popcorn by the monkeys. Debbie stared at a lion that was sunning and licking itself like an ordinary house cat. "Daddy loved the lions. Well, he liked most everything about the zoo, but especially all the large predators that were not in cages." She looked at me and sighed. "I wonder if everything else will seem easy compared to what we're going through now."

I pretended to lick myself and Debbie mimicked me. A few people stared at us, and we got to laughing so hard tears came into our eyes. I licked my shirt and came up with a bunch of fuzz and started coughing. Debbie slapped my back, and I coughed up my gum, which a man passing by stepped on without knowing it. That got us to giggling again. We had just calmed down as the Bodenhamers walked up.

Mr. B sat next to me with Mrs. B on the other side of Debbie. He leaned back stretching his arms straight up and then brought one behind me on the bench. "Those guys are something else," he said gesturing toward two male lions lying next to each other. "It's hard to believe something that big can run fast enough to catch its food." He shook his head and smiled.

"Yeah," I said not knowing what else to say. Mostly I was just glad I didn't have to chase my food.

"Joey, I've got a favor to ask of you." He looked over at his wife, who was talking with Debbie about her latest audition. "A friend of mine at work has a son whose father just died in a car accident. Well, he wasn't in a car. He was walking across the street and got hit."

"Wow."

"Yeah, it's rough on him. I thought if you would be willing to talk with him, it might help."

I stood up and pulled on my pants to be more comfortable and sat down again. "Talk about what?"

"I don't know. Maybe what happened to your father."

"He wasn't hit by a car."

"I know, but he died suddenly. I think the kid is just in shock. He won't go to school and, when he does, he just sits in class, looking dazed."

I knew this was a good thing to do, and I knew that Mr. B would think more of me if I did, so I said, "Sure," as I was already trying to figure out a way to get out of it.

"Great. I'll ask him to join us the next time we all go to the beach."

Mrs. B and Debbie had been quiet for a while, probably because Mrs. B had been waiting until Mr. B and I were finished talking. "George, ask this young lady what her next acting job is."

"I thought you were only doing internships. You mean you're going to be making money?"

Mrs. B nodded vigorously. "You're darned right. We should get her autograph now while she's still willing to talk to us."

Debbie shook her head to pretend they were exaggerating, but I think she felt they were just stating the obvious.

"Okay, what will you be doing next, Miss Norton? Or will you be using a stage name?"

"Debbie's good enough. I've got a part in *Romeo and Juliet*."

"Here at the Old Globe. Starting next month, right?" Mrs. B said turning to Debbie.

"Previews start on November twenty-seventh and we open in December."

"Tell him who you're playing." Mrs. B was like a kid on Christmas morning who's seen the presents already and can't wait to tell everyone.

"So, who are you…"

"I'm Juliet."

"The star of the show, no less."

"Well, Romeo has got a lot of lines, too."

Mr. B offered a hand to shake and then pulled her in for a hug. "Congratulations. Your father would have been proud."

We walked through the reptile exhibit and had snow cones near the gorillas at the entrance. During the ride home, the Bodenhamers reminisced about all the times they had been to the Old Globe over the years and said they were ordering tickets as soon as they figured out a date they could go. I felt proud and wondered if any of the guys in the neighborhood would be impressed.

CHAPTER THIRTY-THREE

THAT NIGHT, DEBBIE WANTED to watch *The Rebel*, and Maw-Maw wanted to watch *Wagon Train* right after it. I didn't care as long as we watched *The Dick Van Dyke Show*, which came on after both. Reluctantly, Maw-Maw allowed us to eat off TV trays while we watched.

Because Maw-Maw wanted to give us a little more freedom, I was staying up until eleven o'clock (almost two hours later than the twins). For dinner Maw-Maw had fixed a chocolate cream pie for dessert, and we all had an extra piece in the kitchen just after Dick Van Dyke. Debbie was pretty talkative for a change, maybe it was the pie, and told us all about her time in Los Angeles. I don't remember her ever doing this with Mom. Maybe with Dad, but definitely not Mom.

"We put on five children's stories, and I had a role in each one. I was the only one. My favorite was *Little Red Riding Hood*."

Maw-Maw asked who played the wolf, and Debbie blanched like Maw-Maw discovered a secret.

"Some guy named Jeff. He lives in Pasadena with his father." She licked some chocolate off her fork. "His mother died last year." I thought I saw her begin to tear up. She got a paper towel from above the counter and blew her nose.

"Well, I'm happy for you. If that's what you want," implying that an acting career wasn't exactly what Maw-Maw had in mind for her. "I'll pray that you get more roles." Maw-Maw didn't know that getting to play Juliet at the Old Globe meant she had already gotten a pretty good start.

Another surprise from Debbie in a whole string of them recently: "Thanks, Maw-Maw. I would appreciate that."

Maw-Maw started to stack and rinse the dishes, but Debbie said she would do them. Maw-Maw hesitated probably because she thought she had misheard, but Debbie was already adding soap to the water in the sink and submerging the plates and silverware. Maw-Maw hugged Debbie from behind, I suppose because of Debbie's willingness to help, but probably more for her openness to receiving what Maw-Maw had to offer spiritually. She signaled for me to get a hug, too, which I did, and she left the room with smiling eyes.

When we heard Maw-Maw close her bedroom door, Debbie sat down at the table and motioned for me to sit across from her. "Don't worry, I'm going to take care of the kitchen, but I want to talk to you first."

In spite of how nice she had been to me lately, I knew there was a lecture coming. I know it was a common story: the older daughter taking over when the mother dies. Sure, Mom wasn't dead, but it didn't look like she was coming back any time soon, so Debbie saw her opportunity. It wasn't that surprising since she was always acting like she knew more than Mom and Dad when both of them were still at home. Now she only had Maw-Maw to compete with. She took out the rubber band from her ponytail, flipped her hair forward, and then put it back, but a little tighter.

"You know what I was saying about the narcissistic mother."

Things had been going so well between us I wished she hadn't gotten into this again, but I was tired after the zoo and the visit to Mom and just wanted to stay up to watch *The Steve Allen Show* unmolested, so I hoped if I listened for a while, she would leave me alone.

"Look. You know what incest is, right?"

"So?" I only knew that it was something bad.

"Joey, you're not to blame."

"For what?"

Debbie looked at me like she just realized this was going to be much more awkward than she thought. "Mom is sick."

"I guess that's why she's in a hospital."

Debbie chuckled, maybe enjoying that I was mimicking her kind of response.

"I mean, she's mentally sick."

"Would that be why she's in a MENTAL hospital?" I said with a gesture that meant that I thought she had said the most obvious thing in the world.

"Look, you little twerp, I'm trying to help. Dad had a mistress for years, and Mom lies with you at night. That's a problem. Also, I know about Sandy and the Twambley girls."

I wanted to know what she knew, but I didn't want to hear her say it. I wondered if she knew about Tamara, too. I didn't care any more about Steve Allen. I just wanted this to be over. She would have had to have more than one source, and the thought of people in our neighborhood talking about me was horrifying.

"I have a friend who was taken away from her family because of stuff like this."

"Like what?" I regretted asking as soon as the words left my mouth. "Never mind." I got up to leave.

"Sexual stuff between the parents and the kids."

I sat down wondering if Debbie thought that Mom and I had done what I did with Tamara or what I wanted to do with Sandy and the Twambleys or even the relatively innocent stuff with Gloria. Again, I wanted to know, but I didn't want to hear it out loud.

I went to the sink, picked up a plate, and slowly sponged it off if circular motions. It was plastic, but I placed it in the rinse water like it was made out of the most delicate china. Debbie picked it up and, taking her cue from me, slowly wiped it dry and put it away. We finished the dishes without talking. After Debbie covered the pie and put it in the refrigerator, she said, "I'll wipe the table and sweep the floor." I nodded and went to bed.

CHAPTER THIRTY-FOUR

THE FOLLOWING SUNDAY THE church was having a picnic at La Jolla Shores. Mr. and Mrs. B were organizing it, and Mr. B asked Debbie to be in charge of a Frisbee game for the younger kids. In keeping with her new improved self, Debbie agreed and even asked me to help her. Pastor Bob was on vacation with his family, so the Bodenhamers were really running things. In the morning at church, the Bs passed out flyers with food assignments and a warning about riptides.

Debbie, who got her driver's license just before she went to Los Angeles, drove Maw-Maw and me to church. After the morning worship service, I was following her to our car when Mr. B pulled me aside. "Remember the boy whose father was killed in a hit and run? He's in juvenile hall." He nodded at me, raising his eyebrows. "I couldn't get him to join us for any of the beach trips."

I nodded. I could see he wanted me to take it as a warning. He didn't know it, but I had thought of doing stuff like shoplifting or sneaking into some house at night or just grabbing some woman's purse and running away. Not because I wanted something we couldn't afford, but just to do something I shouldn't, like it would be payback for having the stuff done to me that wasn't fair.

Debbie drove home like an old lady, waiting extra long at stop signs and staying at one intersection with a green light until she had looked both ways at the cars that had the red light! I was about to tell her to let me out so I could walk home when she asked Maw-Maw a question.

"Can Tamara come with us to the beach?" Debbie looked in the rearview mirror at me.

"Sure, honey." Maw-Maw turned slowly and stiffly toward me. "You bringing someone, too?"

I had thought of asking Billy, but he hated the ocean. He had gone out during a storm on one of their trips to Hawaii, and a wave had kept him under just long enough for him to promise never to come back, calm weather or not, Southern California or not. I also thought of Gloria, but, even if she were out visiting, I didn't want her to be in the same car with Tamara and me.

"Nah."

Tamara arrived at our house just as we had finished loading the food into the trunk. She smiled at me, but I couldn't tell what it meant. I was pretty sure no one would have had any idea of what we had done in the fort from the way she looked at me, but she made me nervous. I smiled and got in the backseat. Debbie was driving again, with Maw-Maw in the front. At first I thought Tamara had on a red bra under her sleeveless blouse when she sat next to me, but I soon figured out it must be her bathing suit. I stared out my window just like I had on the way back from the hospital after Dad had died.

I wasn't seeing the scenery because my skin was tingling like I imagined it would feel after being stung by jellyfish.

At times I could see her in the window reflection. When I couldn't, I imagined her in the fort. For a while I had a buzzing in my ear to match the tingling. If she had touched me, I would have screamed. I was relieved when we finally got to La Jolla Shores and I could concentrate on important stuff, like how skinny I was compared to all the normal kids.

In one of the grassy areas next to the parking lot, two of the older Royal Ambassadors were already choosing teams for a softball game. Mrs. B had sectioned off an area closer to the beach for the sack race that was to follow. I helped Maw-Maw take the food to the picnic tables that would soon be covered with enough for the whole church even though only a fraction were coming.

When it was decided that the Frisbee game would follow the sack race in the same place and Debbie wouldn't need me yet, I went back to the car to get my baseball glove to warm up. Walking past a tall palm, I passed two women talking. I recognized them from church but didn't know their names.

"Pastor Bob is on vacation, all right." The rhythm of her high voice sounded like the "Pick a Little" chicken song in *The Music Man*.

"You mean she finally found out?"

"Oh, come on. She's known for years. Get this. After the Norton funeral, Mabel heard his daughter yelling when she caught Bobby and Dorothy in the garage."

"Doing what?"

"Oh, nothing much, but just a little too friendly, shall we say." I couldn't see Mrs. Hen, but I imagined her clucking and shaking her head.

I wished Debbie had been there. She would have thought of some subtle but crushing comeback. Or she might have decided to wait until she could catch the women committing some hypocrisy of their own and let them have it. I was angry, probably because I knew what they said about Mom was true.

By the time I came back from the car, the women were talking about the time Pastor Bob's wife stayed behind with her parents in Mississippi for two months after they visited over Christmas. They also mentioned the sudden departure of a choir member who was a regular soloist at the same time with as close to the looks of a model as anyone in the congregation, except maybe Mom.

"They won't last much longer, I bet." They were whispering now but still loud enough for me to hear. "Someone said Dorothy went off the deep end because of him, not because of Sam's passing."

Having already thought about what Debbie might do gave me the courage to speak. I walked around the tree into full view of them. "Hi, I'm Joey. My mother is Dorothy Norton. She's in the hospital because my father just died. Hope you enjoy the picnic."

I hardly looked at them while I was talking, but enough to see that both were Mom's age, only fatter and paler. When I also said that they wouldn't have to worry about anyone wanting to commit adultery with them, I knew I was successfully channeling my sister.

I walked back to the area for the softball game just in time to get picked for the team Cindy, Tamara, and Debbie were on. I couldn't concentrate on the game, not even on Cindy or Tamara. I played left field and missed the first ball hit to me. It flew over my head and, by the time I had chased it down, the batter had walked across the pie tin serving as home plate. I asked a father of one of the RA guys who was watching from the sidelines to take my place. It was seen as generous on my part, but I just wanted to get further away from the palm women.

I walked toward the waves until the sand became wet. I stood still when the foam from the next wave passed over my feet, leaving me slightly sunk into the sand. I wondered how long it would take to submerge my whole body. It had been a while since the shark movie at school, but I was still a little uneasy, even on shore.

"Going in?" I hadn't noticed that Mr. B had walked up beside me.

"Not yet." Or ever, I thought. I should have invited Billy because he would have understood why I wanted to stay on shore.

"Did you know Cindy's going to give some surfing lessons?"

"No."

He was smiling, and I hoped this meant that what happened on the rafting trip and before in his house was not a problem anymore, that he could trust me around his daughter. I had no idea since it was the middle of the day.

"She's going to offer it to the older kids who don't want to do the sack race." He stopped as if he knew about me and the sharks. "She'll have them practice on shore before going in the water. You caught on fast last time. Maybe you could help." He turned his body toward me. He had on a tight T-shirt and long surfer jams. He looked young enough to be my older brother. "How're you doing?"

I wanted to ask if he was talking about girls in general, Gloria in particular, Dad, Mom, or my career prospects, but it didn't matter. Dad was gone for good—actually for bad—Mom seemed almost as gone as he was, and nobody, even Tamara, made up for not seeing Gloria.

"I met this cousin in Texas."

A kid came running by, close enough to splash us. A man was telling him to stop and apologized to us as he ran after him. Compared to the kid, he was going pretty slowly, so the only chance he had of catching him was if the kid obeyed his voice.

"Boy or girl?"

"Girl," I said, feeling my face heat up.

"First or second cousin?"

"I don't know, but not first."

Was he worried about whether we could marry? We stood watching a few surfers catch waves and then immediately fall off, one rather spectacularly, his board flying up in the air.

The boy and the man came back by with the man almost dragging the boy behind him. Both of them splashed us, but the man was too angry to notice. He alternated between whispering loudly right in the boy's ear and then continuing to drag him. "This is it. You have done it now," I could hear him say.

Mr. B looked at me with raised eyebrows and then the man and boy. "Ain't easy being a parent." He looked down at me. "Ain't easy being a son, either. What's her name?"

"Gloria."

"Lovely." He looked out toward two surfers paddling furiously to catch the same wave. "Have you been in contact since you left?"

If there was any adult that I might be willing to talk about Gloria with, it was Mr. B. It just occurred to me that he looked more like the twins than Captain Carroll did: the broad shoulders, the haircut, the defined pecs and biceps. If I wasn't so unsure about how I stood with her, I might have been able to tell him about the late-night calls, the cancelled visit with her father, even the Monopoly board kiss. But I couldn't.

"Not really. Do you know why the pastor isn't here?"

"He's on vacation with his family." He answered quickly and looked at me a moment before a Frisbee flew above us. It was snatched in midair by a Weimaraner with those spooky yellow eyes.

"I heard some women talking about him, and they said he went on vacation because of two church women. And my mother." Was I testing him the way the soldier son did in the story the pastor told a few weeks back?

"Joey, have you ever had someone surprise you by doing something completely out of character, or at least the character you knew them for?"

"Are you talking about my dad?"

He put his arm around me. "Well, I wasn't thinking of him. But he would work."

"You know about him and Laura?"

"I didn't know her name, but, yes, I had heard about another woman."

"I don't know why he did that." Certainly not because Laura was more attractive.

The two surfers we had been watching had both fallen off their boards and were running in the shallow water to retrieve them. They talked for a while before one guy picked up his board and started walking in. The other turned toward the ocean and began paddling back out on his knees.

"What did he tell you about it?"

413

"Nothing. We only found out when he was dying." I didn't want to talk about it anymore. I didn't care why Dad did it, and I didn't care what the women said about the pastor either. I looked back at where they were setting up the tables with food. "I'm hungry."

"Well, we have the remedy for that." He put his arm on my shoulder. I let it stay there for a few steps and then ducked out from under it and ran to the food.

It was the usual picnic fare: hot dogs and hamburgers cooked on charcoal grills, fried chicken, potato salad, coleslaw, Jell-0 with grated carrots, and enough pies and cakes for an army. I ate with the Bodenhamers but said little. The two palm tree women decided that one plate each was not enough and had their husbands load up a second plate of desserts before their guys had gotten anything for themselves.

Mr. B said something to his wife that I couldn't hear and scooted over to me. "Grab some dessert and come with me."

The Garner brothers were fighting over who would get the last chocolate cookie and dropped it on the ground. That led to a "See" from their mother and a threat to take them home if they didn't behave better.

I took a big helping of banana pudding with vanilla wafers that Maw-Maw had made. Mr. B put a brownie on his plate and a small dollop of whipped cream on top because it was the last in the can. That sputtering sound usually sounded funny to me, but not now.

He motioned for me to sit with him on a hillock of grass that dropped off a foot or so to sand below, perfect for our feet. We both ate without talking. When the bulk of the brownie was gone, he ran his finger over the crumbs left on the plate and licked his finger. I wanted to do the same with the pudding left but settled for running my spoon over the plate again and again until there wasn't much left to get with a finger. I would have had to lick the rest off with my tongue, but even my outdoor meal manners didn't allow that.

"When I asked you earlier if anyone had done something out of character, I really meant to ask if anyone had ever disappointed you. I'm not talking about your father. I'm talking about Pastor Bob."

He went on to explain how people who are leaders sometimes have temptations the rest of us don't encounter and that the pastor was getting help, that to him being the most important part. "All of us screw up. The men we respect aren't naturally better people, just people who have been willing to get help when they needed it."

He looked at his plate like he couldn't believe he had already eaten all of the brownie. "See, I know. I've been in a group called AA for years. Do you know what that stands for?"

"I guess it's not American Airlines."

He laughed. "No. But I often felt like I was flying, way above everyone else. It's for people who can't control their drinking. It's Alcoholics Anonymous. It's the best thing that ever happened to me. When I was drinking, I used to do lots of things I'm not proud of, and one was to look into windows at night."

I thought the last thing I needed was to talk to someone about this. I was ashamed. All I wanted was some relief from the anxiety I was feeling and that wasn't possible right now. Also, I wanted desperately to make some kind of loving connection to a girl and, until I met Gloria, I only got it with magazines and windows. Well, until Tamara.

Cindy walked by and said to me, "So, are you going to eat all day or do you have some time to help me?" She was carrying a board and about ten kids were following her, mostly boys.

Mr. B got up. "There'll be plenty of food left if you're still hungry. Go catch some waves."

I got up and started to take my plate to the trashcan.

"I'll toss your plate for you."

A little closer to the water, Cindy had us all stand around her in a large enough circle that no one was standing behind anyone else. It was hard to listen to her and look at her at the same time. I had already seen the same suit on the Grand Canyon trip but that didn't make it any less interesting. She wasn't any Marilyn Monroe, but her proportions were perfect and all the guys around her had probably already estimated her measurements. In one of Billy's *National Geographic* magazines, I had read that cleavage was attractive to men because it reminded them of the slit between the buttocks. That seemed gross to me because it was the breasts themselves—what I saw and what I imagined—that I couldn't get enough of. Fortunately she was talking without looking at me so she had no idea.

"Joey, you show them."

"What?"

She said it slowly like part of my problem was that English was not my first language. "You lie down like you're going to do when you paddle out. Stroke the sand a little to pretend. Then put your hands on the edge of the board and start to do a push up. If you're right-handed, get your right foot behind your left foot and stand sideways but look forward. When you catch a wave, get into position quickly. It will make it easier to keep your balance."

I listened this time, but it was hard. I kept imagining I was her board and she was paddling on top of me.

"Okay?"

I nodded and lay down on the board. It was a little hot, but I didn't say anything. I brushed my hands through the sand and stood up quickly. I didn't jump up into position like I'd seen some of the surfers do today, but I was pretty fast. I had learned from the last time she and Loopy showed me.

"So you're left-handed. I mean, left-footed."

I switched immediately so my left foot was forward. She adjusted my position slightly by grabbing my shoulders. The other guys now had a dilemma: to get in the right position to please her or to be just enough off that she would have to touch them.

There were only two girls. Cindy let them go after me and then she let all the boys practice. One guy kept losing his balance, so she let him practice longer. He was not quite as athletic as the twins, but he was close and certainly not nearly as clumsy as he was today. Once he got up perfectly, only to teeter and fall over like we had just had a small earthquake. She was onto him now and said we were all doing well enough to try it in water.

"We're going to practice where it's shallow first and then try a wave or two further out. It's much harder to balance when the board is not moving across a wave, so don't worry if you can't stand up easily here."

Cindy started to pick up her board, but Kerry and Stan, who had been standing closest to her during the whole onshore demonstration, grabbed opposite ends and stood waiting for her to proceed them into the surf. They were both in high school, but only a little taller than me. Each already had enough body hair and large enough heads to look like adults, at least when they were sitting down. They had been best friends since I had first met them at church and were both phenomenal singers. They had already won some citywide music contests, but never used their fame to put you down. They loved doo-wop and would entertain us on RA campovers with Mr. B well into the night. Mr. B would sing the melody and they would take turns being the one just above or the one just below him, like his wife and daughter did on our trip to the Grand Canyon. They never seemed to get tired of our perennial request: "Put Your Head on My Shoulder."

Cindy stationed me to watch for incoming boards that some surfer further out might lose control of while she got everyone up, whether she had to hold them in place or not. She asked the doo-woppers to help Mr. B bring the other boards he had brought in their wagon.

CHAPTER THIRTY-FIVE

THE SUN WAS NOT quite low enough to blind you, but it was hard to look for the next wave without shading your eyes. Cindy put Kerry and Stan on either side of the girls, holding them up so they could at least feel what it would be like to stand. Cindy kept repeating that it would be so much easier when they were actually moving on a wave, but I don't think they were convinced. I had kept two boards from hitting them and got thanks from the surfers they belonged to because it meant they didn't have to swim all the way into shore to get their boards, not necessarily because they were worried about hurting anyone.

"Want to try a wave?" Cindy followed her offer with some enthusiastic nodding, but the girls were having none of it. Apparently they were already worn out from the simulations, both being quite skinny. Besides, they were already getting sunburned. Their skin looked more like a bright red version of the white butt that the dog in the Coppertone ad revealed.

"Okay. How about everybody watch me catch a wave, and then we'll see who wants to give it a try?"

Stan and Kerry nodded a little too enthusiastically. I was in water up to my calves and felt I had already accomplished a heroic feat, so anything to put off the inevitable was welcome to me. Cindy turned the board toward the horizon and began to paddle out. Her butt swayed ever so slightly as she churned over the first few breakers, not that that was all I was watching. The waves were a little shorter than me, but still high enough that her board went up and down as she passed over them, like she was simulating a seesaw. When she was on the other side of all the breaking swells, she turned the board toward us and waved. For the next few minutes, her body faced us while she looked over her shoulder for a wave to catch. She had told us it would take a little practice to know when to begin our paddling. She said speed mattered some, but timing would get us waves that stronger guys couldn't catch.

She waved again just before she began to paddle. At first she alternated arms but after a few strokes, she began to punch the water with both arms simultaneously like a swimmer doing the butterfly. The wave passed by without taking her along. She sat up and did an exaggerated version of a shrug before paddling back out.

She tried twice more before she caught a wave, which seemed a bad omen for us beginners. As soon as her board picked up momentum, she stood in the surfer crouch and turned to the right, sliding down the wave like that was its sole purpose. When the wave broke, she continued across the face and then turned it back over the wave and got off in water up to her hips.

She walked to us. "Well, what do you think?"

Stan said, "I think you know how to surf."

She laughed. "I've been doing it for a while, but the waves aren't very big, so if you fall off—"

Kerry interrupted, "You mean *when* we fall off."

"If or when you fall off," she smiled at Kerry, "it won't drive you under the water much."

That "much" seemed scary to me. I was already concerned about what was touching my legs while we were waiting in the shallows for her, without my head having to go under, too. She asked who wanted to go first, but she was looking at me.

Mr. B had already told me that there had not been any shark sightings at La Jolla, much less attacks, in all the years he'd been a lifeguard. That was the main reason I had been willing just to go as far as I had. Cindy pushed her board toward me and went for the board Stan and Kerry were holding onto. They relinquished it to her after making it clear they were ready to go next.

I wanted to paddle on my knees like I'd seen most of the other surfers do today, but it was too difficult. First, it hurt my knees, and second, I kept losing my balance, not enough to fall off but enough to put me six or seven board lengths behind Cindy in no time. In the beach party films, there were always plenty of girls to witness successful surfing attempts. I imagined Gloria kissing me before I paddled out just in case I never came back alive. I would then wave to her in the midst of some spectacular trick with my board. Of course the spectacular trick I would be doing today would be to catch a wave, much less stand up. It looked pretty easy as I watched a few guys take off. Cindy watched them, too, and I wondered if you had to be an experienced surfer to get her respect.

"Joey, get ready. There's a set coming in now. Do you see it?"

I knew a set meant more than one wave, and I guessed I saw the rises in the water she was referring to.

"Just get in position now. Start paddling as hard as you can when I say 'go.'"

I lay down on the board and looked back at her. She had her arm in the air like the guy with the starting flag at a car race. She looked back at me and then out toward the set. One wave was coming by, and she shook her head. For the next she gave a nod and held up her hand to wait. Then down her arm came, and I took off.

I had never done anything so fast in my life. I did what she had done first, alternate arms. I was moving pretty good, but she yelled out to go faster. "Both arms," she yelled. "Both arms at the same time."

I almost levitated off the board I was pumping into the water so fiercely. I could feel my arms start to burn at the point they were sliding against the board. I had to angle my arms out because the board was much wider than my body. Every time she yelled "faster," I punched the water a little deeper. When she said, "That's it; you've got it," all I heard was faster.

"Joey. Stop." I thought she meant I was about to hit someone, but what she meant was that I had caught the wave and it was time to stand up. Then everybody started yelling, "Stand up. Stop paddling and stand up."

I did and in one sweet motion of futility, I began to turn the board to the right. Unfortunately, we had drifted over enough to be in a set that was breaking left and I turned right into the full force of the breaker.

I never had swallowed so much water. I couldn't breathe. I couldn't see. I couldn't tell which way was up and which way was down. I heard later that some guys called me a few unpleasant names as my board popped into the air and almost hit them.

I was still in the water but above the surface now, so I could breathe. I was completely worn out, like I had just run an 880 at sprint speed. Gradually my breath was coming back. I heard cheering and applause and looked out toward the waves to see who was showing off.

"Wow. I mean, cowabunga." It was Cindy not far from me on her board coming over to boost me up and ride me in.

"I can swim in." I felt that I should pay at least some for not making it. I would have thought they were making fun of me if Cindy hadn't been in on it, too.

"That time with me and Phoebe was the first time you've been surfing?"

I nodded.

"This was the first time you've caught a wave?" she said like a lawyer who doubts the truth of a witness's response. I nodded waiting for the Debbie-like zinger, even though Cindy had never been that way with me.

"Do you realize how long it took me to catch a wave? I would go out with Dad and just practice paddling. For weeks."

Kerry had saved the board I was on from going all the way back in. Looking toward the sun, everyone was a silhouette, like two-dimensional cutouts for a shooting range. Kerry pushed the board to me as if I were a celebrity he wanted to please. His upper body looked massive. He appeared tall because he was in water up to his waist and you couldn't tell whether he was over six foot in four-foot deep water or barely five four in three-foot water, which was closer to the truth.

Cindy was ahead waving me out for another try. I was especially nervous now because I "knew" everyone would expect me to stand and turn, that is, to accomplish the whole point, riding a wave. I had seen enough surfing movies, documentary and fictional, that I had a pretty good idea of what I wanted to look like, and I don't just mean the massive, well-developed lats and chest. I could almost feel myself in that crouching position, arms outstretched at first and then down by my sides, as comfortable with surfing as I was with throwing a baseball. I even saw myself walking forward on the board, not enough to "hang ten" or even "five," but to show that I had control of the wave.

Cindy was smiling widely. Her hair hung straight down and framed her face like a museum painting. I wanted to tell her how beautiful she was and that I would do anything to be her boyfriend if things with Gloria didn't work out. I was caught in the reverie of imagining myself sliding down the wave atop my board and hearing Cindy say she'd be glad to go to a movie with me, when she yelled out, "Here it comes."

The "it" was a bulge in the water that seemed to suggest the surfacing of a whale. It was already starting to foam a bit at the top, it was so steep. I swallowed and followed her command to paddle, even though it seemed I would be on shore before it broke. I was wrong. It passed under me but carried Cindy with it. She was screaming with delight, the kind of scream I came to associate with another exciting pleasurable activity.

I sat up and watched her as best I could. I could see her catch the wave and then begin the drop down until she was almost out of sight. Next it broke with a sound that said you better take me seriously or I will crush you and your flimsy fiber-glassed gear. I watched her try to kick back over the wave, saving herself from a wipeout and avoiding the exhausting swim back to shore to get her board. Instead, she went further down and the board popped up in the air about twenty feet. She was just below it, and I could see it was headed right for her. She managed to move out of the way just as another wave came in that was carrying a guy who tried to avoid her. Both of them moved into each other's path, like two people doing the dance that follows a chance meeting on a sidewalk, each assuming the other is moving in the opposite direction.

At the last minute, he pulled out of the wave just like she had tried to do. He was not able to get the nose as high as he wanted for a clean break and caught her on the side of the head. I was stunned. I looked into shore. For what I don't know. Maybe it was to see if Mr. B was watching and would be swimming out to save her. As I learned later, he did see it happen, had borrowed a board, and was paddling furiously out while I was going to her. It was a good thing I didn't see him, or I might have just sat there waiting until it was too late.

I could not see her above water but she could have just been on the other side of the swells that seemed to be coming in at a much faster rate than I remembered they had been doing a few minutes ago. It was like the big swell had pulled along all the others faster than they would have gone normally. The guy that hit her was going up and down like a bird diving for food. He came up again just as I paddled over. "She's right here somewhere," he said going down again.

He was wrong. I saw her head, but not her face, a few yards toward open water, and paddled furiously to get beside her. I pulled her up by the hair. I did it with one hand, so it was not my normal strength that was responsible. I had read about the mothers who lifted large sedans off their children when it would normally take a few NFL linemen just to lift one end of a VW Bug. Anyway, I pulled her face above water but did not see her gasp for air. She looked a lot like she was unconscious or, worse, dead. I had seen people revived in movies by alternating putting pressure on the victim's chest and lifting their arms, but that required the victim to be lying on something solid, like the edge of a pool.

Later I found out that Mr. B had been yelling to keep her above water. Fortunately, even though I didn't hear him, that seemed like a pretty obvious first step. I managed to get her closer to my board to try to get her on top, as if the danger was her being wet. She had made no sounds at all by this time. Then, I channeled the Cagney movie from a few nights ago like Debbie had with Mom and slapped her, not hard, kind of like a trial to see if I could get the force just right, not too hard to hurt her, but enough to wake her up, if she could be woken up.

I knew then anyone unconscious needed to breathe most, so you do whatever you can to get their lungs working. I slapped her again and yelled, "Wake up, Cindy. Wake up." If Mr. B had gotten to her a little sooner, he might have reasonably disapproved and she might not be alive today, but somehow I got it in my mind that I should hit her, harder and harder, until she showed some signs of life.

She woke up after a few more smacks and grabbed my hand. "What the hell are you doing?" Except for Debbie, I never heard anybody at church use hell, unless they were referring to where we weren't going and where all the people who didn't understand the Bible the way we did were. She sank down and then popped up again, gasping for breath the way anyone might who's fallen off a board and been pushed under by a big wave.

By this time Mr. B had made it within earshot (and eyeshot) of us and was yelling for me to keep hold of her. She had slipped off the board, so I reached down to pull her up, but felt I shouldn't be pulling on her hair this time. I tried to reach under her arms and couldn't get a place to hold her. When I tried again I grabbed her top and thought that might work until Mr. B came over to help pull her completely out. Instead her top came off. When I saw it was in my hands, I looked helplessly at Mr. B, who was much less concerned about a topless daughter than a dead one. "Grab her, dammit," he yelled. I did and tried not to notice what I felt. In any case I got her above water again. She was aware enough to grab her top and try to put it back on. Now her father was yelling at her. "Fuck that and grab on to my board."

She did, resting her upper body against it so you couldn't tell she was down to only half a two-piece. Her father grabbed her head, kissed her, and pulled her onto the board.

"Paddle in ahead of us and get a towel." I thought he was going to add, "And never touch my daughter's clothes again, whether they're on or not."

I wanted a towel, too, because I now noticed I had a hard-on and the greatest fear of my life would finally happen, that I would be out in public and people would notice that I had a penis, even with my clothes on. It was the reason I usually wore a jacket that came below my waist to school, even on hot days. Having someone ask why you had on a jacket when it's in the eighties was much preferable to someone asking what you got in your pants there, pointing to your crotch. Mae West's gun in your pocket was funny if you weren't the one with the "gun" and around the merciless boys that inhabited the hallways of my junior high.

I didn't know what to do. I had to get the towel for top-less Cindy. Even more I had to do what Mr. B asked because of all the adults I knew, I wanted to please him most. Fortunately my trunks were fairly large and by the time I made shore, I was able to carry my board so nothing would show. I asked for two towels like one was for Mr. B and held on to other when I handed the first to Mr. B for Cindy.

Cindy was able to walk, though a little unsteadily, with the towel wrapped around her and dragging in the water. A crowd had formed by this time and one of the lifeguard jeeps was parked right in the water with two guys bringing over a canvas stretcher. Cindy refused to lie down, but they, along with her father, convinced her she had to go to the hospital and the only place they had for her was in the back where the stretcher went. Mr. B stood behind her as they rode up the beach through the parking lot and on to the hospital.

CHAPTER THIRTY-SIX

I THINK THIS WAS the first time I ever became aware that you could have feelings that have nothing to do with what is happening. I know now that unresolved pain from the past can fester until it appears at the most inopportune times. For days, no matter who brought up my heroics with Cindy, all I wanted to do was cry.

On the way home from the beach that day, Maw-Maw, Debbie, and I visited Mom in the hospital. Debbie tried to tell her about me saving Cindy, but she got Cindy confused with Sandy and thought she had almost drowned in her family's pool. She would nod at almost anything we said, like someone who didn't understand the language we were speaking but didn't want to admit it. Every so often she would abruptly ask when Dad was coming to visit.

"Soon," Maw-Maw said for the twentieth or so time before ushering us out of the room.

Her roommate had been released, so Mom had the small space to herself. It was hard to tell if Mom needed company or was better off without it. The last I remember of that visit was her standing at the window, her hospital gown not quite covering her behind. She was waving good-bye like we were on the other side of the window walking

429

across the lawn. Debbie walked up behind her and hugged her, but Mom just kept waving to her imaginary family in the distance.

The church decided to have a recognition service for what I did. I only remember something like this being done for returning missionaries or for one kid who was going to train to be a pastor after he had graduated from college. It turned out that Pastor Bob was not just on vacation but had taken a leave of absence. The interim pastor seemed to think a gathering to honor someone would be a good way to get people's minds off the pastor's shenanigans and help out a family that his shenaniganizing had touched directly. I should have been excited—even the twins hadn't ever gotten this much attention as far as I knew—but I just wanted to be in Texas.

Besides, as the cliché goes, I just happened to be in the right place at the right time. But no one would accept that. It was like this was an excuse for them to tell me how much they liked me. I finally got the praise I always wanted and it only made me uncomfortable. I worried it was setting me up for some major disappointment.

Some deacons wanted to wait until Sunday when there would be more people, but the majority wanted to do it as soon as possible, so the Wednesday service won out. Most in the congregation thought the pastor was only on vacation. This gave the interim pastor something to do before the official ceremony to make him the new pastor. Besides, on Wednesday the congregation would have a chance to meet with him, his wife, and his eight children more informally.

With that many children, his wife would get the sympathy of the women immediately. The youngest was still nursing and the oldest was barely a teenager, so Pastor

Thomas and his wife had been at it pretty regularly. I heard one of the gossips from the picnic say that it seemed a little Catholic, but even they were won over because the kids were so well behaved.

Mr. B was working with Pastor Thomas because it was Mr. B's daughter that was saved and because he was the ranking deacon. Mrs. B planned the food for after the service, much like Mom would have done in the past.

Maw-Maw said I had to dress up. Even Debbie agreed, so here I was sitting in a chair on the "stage," just outside the choir area and behind the pulpit in a dark blue suit and red tie. Mr. B kept winking at me as the people poured in. We had at least as many as we had on normal Wednesday nights. The phone bank had been activated, and Mrs. B said they made at least 200 calls. There were no answering machines then to leave a message, so many of the 200 never knew they got a call.

Debbie waved from the front row. So did Tamara. They pointed to the back, apparently so I would notice who was coming in. I already knew that our neighbors were coming so I wasn't sure what they were pointing to. Then I saw a man who looked familiar and didn't realize who he was until a girl stepped out from behind him. She was in white, like a bride but without all the extra petticoats or fancy sleeves. She had on red shoes that matched my tie and would have rivaled Dorothy's in *The Wizard of Oz*. Her hair was pulled straight back from her temples and braided down her back. I couldn't see the greenish-gray color of her eyes from so far away, but they seemed to sparkle anyway. She was smiling that large smile that Mom used to be so famous for. I hadn't noticed the similarity until now.

I stood up and thought about escorting her to a seat. Mr. B saw something was going on and put an arm in front of me, motioning for me to sit down. Gloria mouthed some words to me, but I couldn't make them out. She and her father sat down next to Debbie and Tamara, and Debbie immediately began to talk to her. She must have been asking about Gloria's brother.

Cindy came up the carpeted steps past the pulpit and sat next to me. I didn't know if this meant she was going to say something or that she wanted to know who the girl was. It was like going to heaven and God asked you which girl you wanted and put them all together so you could decide. Now all we needed was the Twambley girls to arrive.

They did come, but only after the Carrolls and Bradleys had arrived. I had thought of running up over the choir chairs and jumping into the baptistery and swimming my way out. It might have been fitting since we were there to celebrate what happened in the water. But I couldn't leave now that Gloria was here. It was like I was receiving energy from her. She kept looking at me and smiling, the same way she did back in Dayton when she said she would stay faithful to me. And here I was, more unfaithful than the pastor or the prodigal son or even Dad. Tamara and Sandy and Cindy and the Twambleys, any one of whom I would have at any given time, and in Tamara's case I did, thrown Gloria over for.

They were all beautiful in their own right, and it never occurred to me how unusual it was that so many pretty girls could be in such close contact with me and me still feel so unattractive. In fifth grade I had thrown rocks at two girls I adored. One had brown hair to her shoulders and the other blond hair that reached down her back. They were the prettiest girls in the school, and I only knew to get their attention by being mean. Though, to be fair, I never hit them, and they would wait until I came out of class every day so they would be sure to get the rock treatment.

It turned out that Cindy was not going to speak but sing. With accompaniment from the choir director at the piano, she sang "Nobody Knows the Trouble I've Seen." To compare her experience in a surfing accident to the travails of slaves was a bit much, but she looked great in the maroon choir robe and sounded heavenly. Besides, few knew how much trouble she had really seen after the board had whacked her on the head and she had stopped breathing.

When she finished, Pastor Thomas explained briefly that he was taking over temporarily for Pastor Bobby. That set a few heads to wagging. Others were obviously hearing it for the first time because they began to look around for someone they could talk to later who might have more of the details.

"We had quite an event last Sunday afternoon. Now, how many of you were there?" About half the congregation raised their hands. "That's nice. That's nice. Wish I could have been." He was rather short so he stayed on the pulpit stand while he motioned Mr. B over.

"Here's your Mr. B, church leader and proud father of the one who was rescued." I hadn't heard any adults use his name like we kids did.

"Good evening and thank you, Pastor Thomas. I know you're going to do a great job while Pastor Bobby and his family get the rest they need. And Cindy. Wonderful." He bowed to her in the front row where she had gone after singing. She still had the choir robe on and looked a lot older. From here I noticed the wound on her head that had required a few stitches.

"Well, if our wonderful phone bankers didn't get a hold of you in the past few days, then you found out when you came in the door tonight that we are not having our usual Royal Ambassadors and Girls Auxiliary meetings or our normal prayer service. We're still going to pray, but we're starting with something a little different." He turned around to look at me. I could think of nothing to do but wave and felt like a dork immediately.

He smiled and faced the congregation and spoke again into the microphone. "Every once in a while someone does something that is so wonderful that the only way we can deal with it is to tell that person in public how wonderful it was." Again he looked at me. "Last Sunday afternoon, my daughter, Cindy, was teaching some of our kids to surf. When a wave she was riding broke too soon to catch, she spun out. Her board shot up in the air and, while she expertly avoided it, the board of another surfer caught her in the temple and knocked her out. Joey," he gestured toward me, "was watching the whole time and paddled over to pull her above water until she could start breathing again."

The more Mr. B described it, the more what I did seemed so minor and lame. If Mr. B hadn't gotten out there quickly to pull her onto his board, I doubt she would have made it, but every time I looked at Gloria, she was staring at me with admiration. I loved it, but it was embarrassing, too. I wished it were just her and me playing Monopoly back at Dayton.

"Joey saved her life." Mr. B was weeping and came back to give me a hug.

Pastor Thomas hugged him with a quick pat on the back and took over. "Now, Cindy is not the only one to celebrate being saved. By the blood of Jesus, we all can be saved and only need to claim that for our own salvation." He gestured for the pianist to begin and asked us to turn to "The Old Rugged Cross."

During the instrumental intro, before anyone started singing, I began to cry. I don't know who noticed, but someone had to since I was in front of the whole church. Mr. B did and came over to hug me again. He whispered that I was wonderful, which just made me sadder and unable to hold back heaving sobs. By now I was totally ashamed and thought again about escaping through the baptistery, but some sanity prevailed and I just walked down the steps, off to the right, and out the closest exit.

I felt like I did when I wouldn't let Mom touch me, but sadder and more out of control. I didn't want anything, not even Gloria. I hoped she wouldn't come out because I was afraid of what I might say to her. Somehow every mean thought, every sexual fantasy, everything I had ever imagined that I would never want anyone to know about me flashed before me in the distance for everyone to see, like a drive-in movie. If an animal were nearby, I would have tried to kill it. If someone said anything to me, I could see only one possibility, doing whatever I could to drive them away.

I imagined riding out of town on a horse like I was in some Western. I would go from town to town doing good for others until I began to forget about my own pathetic life. Or I would drive away in a car and go on a robbing and killing spree and get riddled with bullets from a machine gun like some prohibition gangster, jumping and squirming each time a bullet hit my body.

I walked toward the Sunday school building and then, instead of going in, sat on the back stairs that led down to the street behind the church. From here you could see the Catholic university and the area near Mission Bay that

SeaWorld would build on in a few years. I had stopped crying and was feeling numb like you do when you're so tired you can't go to sleep but you have no energy to get out of bed.

I watched a rat scurry from under the stairs and into the ice plant on the hillside. A hummingbird hovered about eye level, twitching back and forth and then flew almost straight up. I used to play "Emperor of the Universe" with Debbie on our trips to Texas. As emperor she would eliminate smoking and provide scholarships for young actors to go to New York. I tended to be more personal and would make myself bigger and stronger and older before I became a Yankee outfielder or a rock and roll singer. As emperor now, would I eliminate death? Would I make Mom well? Would I get my faith in God back? I think I would just have some barbeque ribs and homemade ice cream delivered after having sex with all the girls in that front row.

"You coming back in?"

It was Gloria. Her eyes were moist, and she seemed much less confident than I remembered her in Dayton. She was trying to get a strand of hair to stay behind her ear. All I could think was that she was too good to want me. The freckles on her face made her look like she was way younger than she was. She had perfect teeth that she was displaying now in a sort of grim smile, the kind I got at the reception after Dad's funeral.

"I don't know." That was true. I didn't know. I didn't know anything. I just wanted to stop feeling like I had missed out on life and that nothing good would ever happen again.

"Can I sit?"

She meant to say "may," because obviously she is capable of sitting down, but I didn't correct her. I started to say that it's a free country but just shrugged instead.

"Debbie called about an internship at the Globe and Dad was feeling so bad about not getting to San Diego on our trip that he agreed to fly me out. I didn't beg him, but he knew it was important when I said I had enough in my savings. I think Debbie told me about it as much for you as for me."

She was still surprisingly pale the way pretty actresses who spend all their career on stage can be. Instead of looking sickly, it made her dark hair glisten all the more. From those early adolescent years until now, I find pale, round shoulders under cascading dark hair to be the most attractive of anything I ever see in a woman. I suppose Gloria set the standard and, if we had stayed together long enough, I would have had my daughters with her, daughters with long black hair draped over thin but perfectly rounded shoulders.

I was supposed to say "thanks" now and did, but it sounded, as Debbie would say, like some bad actor's line reading. We both looked up when we heard talking around the "corner"—though there were no corners since the church was round—and realized that the service must be over. The sun had set in the meantime.

I had every reason to feel the best I had ever felt. No one could have written a script that would have come out better than this: saving Cindy, praise from the Bodenhamers and the church, our whole neighborhood coming to see me, and, to top it all off, the surprise visit by Gloria. But I didn't.

Mr. B appeared from the direction of the crowd noise. "May I join you?"

I could tell from the way Gloria looked at him that she thought he was handsome. He had on a dark suit with a white shirt. Nothing special, but he had a deep tan so the shirt looked even whiter than it normally would. The suit fit so well that it was not difficult at all to imagine the muscular bulk that it barely hid.

"Your grandmother wants some of us to come back to your house for a late supper. Something about fried chicken, lemon pie, and root beer." I realized at that moment that I was starving. Gloria reached for me, and I fought back tears again as we followed a few steps behind Mr. B hand in hand.

CHAPTER THIRTY-SEVEN

WHEN MR. B, GLORIA, and I were in view of everyone leaving the church, a few started to applaud and the rest, when they saw who was being congratulated, joined in. I thought for sure Maw-Maw or the new pastor would say something about giving the praise to God, but they were clapping, too. A reception line formed on the way to the parking lot, and I was given long hugs by the women and some of the girls, but quick hugs with rapid-fire pats on the back by the men and a few boys. The rest shook my hand or nodded as they walked by.

I didn't know what to do but to say thank you over and over again. I wanted to try to say something about not being deserving but seeing the twins and their parents in line made me change my mind. Deserving or not, I had been made a hero. That could never be taken away from me, but I still felt like a fraud.

By holding hands with Gloria, I made it pretty clear to everyone she was my girlfriend. That alone would have been enough to impress the guys my age. That I saved another girl who was equally attractive made me seem like a movie star, too, not that anyone thought Cindy was interested in me the way Gloria was. A few of the younger RAs started calling me Rock Hudson.

Like Mr. B had told me earlier, Maw-Maw had invited the Bodenhamers and a few other people from church to our house. Just like at Dad's funeral reception, all the neighbors were there. I figured they liked being there better this time since it was for something other than a death, not because they wanted to be there for me. Each of the Twambley girls made a point of kissing me lightly on the cheek. Even the neighborhood wives gave me a peck. I had been wearing a suit, but Maw-Maw let me change into something more comfortable, and I had enough foresight to put on my baseball jersey because it hung well below my waist. I still could not believe all the attention, from girls in general and from Gloria in particular. Tamara made a point of kissing me on the lips, not long, but with enough force that it hurt my lip.

People were enjoying the food and each other enough that the twins, Billy, and I weren't noticed when we slipped out for some football. The street lights were enough for us to see each other and the glowing ball Billy brought. In keeping with the specialness of the day, Billy and I decided to face the twins as a team. Jerry nodded with smirk, as if to say, "Okay, you asked for it."

Billy was so confident that he said, "We'll kick off to you guys."

Captain and Mrs. Carroll left at the same time we boys went outside. They were talking heatedly from the minute they got to the sidewalk and all the way to their front door. I had never heard anyone in their family arguing with each other before. Jerry and Terry stopped and stared. Apparently they hadn't either.

Captain Carroll said, "That *is* where I was. I just wasn't there the whole time."

Mrs. Carroll shook her head like people do to tell you that they know you're lying and you must think they're idiots to buy such a flimsy story. When Captain realized we were all watching and listening, he ushered his wife inside. Or at least he tried to. She moved away from his arm and went straight to their car. Inside the car, after the motor was running, she looked at him one more time, with the same disappointed shaking of her head. As he walked toward her, she drove off.

Their other car was in the shop, so I thought he might ask to borrow our car to go after her, but he resorted to the same head-shaking gesture and went in the house. The twins lost all focus, and every move they made was just a little bit slower than usual. They got fooled with the cheapest tricks, like me running back by Billy and pretending to take a handoff so I could pass to him but he had kept the ball. He just loped over the goal line, if someone Billy's size can ever be said to lope. Once Billy and I were ahead by two touchdowns, I said I had to get back to the party. After all, it *was* for me.

Gloria had been watching from the porch and put out her hand for me to hold as I walked in. I looked back over my shoulder to see if any of the guys were watching, but the twins were gone and Billy was already headed for his jeep.

We passed Tamara, and I thought I detected the slightest look of disdain. It was as if her thin nose had become longer, so she had to lean her head down to keep it from touching other people. She smiled, but it was more the smile of a car salesman who's been asked one more time why the price advertised in the paper is so much less than what he has just told these latest customers.

Maw-Maw had set up the food buffet style in the dining room using Mom's china, crystal, and silver, which Mom never used, except for one Christmas when the pastor and his wife came over for dinner. Maw-Maw must have had other people doing some of the frying because she wouldn't have had time to cook enough to fill the three platters. There was A&W root beer in large cups that someone had picked up from the drive-in near the high school. She had also fixed dozens of ears of corn on the cob. She had two bowls of collards for the few who needed something green. Cooling on the kitchen table were four lemon meringue pies. A few more were in the oven. Even though others brought some of the food, she had to have stayed up all night.

Gloria offered to fix a plate for me, and I let her. Debbie rolled her eyes but then laughed and said in my ear, "You deserve it."

Sudden kindness is just as disturbing as sudden cruelty. I don't mean Debbie or the rest of them had never been nice to me, but I certainly never had such an outpouring. It made me so nervous I wanted to go to my room and masturbate just to relieve the tension. Actually, I most wanted to return to the fort with Tamara. I got red in the face thinking of it because Gloria was being so attentive.

"Joey, I would never have guessed how much people admire you from the way you have described yourself. Is it true you just got top student in the seventh grade?"

I nodded, and didn't know whether to be grateful to Debbie, who must have told her, or to be angry that Debbie had blabbed. I didn't see the award as a big deal because I liked to study, I liked to do well in class, and it all came easy to me. Of course, I didn't realize that if any of my friends had spent half the time I did studying they would have been getting A's too.

I looked at Gloria and smiled.

Gloria looked at me. "What?"

"Nothing."

"Come on."

"I don't know. You just reminded me of when the principal pulled me aside."

"You were in trouble."

"That's what I thought, and that's what the guys who were watching thought."

We were interrupted by a couple that used to go out dancing with Mom and Dad. They offered their congratulations as they walked out the door.

"The guys in the hall made the naughty/naughty sign with their fingers, because they thought Mr. Rose was about to scold me. Instead, he said that he had never had so many teachers praise one student to him and that he had to tell me in person. He also said that he would pretend to be angry with me about something so the other guys wouldn't make fun of me for being praised by 'The Hose.' I was surprised to find out he knew what we called him."

Gloria pushed a few strands of hair off my forehead. "Joey, will you come to see me in *Romeo and Juliet*?"

"Of course." Besides Debbie was playing Juliet. Gloria was hoping for a miracle, that she would be chosen as Debbie's understudy. Of course, her being here was already a miracle. Why not another? Wouldn't put out God too much now that He's on a roll.

Once the rest had said their good-byes, Mr. B took me out back. We stood near the pitcher's mound. "That Gloria is something else. You said she's a second cousin, right?"

I looked at him with a frown, but he just winked and smiled. "You're a wonderful kid. If you ever want to talk about you know what, I'm available." He winked again and gave me a hug.

Gloria was going to live with us during her internship. Maw-Maw put her in the only free bedroom, Mom and Dad's. Earl took to her immediately. I almost suggested she could have him stay with her at night, but I hadn't slept without him since we got him, except for the night at the Bodenhamers and the trip in the Grand Canyon. No matter how bad I felt, when I saw him in my room, or felt for him with my feet in the middle of the night on my bed, I got better. If God wanted to really be cruel, he could do something to Earl. I got angry and frightened just thinking of it.

When we finished dinner, Debbie got the Monopoly board out, but all of us were too sleepy to play. Debbie and Maw-Maw used the bathrooms first. Gloria was next and, when she came out, I was waiting in the hall. She kissed me goodnight and went to her room. What a crazy world.

I sat on my sofa before pulling out the bed. There would be school tomorrow. Gloria would be going to mine while she was living in San Diego. What would happen when people found out she was my cousin? Would she find out about Tamara? Would we get to stay girlfriend and boyfriend or would she find someone else?

Gloria's father had agreed to let her stay until Christmas, so she would be sleeping in the room next to me for about three months. I would see her when she got ready for bed

444

and on the ride to school with her. We would have breakfast and dinner together. Lunch maybe.

Over breakfast Monday morning, Gloria told us, "Dad and Mom had one requirement: I had to call them every night, any time after the cheap rates started, but didn't have to be the cheapest." She looked at me when she said this.

She had gotten up before me, and, when I first saw her at the kitchen table, for a moment I thought I was back in Dayton. I couldn't believe that she ate Grape-Nuts and, just like Dad, soaked them first in milk. She looked funny because she had forgotten to pack her pajamas and had borrowed Debbie's, the ones that had dozens of Bozo heads at random on the top and large yellow-and-red polka dots on the bottoms.

School was horrible because I didn't know how to act. I was afraid to establish we were boyfriend and girlfriend for fear that some of the bigger guys would make fun of me, hoping I would fight back and give them an excuse to beat me up in front of her. I was afraid of what they would say about her if they found out she was my cousin, too. Fortunately I had volunteered to help sort textbooks in the library during lunch, so I didn't have to see her on our longest break.

When Debbie came to pick us up, I was waiting at the curb before Gloria got there. Gloria showed up followed by a half dozen boys. It looked like they were planning to come with us.

"So how'd the first day go?" Debbie asked.

"Fine." Gloria waved at the boys and then looked at me. "But it was weird. Joey wasn't in any of my classes, and I only saw him on one recess all day." Exaggerating a frown, she looked at me. "I think you were trying to avoid me."

I shook my head and laughed. "I know, it was weird."

We had most of the same teachers, just different periods. Her favorite was mine, too, Mr. Langley. He was famous for doing crazy things during class, like hiding in the closet during A-bomb drills. He would run into it, close the door, then pop his head out to say, "Sorry only room for one." To protect ourselves we put our heads on our desks on top of one arm while the other arm was on top of our heads! Of course, we all would have died with or without the closet and with or without our arms around our heads, but the whole scary and ridiculous exercise was made somewhat tolerable, if not enjoyable, by him.

That afternoon Debbie and Gloria went to the Old Globe in Balboa Park for the first meeting of the interns for *Romeo and Juliet*. I knew we wouldn't play Monopoly every night and soon Gloria would be busy going to rehearsals, but I wanted to play as much as possible in the evening, before or after TV. I was tired last night, too, but would have played if Gloria had been willing. I didn't even care if Debbie joined us.

The night before last I had had a dream that Mom came into my room as usual, only when she got in bed, she turned into Gloria. When we started to mess around, her nose began to grow like Pinocchio until she turned into Tamara. Tamara began to make noises like she did in the fort, but so loud that Maw-Maw and all the neighbors—the adults and the kids—heard and were standing in my bedroom shaking their heads in disgust.

We started our Monopoly game after all three of us had done some homework and stopped when Maw-Maw said, "Time for bed," at 10:00 p.m.

Debbie got up and stretched. "Lucky for you two." She smiled ever so condescendingly at us, the financial dummies.

We hadn't been playing quite a half hour, but Debbie already had Boardwalk and Park Place plus all the railroads. Both Gloria and I had lots of property but not a monopoly that allowed us to buy houses and hotels. It put Debbie in a good mood, so she was funny without being too sarcastic. Or she was just being nice because Gloria was there.

Before I picked up the pieces, I thought of all the property I could have sold (or given) to Gloria, so she would have beaten Debbie, but she didn't have Debbie's killer spirit. Gloria played games to have fun and be with people she liked. Debbie played to win, which was how I played when Debbie was the only opponent.

I wanted to ask Gloria what her favorite TV shows were so we could plan the rest of the week, but she was pretty sleepy and asked if she could use the bathroom first. I said I would pack up the game so Debbie could use the other bathroom ahead of me.

When Gloria had brushed her teeth and changed into her pajamas, she went to the kitchen to wait for her parents to call. They always called on the half hour and would tell Gloria exact time the night before. I was jealous that they were calling her instead of me calling her, even though she was here in the flesh. I wanted to hold her while she talked to them like I'd seen two lovers do in a film. I wanted to know what her parents said to her and if she said anything about me. Even though I had avoided her all day at school, or maybe because of it, I wanted to be with her every moment at home.

When they called, I went to my bedroom. In about fifteen minutes, I heard five knocks on my door in that rhythm that reminds you of something bad about to happen: dum, da dum dum, duuuum.

"Joey?"

"Yeah?" Who did she think it was?

"It's Gloria." Like I didn't know her voice? "Can I come in?"

I opened the door. "Mom says you can come back with me when I return to Texas." She was smiling like she had just been told Santa was bringing her an Earl lookalike puppy for Christmas. At her voice, *my* puppy walked over sluggishly because he was already well into his hundredth nap of the day and began to lick her ankle. She laughed and bent down to pet him.

"No, no, no," I said as he started to get into peeing stance. I made it out the door to the patio and almost to the dirt. At least I had learned how to hold him so he didn't wet me.

Gloria was waiting at the door when I led Earl back in. He still had a little trouble coming up the steps but not for lack of eagerness. She bent down to him but asked me permission before petting him again.

"It's all right, now." His fur was almost the color of the yellow dots on her pajama bottoms. The two people I loved most enjoying each other. A little more of this and I might start praying regularly again.

She led him into my room and onto his pad. I followed them and didn't tell her that at night he would be sleeping with me on my bed. She turned to me, held my shoulders, and leaned in to give me a kiss, right on the lips. Then she pulled back, looked into my eyes for a few moments, and said, "Goodnight, my love."

I could hardly breathe. When I could, I said "goodnight" a little too loudly since she had already gone to her room. I picked up Duke of Earl and set him near the bottom of my bed in the bunched-up blanket I kept there just for him. I had the windows open, and it was already cooling down nicely.

Gloria was only a few feet away and would be there all night. Wow. I didn't know what to do with all these extremes of life. Maybe Tamara would have a sleepover with Debbie and sneak into my room. Maybe Maw-Maw would die and Mom would come back home. Maybe Mr. Bodenhamer would train me to be a lifeguard. Maybe Billy would have a car accident and become a paraplegic. Maybe I would be written up in the paper for saving Cindy. Maybe I would grow up to teach at UCLA. Maybe an escaped convict would kill us all in our beds.

I thought I heard singing and got up to see if it was coming from Debbie's room. No, it was either Maw-Maw or Gloria. I could get close to both bedrooms at the same time since they shared a wall at the back of our house. Faintly I heard what I thought was "Sealed with a Kiss." It couldn't mean she was going to say good-bye to me since she just got here, and the summer of the song was already over for us.

I went back to bed and stroked Earl's fur the wrong way so it stood up. He wiggled under my touch but didn't open his eyes. Then I got this idea that Gloria was waiting for me.

I want to be very careful how I explain what happens next. I don't want you to think that I am editing out the parts that are somewhat embarrassing to me today, but I don't want to linger on them either out of some desire to get your absolution. Kids do stupid things and sometimes things that are adult in their seriousness, as Mr. Bodenhamer had said.

If I can excuse my behavior at all, it would be by reminding you all what had happened in a very short time: losing

Dad and Mom, being seduced by Tamara, practically being adopted by the Bodenhamers, saving Cindy, having my first girlfriend live with me, all the while being totally obsessed with sex. Mom had created in me a need for love that got all confused with an obsession with the female body. I was desperate for love and desperate for girls/women to supply it. I could only see sex as a way to get that intimacy that my mother had teased me with and so longed for herself.

I lay awake for about an hour, thinking of all the things that Gloria might be thinking since I was sure she was having as hard a time sleeping as I was. I went toward the kitchen, pausing by Debbie's door to see if I could identify what was on the radio, but she had it turned down lower than usual and I could only hear the backbeat. Without turning on the lights, I got an open bag of potato chips from the cupboard over the stove and put a bunch them on my T-shirt as I held it out from my stomach, like some farmer woman collecting eggs for breakfast.

Back in my bed, I gave a few chips to Earl, and then ate the rest, one at a time, sucking out all the salt before chewing and swallowing. I smelled the oil and salt on my fingers and licked them after bringing each piece to my mouth. I wished we had an intercom or Gloria and I each had walkie-talkies. I didn't have anything to say. I just wanted to be in touch.

I got up and went to the kitchen again. This time I got a Coke. Back in my room, I thought of offering some to Earl but had heard some human food was dangerous to dogs and thought that might be true about soft drinks. I had a science teacher who put an egg in Coke, and we watched it dissolve a lot faster than we would have anticipated. I sat up in my bed leaning against the sofa back. I took small swigs, pretending I was drinking whiskey in some motel after my girl had just left me. The more I pretended, the more I wanted to be near Gloria.

I took two long pulls on the bottle to finish it off. I wiped my mouth with the back of my hand and stood up. Should I slip a note under her door? No, she might not notice it until morning. I could knock softly. But if Debbie had turned off her radio, she might hear first. At least I didn't have to worry about Maw-Maw. I decided I would sneak in and surprise Gloria by climbing into her bed.

I changed into my plainest pajamas. I could taste Coke and potato chip and wondered if I should brush my teeth first. I opened and closed the bathroom door slowly, turned on the light, and stood in front of the mirror. I could see a pimple forming on my right cheek. My nose seemed larger than usual. My right ear—I had never noticed before—stuck out a little more than my left ear. My chin looked okay from the front but almost disappeared into my neck when I looked at my profile with Debbie's hand mirror. I did push-ups on the floor until my chest was red and slightly pumped up. If only I had started weights a few months ago. I was about to flex my biceps when I heard the other toilet flush.

I waited until I heard a bedroom door open and shut but it didn't. Was Debbie waiting in the hallway like she had the night she discovered me helping Mom? If she were there, I would just go back to my room and wait until she was back in her bed.

Maw-Maw liked to leave one lamp on in the living room, so when I stepped into the hallway, I could see easily that no one was in the hall. I carefully lifted each foot and placed it down toes first. I paused halfway between my room and Gloria's. No sound was coming from anywhere, from Debbie's room or Maw-Maw's. I stood outside Gloria's door and listened like I'd seen actors do in countless movies. I even put my ear on the door. Nothing.

I turned the knob slowly as far as I could and slowly pushed the door open. It smelled of something sweet. I think it was her shampoo. Holding the knob fully turned, I shut the door and turned the knob in the opposite direction until it was back in its original position. There was light coming from the window, a full moon just high enough for me to see a part of it. It did not fall on part of her face like it would in a movie.

I stood next to the bed. She was sleeping all curled up on one side, like she was expecting someone to join her. I felt like a vampire waiting for her to expose her neck. I leaned down to hear her breathing. I started to kiss her, but she turned to her other side. I walked to the other side, where there was plenty of space and slid under the covers. I thought I could hear my heartbeat echoing off the ceiling. I lay on my back staring straight up. I scooted my hand across the sheet until it touched her arm. She mumbled something and turned back the other way, as if her right side was the side she was supposed to sleep on.

I started to get up and then began remembering the time she said she loved me: in Dayton, on the phone, when she came here, and before going to bed last night. I started counting and came up with twenty-four times. I rolled to my right and snuck an arm around her waist and under her arm. She pulled my arm into her chest like she was expecting me. I did not realize at the time that her not waking up or being weirded out by having someone in bed with her was unusual and said more about how soundly she was sleeping than about how welcoming she was to me.

I could smell her hair now and thought it would be enough to just lie awake next to her all night. Then things started to change in me. I began feeling this tingly in my groin and felt like my erection was about to push the sheet and blanket straight up. I turned to my side away from her but couldn't control this overwhelming desire to lie next to her and rub up and down. I had no intention of doing anything else. Unless she offered. I thought I might be able to get relief without even waking her. Then I would go back to my room calm enough to sleep. Kind of a normal night except for being next to Gloria.

I started the up and down and took almost no time to fire off. Just as I did, she reached over to feel what or who was next to her. She touched me right where I had ejaculated and screamed.

"Eeeuuu. What are you doing?" She scooted away. "What did you do?" Then she screamed like I had tried to rape her or something. "Get out. Get out of here."

She screamed the last so loudly and meanly I was afraid she would wake up Maw-Maw.

Debbie had heard, with or without her radio still on. She burst into the room with a trophy she had won for a musical, planning to use the base to whack the intruder on the head, I guess.

"Joey? What the hell?"

"Get him out of here." Gloria was crying now. Debbie had turned on the light and was staring at the big wet spot on my pajama bottoms.

"Good Lord." That was what Maw-Maw said when something surprising or horrible happened. "Go to your room." She said it with such parental authority that I went after looking back at Gloria, who was sobbing into her hands.

I thought of saying that I did more with Tamara, and she didn't even love me. I might have actually done that, but Debbie and I years later could not remember if I had.

Later, Debbie found out about Tamara and me and confronted her about it. She admitted it, and they stopped speaking until Debbie found out about what Tamara's uncle had done to her in a newspaper article after he committed suicide.

I closed my door and went into my closet. I didn't know what I had done wrong. I mean, Gloria and I loved each other. I didn't hurt her. But I knew Debbie thought I was bad, and Gloria was crying. I wanted Mom back. I wanted to be with Tamara. I wanted to hurt myself.

I leaned forward and, on my knees, began to bang my head against the floor of the closet. It was carpeted and I couldn't get it to hurt enough, so I started banging my head against the wall. I kept hitting my head until it hurt so much I couldn't continue.

CHAPTER THIRTY-EIGHT

No child wakes up one day and thinks it would be a good idea to look through windows at girls undressing or to surprise a sleeping house guest/girlfriend awake by slipping into her bed and masturbating next to her. I suppose there are psychopaths whose genetics predestine them to commit heinous crimes, but I bet most, if not all of them, had something done to them in childhood that, at the very least, pointed them in that direction.

I don't blame my mother now that I know so much more about her and what she had to put up with from her father. I only found that out a few years ago. She was locked in a closet for punishment and watched her father go crazy strapped to a bed because he got syphilis before penicillin. Still she did things she shouldn't have and, if it hadn't been for Mr. Bodenhamer drawing on some similar experiences when he was young, I wouldn't be married today with two beautiful daughters and an overwhelming appreciation from my students.

Gloria went home in a few days, telling her parents she was too homesick to stay in San Diego. Maw-Maw and Mr. Bodenhamer managed to get me off from school for a few weeks, and I spent all my time with him. During that time

I admitted that Mom had done a little more than I let on at first. I had hid it because I was such a willing partner. Mr. B paid for me to go a therapist while I tried to sort it all out. When it looked like Mom might come back home, her doctor was told about her relationship with me. He confronted her with it, and it set her back into a semi-vegetative state.

Maw-Maw agreed to stay with us until I could go back to school. Then the Bodenhamers took Earl and me in, Maw-Maw went back to her commune, and Debbie left for a full-time job with an acting company in Los Angeles. It was more than I could hope for and got me through the many nights of sobbing into my pillow over Gloria. By the time I got to high school, I actually had recovered enough to have my second girlfriend. We were together for a few years. My third, Shirley, I met in college and we are married today, though we separated a few times and avoided divorce because we already had the girls and because we spend a lot of time and energy on therapy. I still struggle with understanding and engaging in healthy sex, but we're working on that, too.

Gloria and I met up just a few years ago, here in Pasadena. She had come out for a vacation with her husband and twin boys. We didn't talk directly about what happened that night, but she did say that she wished she hadn't so freaked out over it. She explained that her mother had been attacked in her own bed by a cousin who was staying with them and that had made Gloria super paranoid.

"God, you have a lovely house. And backyard." She looked at the bougainvillea and pointed at a hummingbird that was hovering in front of the tiny white flowers until it realized they had little nectar to offer. "It's almost silly how far I got in fantasizing our life together."

I felt a flutter in my chest and wondered if we would now spend some time matching each other's fantasies.

She smoothed her pants and scratched a bare shoulder. Her yellow top seemed to make her lightly tanned skin glow, and she had not gained a pound since I last saw her during her short stay with us.

"Do people still ask you if you're related to Elizabeth Taylor?"

She nodded, blushing.

"I've got to go. We're going to Disneyland." She looked at me. "Remember when we were going to go together?"

I nodded and stood up when Shirley came out with iced tea. "Thank you so much. It makes me feel at home, but I've got to go."

Shirley looked at me as if to ask if the time with Gloria went okay. I nodded. Shirley is a little plumper than Gloria and has always had to fight acne, but she's the kindest smart person I know and glows the way only lesser beauties can. How I got hooked up with someone so sane and compassionate is still a mystery.

The short time with Gloria *had* gone well, but I could still feel a little regret. I had gone through so much inner work since then that the Joey who was accused of attacking his girlfriend in bed seems like someone else, but I still struggle, as I already mentioned, with some of the same sexual issues.

Our neighborhood in San Diego was never the same once Dad died and Mom was committed. Not that my parents caused it, but I sometimes wondered. The Twambleys kept Leslie's baby as if he was her brother, but divorced when another daughter got pregnant but *did* go through with an abortion. The Carroll twins never recovered from finding out that their parents were so strict with them, especially about bedtimes, only because they wanted to make it easier to go out on each other. Neither of the boys made it through college or into professional sports. The last I heard they were both still in San Diego. Jerry was working at a gas station, and Terry was an elementary school janitor.

The Bradleys have done best of all. The parents stayed in the same house even though, for years, they talked of moving to Borrego Springs when they retired. Billy owns a speed shop and Sandy became a model. I saw her in a shampoo commercial a while back. Sandy never married but both she and Billy, who married right out of high school, have children and visit the grandparents on Clancy Street regularly, according to Debbie.

Debbie knows because she became a dental hygienist at an office in the strip mall near Clancy. She had gotten a recurring role on a sitcom but became disenchanted with the Hollywood scene. She still will take a small part in a play at the Old Globe in Balboa Park now and then since she has such a good reputation among the stage acting community, both for her portrayal of Juliet those many years ago and her decision to turn her back on TV. She even got a singing part in one of the Starlight Theatre musicals during the summer. She plans to buy our house back if it ever comes on the market.

Mr. Bodenhamer retired from lifeguarding after his children finished college, at least those who wanted to go, and became a therapist. He had plenty of preparation in saving me from me from psychological self-immolation over Gloria. I'm now an English teacher at a community college in Pasadena and have never been happier. The drama is in the literature now. Mostly.

Gloria ended up having the career Debbie always dreamed of. She recently settled in San Diego but spends a lot of time commuting to Los Angeles for various TV series.

Last week Debbie came up for the weekend. My girls adore her and can't understand why she gave up acting. She brought with her dozens of photos of our family in front of that bougainvillea.

I don't know a lot about life, but I do know this: the most important discovery one can make regards love, how to give it and how to receive it. For many of us, the receiving is the hardest part.

The good news for me? I can look at those old family photographs, on my patio in front of *our* bougainvillea, my wife puttering in the yard, my daughters arguing in the living room, and feel at peace.

By the way, when Earl died, Debbie brought him up here, and we recited a ceremony I wrote for him before we buried him just behind the bougainvillea.